The Seven Year Itch

The Seven Year Itch

Josie Lloyd & Emlyn Rees

WILLIAM HEINEMANN: LONDON

Published by William Heinemann 2007

4 6 8 19 9 7 5 3

First published in Great Britain in 2007 by
William Heinemann
Random House, 20 Vauxhall Bridge Road,
London, SW1V 2SA

www.randomhouse.co.uk

Addresses for companies within The Random House Group Limited can be
found at: www.randomhouse.co.uk/offices.htm

The Random House Group Limited Reg. No. 954009

A CIP catalogue record for this book
is available from the British Library

ISBN 9780434011490

The Random House Group Limited makes every effort to ensure that the papers
used in its books are made from trees that have been legally sourced from well-
managed and credibly certified forests. Our paper procurement policy can be
found at: www.randomhouse.co.uk/paper.htm

Typeset by SX Composing DTP, Rayleigh, Essex
Printed and bound in Great Britain by
Clays Ltd, St Ives PLC

For everyone who read *Come Together*

ACKNOWLEGEMENTS

Firstly many thanks to our wonderful agents, Jonny Geller and Vivienne Schuster, Carol Jackson and everyone at Curtis Brown. Also to our fabulous supporters at Random House, in particular Susan Sandon, Georgina Hawtrey-Woore, Claire Round and Cassie Chadderton for all their hard work. Congrats to Kate and Faye! As usual, we are extremely grateful for the invaluable input from our friends – you know who you are – and the on-going support of our family, particularly our two little angels.

The Seven Year Itch

The important thing about the social phenomenon known as the Seven Year Itch is not whether this urge towards marital infidelity is universal, or whether it really is most likely to strike seven years into a marriage, or even whether you actually believe in it at all. No, the only truly important thing about it is this: if you *do* feel the Itch, will you choose to ignore it, or will you start to scratch?

1

amy

The Vipers

When I was eight, my grandfather wrote in my autograph book: *When three or four women come together to chat, God help the first woman to leave.*

I never truly understood what he meant until I joined the Vipers.

It's our bi-monthly meeting and I'm late. Personally, I don't think of them as vipers, more as a close group of fellow first-time mothers, but Jack's always referred to them as that, or the Coven, which is just as bad. It's fair enough, I suppose. My poor long-suffering husband bears the brunt of the processing I have to do, to get over the veiled comments and insinuations made each time the Vipers meet.

Jack, of course, doesn't understand why I still see them at all, but it's like the Mafia: once you're in, you're in for keeps. I know these women and they know me. We're bound together by pain and ugly scenes of uncommon emotions. If I did leave, I'd be a traitor forever. They'd spurn me in the park and not invite me to birthday parties, and before long, I'd wake up with a severed horse head – well, a 'My Little Pony' head at the very least – in my bed.

I hurry through the gates of Queen's Park and take the short cut past the tennis courts. It's a cloudless May day and the horse chestnuts are loaded with cones of blossom, but I

1

hardly have time to notice. I'm sweating as the buggy rattles over the grass.

There's a young guy playing tennis with his coach on the court. His legs are tanned and supple and there's an athletic spring in his step. As a peel of his laughter reaches me on the breeze, I'm reminded of how Jack once was, before too much work, parenting and our on-going financial crisis made him so serious.

Back then, Jack and I always used to talk about how we'd meet up at lunch time to play tennis once a week together. Being able to do just that was part of the reason we chose to buy a flat as near to the park as we could afford. But in the three years that we've lived here, we haven't once met up for lunch, let alone played tennis, and now we've stopped talking about it altogether.

Before I get within sight of the playground area, I stop and pull out *Buster's Bedtime*, my son Ben's favourite book. I open it at the bit where Buster cleans his teeth. The illustration has a tin foil mirror in it. I search my own distorted reflection for any signs of the illicit croissant I had earlier, or yesterday's smudged eyeliner. I'm clear, but even so, I wish that I'd washed my hair. And wish that I'd had my roots done. And wish I didn't look like one big frown. And, as I chuck the book back into the netting at the bottom of the buggy, along with the rancid assortment of banana skins and sandy nappy wipes, I wish most of all that my appearance didn't matter. But it's the Vipers and it does.

Believe me, with them everything gets exaggerated. You put on new heels, you might as well be wearing stilts. You put on lipstick and you're having an affair. And if you put on a pound, you might as well have put on a stone.

It's like playing spot the difference for a living, and every difference spotted involves a judgement or a criticism of some sort. Which is why I take out the book again and carefully touch up my lip-gloss so that it looks like I haven't got any on. Because I hate coming away from these meetings

2

feeling crumby. It leaves me feeling downtrodden, and I just don't think I can face it today.

The Great Female Conspiracy

Of course, it wasn't always like this. At first being with the Vipers was great, because when I fell pregnant with Ben, the initial euphoria of the thin blue line on the pregnancy test quickly wore off, and the terror I felt at the prospect of giving birth equally quickly kicked in.

Of course, I knew I wasn't supposed to feel like that. I was supposed to be all earth mother and smugly proud, but inside I felt like Sigourney Weaver facing the drooling alien, and as I got bigger, I started to feel like the alien had impregnated me and it was only a matter of time before its offspring punched its way out.

So when I joined the local group of expectant mothers and found that I wasn't alone in my fears, I clung on to them like a life-raft. They made me feel normal. They talked to me like I still had a brain and wasn't just a walking brood mare, and in no time at all, we were bonding over the horrors we tried to hide from our men-folk: varicose veins that crawled like feeding worms across our groins, and piles that a mole would be proud of; stretch marks that appeared on our bellies like contours on a map, and aching hips that made us hobble like little old ladies. Not to mention tits that leaked like Mr Whippy ice-cream dispensers, warts and beauty spots that went weird and itchy and our unfeasibly bushy bikini lines (less Brazilian, more Cuban – as in Fidel Castro's beard).

We learned to laugh about it all, just the same as we did about how fat our faces felt and how we regularly got stuck in the bath, whilst assuring one other that we were just 'all bump' and hadn't put any weight on at all.

But then came the births in quick succession and, ashen-faced, we clung to each other with renewed neediness, glad that there were others out there who also felt like they'd narrowly survived a terrifying car crash. ('Vietnam.' That's how film-crazy Jack described Ben's birth. 'Like spending a night on Hamburger Hill.' He was right, in a way. We did feel like war veterans.)

It was the betrayal that was the worst. The discovery of the Great Female Conspiracy. I guess it exists to keep the human race going, but the fact is, that nobody – especially other women – tells the truth about giving birth.

They never tell you about the full gynaecological horror that involves delivering another human being into this world. They never prepare you for the moment when you discover that you're made of meat, not make-up; that you're actually more butcher than Bodyshop; and that this epiphany changes you for ever.

So in the weeks that followed these birthing experiences, we comforted each other, us Vipers. We shared in horrified whispers the gory details of what we'd been through. We cried on each other's shoulders as we tried to come to terms with stitched perineums, cracked nipples and sleepless nights, whilst we pretended to the rest of the world that we were glowing with maternal serenity.

But the problem with any group of women (as any woman knows) is that over time it becomes a hornets' nest of covert competitiveness. And once our babies stopped being newborn? We were on bitchy quicksand.

It shifted from being about how we were *feeling*, to how we were *doing*. We started sizing each other up, scrutinising and comparing our new mothering skills – and found each other lacking.

A Test Of Faith

I take a deep breath and smile brightly as I approach our usual tables by the toddler sandpit. They're the wooden type you get in pub gardens with the benches attached. I remember that Jack had one in the garden of the house he shared once with his best mate, Matt. Only this one is a lot

4

less enticing, of course, on account of a deficit of peanuts and ice cold lagers, and a surfeit of tasteless breadsticks and sticky juice cups.

In the sandpit, I can see several of the kids I've known since they were born tearing around. One of the biggest surprises about becoming a parent is that, despite all the gumph they tell you on the TV, it really is nature not nurture. These kids were all born with their own personalities. The cute ones are cute, right from the start, and the mean ones are mean. Not that you can ever say this out loud, of course, any more than you can say that it's possible to really loathe other people's kids.

Don't get me wrong; some of these offspring I love. I really mean it when we joke about dancing embarrassingly at their twenty-first birthdays. But between us all there are eight kids. Statistically, one of them is going to turn out to be a nasty crim of some sort.

The Vipers are all present and correct, surrounded by a protective shield of buggies. Camilla is holding court. I swear she's had a fake tan. She's wearing a pretty summer skirt and Converse trainers and she's sitting astride the bench, one hand rocking her Bugaboo Buggy (the most expensive in the range) where demon Tyler is mercifully asleep. Her other hand (complete with diamond studded eternity ring, presented at her bedside in the private maternity hospital, by BBC exec hubby, Geoff) is resting ostentatiously on her swollen belly. She's sixteen weeks already. She laughs up at Sophie.

Sophie does combat yummy mummy. She's pretty in a freckly, turned-up nose kind of way – all khaki pants and headscarves and glimpses of her flat midriff and the top of her tattoo. 'Womb Raider' Jack's always calling her with a worrying twinkle in his eye, the same as when he watches the real Angelina Jolie on the screen. I'm not losing any sleep over it, though. Jack may wonder, but he's not the type to wander. Not these days, anyway.

And patting the space beside her, when she sees me, is over-enthusiastic Faith. Fashion-wise, Faith seems to have stuck in the nineties, with an original Rachel-from-*Friends* barnet, but today I notice that she too is wearing new Converse trainers. It crosses my mind that she might have actually followed Camilla and bought the same trainers in secret. Put it this way: Camilla isn't copying *her*.

'Ah, there you are, Amy,' Camilla says, smiling. We do kisses all around and I climb into the space next to Faith.

I've been kind of looking forward to today. Let's face it, there's not much in my day-to-day diary to get excited about. So little, in fact, that I don't actually use a diary any more. There's the on-going activities that fill up my time: the rota of dishwasher emptying, food shopping, nappy changing, cooking and washing machine filling. Then there's my routine with Ben: Aquababies at the pool on Monday, Boogaloo Bunnies on Tuesday, Monkey Music on a Wednesday and Park Pranceabout on Thursdays. (Fridays, obviously, we go wild and crazy.)

And then there's these occasional get togethers with the Vipers.

But the second I'm subsumed into the group, I remember what I loathe about it. Motherhood, I've discovered, is the great leveller. I could be a brilliant lawyer, or an architect, or yes, even a celebrated fashion designer (as I once thought I would be by this age), but it counts for nothing here.

Apparently, because I have a child the same age as Faith's, that makes me *the same* as Faith – And call me a snob, but Faith is really quite thick. Being 'the same' as Faith makes me want to break free and do something terribly rash. Like telling her that I find her constant bonhomie false beyond belief and her annoying assumptions about my life ignorant and inaccurate. Or that beneath the virtuous veneer, I suspect her of being the most venomous viper of all.

'Aw. He's still got that nasty skin rash then,' is Faith's opening gambit, pointing down at Ben, who's asleep, wrung

6

out from the eye-rolling, toy-tossing, tonsil-tearing tantrum he had earlier about being strapped into his buggy. (Anyone would have thought he was an innocent death row prisoner being dragged to the chair.)

I reach out and protectively cup my darling boy's angelic face. A few hysteria-induced blotches are hardly a nasty skin rash. I feel my heart flip with guilty love for my little boy. In the WWF-style wrestling match I had with him, I wish now that I hadn't lost my temper and called him a 'little fucker' for making me late.

'He's fine,' I state, in the kind of tone I hope will kill this line of conversation dead.

But Faith is to empathy what Stalin was to public relations.

'Could be the start of chicken pox,' she speculates.

She really hopes it is, clearly. I'd never dream of criticising her daughter Amalie, or keeping tabs on *her* illnesses, as if they were weaknesses. I wouldn't dare offer an opinion on the fact that Amalie looks – in Sarah's words – 'slightly touched'.

'It's understandable really though, isn't it,' Faith continues. 'Poor Little Ben's probably got low resistance after that horrible cough he had last time . . . it's going around.'

I smile as blandly as I can. 'Or maybe it's bird flu,' I suggest. 'You never know . . .'

For a moment, I hope Faith might see this statement for what it is: a joke. No such luck. She leans in close.

'I've got some Tamiflu,' she confides. 'I've been stockpiling for months. I've got enough to give you a box or two. Or I could give you the website, if you like?'

I'm at a loss as to how to respond, because my first instinct is that if Faith is the kind of person who's going to survive a pandemic, I'd rather perish with the masses.

Fortunately, our attention is drawn to Camilla, who leans in conspiratorially and rattles a pink bottle of pills, and glances at Sophie, eliciting giggles and coos from the group. Of course, that's what Camilla and Sophie are looking so smug about: Sophie's pregnant.

Then it turns out, in a sudden splurge of confessions, that Faith, Linda and Abby are all actively trying for 'number two' as well. Lan simply holds up two hands with her fingers crossed and stares down at her belly (although it's so tiny, it's a wonder that anything as big as an olive, let alone a foetus, could fit in it). Camilla squeals with delight and starts handing out folic acid vitamin pills like a teenager dealing Ecstasy.

And they're off.

The Second Coming

Over the last two and a half years, many topics have been aired and debated at these very tables. Some of them, looking back, have been ridiculous. Like the endless pre-birth pain-relief-versus-natural-birth debate. Laughable now. The moment we went into labour, we were all screaming for drugs. Abby's water-birth pool stayed in the boot of the car, Linda drop-kicked the hired back massage machine against the wall, Lan stabbed Phil in the balls with her acupuncture needles when he suggested they might help, and Sophie screamed hysterically over her Yogic-Breathing-Through-It tape.

Post-birth, of course, the Vipers' conversational topics became much more specific. There was will-he/she-take-a-bottle? month, followed by how do-I-know-if-he/she-is-ready-for-solids? Then we were on to is-it-too-early-for-potty-training? And the on-going nanny-or-nursery-or-me? debate.

These conversations are so inane, they make me want to shoot myself.

And this one is no different. Soon, we're past dates of last periods and on to the justification for having another child. The big question is, why do it all over again?

'What about you, Amy?' Camilla asks, eventually. 'You're very quiet. Any thoughts on number two?'

'You've *got* to get pregnant too,' adds Faith, 'otherwise you'll be left out.'

I'm in the spotlight.

The truth is, I do want another child. The only problem is, the reasons I have for wanting another one I could never, ever admit to the Vipers. Because if I'm very honest, this is what I think about having another baby:

1. If I get up the duff now, then I don't have to worry about sorting out the next stage of my career for a few more years and can spare myself the inevitable humiliation of failing job interviews. It's been five years since Friers, the fashion company where I worked, was taken over and I got made redundant, and three years since I quit a dull and stressful job as an office manager in a bookings agency.
2. If I have another baby, I can get thin after that one.
3. If I get pregnant now, I can put off starting the sit-up regime I've promised myself I'll start any day now and then I'll have a good excuse for my flabby tummy next time I'm in a bikini.

'Oh . . . Jack and I haven't really discussed it, yet,' I lie.

(We have. He's said no way.)

I'm aware that I've fallen once again for the Vipers' old trick. They've managed to turn reproduction into a group activity, and now I feel that I'm on the wrong side of a divide.

'I loved discussing it with Ed,' Sophie gushes. 'It's so different deciding to go for it the second time around, isn't it?'

Camilla, Lan and Sarah heartily agree.

Sophie adds a cheeky guffaw. 'I had no idea it would happen so fast. I was rather enjoying all the trying!'

I cringe at the cliché, but can still feel my heart racing with childish jealousy. I've always considered myself to have a better, healthier relationship with Jack than any of these women have with their fellas. I hate the fact that they've all made the decision to reproduce again – on the assumption that it'll happen just like that – and are all apparently enjoying wonderful, intimate sex sessions trying to conceive.

I look down at Ben. I can feel Camilla staring at me.

'I'm not saying Jack and I won't go for a second,' I say, trying to keep the defensive edge out of my voice, 'but I'm just *so* enjoying being a mother at the moment. It's just so great. I really don't want to spoil things for Ben. And besides, the thought of being pregnant again –'

'Oh God, yes,' Faith interrupts. 'Poor Amy. Do you remember how sick you were last time?'

That's rich. *She* was the one who bellyached all throughout her pregnancy. Not me. This girl projects so much, she should get a job at the cinema. It's typical of her to re-write history.

'And I suppose you would need to be out of the flat before you had another baby,' Camilla adds in her best sympathetic voice. 'I mean, it's lovely and everything, but there's not exactly enough room.'

Jack's right: they're Viperous Witches.

Shooting Myself In The Foot

'Now then, before I forget, Yitka is after some evening work,' Camilla announces. 'If anyone can use her? Amy? Weren't you saying last time you needed a babysitter?'

'Well, it's our wedding anniversary next week –'

As soon as I say it, I feel as if I've thrown a fresh haunch of venison to a starving pack of wolves. There's a round of anniversary celebration one-upmanship, during which we learn that on their last anniversary, Camilla's Geoff planned a romantic 'seasonally-based' meal at home cooked by a minor celebrity chef, and Faith's husband, Craig, has a tradition of buying her a red rose for every year they've been married.

Sophie shares that Ed is planning on taking her to Paris for the weekend, without Ripley, next month. It was supposed to be a surprise, but The George Cinq hotel in Paris sent the booking confirmation to her home address by mistake, with the details of the *menu gastronomique*. Shame.

I try and play down our own plans on account of the fact that Jack and I haven't any yet. I can't even be sure that Jack will remember.

Last year, during Jack's political phase (he tore up his supermarket reward card and finally started using the recycling bin), he announced that he had also decided to adopt an anti-Hallmark stance. This applied to Mothering Sunday (American hogwash) and Father's Day (pointless) and wedding anniversaries ('Why should other people dictate when I'm romantic?') and last, but not least, Valentine's Day (which no longer applies to us, apparently, as we're no longer single). It was only when I threatened not to let him have a Playstation 3 for his birthday, that he agreed that birthdays should be the exception to his bah-humbug rule. So, even if he does remember our anniversary, we certainly won't be doing anything lavish.

'We'd just like to spend the evening together,' I mumble. 'You know, maybe go to the cinema –'

'I'm sure you can do something *much* more exciting than the cinema, but whatever,' Camilla interrupts, 'you simply *must* borrow Yitka.'

Thanks. I can borrow her, can I? Like she's a cardigan, not a girl with an honours degree in psychology, who lives here, pays tax and speaks perfect English and is brilliant with kids. I don't have the nerve to say it.

'Well, you know, Yitka might have plans,' I suggest, instead.

Camilla looks at me, confused. 'Plans? You mean social plans?' She laughs, as if I'm crazy. 'Yitka doesn't have plans. As I said, she's great. She's really hard working. I don't think she even *has* friends.'

And why would she need any, with a boss like Camilla?

'But you've got to watch out for her,' Camilla says. 'She was angling for a rise to seven fifty an hour.'

So . . . let me get this straight. Camilla's happy to entrust the care of her precious only son to Yitka, holding Yitka

11

personally responsible for his safety and happiness and early education, only to then try and screw her out of fifty pence per hour?

And this from the woman who justified spending six hundred and fifty quid on a cashmere jumper dress in Matches, by saying it was only £2.50 per wear.

Honestly.

Fortunately, at that moment, Tyler wakes up. His scream is so loud, he wakes up Ben. There's a flurry of Tupperware and half an hour of organising the fair division of carrot sticks between the kids, plus a ten minute conflab about the new management in the park café and whether we're all 'doing cake' today or not. For huntin' shootin' fishin' big girl Sarah, that's like asking whether we're 'doing air'. The lattes are off, caffeine hindering conception, apparently.

Finally we're all settled, and it's time for the regular update on each child's digestive quirks. It's riveting stuff. Really. Pithy, quick-fire dialogue. Seriously. It's a wonder Spielberg doesn't call.

I don't have the heart to admit that Ben is on day three of a hunger strike (salt and vinegar crisps excepted) and frisbees any bowl of food I give him at the wall.

'Goodness,' Camilla says, 'looking at everyone now, I can't believe how big Tyler is compared to the others. You know he's in size five Huggies!'

She makes this declaration in the same way I imagine a nudist on the beach might boast about her husband being hung like a baboon. Everyone can see it, but she's going to rub it in anyway.

In fact, nobody is given a chance to retort before she adds, 'So, what are we doing kids' birthday-wise? Are we going to do a joint one again, this year?'

I groan. Last year, on the exact day between all the kids' first birthdays, we lined up all the babies on a sofa and took photos of them, whilst Camilla made us all feel grateful for being in her huge mansion.

'Only last year was such a hassle, having *two* parties,' Camilla continues.

This is news to me. And deliberate news, I'm guessing, from the way in which she leaves the comment hanging in the air. I had no idea she had hosted another party as well as the one for the Vipers. We certainly weren't invited. Or *I* wasn't, at least.

'So this year, I think we should all do a party for our own child. It's easier that way.'

And more competitive.

'I've already booked out Pizza Teca on the 27th for the whole afternoon and Bella Bubbles will be there for entertainment,' she says, confirming my suspicions.

There are general impressed murmurs all around.

'So now, let me see . . .' She waggles her fingers. 'Amy, it's you first, isn't it?'

Too late, I realise that I've totally shot myself in the foot. In public, I've declared that I'm not having another baby because I'm enjoying motherhood so much. So telling the truth – i.e. that up until this moment, it hadn't crossed my mind that I'd need to have a party for Ben, on account of the fact that he's only two and won't remember it – won't wash with the Vipers.

'Yes. Sunday after next,' I say breezily, as if I have it all worked out. I pretend to look in my handbag. 'The invitations are . . . Oh dear, I left them at home,' I lie. 'Anyway, I hope you can all come?'

Everyone nods and looks generally pleased.

'Husbands too?' Sarah asks, through a mouthful of muffin.

I nod in a friendly way, a horrible sinking sensation in my stomach.

Jack said last time that he'd rather stab himself in the head with a fork than spend a minute in the same room as Sarah's husband, Tory Rory.

Oh God. What have I done?

13

2

Jack

Boomerang Boy Does The Praying Mantis

When I open the front door to our flat and the smell hits me, the first thing I'm reminded of is the school French exchange I went on when I was thirteen years old.

Long-suppressed memories strobe through my mind: *pain au chocolat*, butterfly knives, *petards*, Gauloise Blonde cigarettes . . . and a cute, spotty dishwater blonde called Marianne, who had tits big enough to ski off, a smile wide enough to break your heart, and who taught me how to kiss with tongues like they did in the movies, and promised she'd write to me in England, but never did.

Exhilarating times, perhaps, but it's the smell of the suburban maisonette I lodged in that sticks with me most.

The Legards were butchers. Mme Legard (face of an ageing Bardot, body of an ageing Sumo) had six kids, and spent her life grilling offal and frying onions, boiling cauliflower, changing nappies, making beds and running baths.

Their house smelt of feeding and breeding, laundry and drains.

It was an overwhelming, suffocating smell. It left me gagging and reeling, claustrophobic and trapped.

Which is why – Marianne's gargantuan charms notwithstanding – I was glad when my brief European *sojourn* came to an end.

In between sucking up the fresh sea air on the P&O ferry on the way back home, and chucking up illicitly purchased Martini Bianco into *La Manche*, I thanked God that I'd only been a *visiteur*, and that the rest of my life was still to come.

Yet, here I am – with twenty years having whipped by in the blink of an eye – and my own home smells exactly like the Legards' did then . . .

It's like I've come full circle, like everything I once ran away from has suddenly tracked me down. It's like I've become the Boomerang Boy.

I stare along the cramped hallway of my flat like it's the barrel of a gun.

Cloying with the *bouillon* whiff emanating from our kitchen, there's the nose-wrinkling, dry dairy tang of dribbled, soured milk, which patterns the upholstery of the blue gingham buggy that's currently blocking my path.

Added to these smells is the all-pervasive, meaty guff drifting out of the nappy wrapper in Ben's room. This rank contraption's Satanic purpose is to wrap and store used, disposable nappies in lemon-scented cellophane, like a string of pooey sausages.

Quite *why* this invention exists is beyond me. I mean, *why* would anyone conceive of wrapping a shit? Wrapping is what you do to presents, and it's not exactly like you're ever going to tie a gift tag to one of these stinky little numbers, and adorn it with the words: '*As soon as I saw this, I thought of you . . .*'

But what does my opinion matter? The nappy wrapper was brought here by my mother-in-law, and as such, I cannot do with it what I otherwise would – i.e. chuck it out, incinerate it, donate it to medical science, or, indeed, detonate it with a high explosive charge . . .

Instead I must live with it.

And accept it.

Just as I accept the other odours in my life.

Because it's nobody's fault really, of course . . . these whiffs

15

and pongs. It's just parenthood. We *do* clean, Amy and I. We vac and we ventilate. We mop and we scrub. It's just that sometimes – meal times, bath times, nappy times – the smell takes over, especially in a two bedroom flat like ours.

Sometimes it leaves me wanting to turn around and flee, to hunt out wide open spaces, the same as I did when I was a kid, and run with my arms outstretched like a plane, hoping beyond hope that I might actually take off and fly across the sky.

But I don't run. Because I'm not a kid. And because I know now what I didn't know then: that even the fastest of planes has to land somewhere.

And I landed here.

So I kick off my muddy work boots and close the front door behind me, and tell myself this:

So what if my life occasionally stinks? There's so much more to it than that, right?

And then I search for proof that this really is true.

And I'm lucky. I don't have far to look.

After contorting my way like Houdini through the obstacle course of the half-collapsed buggy, the upturned car seat, the wooden block trolley, and the soft toy wicker basket, I find that the first piece of evidence pertaining to the general munificence of my life is standing with her back to me just inside the kitchen doorway . . .

Amy Rossiter: the yin to my yang, the rock to my roll, the Moët to my Chandon, and the fish to my chips.

She's dressed in a tight black cotton top, with her hair tied up in a blue and white chequered scarf thats she's knotted at the nape of her neck. Her hair's downy there, kissable. Her top's ridden up slightly from the brown leather belt of her blue jeans, revealing a sensuous strip of skin at the base of her spine.

She doesn't turn round. She hasn't heard me come in. She's stirring a pan of cauliflower cheese that's blistering and popping on the gas stove, and looking like the surface of the moon. The extractor fan above the cooker is humming away, and the iPod's turned up loud, pumping out Marvin Gaye's 'Let's Get it On' . . .

It might be the sensuous strip of skin that does it. Or the redneck scarf, which, I admit, does add a certain Daisy Duke fantasy element to the scenario. Or it could be the song. Or even that the song isn't 'Teletubbies Say Eh-Oh', which is more often than not what I return home to these days.

Then again, it might just be that Amy's bum, snuggled tight inside her jeans, now starts swaying gently – hypnotically even – from side to side . . .

It could be any combination of these audio-visual factors that triggers my dormant libido, but the result is the same: I suddenly get an overwhelming desire to jump her.

Overwhelming desire to jump and actual ability to jump rarely coincide in my life these days.

This is largely to do with the fact that Amy and I are rarely alone together. And also largely to do with the fact that when we are, we're usually so exhausted that the attraction of slumping on the sofa often outweighs the attraction of humping on the bed.

Long gone are the bawdy pre-work bunk-ups upon which our relationship was built.

Lost to the mists of time are the occasional rude and rampant, raunchy lunch time rendezvous which spiced up our working days.

Dear-departed are the cheeky weekend getaways, spent speeding down motorways in search of cheap country B&Bs with creaking bedsprings and snug warm fires.

And all but a fond memory are the lewd and lascivious evening-long sessions of steamy baths and slow massage.

Instead, Amy and I have become the Sultan and Sultana of Speedy Sex, the Prince and Princess of Pragmatic Porkings, and the King and Queen of Calculated Quickies.

So long as we're not hung-over (which we frequently are),

17

we'll attempt to do it on a Sunday morning, before Ben wakes up.

So long as we're not seeing friends (which we frequently are), we'll attempt to do it at lunch times at the weekend, while Ben is taking his afternoon nap.

And so long as we're not hung-over, seeing friends, or dead on our feet (which we frequently are), we'll attempt to do it on weekday evenings, after putting Ben down and reading him *I Want My Potty* (which, I'm guessing, is *not* a text regularly recommended by sex therapists for its aphrodisiac qualities).

In other words, Amy and I get it where we can. Where sex was once a chef's gourmet tasting menu, it's now become a Subway sandwich. It's something you have on the run, something you squeeze in between other appointments and commitments – and as with all fast food, while the filling is perfectly tasty, it's rarely satisfying for long.

But this moment – here in the kitchen, straight after work – this truly is something of an anomaly. It's a window of opportunity I'd long ago thought bricked up.

So surprised am I, in fact, by the absence of my son at Amy's side, or some other local mum who's brought their kid over for tea, that I'm unable to resist stepping forward and issuing a mock-pervie, 'Phwoar!', complete with an affectionate pelvic thrust to Amy's well-presented behind.

I feel her flinch, surprised, as my arms slide automatically around her waist, and begin snaking up towards her breasts.

There are certain reactions you expect when you make such a covert amorous move on the woman you love.

The spooked: 'God, you made me jump!'

The ever optimistic: 'Grow up!'

Or even the aroused: 'Mmmm . . .'

But what I actually hear is: 'What za fuck are you doing?'

And the reason for this bellowed demand becomes glaringly apparent the moment she twists angrily round to face me.

She is not the she I thought she was.

This scarf-wearing woman – against whose buttocks my groin has just been grinding, and around whose breasts my hands have been circling like vultures – is actually someone I've never seen before in my entire life.

And as if any further proof of this horrendous, gut-churning fact were needed, it's provided now by Amy's appearance in the kitchen doorway, with Ben hitched up on her hip and gripped in the crook of her arm.

My mouth dries up like I've just bitten into a sack of salt.

'What the fuck *are* you doing?' Amy demands, glaring first at me, and then at the puce-faced, scarf-wearing younger woman, who's now staring at me in silent outrage, like she's just been plugged into the mains.

Horror fills me, as I follow the woman's stare, first towards my hands, which are still stretched out before me, incriminatingly cupped.

And then towards my hips, which I only now realise, are continuing to gyrate away spasmodically like those of an Elvis doll on a car dashboard, like they've somehow become autonomous from the rest of my body.

It's like a documentary I once watched on the Discovery Channel about the mating habits of the praying mantis, where the male's abdomen continued thrusting and pumping long after the female had devoured his head as a mid-coitus snack.

A strange, high-pitched whimper escapes my lips. Inside my trousers, my nuts perform a most un-nut-like manoeuvre, a kind of testicular jiggle, like they've transformed into two baby voles, who, having found themselves faced with a deadly predator, have started scurrying desperately around, seeking the protection of their mother.

I cross my arms, clear my voice and steady my hips.

'I'm so sorry,' I tell the girl in the scarf.

'I can explain everything,' I tell Amy.

'I thought you were Amy,' I tell the girl.

19

'I did,' I tell Amy. 'I thought she was you.'

The two of them exchange glances, like they're deciding whether to castrate me or shoot me first.

And the way I feel right now, the second of these two options would be both a kindness and a relief.

'Daddy funny,' says Ben.

I notice him smiling at me, eyes twinkling, like I'm a particularly clever monkey who's just performed a particularly clever trick. He giggles at me, and points.

'Daddy funny, Mummy,' he repeats, starting to giggle.

Something about the sound makes the scarf-wearing woman relax. I see it in her face.

Hey, she must be thinking, *if the kid thinks he's OK, then maybe he's not a serial sex pest, after all . . .*

Ben makes me relax too, the same as he always does the moment I see him, the same as the sight of my mum always used to when I was a kid. Ben makes me feel solid, a part of something bigger than myself. He puts my problems in perspective and makes me feel safe and strong.

I walk right up to him and kiss him on the nose.

I don't take my eyes off his for a second.

My son, my boy, the apple of my eye, the kid I'm looking forward to playing football with when he's seven, and who I'm itching to buy a beer for when he's seventeen . . . the kid who lights up my day, every day.

'Buzz, buzz,' I tell him, pressing his nose like it's a bell.

'Buzz, buzz. Buzz, buzz,' he repeats, grinning with delight.

If only adults were this easy to please.

But one glance up at Amy's glowering face tells me that this isn't the case.

Michael Douglas's Wrinkly Finger

'I can't believe you just did that,' Amy says.

She's standing with her back to the closed bedroom door, which has got so much paint peeling off it that it looks like a eucalyptus shedding its bark. She's just followed me through from the kitchen, leaving Ben with the woman in the scarf, who I now know to be none other than our new babysitter, Yitka.

'I already told you,' I answer, as I perch on the edge of the bed and haul off my sweat-heavy socks, 'it was an accident. I'm not to blame. She was in disguise.'

'In disguise?'

'She was wearing a scarf,' I remind her.

'Oh, right, well, that *does* make it her fault, then, doesn't it?'

I knew Amy would see reason in the end. 'Exactly.'

'And to avoid any possible confusion in the future,' Amy continues, 'perhaps I should ask her to wear a sign on her back, saying, "My name is Yitka, not Amy. So please don't grab my arse or squeeze my tits." '

'I didn't squeeze them, actually,' I point out. 'I merely caressed.'

This important distinction seems to pass Amy by.

'I'm surprised she didn't run out screaming into the street,' she says. 'Not that she could,' she adds, staring accusingly at my midriff. 'Not with you wedging your packet up against her like that.'

I groan, as I begin unbuttoning my shirt. 'Can we just drop this? I only goosed her, OK? By mistake. It's hardly the sex crime of the century.'

Amy's upper lip curls in distaste, as I stand up and drop my trousers. 'Rubbing yourself against her like that . . . like . . . like a dog on heat . . . it's disgusting . . . God, the poor girl. It must have been like . . . I don't know, like being assaulted by a male version of Mrs Robinson.'

'Hah,' I tell her triumphantly, standing here naked now, with my hands on my hips, 'so *that*'s what this is really about. Not *what* I did, but *who* I did it to. Not the crime itself, but the profile of the victim. You think that what I did is worse, because of Yitka's age.'

'I never said that.'

21

'Yes, you did. You just accused me of being a stubbly Anne Bancroft.'

Amy says nothing. Because she can't. Because her Freudian slip has clearly betrayed the fact that my inadvertent groping of another woman is nothing, compared to the fact that this other woman is younger than her.

It should make me laugh, of course, how ludicrous this is, but what it actually does is rile and depress me in equal measure.

Because there was a time when it would have been considered perfectly acceptable for me to have made a move on a woman Yitka's age. But it seems that time has passed. In Amy's eyes, I've clearly crossed that fine line from Lothario to . . . pervert. Another couple of years and I'll no doubt be promoted to the rank of Dirty Old Man (trench coat and *Razzle* magazine subscription *de rigueur*).

'Which is typical,' I add.

'Of what?'

'Of you. Of women. Of women's attitudes to men and younger women. I mean, sure, it's fine for Demi Moore to go out with Ashton Kutcher. Or for Diane Keaton to see Keanu Reeves. That's feminism in action. But the moment Michael Douglas lays one wrinkly finger on Catherine Zeta-Jones . . . well, everyone slams him for being a dirty old man.'

'Which is probably exactly what Yitka thinks of you.'

I grab a towel from where it's hanging on the back of a chair. 'Rubbish. And besides, Yitka's only a few years younger than me.'

'Just a few?'

'OK. Several.'

'Seventeen, actually, Jack. You're thirty-five and she's eighteen. You're old enough to be her father.'

'Well, biologically, I suppose,' I concede.

'And legally. And normally. There are plenty of thirty-five-year-olds with kids her age.'

I have to admit that these cold statistics do come as

something of a shock, but I'm determined not to let them put me off my stride. Or put me in the wrong.

'Which is exactly why,' I continue, 'if anything, you should take what happened in the kitchen just now as a compliment.'

'A *what*?'

'Well, Yitka's clearly a good-looking girl. So my mistaking her eighteen-year-old rump for yours *has* got to be flattering, right?'

'Oh, and there was *me* thinking that someone telling me I've had a smart idea, or that my hair looks great today is flattering . . .'

I notice that she has indeed had her hair highlighted and trimmed. 'Your hair does look great today,' I hurriedly say, trying to make amends. It does, too.

'Spontaneous, Jack. Why don't you look it up in the dictionary? You'll find it there between shithead and stupid.'

She turns to leave, but I catch her by the elbow.

'Come on,' I say gently, stepping up close to her. 'Let's not argue. Not tonight.'

There's an instant, as her eyes narrow, that I think that my attempt at appeasement has come too late, and that we're about to tip over from argument into full blown row, an event which seems to happen all too frequently and easily these days.

But then her expression softens and I feel her arm relax.

'You need a shower, shit seller,' she tells me, affectionately, screwing up her nose.

I slowly smile and shrug because there's no denying it. It's smeared across my work clothes, and even encrusted under my un-manicured nails: horse manure.

It's what I've spent my afternoon doing, spreading horse shit on Mrs Wilson's flowerbeds. Thoroughbred horse shit, mind you – driven in from an Essex stud farm at a quid a kilo, no less.

That (amongst a few other things) is what I do for a living now: sell shit to people richer than myself.

Or as Amy once put it: 'You used to just talk it, but now you flog it as well.'

This isn't to say that she's ashamed of what I do. It's just that sometimes I think she wishes it was a tad more glamorous. It's not surprising, really, when you consider that that's how things really were for a while, back around when we got married. When she was still working in fashion and I was still making a decent living selling my paintings to city firms.

But then Amy got pregnant. And my corporate commissions tailed off.

I had a crisis meeting with my old friend Chloe, who's now a financial adviser down in Brighton, and we talked through what I liked doing and what I could do – and *actually get paid for*.

She shot down my first idea: a Mafia-themed sandwich shop, called Baguetteaboutit.

But she went for my second: landscape gardening.

And so I took out a bank loan and did a twelve week course, and then I got the job at Greensleeves, a London-based firm that designs and manages rich people's gardens.

I work for them five days a week, and then help staff their organic veg store at the Queen's Park Farmers' Market every Sunday.

I slog my guts out, in other words. But then I have to: I need the money.

We're mortgaged up to the eyeballs on the flat, and I'm still paying off the loan I took out for the gardening course, as well as juggling various credit card debts and our overdraft.

There's not a lot left, in other words, at the end of each month. Especially now that Amy's no longer bringing in a wage. But we do get by. And we don't complain. Which keeps me going and keeps me proud.

Just like Amy's smile does now, as she watches me wrap the towel around my waist and pick up my trousers and shirt and chuck them into the laundry basket.

I'd normally leave my work clothes at the Greensleeves store over in Queen's Park, where I'd normally shower and scrub up as well, but I was in a hurry to get home tonight.

Tonight is special. It's my wedding anniversary. It's seven years since I married Amy Crosbie, the love of my life and the mother of my child. It's seven years today since I said the only two truly smart words of my life: 'I do.'

'Hurry up and shower,' Amy says, taking out a lip liner and crouching down and applying it in front of the mirror on the bedside table. 'I've got the cinema booked for half past.'

'Yeah, right,' I say. 'The cinema. I can't wait.'

Let's Talk About Sex, Baby

We never actually reach the cinema, of course, in spite of the fact that we've already prepaid for our tickets online.

What we do is walk down Mortimer Road and stand alongside a trio of gobbing, shuffling, teenage hoodies by the bus stop on Kensal Rise, and wait for the Number 52 bus that will deliver us to the Electric Cinema on Portobello Road.

And while we're waiting, we stare enviously, like a pair of starving Dickensian waifs outside Ye Olde Candee Shoppe, at the couples framed like magic lantern cut-outs in the warm amber glow of the pub windows opposite.

Wordlessly, we watch the bus arrive. Wordlessly, we watch the hoodies get on. Wordlessly, we stay right where we are and watch the bus depart.

Then, like two school kids cutting class, we scamper back across Chamberlayne Road and into The Greyhound pub.

This undebated, yet unified, change of destination comes as no surprise to either of us, because this is what we always do. We book tickets for things, for movies, or musicals, or comedy shows, because such cultural excursions justify the expense of a babysitter. (Which going to the pub clearly doesn't, as we could just as easily get hammered at home.)

'We don't use London enough,' we'll austerely bemoan, as

25

we studiously surf theatrical websites and plan our nights out.

'We put up with all of this city's downsides: the traffic, the taxes, the packed-out tubes,' we'll wisely declare, as we book in a babysitter, 'when what we should be doing is immersing ourselves in its great cultural wealth.'

And yet, always, lurking behind these verbal charades of intellectual self-improvement, there's the tacit agreement that we'll never actually see any of these theatrical productions.

They're facilitators, excuses, a means to an end.

They allow us to exit the house kid-free, and rewind time and feel young again, and hang out in the boozer the same as we always used to before we had Ben.

It's the best way we know, in other words, to get back to *us*.

Or at least it should be. It used to be.

Only, two hours after entering The Greyhound tonight, I'm no longer sure that this is the case.

It's not the pub itself that's the problem. The pub's fine. It's busy and vibrant and the food's awesome They've got the Gotan Project's latest coming out through the Bose, and all the other punters seem chirpy and relaxed.

No, the environment isn't the issue here. It's us. Amy and I. We're the ones who no longer fit in. Where we used to slide smoothly into pub-mode (rolling conversations, flirtation, and fun), we now seem to remain locked in home-mode – witness what we're talking about now . . .

'Can you believe she actually said that?' Amy's asking me. 'I mean, can you believe that she actually used the phrase "Shrek-like"? Don't you think that's incredible?'

'Gobsmackingly so,' I answer, but not because I cannot actually believe how vile Faith was to Linda about the shape of her kid's ears.

No, my incredulity stems from the fact that I cannot actually believe that Amy thinks this story is worth repeating. Especially in the hallowed adult environs of the pub.

Even more so on our wedding anniversary, with less than an hour to go before our Cinderella-like excursion into the nocturnal world of adults draws to an end.

Amy takes another sip of white wine and continues to tell me what happened next between Faith and Shrek Senior, but it's hard to stay focused on what she's saying.

This isn't because Amy's a boring person. She's not. (For example: I hope and suspect that she's only relaying these domestic titbits to me now, because she thinks I'm missing out.)

And it's not that I don't care about her. (I do. Just like I care about Ben. Passionately.)

It's just that motherhood's a boring subject. As in coma-inducing. At least it is to me (and, I suspect, to anyone else who's not a mum).

It's the relentless tedium of it all: the daily routine; the petty politics up at the park; the tiny, frankly imperceptible, daily steps taken towards maturity by my son . . .

Being subjected to this mountain of mundane details is like being forced to watch the news when you're a kid, or the Queen's Speech on Christmas Day. You know it's important, but, really, wouldn't it be much more fun to watch cartoons or a Bond film instead?

Most dads I know feel the same way. Which is why you'll never find us in a group discussing motherhood. Or father-hood, for that matter. Or anything else to do with rearing kids.

If a dad asks another dad the question, 'How are the kids?' the answer – excepting serious illness or death – is always the same: 'Fine.'

Whereas if a mum asks another mum the very same question, the answer always begins with 'Well . . .' and can go on for hours.

This isn't because dads love their kids any less, it's just that we know less about them than the mums. Most dads I know are parenting part-timers, temps, good for the odd bit of emergency cover, but not a lot else.

27

The plain fact is that we just don't get it.

And that makes talking about it all a bit women's turf, like detox, or exfoliation – and all the other subjects we don't discuss, not because we don't want to, but because we don't know how.

'So what do you think we should get him?' Amy asks.

'Who?'

'Ben. For his birthday.'

'Oh.' I picture all the toys we've got left over from Christmas which he hasn't even looked at. 'I don't know,' I reply.

'Well, think,' she tells me. 'It's important.'

'It is?'

'Of course.'

'Only, in case you don't remember, the last present I gave him – the Fireman Sam engine – he rammed it down the toilet and flushed it so many times that we had to get a plumber round to fish it out.'

'He thought it was a submarine,' Amy says defensively, the same way she always does whenever I criticise our little boy. 'He didn't mean to –'

'I know, I know, but all I'm saying is, I don't think he really cares what he gets for his birthday. We could get him a Bob the Builder house and he'd demolish it. Or a Star Wars doll and he'd decapitate it. The fact is, he'd probably be just as happy if we gave him a metal frying pan out of the cupboard and a wooden spoon to hit it with.'

'Or perhaps we could give him a wooden spoon to hit *you* with,' Amy says.

I notice that she's giving me that tetchy look, the one she holds back for traffic wardens and people who let their dogs crap on the pavement.

'I'm only expressing an opinion,' I say.

'Which is what, exactly? That we should give our only son two second hand kitchen utensils for his birthday?'

'If we wrapped them up nicely, he'd never know the difference.'

I might as well have just suggested that we give him a dose of anthrax.

'No, Jack. Birthdays are special. Which is why we need to get him something special as a present. Something he'll remember.' She tells me this slowly, I notice, like *I'm* the child.

As Amy launches into a sociology thesis on the importance of parenting not how we were parented ourselves, but how we *wish* we'd been parented, I once more find my attention slipping away from her like sand through an hourglass.

Instead, I begin surreptitiously checking out a girl who's perched on one of the high stools next to the TV. She's younger than Amy by around five years (*not*, then, young enough to be my daughter, biologically, or otherwise).

I watch her bright green eyes flash sexily through the gloom of the pub, as she laughs at something her friend's just said. When she stands up to go to the bar, I can see the outline of her lacy bra (black) through her frilled, embroidered shirt (white). I notice with approval that she's got the kind of legs and arse that it would be fun to play wheelbarrows with all night.

It's wrong, I know, to eye up a stranger like this. More wrong, I completely understand, to do so when I'm here with my wife. Most wrong of all, of course, when it's our wedding anniversary to boot.

But all men look at other women. All men look at *all* other women. From the moment we first spot the link between erections and sightings of the opposite sex, we perve, we wonder and we assess.

Sure, it's the kind of behaviour you're better off masking. Personally, I like to give the outward impression that I'm beyond that sort of primitive sexuality, that I'm evolved, that I'm nothing like those leering men apes you find jamming the West End bars at the weekend, swigging down pints of Stella and goggling at anything with tits that can walk.

But the truth is, I'm just the same. I'm just more subtle about it. I glance, rather than stare.

29

Just like I'm doing now.

And, I wonder idly, innocently, what *would* happen if I *wasn't* married, if I *did* go up to this girl and try on the old charm?

I mean, *do* I still have what it takes? *Could* I, with this green-eyed girl? *Would* she? With me? Tonight? Or would it take longer: flowers, dinners, jokes and real emotions? In a parallel universe, might we even have ended up falling in love?

Or have all such possibilities already been terminated? I think gloomily. In life's great sexual supermarket sweep, have I already passed my expiry date? Am I lying here on the discount shelf, next to the economy sausage rolls and shop-brand rhubarb yoghurts, unlikely to be picked up by anyone more discerning than bargain-hunting winos and OAPs?

As I drain my pint, I force my attention back onto Amy.

'He needs a special present and a special day,' she's telling me, 'and that's another thing I wanted to check with you . . . I thought it might be nice if at the weekend we asked some people –'

'Listen,' I interrupt, 'and I don't want you to take this the wrong way, but –'

'But what?'

'But can we just not, well, not talk about kids for a while?'

'We're not talking about kids.'

'We are.'

'We're not. We're talking about one kid, *our* kid. Who happens to be turning two this weekend.'

I rock back in my chair and fold my arms. 'We used to talk about other things,' I say.

'We still do.'

'When?'

'All the time.'

'So why not now?' I say.

She looks at me suspiciously. 'What do you want to talk about?' she asks.

'Don't say it like that.'

'Like what?'

'You know like what. Like that. Like I've got an issue.'

'An issue?'

'Yeah. An issue. Like I've got an issue I need to discuss,' I explain. 'Like that's the only reason I said I wanted to talk.'

She frowns at me, uncertain. 'Well, isn't it? Haven't you?'

'No. There is no issue.'

'You just want to talk?'

'About things.'

'So long as those things aren't kids?'

'You got it. Just like we used to.'

She looks around the room for a second or two, then laughs. Her cheeks flush, embarrassed, giving her this sexy sheen, like she's been caught out naked.

'What *did* we used to talk about?' she then asks. 'Because I don't remember any more.'

I grin back at her. 'Me neither. Which means it must have been a while.'

'I mean,' she stipulates, 'I remember *doing* it. Staying up late, drinking wine, but I can't remember anything that we actually said.'

'Maybe we're going senile,' I suggest.

'Maybe we are. Or maybe we've just forgotten how to relax.'

'I know,' I say, 'what we used to talk about . . .'

'What?'

'Sex. We used to talk about sex. One of the things, anyway.'

She laughs. 'You want to talk about sex?'

Leaning back the way I am, I can see the curve of her calf underneath the table. 'Not as much as I want to do it.'

'With me, I hope,' she warns.

'You're nearest,' I tease.

'Well, thanks . . .'

'And fittest.'

'That's better.'

31

'So fit, in fact,' I tell her, 'and so near . . .' My heart begins to drum. '. . . that I thought I should give you this . . .' I reach inside my jacket pocket and take out the simple silver necklace I picked up from Amy's favourite jeweller's during my lunch break this afternoon.

I walk around the table and she lifts up her hair as I put it round her neck and fasten it.

As I softly kiss the back of her neck, I wonder how I could ever have mistaken Yitka's neck for hers. Amy's is by far and away the more sensual of the two.

'Thank you,' Amy says, blushing. She cradles the necklace in the palm of her hand, before letting its silver links trickle through her fingers like water. 'It's beautiful,' she says.

I kiss her. 'Just like you.' And I mean it. Looking at Amy now, the green-eyed girl behind me suddenly no longer exists.

'I hope it wasn't too expensive,' Amy says, her face flashing with concern, as I return to my side of the table.

It was, but I don't tell her that. Besides, it's nothing I can't handle, not with the overtime I've already booked in at work. I'm just pleased she likes it.

'You are naughty, Jack. I thought you said no anniversary presents. I feel awful now. I haven't got you anything.'

'I'm sure we can come to some sort of arrangement . . .'

She laughs, taking my hand in hers as I sit back down. She stares into my eyes. 'Would you like me to seduce you?' she asks.

I smile back at her. 'I thought you'd never ask.'

The Horizontal Tango

Some things in life combine perfectly. The voices of John Lennon and Paul McCartney. The Grand Canyon and sunrise. Coffee and TV. Strawberries and cream. Amy's body pressed up against mine.

Not only does it feel right, it *looks* right. Like a great painting, it's a triumph of content and form, where every

32

brushstroke is how it should be, how it *has* to be, for the *tableau* to work as a whole.

It's like it could only ever have been this way, with *these* parts of my body, working together in perfect harmony with *those* parts of hers.

And, once more like a great painting, it's a sight I never get tired of. Each time I see it, I find myself staring in wonder, fascinated by some new facet.

Amy is a true instrumentalist. She's like Vanessa-Mae on the violin. Or Blondie on the microphone. Or Jethro Tull on the flute.

Euch. On second thoughts, let's put that Jethro Tull reference to one side.

And just think about what Amy's doing instead.

'Aah,' I softly moan.

As I gaze up at the shadows thrown on to the bedroom ceiling by the candles that Amy lit earlier, I think to myself that I could stay like this forever.

But this isn't only about my pleasure, of course.

It's about giving, as well as receiving.

And this is clearly something Amy's thinking about as well, I see, as without speaking, she begins to slowly, smoothly reposition herself on the bed.

Our bodies realign.

To 69.

And I wonder to myself, *Was there ever such a perfect coupling of numbers? Just look at them both, lying there side by side. Was there ever such a perfect inversion, and delicious perversion?*

It's a matter of taste, I suppose.

Time flows past like a warm stream, and soon we're on to dancing the horizontal tango, a routine that should be so familiar by now, and yet somehow still manages to surprise and remain startlingly fresh.

There's a brief moment of personal discomfort, when I find myself removing the paw of a Boo-Hoo Bear that Ben's left in

33

the bed from my butt cheeks, but apart from that, everything goes swimmingly. We're like two otters at play.

Right up to the point where Amy's sitting astride me, riding me hell for leather, like there are only a couple of jumps to go before the Grand National will be hers.

'There,' she's crying out encouragingly. 'Right there. Oh, mmm.'

'Mmm . . .'

'Oh, Jack . . .'

'Oh, Amy . . .'

'Mmm . . . Jack, oh, yeah . . .'

'Oh, Amy . . . oh, mmm . . .'

'Oh, Jack . . . yeah, there . . . I think I'm going to . . . I'm going to – I *am*, I'm going to –'

'Poo poo.'

Poo poo?

'Poo poo,' Ben confirms from his cot next door.

These two little words burst the balloon of our eroticism like a pin. A terrible transformation overtakes our surroundings. The exotically lit boudoir in which we've been making love reverts to our shabby and cramped candlelit bedroom. The fantasy is flattened. Our flight of imagination has been cruelly shot down.

Amy's hips cease sliding against mine. Her fingers unfurl from my hair, releasing their grip on my shoulders, so that I'm left with my hands locked on to her breasts, like I'm conducting a medical examination.

For nearly ten seconds, all I can hear is our breath, coming shallow and fast, as we pray for the silence to last, signalling that Ben's gone back to sleep.

'Poo poo!' Ben calls out again.

Amy growls with frustration. 'I'm going to have to change him.'

'Into what?' I ask hopefully. 'A mute?'

'Ha, ha.' She starts to roll off me.

'Please don't,' I beg. 'We're nearly there.'

34

It's true. We're teetering right on the edge of Orgasm Cliff, mere seconds away from toppling over into Endorphin Bliss Canyon.

'Just ignore it,' I implore. 'He might go back to sleep. It might not be his nappy at all. He might just be having a nightmare.'

Amy stares at me sceptically. 'About poo poo?' she asks.

'Well, why not? It's possible. I mean, it's not exactly like he's got a huge range of night terror subjects to pick from at his age, is it? Death by excrement avalanche,' I list off, 'death by teddy bear attack, death by breast suffocation . . . Mmm,' I reflect, 'what a way to go . . .'

'Poooo!' yells Ben.

Amy quickly kisses me. 'I'll be back.'

I answer her Schwarzenegger line from *Terminator* with the one Russell Crowe used in *Gladiator*, when he needed his troops to remain resolute in battle: 'Stay with me,' I call out. 'Hold the line.'

But Amy doesn't hear me; she's already gone.

I sigh, turning on to my side and taking a swig of water from the glass by the bed.

She's right, of course. There's no point in us trying to carry on once Ben's awake. Him demanding a new set of Huggies isn't exactly the ideal amorous soundtrack. Nothing to do with kids is (which no doubt explains why Prince chose to write about Alphabet Street, rather than Alphabetti Spaghetti).

'OK now?' I hear Amy ask Ben a few minutes later.

There's only one good answer to this: no answer. Because that would mean that Ben's riding a one way ticket back to the Land of Nod.

Instead he says, 'Milky.'

'Darling, it's the middle of the night,' Amy tells him firmly. 'Please, just close your eyes and go back to sleep.'

'Milky.'

There's a deep sigh-length pause.

'OK, darling,' Amy then tells him, resigned, 'I'll go and get a bottle.'

I listen to her walking through to the kitchen.

'Come back,' I call out, knowing that she won't.

Or rather, knowing that she will – in twenty minutes' time, after trying and failing to get Ben back to sleep – when she'll curl up between him and me in our bed, the same as she ends up doing every night that he wakes.

Feeling my cock slowly capsize, I sit up.

The moment has definitely passed.

Ben starts to cry, mewling like a kitten to begin with, then picking up volume with each new breath, cranking himself up notch by notch like an air-raid siren, as he builds, inexorably, towards what will become a deafening, full blown banshee wail.

Sighing, I get out of bed.

I wince as I stub my foot on the folded-up travel cot which is wedged up against the wall in his room. I bite my lip to stop myself from swearing at the stupid damned thing: harder than a Rubik's Cube to put up; tougher to get down than wrestling a greasy pig to the ground.

Ben's crying hits fever pitch, searing into me like chalk on a blackboard, or polystyrene packing being torn. Shivers splinter down my spine.

I hurriedly scoop him up in my arms. He quietens as I stare into his dark eyes.

He smells of menthol. I'm guessing Vicks Vaporub, which probably means that his tentative a.m. snuffle has turned into a full-blown p.m. cold.

I hope not. I hate it when he's ill. It makes me feel like I've failed, like I shouldn't be bringing him up in London at all, but somewhere cleaner, somewhere with fewer germs. Like the Galapagos Islands. Or that I should have done a first aid course, or become a doctor, or a Nobel-Prize-winning pharmacologist who could prove my love and dedication to

36

my son by conjuring up miracle drugs of my own invention to counter any complaint he may have.

Instead, I hold him close to my chest and whisper that I love him. I listen to him sigh and it melts my heart.

I smile, thinking that I'm a lot better at this than I used to be. I remember the first time I held him, there in the maternity ward, with Amy collapsed like a punctured inflatable doll beside us on the bed.

I was about as flummoxed as a chimp who'd just been sat at the controls of a Space Shuttle and then told, 'OK, we're ready. Now fly us to Mars.'

Looking at Ben and holding him close like this, feeling him here so solid and real, I sometimes get freaked out by the possibility that he might not have ever existed at all.

And that *is* a possibility. If Amy and I hadn't met . . . Or if we had, but we'd broken up . . . Then Ben wouldn't be here now.

It's a repugnant thought. An *impossible* thought. But it's one that keeps on occurring to me and leaves my chest tightened with fear. It makes me believe that actually there could *not* have been any other outcome. Amy and I *had* to get together. Fate's hand was in the mix. Right from the start.

I carry Ben back into our room and climb into bed with him.

Amy comes in a few minutes later and gazes at us and smiles. She looks beautiful in the flickering candlelight. She stays there, saying nothing, then walks quietly round the room and snuffs out the candles one by one.

'I'm sorry,' she whispers, slipping into bed beside us and handing the bottle to Ben, who grasps it and begins to drink.

'For what?' I ask, stroking her arm.

'For having to break everything off like that. Maybe we got his middle name wrong. Maybe instead of plain Benjamin Matthew, we should have called him Benjamin *Coitus Interruptus* Rossiter.'

'It's OK,' I say. 'It's not your fault – and anyway, you know what they say . . .'

'What?'

'Half a fuck's better than no fuck at all.'

'*Who* says that?'

'Parents mostly, I suppose.'

She's silent for a couple of seconds, then giggles. 'A fu,' she says.

'What?'

'A fu. That's half a fuck. So at least we can say we had a good fu.'

'Exactly,' I answer sleepily. 'And who knows? Maybe some time later in the week we might even get to finish it off with a ck.'

She giggles again. 'Play your cards right and I might even give you a *blowj*.'

This time, it's me who laughs. I take Amy's hand in mine and squeeze it tight. Happiness like I never knew before I met her fills me. I close my eyes and let the darkness swamp me.

Then there's just the three of us breathing, lying here side by side, drifting off into our separate dreams.

3

amy

Morning Glory

Good morning. You're listening to Radio CapitalChat with me, Jessie Kay, with you until eleven thirty. And that was 'Waterloo Sunset' by The Kinks, about Julie Christie and Terence Stamp . . . apparently. Should put you in the mood for this fine sunny morning in the capital. Now, this week, we're running a new feature called My Rant. Because I think it's time for you, the people, to have your say. Every day, we want you to ring in and tell us how it really is. Get real issues off your chest. Today's topic is working parents. Just call or text me on 0871 –

'Amy, where's my keys?' Jack yells from the bedroom.

It's nine thirty and I'm trying to coax some Weetabix into Ben, but he's sitting in his high chair at the end of our kitchen table, intent on blowing the longest non-stop raspberry of his life.

At least he looks a little better, I think, feeling his forehead. Since our anniversary last week, the poor little thing has had a shocking cold and has wound up in bed with us every night, which is less than ideal. I would leave him to cry himself back to sleep, but our wanker neighbour upstairs, Passive Aggressive Tim, bangs on the ceiling if Ben so much as whimpers. (It's his own stupid fault for installing trendy stripped floorboards, which provide no sound insulation and we have pointed this out to him in a carefully worded letter, but that just made his behaviour worse.)

But my problems are nothing, apparently, compared to Jack's. I should be able to deal with Ben all night and still be bright, breezy and attentive towards my husband. Yes, even when he's a grumpy bastard.

Because, Ladies and Gentlemen, let's not forget that disturbed sleep is *so* much worse for a man. Yes. Much, *much* worse, apparently. In fact, it's amazing they haven't done a scientific study to prove that it's medically damaging men's health for them to do any form of childcare in the night.

'Amy?' Jack yells again and I turn down the radio.

Why should I bloody know where his keys are? Why does he assume that I have nothing better to do than keep tabs on every single item of his personal belongings? I already do that for myself and Ben. Doesn't Jack realise how much brain space that occupies? Too much is the answer.

'Try your jacket,' I yell back.

'I have.'

'Laundry basket?'

'Not there.'

I can tell just from his tone, that he's standing in the bedroom cursing me. He hasn't even looked.

A second later, he appears in the kitchen doorway, staring at me in a frantic kind of way. Having only got to sleep at four a.m., we've both overslept this morning and Jack should already be at work. He's got bits of blood-stained loo roll on his neck where he's shaved in a hurry. Serves him right for nicking my blunt Venus ladyshave.

'Uh-oh, Daddy's rumbled me,' I say to Ben, scooping up a spoonful of goo. 'You see, Mummy got up in the middle of the night and took Daddy's keys out of his jacket pocket and . . .' I lean in close to Ben and raise my eyebrows in a scary, fairy-story kind of way, '. . . and *hid* them!'

Ben giggles, but Jack's not being humoured. He's got more furrows on his brow than Jeremy Paxman when he's quizzing a slippery politician.

'Amy, I'm bloody late.'

This sentence manages to convey that not only is this somehow entirely my fault, but also that I'm not taking him seriously. Furthermore, his time is more important than mine. Three black marks to Amy.

However, experience has taught me that there's absolutely no point in making him look for his keys himself. If I do, he'll start rampaging through the flat, tearing up sofa cushions and emptying drawers out on to the tables, cursing me the whole time.

On these occasions, ninety-nine per cent of the time Jack finds the article he's looking for (usually car keys, sun glasses, phone or his wallet) about his person, or where he last left them – i.e. in his jacket pocket, slung on the floor.

So it's a tricky one.

On the one hand, if I cave into him and find his flipping keys, I'll not only have reinforced his inability to find anything, but also recommitted myself as a finding things slave. Which doesn't bode well, considering that Ben is turning out to be Jack's Mini-Me in this department.

But on the other hand, if I don't help Jack find his flipping keys, I'll have to spend all day tidying up the resultant carnage.

And the bummer is, that either way Jack will be in a strop.

I dump the Weetabix on the high chair and, sighing heavily, get up and walk past Jack into the bedroom and straight over to the laundry basket. His jacket lies in a heap by its side.

I pick it up and check the pockets. No sign of his keys. So I check under the shorts on the top of the laundry basket. As I suspected.

I hold the keys up for him on my forefinger, expecting an apology, or at least a contrite kiss.

'You see. You hid them,' he says, triumphantly, snatching them off me. 'Why would I think of looking there?'

'I said the laundry basket. You've got to look *under* things, Jack.'

I roll my eyes and head back to the kitchen. He leaves it at that, for once, not demanding the last word. I take it as a thank you of sorts. I wonder, will we still be doing this in five years, ten years, fifty years? Will I be shuffling around on my zimmer frame still searching for Jack's pension book, or his false teeth? I suspect, I might.

'Mummy, look,' Ben says, pointing at his bowl of Weetabix, which lies upturned with sludge splattered up the wall. He surveys this curiosity from his throne as if it has absolutely nothing to do with him.

'I suppose I'll clean it up then, shall I?' I say, to no one in particular. I turn up the radio.

'What's this station?' Jack says, following me into the kitchen, picking up my mug from the table and drinking my tea. 'It's crap.'

'I was bored with the other one.'

This is not strictly true. I'm boycotting the usual station on account of the fact that they kept me waiting on the phone for twenty minutes last week on the afternoon show, when I had all the right answers and could have won a new plasma TV screen – and it pisses me off, because the girl who did win was helped out by the DJ. The fact that we don't have a wall big enough to put a plasma screen on is neither here nor there. It's the principle.

So what's on your mind, listeners? Time to have a rant. You'll feel much better for it. Call me, Jessie Kay. We'll talk to our first caller after this . . .

Oasis's 'Morning Glory' starts playing.

'Who's Jessie Kay?' Jack says. 'She sound like a right old tart.'

'I think she sounds quite nice. You know, I could ring in,' I say, dumping a handful of Weetabix-covered kitchen towel in the bin. 'I've got plenty on my mind.'

'Why don't you, then?' Jack asks.

I shake my head and blow my fringe out of my face. 'Because it's silly. Who'd want to listen to me?'

'Well, it wouldn't matter what you say. Only nutters and bored housewives listen to the radio at this time of day. All the real people are at work.'

'Real people like you, you mean?' I retort, before sticking my tongue out at him.

He's deliberately trying to wind me up, but he doesn't realise how close he's cutting it. He kisses me and then Ben on the top of the head.

'I'm only joking, darling,' he says. 'NSOH, or what. I thought you liked being a lady of leisure.'

A moment later, the front door slams as I reach for the phone.

Radio CapitalChat
Feature: My Rant
Caller: Amy from West London

Well, Jessie, sadly I'm not one myself, but I'm all for working parents. You see, my friend Ali is a working parent and I fantasise about being like her. Because every day she wears high heels, not trainers, and foxy little skirts, not yoghurt-stained jogging pants, and her handbag is filled with lipsticks and digital organisers and not nappies and half-eaten biscuits.

When she gets to her office, people make her cups of tea and tell her lots of juicy, interesting gossip, and people actually value what she has to say so much that they book meetings with her to discuss important issues. Not the frigging Teletubbies *or an update of the latest giant poo being performed. Imagine.*

But the problem is that unlike Ali, I don't have an important career to return to, and now that I've been out of the workplace for over two years, I'm also too useless for temping. What would be the point of paying someone to look after my precious two-year-old, whilst I sit and do a reception job for less money than his childcare costs?

OK, so there's the local nursery, but it's not nicknamed The Romanian Orphanage for nothing. But, guess what? I can't even leave him to beat his head against the padded wall all day because I didn't put his name down for a place on the waiting list the moment my husband was gurning with his final, conceptive thrust.

I should have done. I should have grabbed the phone and said, 'Hang on love, here's the Kleenex – now, where's that local nursery list?'

So I have no choice but to be a non-working parent. And I tell myself that it's better this way, caring for my child in his formative years.

So why do I feel so useless? And why do I feel guilty the whole time? Why do I feel as if I've given up on all my modern feminist female principles? This wasn't part of the plan. I'm sorry, but wasn't I part of the generation who was told we could have it all? Well, let me tell you, it was all a con.

Maybe the only option is to breed more.

Aha. But wait! Aren't I forgetting something?

Oh yes, we can't afford another baby, because I'm not working ...

Let The Boogalooing Begin

It's Tuesday, so it's Boogaloo Bunnies in Notting Hill. It's a schlep on the bus, but hey, what else am I going to do? I've already had my five minutes of fame for the day. Jessie Kay was right: Having My Rant has made me feel a lot calmer.

On the bus, I call Jack to tell him about being on the show. 'How are you?' I ask.

'What?'

'How are you?' I repeat. I'm smiling. I want to tell him how much better I feel.

'I'm fine, Amy.' He sounds both confused and annoyed. I suspect he's with the guys at work. 'In fact, I'm exactly the same as I was an hour ago when I left home. Did you want anything specific, only I'm right up to my elbows in shit. Literally.'

'No, it's nothing.' Backtracking and trying to keep the disappointment from my voice, I say, 'I'm on my way to Notting Hill, that's all.'

44

'Fine,' he says with an exasperated sigh. 'Love-you-bye.'

I growl at the phone. Then I text Ali to tell her that I mentioned her on the radio this morning, but even as I do, I feel like a pathetic saddo. She's in work. It seems impossibly glamorous and a world away from my pavement-pounding reality.

I would leave Boogaloo Bunnies, but I've paid for a block of sessions and I know from the nannies that I'm not going to get my money back. Besides, it gives me a chance to look in the posh shop windows on Westbourne Grove and play shoe fantasies.

More importantly, I pass the newsagent's where I always buy a lottery ticket. This particular newsagent, I know for a fact, has had two big lottery winners. I'm going to be the third.

When I win, I'm going to buy a big fuck off house on the hill with an artist's studio for Jack and a fabulous view over London, and I'll have a second home on a Caribbean island, where Jack and I will spend most of the year. I'll have so many staff, Camilla will choke on her cashmere cardigans. I'll have a sexy personal trainer who'll whip me into shape, and an amazing nanny for the kids (I'll have three more). Jack and I will spend our days together, eating lunch that we've caught from our jetty that morning and having a siesta and making passionate, unbridled love in our architect-designed tree top suite, where there are no neighbours, except for the exotic birds. And, most importantly, the kids can't get in.

I'm just on my way out, negotiating the buggy around the pile of *Evening Standards*, when Ali calls.

'I don't know why I came back to work,' she says, after we've swapped hellos and I've ascertained that she's whispering because she's in the office loo. Even so, I can hear her voice catching in her throat.

'Are you OK, Al?'

'No, I'm not,' she says with a hefty sigh. 'I'm so bloody tired. All the time. I get up at six with Oscar, and then there's the commute and a full day at work, and then I'm treated like a part-timer for leaving at six thirty in the evening. The women at the nursery treat me like scum for picking up Oscar so late, by which time he's tearful and tired, and I'm so knackered, and then I have the onslaught of bath and bedtime. And after that I have to do paperwork in the evenings to catch up with all the stuff I didn't get done in the office . . .'

'But I thought you wanted to go back. I thought –'

'I don't have time to do anything, Amy. I mean *anything*. I don't have time to shop, or clean, or wash my clothes, or see my friends. I can't remember the last time I had sex. My house is a giant pig sty, and I feel guilty all the time. I feel like I'm letting everyone down. I'm crap at my job, I'm a crap friend and a crap wife and a crap mother.'

I'm stunned by her outburst, and confused too in the light of my rant on the radio this morning.

'Hey, you shouldn't feel guilty,' I say. 'I'm the guilty one. At least you're being a useful member of society.'

'And fucking up my child, as a result. I don't know. Enjoy it, Amy. You don't know how lucky you are.'

I'm still confused about Ali's rant as I make my way into the hall. I've been to plenty of playgroups in the last two years and they're all fairly dire. But maybe Ali's right. Maybe I should let myself off the hook and enjoy hanging out with Ben more. However, one look at the Boogaloo Bunnies crowd and once again it's patently obvious that I don't fit in here.

On the one hand there's a group of cliquey uber-posh Kensington and Notting Hill mummies. They all wear size six designer jeans and giant knuckle duster diamond rings and have Botoxed foreheads. And then there are the nannies. They all talk Slovakian to one another, but at least they're friendly (and intelligent).

Boogaloo Bunnies is run by Trish and her side-kick Magda, whose only job is to operate the music system. She has a dyed Cleopatra bob and a manic expression. I don't think she's really all there.

Trish herself is something to behold. Today she's in purple lycra tights. A throwback from her days auditioning for the original cast of *Fame – the musical*, no doubt. Her bug eyes are heavily made-up and red lipstick clogs the cracks around her lips. But you can't fault her dedication to the job.

Personally, I think you've got to be missing the self-conscious gene in order to work with children. There's a kids' presenter on the TV who does the bits between the programmes and Ben absolutely loves him. He finds him hilarious, but I look at him every time and think: How do you do that for a day job and then go home and have sex?

'Can you guess where I am, everyone? Yes, that's right, I'm in bed with my wifey. And look at this lovely pink nipple, just here. Look, you can wiggle it with your finger. I know a little song about a nipple. You can join in if you want: 'wiggle wiggle little nipple, wiggly wiggly woo, wiggle wiggle little nipple, is it nice for you?'

I mean, this guy comes across as an utter berk, but he must have agents and make-up people and accountants. Do they take him seriously? Does he consider it a foot on the ladder to serious TV drama? Does he dream about his big break in Hollywood? Or wowing the critics at the Old Vic?

It's a mystery to me how these people – the bloke off the TV and Trish, here in Boogaloo Bunnies – can do their job. I find singing 'The Wheels On The Bus' in public excruciating. Every time we're asked to join in with the kids, I turn into a sulky sixth former. I have to fight every urge I have to run away to stay sitting on the floor cross legged. I can only just about deal with it by making up alternative words in my head: 'The Mummies on the bus go, "We want Valium! We want Valium! We want Valium!" The Mummies on the bus go, "We want Valium!" All day long.'

Magda presses a button and 'Postman Pat' blares out at club volume. There's a bouncy castle set up in the hall and Ben shoots out of his buggy straight on to it. I can tell from the glint in his eye that he's going to jump as high as he can and, if possible, practise his new skill: headbutting. He's got his sights on posh Jessica. She's six months older than he is and has already mastered the double eye fingernail gouge, so it should be quite a match. I think Ben's got a score to settle.

I've only just had time to kick off my trainers and scramble across the crash mats to intercept him, but not before he's bounced Jessica's mate out of the castle. Her mother gives me a wounded look. As wounded as she can, considering she can't move her Botoxed forehead. Silly cow.

There's twenty minutes for 'soft play' before the Boogalooing begins, which involves me trying to minimise the injury caused to the entourage of toddlers my son gathers in a pied-piper-like way to do what looks like rugby squad training with the various padded cylinders. There's nothing remotely 'soft' about it.

In between the tears and scuffles, us grown-ups attempt to make small talk. Jack thinks that I hang out all day with other like-minded women having a good laugh, nattering and yacking away in an endless stream of amusing banter, but he, like every other man I know, has never been to one of these playgroups. If he had, he'd quickly realise that they're social Siberia. Adult interaction is pitiful at best.

There seem to be ludicrously small parameters for conversation. There are no hellos or how-are-yous, for starters. Personal information must be kept to an absolute minimum, even down to names, and since we're there as carers, we have to appear to be looking after our offspring at the same time and therefore not give any conversational gambits our full attention. And subjects for these are tough. The décor and surroundings are too dull to comment upon, and, as half the women aren't British, comments about the weather are met with confusion. So that only leaves the kids for conversation.

'So how old is your little one, now?'

'Nearly two.'

Understanding nod.

Next.

These conversations start nowhere and end nowhere. That's the problem. Even if I did have anything in common with any of these women, I'd never get a chance to find out.

Trish calls us into a circle.

She means business. She turns off the air to the bouncy castle and it promptly slumps in the corner like a drunk.

We all sit dutifully. Trish prances into the middle of the circle.

'All the children, here we go,' she chirrups, nodding to Magda who presses the button on the CD machine.

But it's the wrong song. Furious, Trish bats her hand, eventually stomping off to the corner to tell off Magda.

Finally, the right music comes on.

'And, five, six, seven, eight,' Trish announces, smiling broadly and pulling all the children into a conga formation.

'No, Mumma, no,' Ben says, crawling into my lap and burying his head in my shoulder. He always calls me Mumma when he's being particularly affectionate. He smells delicious – of fabric softener and baby shampoo and Marmite toast.

The problem is that I'm kind of with him. Trish looks scary to me, let alone to a nearly two-year-old.

'Home,' he says, pulling back and gripping my shoulders with his little hands, so that he can look at me with his huge brown eyes with their impossibly long lashes.

My heart swells. Part of me wants to wrap him up and take him home and protect him from the perils of other children and the awfulness of having to join in with them.

Maybe it would all be simpler if I let him sit at home in front of CBeebies all day until he's school age. Perhaps that would be educational enough. After all, who's to say he should be socialised? And why should he socialise with this lot, in particular? They're not exactly scintillating company for an adult, either.

But no. I'm doing this for him. For his benefit and he's

49

going to join in whether he likes it or not. Besides, I've paid for it.

I gently push him away. 'Go on, darling, it's OK. Mumma's here.'

Trish homes in on him and grabs him. The more I look at her, the more I think there's definitely something Wicked Witch of the West about her. Her nails are painted purple and look like talons on her wrinkly hand. I half expect an evil hoard of monkeys to appear from somewhere.

Ben's eyes grow wide with horror and tears. He looks at me as if I've totally betrayed him, as the Wicked Witch hauls him away. Like Dorothy would if Toto had taken a leak in her red slippers, before selling her out for a can of Pedigree Chum.

'No like you, Mummy,' he calls back.

Ouch.

Meltdown

Of course, by the end of the session, Ben's loving it and he doesn't want to leave. I have to drag him away, carrying him under my arm out of the hall. Kids are like that. They hate what they don't know. They love what they do.

I'm just crossing the road to the bus stop, when my phone rings. I'm hoping it's Jack and, juggling Ben and the buggy, I somehow manage to press the answer button. It's only then that I realise it's my mother.

'Now, Ben's birthday . . .?' she says by way of greeting. There's an expectant rise in her voice, the kind that manages to convey that she's slightly miffed she hasn't yet received a handmade invitation (one of Ben's potato prints maybe?) through the post.

'Ben's birthday?' I ask back, ignoring the obvious impli-cation. I lift Ben up, gripping the phone against my shoulder, as I manhandle the buggy over the high kerb. A car beeps me.

'Piss off,' I yell, somehow managing to find a spare finger to flip at the driver.

'What did you say?' Mum demands.

'Not you. Someone else.'

'Who?'

'It doesn't matter.'

'Well, clearly it does, or you wouldn't be using language like –'

Ben tries to headbutt me. 'Stop it,' I warn.

'No, I will not,' Mum says.

'Not you,' I repeat, exasperated. 'Ben.'

'Ben's with you? Well, that's even more reason for you not to speak like that.'

Lord, Give Me Strength.

I let go of the buggy and put my finger to my lip, to tell Ben to be quiet, but he's not happy and repeatedly attempts to slap my face.

'Mum. Look I'm really busy. Was there anything –'

'So when's his party?' my mother asks, clearly annoyed that I've forced her hand.

I lower Ben into the buggy.

'When is his party? Um. Well, I wasn't thinking of doing a party, Mum,' I lie. Actually, I've been thinking about nothing else since I was forced into it by the Vipers, but there's absolutely no way I can ask any family. That ups the numbers to far beyond the capacity of our flat and I've left it too late even to think about hiring somewhere else.

Not that we've got any money for hiring anything much more than a DVD right now. Not after Jack bought me that necklace. I felt so bad at the time for having doubted him and for having assumed he would have forgotten our anniversary. I felt like such a low-down doubting Thomas that the next day, I ransacked the flat until I found the receipt for the necklace and read it (naughty, I know). I guess I was hoping to assuage my guilt, but the receipt only confirmed that Jack had pushed out the boat and made a truly romantic gesture and bought me the kind of gift that he knew I'd love – the kind of understated-but-nevertheless-unmistakeably-expensive necklace that rich girls (like Camilla) receive. I love Jack

51

for doing it (I haven't taken it off yet), but really, our bank account is about as healthy as a corpse, and, since I was so in the wrong about our anniversary, I still haven't found the right moment to break it to him that I've invited all the Vipers plus husbands, plus kids over for Ben's birthday. If I compound my hideous error by asking Mum too, he'll go bonkers.

There's a short intake of breath, as Mum contemplates the horror of what I've just said.

'But you've got to have a party, darling. Think of the child.'

The child. She always says this. Not, your son, or my grandson, or even his name. No, for important conversations where she needs to upgrade Ben's status and downgrade mine, he's *the child*. It would be fine if instead of living in NW10, I lived in Galilee and was, in fact, the Virgin Mary. I'd get used to people referring to my son as 'the child'. But as it is, it gets right on my tits.

'I *am* thinking of Ben, Mum,' I say pointedly. 'I'm thinking that he's two, and that we live in a tiny flat, and he's not going to remember it anyway –'

'How can you possibly say that?' she interrupts. 'Of *course* he'll remember it. I mean, not physically probably, but emotionally . . . they say that celebrating birthdays with the child's close family makes a huge impact . . .'

She says this as if she's reading it from a parenting manual – the kind of manual I've never bought, but she has a shelf full of them purchased on a month-by-month basis since Ben was born.

I try to do the straps up on Ben's gingham buggy, but he's not having it. He emits a low screech-growl and his cheeks go red.

'Please,' I hiss at him, through gritted teeth. Not again. Not today. I jam my forearm across him, my face tensed for war. I lean in close. 'Stay in,' I threaten. 'Or else –'

But it's too late. It's a code red. Ben has clocked that conditions are right for a full blown tantrum.

Hungry. Check. Tired. Check. Bus stop full of bored on-lookers with nothing better to do than provide captive audience for tantrum. Check. Mother distracted. Check. Even better . . . mother on phone to grandma. Check . . .

Ben does a violent back arch. His arm punches out at full force, catching me on the nose with a right hook Mike Tyson would be proud of.

'No! No buggy! NO BUGGY!!!' he screams, thrashing around.

'Mum . . . Mum . . . can I call you back?' I ask politely, trying to keep calm, as I hold my nose. My head's spinning. I check my palm. There's blood.

Incredibly, Mum's still talking.

'I've got every one of your birthdays in a photo album,' she continues, oblivious to my tone. 'I can bring it over. *Your* second birthday was wonderful. Alice and Richard and all the old gang were there.'

She thinks this gives her top marks for parenting. If she had one ounce of parenting skills, however, she would suss that I'm in the middle of a crisis and stop playing 'I'm a better mother than you'.

Ben continues thrashing. He's screaming so loudly and bucking so violently that a cyclist stops to stare at him, then looks around to check for hidden cameramen. Like this might be some kind of stunt.

Why is it that, all my life, for as long as I can remember, I've slogged through exams and tests and been forced into accruing tonnes of useless, impractical knowledge – how to dissect an earthworm, how to ask the directions to the nearest carpark in German (Wo is das Parkplatz, bitte?), how to master Word Perfect, how to use all those brown logarithm keys on a calculator – instead of anything that might come remotely close to teaching me how to deal with a toddler having a hissy fit?

I can feel the eyes of the bus-stop on-lookers boring into my back. I can feel the weight of their expectation.

53

But how the fuck should I know what to do?

OK, so I *know* I should be taking control. He is, after all, my son. But if I lift Ben up, there's every chance he'll headbutt me and I'm injured enough already. If I let him out of the buggy, there's every chance he'll start headbutting the pavement.

But what am I thinking? I can't lift him up, or let him out. I can't let him win. He's nearly two. If I let him win, I'm stuffed for life. He'll think I'm weak. He'll assume he's in charge, and the next thing I know, he'll be fourteen years old and skiving off school and shagging his girlfriend, and staying out clubbing and driving drunk on his moped. I know. I've been there. Done that.

So I'm not going to give in to him. No way.

I keep him pinned exactly where he is and try again to fasten the straps.

But playing by my own rules is extremely hard. I'm being verbally and physically abused. In public. Shouldn't a UN Peacekeeping Envoy be here any second? I turn desperately to the crowd, but they're all staring at me. It's clear that none of them has any intention of helping.

Desperately, I look up at the sky. Where's my chopper with a rescue ladder?

'Well?' Mum says, waiting for my response.

I'm forced into crisis management. I'm simply not strong enough to stand up to two generations at once. Hating myself and knowing that I'm going to regret it, I make a snap decision on potential long term damage. I give in to my mother.

'OK, OK, OK, come on Sunday then. I'll have a little party,' I bark at her, shrinking inwardly at my own weakness. 'Now I've got to go, I think I'm running out of –' I say, pressing the button and cutting her off.

I throw the phone into my bag and give Ben my full attention. I pinion him into the buggy, forcing myself not to swear at him. And . . . ha! I finally lock the straps.

Ignoring his piercing yells of fury, I set off at a ripping pace up the road. Sod the bus.

'Poor little scrap,' a lady says as I pass the bus stop, looking down into the buggy and then up at me. 'He's probably just hungry, love.'

Well, wouldn't you just know it. Just when you least need one. Who should turn up? A genuine MOB (Meddling Old Biddy). Typical.

You meet MOBs all the time. At first I was truly shocked when I discovered their existence, because, as a female, it would never occur to me to dole out unwarranted, slightly critical advice, to a stranger, when they're obviously stressed. It's just not done. It goes against every code of social etiquette.

That is, unless you're a MOB. MOBs are a breed unto themselves. And new mothers are fair game to them. They seek you out and time their strikes for when you're at your most vulnerable. 'Are you going to feed that baby?' (Tesco's dairy aisle, when Ben was two weeks old and hyper-ventilating with fury.) 'He's too hot, he'll overheat. That's why he's upset.' (Stuck on the Piccadilly Line, at midday, during a heat wave.) The list goes on . . .

But the golden rule of dealing with MOBs is never to engage with them. Because they really do think that they know more about your baby than you do.

Back off Hag, I think to myself, pushing on past, but I still feel the curse of the MOB upon me. I feel low down and depressed.

There's only one thing for it: sugar fix.

I dive into the nearest shop and buy myself a bar of chocolate. There's a *Win A Shopping Trip to New York* competition on the wrapper. Yeah. Right. Like that's ever going to happen.

But I still read all the details, as I stand on the street. Ben's fallen asleep. I finish the chocolate in one go, and I'm about to set off again, when my phone rings.

It's Alex Murray, the producer of Jessie Kay's show on Radio CapitalChat. I'm so flummoxed that it takes me a while to understand what he's saying. It seems that my rant this morning on My Rant has prompted a really good response from callers. And they all feel exactly like me. And now Jessie Kay thinks *I'm* chocolate. And she wants me on her show again.

Ha!

See Jack, I think, wiping the blood off my nose on the back of a nappy, I'm not just a bored housewife or a nutter.

I'm a real person, after all.

4

Jack

The Exorcism Of Amy Rossiter

I flick the radio over from Radio CapitalChat on to XFM and take off my jacket and stretch and yawn. It's Saturday morning, just gone eleven, and I'd give anything to still be in bed.

Out through the kitchen window, warm sunshine filters through the eucalyptus tree. It dapples our back garden, which is the same shape as a slice of toast and not a lot bigger.

Delicate yellow jasmine flowers are scattered like Christmas lights along the garden's ivy-covered rear wall. Honeysuckle hangs from the worn wooden side fence in a candy floss of white blossom, and the Cornelia roses I planted last year for Amy's birthday are out in full bloom, and glistening from where I watered them earlier.

It's as good a day as any, I suppose, for the barbecue that Amy's got planned, and I almost wish I'd asked some of my friends over.

The problem is, most of them (like Ug, Chas and Mikey) don't yet have kids, which means that kids' parties are still high up there on their lists of 'Extremely Uncool Things To Do' (along, one suspects, with *getting up before lunchtime at the weekend, staying at home on a Friday night* and *listening to James Blunt*).

And as for the friends of mine that *do* have kids . . . well, it wouldn't be fair to ask them either. For one thing, they're probably suffering from kiddie fatigue themselves, and for another, none of them lives nearby any more. They've been scattered across the country by parenthood, as if by a war. Forced to enlist in the ranks of new social tribes, in safer communities, with cleaner streets and better schools.

'Look, Dadda . . .'

I turn and smile at the birthday boy himself, who's sitting in his chair at the end of the kitchen table, smearing Marmite all over his face. I kiss him on the brow and he giggles my name.

'What's *that*?' Amy demands, coming through from the bedroom, and staring down at the two Sainsbury's bags I've just dumped on the kitchen table.

She's dressed in jeans, open toe sandals and a loose green top. She's looking rumpled and sexy, the way she always does in the morning, before she's had a chance to shower and do her hair.

Or maybe it's just stress.

'The shopping,' I answer.

'Where's the rest of it?'

'The lager's in the car. I picked up an extra slab. Along with some vodka. You know, just in case . . .' Just in case Ben's birthday party turns out to be fun, I'm thinking. Which is about as likely as Jim Carrey and Mike Myers turning up in person to do the kids' entertainment. But still, you never know . . .

'No, I mean where's the rest of the food?' Amy asks.

'There is no rest. That's it.'

'But . . .' She starts rummaging through the shopping, like she's a customs official at Heathrow Airport acting on a tip-off. 'But what about the organic chicken nuggets?' she demands. 'And the manuka honey? And the Belazu olives and sesame seed bread sticks? What about the guacamole and haloumi? And . . . and *everything* else that was on the list I gave you?'

She stares at me in exasperation, like it's me, not her, who's suddenly started speaking fluent Martian.

'Oh, that,' I say. 'I didn't get any of that.'

'What?'

'I decided it was overkill.'

'*Overkill*? *You* decided? *You*, who've put so much effort into arranging this party . . .'

'Oh, come on. We've already got plenty of meat defrosting for the barbecue, and most of that other stuff you wanted would have ended up in the bin. It would have been a complete waste of money.'

Amy doesn't answer. Or not in words at least. What she does is growl. It's the kind of growl a Rottweiler dog might make if you tried to take its favourite bone off it, the kind of growl that says, *Back off, pal. Or walk with a limp for the rest of your life.*

I watch in bewilderment as Amy snatches three cartons of milk from me and rams them into the fridge like artillery shells into a cannon.

I'm about to point out to her that her current level of anger (a 7.9 on the Amy-Richter Scale) constitutes a completely disproportionate reaction to my entirely sensible rationalisation of her overambitious shopping plan, when another possibility springs to mind.

'How many people *have* you invited?' I ask.

'I already told you: a few.'

'How many?'

She slams the fridge door and rears up, spinning round to face me. 'Thirty.'

'*Thirty*?' I blurt out. 'But we don't even know thirty people.'

'Ben does.'

I stare at her, astonished by this claim that my two-year-old son's social life has apparently eclipsed my own. 'Name them,' I challenge.

So she does. And as she rattles them off, I start groaning like an asthmatic having an attack.

It's like a hideously inverted version of *This is Your Life*.

Instead of being presented with a much-loved parade of people from my past (each prepped with a suitably hagiographic and quasi-comedic anecdote, paying homage to the Wonder of Me), what I actually get is a pantheon of randoms, dullards, half-acquaintances, and bores (most of whom couldn't even name me on sight).

But Amy appears completely oblivious to any discomfort I might be going through. Ignoring me, she marches back past me and noisily upends the first of the shopping bags on to the table.

She stares down at its disgorged contents in the same way I imagine a panicked rookie Army surgeon might when presented with their first critical battlefield casualty.

Why me? her expression seems to be saying. *Why now? I never wanted to be a surgeon. I never wanted to go to war.*

The Sainsbury's bag's entrails consist of the following: an assorted pack of Discos crisps, six bright blue jellies in pots, a party pack of pink flumps, eight bags of Chewits, a pink and yellow chequered Battenberg cake, and a discounted tin of Christmas biscuits with some badly painted shop-brand generic cartoon characters on the lid.

Amy's diagnosis is: 'There's enough saturated fat in there to sink an aircraft carrier.'

But I'm ready for this. I tip out the contents of the second bag and point out the two carrots *and* the apple which I considerately bought.

'I thought we could make sticks out of them,' I helpfully suggest. 'You know, batons . . .'

Amy seizes on the family-sized bag of salted mixed nuts, and holds it up before her like Poirot might a loaded gun.

'What's wrong with that?' I ask.

'You can't serve nuts at a kids' party, Jack. Haven't you heard of anaphylactic shock?'

'The punk band?' I hazard.

She groans and grabs the Smartie cake, which suddenly doesn't look quite as big, or as smart, as it did on the supermarket shelf. She starts to tear the brown icing-smudged wrapper off, but then she just stops. Her shoulders sag. She stares forlornly down.

'I'm not Jesus, Jack,' she groans. 'How do you expect me to feed them all with this?'

'Well, if you'd told me the truth about how many people were coming –'

'You'd just have got angry,' she yells, gripping the edge of the table like she's on a ship in a storm. 'Just like you are now.'

Me angry? *She*'s the one who looks like she's auditioning for *The Exorcism of Emily Rose*. I check her ears for signs of blood, or steam, but then her face crumples in anguish and I start to feel sorry for her.

'Oh, God,' she wails, 'my mother's going to think I'm such a failure . . .'

My sense of pity evaporates like a droplet of water on the surface of the sun. It's my turn for am-dram antics now.

'Whoah,' I say, holding up my hand like a copper stopping the traffic. 'Your mother? Your mother's coming here?'

'Yes.'

'Today?'

'No, Jack, next bloody millennium.'

'Hah. More like that's when she's planning to leave.'

'She's only coming over for an hour.'

'An hour,' Ben mindlessly agrees.

'Right, and the last time she said that she was still here three days later,' I remind her.

OK, time out. I know. The Mother-in-Law of Doom (MILOD). It is, of course, a bit of a cliché, but there's no smoke without a fire. And MILODs really do exist. I know. I have one myself. She inveigled her way into my life, shortly after I inveigled my way into her daughter's knickers. And she hasn't left since.

'This isn't about you, Jack,' Amy complains. 'This isn't your party. This is about Ben.'

61

'Ben,' says Ben, as if to emphasise this point.

But I'm not in the mood for being ganged up on, and I've had enough of being vilified too. I've been up since seven. I've done the shopping. I've agreed to do the barbecue. I'm here, aren't I? I'm doing my bit, goddammit.

'No,' I say, suddenly feeling more snappy than a piranha with a period, '*this* is about *you*. About you showing off to your friends and your mother . . . It's about you saying, "Look at me. Aren't I a great mum?"'

Ben starts to cry.

'Now look what you've done,' Amy and I bark in unison, before lunging at our son in an effort to claim the parenting moral high ground.

Annoyingly, Amy gets there first. She snatches Ben up triumphantly and kisses him rapidly and repeatedly on the face, before holding him tightly and melodramatically to her chest, like she's sweet little Nancy trying to protect Oliver Twist from the murderous claws of nasty Bill Sikes.

'Horrid Daddy,' she tells Ben, 'making you cry like that.'

'Nasty Mummy,' I retort, 'shouting all the time.'

'Prick,' Amy hisses.

I open my mouth to swear back (I was considering either a *shithead*, an *arsehole*, or a *twat*), but then I close it again, because the route back on to the moral high ground has opened up wide before me. *I* don't need to resort to petty profanities. *I* can rise above all that.

'Don't swear at me like that in front of him,' I say. 'Apologise. Now.'

But my valiant defence of civility and good old-fashioned family values appears entirely wasted on Amy.

'Piss off,' she shouts, before bolshing out of the kitchen and up the corridor like a hormonal teenager.

'Oh, fine,' I call after her. 'Walk away. That'll solve everything.'

'No, Jack, it won't,' she flares, 'but going to the corner shop will. And getting everything *you* should have already got.'

But just as Amy reaches out to open the flat's front door, the doorbell rings and I watch her freeze.

'Who's that?' she demands, suddenly looking back at me. 'No one's meant to be here for another hour.'

I fold my arms across my chest and smile. 'Gosh, I wonder...'

Amy's eyes glint with feral menace. 'You don't know it's her.'

Oh, but I do. As surely as Harry Potter can sense the approach of a Dementor coming to suck his very life force away...

I walk up behind Amy as she opens our flat's front door. As we peer across the small, tiled communal hallway, we both see that I'm right.

A large-barnetted woman is clearly silhouetted there on the other side of the building's stained glass front door. It's instantly apparent that there are only five possibilities as to who this is: Marge Simpson, Dusty Springfield, one of the two chicks out of the B52s or ... Amy's Mum.

Step Aside, Sperm Provider

'Shit,' Amy says. 'Stall her, will you, Jack? The cake wrapper. She'll see it. She'll know I didn't make it myself.'

So *now* she wants a friend ...

As paranoid as she might sound, Amy's panic is actually well-founded. Her mother, Jan, is something of a pre-feminist, 1950s throwback, who genuinely believes that any woman worthy of the name should be capable of knitting a shawl, ironing a shirt, milking a cow, and most importantly of all, baking and icing a moist Victoria sponge cake.

Any woman failing to live up to these high-faluting standards is liable to incur Jan's tut-tutting disapproval, no matter what other great achievements might have peppered their life.

I once heard Jan comment, after reading an article on

Andrea Dworkin, 'With an attitude and dress sense like that, it's no wonder she's still single.'

Panicked, Amy puts Ben down and tries to squeeze in between me and the Blue Gingham Buggy from Hell, so that she can get to the kitchen.

But I am Prometheus. I don't budge an inch.

'Move,' she tells me.

'What's the magic word?' I reply.

'The *what*?'

'You heard.'

'Please,' she hisses, pressing herself up against me and trying and failing to force her way past.

Again the doorbell rings, but again I stand my ground.

'I mean the other magic word,' I say. 'The one you use when you want to apologise to someone for calling them a prick in front of their son.'

In answer to my not unreasonable request, Amy mumbles something that even a bat with an ear trumpet would have difficulty hearing.

'I didn't quite catch that,' I say.

'I said I'm *sormomr* . . .' Amy growls through gritted teeth.

'*Sormomr*?' I query, turning my attention to Ben, who's standing behind her with his thumb in his mouth. 'I'm not sure that I know what *sormomr* means. I'm not even sure if *sormomr*'s a real word. Are you, Ben? Have you ever heard that funny little word before?'

'Who door, Daddy?' Ben asks, as the doorbell rings for a third time.

Amy finally looks up at me. 'Sorry,' she spits.

I smile benignly. 'There. That wasn't so difficult, was it?'

She's almost too furious to reply as I finally step aside to let her past.

Almost, but not quite. Because she does manage one word.

And that word is: 'Cunt.'

I don't have time to dwell on the fact that this is the first time either of us has ever addressed the other this way. Nor

64

do I have time to throw an insult back (though quite how you trump a *cunt*, I don't know. I'm guessing that it would take a *motherfucker* at the very least).

The doorbell starts ringing again, and keeps ringing, like whoever's outside has died from boredom and slumped inert against the bell button.

But as I open the front door, I see that my mother-in-law is perfectly well, and smelling mildly of Dettol and chomping vigorously on her customary antacid tablet, in the same way that Clint Eastwood might once have sucked on a cheroot.

'Hi, Jan,' I say. 'How nice to see you.'

Of course, I could just as easily have said, 'Hey, Jan, show us your growler!' for all the reaction I get.

Because there is no reaction. Because Jan's not listening. Or not to me anyway. Because, to her, I am Mr Cellophane.

I smile awkwardly, as she looks straight past me like I'm a particularly uninteresting piece of furniture. As with her failure to greet me, this is an incidental form of insult to which I've grown accustomed, ever since Jan first barged me aside like a professional wrestler as I greeted her at the maternity ward doorway.

Her continued attitude towards me since the arrival of her only grandchild can be summarised thus:

Step aside, sperm provider. Your work here is done. We have your DNA, and no further use for you. For now . . .

Jan, in other words, is not here to see me. Come to think of it, I'm not even sure that Jan *can* actually see me any more, so insignificant have I become in her scheme of things.

This could even be a medical condition, I consider. Perhaps a bad dose of *witchus myopus discourteoso.*

Her eyes scan the area around me like the missile-targeting system of an Apache helicopter, before locking on to Ben.

Like Gollum, Jan only has eyes for *The Precious*, aka my son, and it's only now as she spots him that she smiles.

'There's my gorgeous boy,' she coos, shoving past me and crouching down to Ben's level, as her expression sets into that screwed up come-hither-child-and-kiss-my-moustachioed-lips look that grannies do so well.

Grandparenting College

I sometimes wonder if there's a college grandparents enrol at the moment they discover that their offspring are having offspring of their own.

Modular learning units to be practised in the months leading up to the grandchild's birth might include:

- *COURSE UNIT ONE: Turd sniffing*. A popular *distrust* method employed by grandparents to reinforce their own status as authority figures, by undermining their own children's parenting ability. The novice grandparent would learn a variety of methods for detecting soiled nappies, from the simple but effective *nose twitch*, to the infinitely more dramatic *nappy snort and retch*, to the extremist *dip 'n' sniff*.
- *COURSE UNIT TWO: Traipsing*. A horse and cart method, whereby grandparents never let their grandchild out of their sight, whilst simultaneously providing frequent criticism and advice, but never any actual form of practical help.
- *COURSE UNIT THREE: Repeating long-since discredited parenting advice* from the 1950s, 60s and 70s, such as, 'What that child needs is fattening up', or 'A good glug of whisky in your formula always used to get you off to sleep', or 'We used to spank you black and blue and it never did you any harm'.
- *COURSE UNIT FOUR: Indulging in genetic one-upmanship*, whereby any attractive biological traits displayed by the child (such as beautiful eyes, or a well-proportioned nose) are immediately attributed to the superiority of one's own gene pool. Conversely, any less attractive character traits or physical qualities (triple nipples, etc) should be immediately palmed off

66

on the murky genetic waters of the good-for-nothing spouse.

One thing I do know is that, were there such a thing as Grandparenting College, then Jan would get a first class degree, no sweat.

The Curious Incident Of The C*** In The Daytime

Still, it's not all bad. As Jan scrabbles around my groin, in an attempt to get hold of Ben, who's suddenly gone all shy on her and is making a doomed attempt at evading her Cruella de Vil clutches by clinging on to my leg like a randy dog, I notice with relief the absence of an overnight bag, or indeed an estate agent's prospectus for the property next door (my ultimate fear).

'Come to Granny,' Jan warbles, puckering up now, closing in for the kill.

But Ben's not having any of it. He's been tickled by that little mustachio before.

And besides, he's a boy. And Amy's mum, an embittered divorcee of fifteen years, has forgotten how us boys operate. The more affection you give us, the less we're likely to give in return.

Ben blows a king-size raspberry at her and Jan glares up at me, as if his current rejection of her is in some way my fault.

'Look who it is,' I tell him in that fake rhetorical sing-song voice that parents seem to reserve exclusively for addressing their kids in front of their in-laws. 'That's right, it's Granny. Now what do we say to Granny?'

Ben grins at me. 'Cunt,' he says.

Time slows. Tumbleweed blows past. Somewhere in the distance, a lone wolf howls at the moon.

So here we have it. The daddy of all swear words. Possibly the last remaining word in the English language guaranteed to cause offence. But particularly when spoken by a two-year-old child. On his birthday. To his dear Grand-Mama.

'Can't. Can't. Can't. Can't,' I half-say, half-sing, smiling inanely down at Jan, as if there's *absolutely nothing wrong*.

But my plan to distract Ben drastically backfires, as he sings straight back at me: 'Cunty-cunty-cunty-cunt . . .'

I stare down at my son in horror. He can't even pronounce his own name clearly, but he's somehow managing to enunciate this choice piece of Anglo-Saxon with all the authority and precision of a BBC newsreader.

Jan's eyes fix on mine. And there it is again. That look – the only look I ever get from her these days – the look that says, *Well, it's not hard to see where he gets that from.*

It's right then, as my cheeks are burning bright with shame, that I notice Amy standing, listening just outside the kitchen door, and both of us start to laugh, and just can't stop.

This last bit, of course, is all in my mind.

Amy and I don't start to laugh, and just can't stop. This is what I wish was happening. Just like I wish that Amy and I would continue our display of solidarity in the face of her mother's damning judgementalism, by telling Jan to chill out and back off. Just like I wish the phone would ring right now and it would be Bill Gates telling me that he's plain sick of being the richest man in the universe, and that he's picked my name at random off a worldwide phone directory, and wants to swap places – and, crucially, bank account details – with me, for today, and forever more.

But like I say, this is all in my mind.

In reality, what happens is that Jan tells me, 'You should be ashamed of yourself,' before snatching Ben up from the floor and cradling him protectively in her arms, in *exactly* the same way Amy did in the kitchen less than two minutes ago.

I glare after her, as she follows Amy into the kitchen.

And what I think to myself, as I stand here, an outcast in my own hallway, is:

Yeah, and it's not hard to see where Amy gets it from either . . .

The Slow And Sensual Orgasm Of Sharon Stone

I don't know when it happened, this renewed expansion of the gender gap. I don't know what prompted this San-Andreas-style seismic shift that drove us men and women back apart.

It was there in primary school, of course, a gaping chasm which I refused to cross, so that I only made friends with other boys, and eschewed the company of girls on account of the fact that they were sissy and gossipy and couldn't throw properly.

But then I hit puberty and came to see women in an altogether more attractive light. So much so that I spent my whole teenagehood and early twenties trying to butter them up, by proving that us boys weren't so different after all. I worked on my listening skills. And my sensitivity and charm. I became a shoulder to cry on. And a hand to hold.

I even bought into it myself. I played after-work softball and pretended that the ability to throw straight didn't really matter at all. I stopped talking about cars and football and all that other tosh that was meant to be the exclusive preserve of men. I started talking about people instead, and what it was that made them tick.

It was well worth the effort. Because I worked out how girls ticked as well. And I ended up with a lot of them as friends. And, just as important at the time, with a lot of them as girlfriends too.

Yet here I am at a party, manning the barbecue at the end of the garden, at the centre of a scrummage of men, while all the women are clucking around the kitchen doors with the kids.

Equal opportunity, it ain't.

And this separation, between us Mums and Dads, it's permanent. We've become like water and oil. We no longer mix, because we no longer need to. Just like we don't flirt any more, because it's no longer necessary. Because our big decisions about the opposite sex have already been made. Because we've already found our mates, and already bred.

So instead of mixing, we commiserate with each other in polarised camps, the Mums with the Mums, and the Dads with the Dads. Like we're members of support groups. ('Hi, my name's Jack Rossiter and I'm a . . . parent . . .')

We pass round joints behind the kids' backs, while we talk about lack of sleep and lie-ins, intrusive in-laws and school waiting lists, and about the good old days, *always* the good old days, about how we met our partners, and all the crazy stuff we *used* to do, about our exes and our bad *old* habits, just to remind each other – and ourselves – that *we haven't always been this dull.*

'Great steaks,' drawls Rory (married to Sarah and father of Gooey Louis – pioneer of the portside nostril permabogey), who's currently ruminatively chowing down on his sandwich, like a Disney talking cow.

Metrosexual Ed (partner of Sophie, father of Ripley) nods in agreement. He's dressed like he's just got back from a stint of photojournalism in downtown Basra, and is wearing shades so big he looks like he's auditioning for a remake of the remake of *The Fly*. He hasn't said a single word since he arrived, making me think he's either catatonically stoned, or simply *trop chic pour moi.*

'Thanks,' I say, eyeing Rory warily. I've had the misfortune of conversing with Rory the Tory before. I use the term conversing in the loosest sense, of course, in that Rory tends to talk *at* people, rather than ever actually *listen* to a word they say.

Even though it's a Saturday and the year is 2006, not 1986, Rory is wearing a blue blazer with brass buttons. And jeans (ironed, creased, Armani natch), which are much too tight for him, and into which he's secreted the lowermost part of his belly, so that he looks like he's wearing a colostomy bag.

If Rory's making a fashion statement, I'm guessing that statement is: *Look at me, I'm a tosser.*

'Organic or normal?' he asks, wafting a dribbling sausage sarnie towards me in a way that makes me wish I was vegetarian.

Klingon or human? I consider answering him back, but instead reply, 'Organic.'

This is, of course, a lie. The sausages are from the darkest recess of the corner shop's freezer. They're economy range, reduced to clear, and probably contain several pigs' foreskins a-piece – a fact that cheers me up no end, as I continue to watch Rory munch.

'Butcher or market?' demands Rory.

'Market,' I plump for.

'Borough or Queen's Park?'

'Queen's Park.'

'Heard you've got a stall there,' says Geoff (Camilla's husband and father of Tyler – who can only, surely, have been named after the psycho in *Fight Club*).

Got, as in a possession (rather than a place where I'm employed). I could correct him, but I don't.

Geoff is a pale-skinned, lanky guy, who does something with contracts at the BBC. (His responsibilities could well be limited to stapling these contracts together, I'm guessing, seeing as so far today he's displayed all the dynamism and personality of a bivalve.)

'That's right,' I answer.

In fact, I think, I'd much rather be there now, working my guts out with my fellow Greensleeves wage slaves, Dom and Lee (or 'Tweedle-Dom' and 'Tweedle-Lee' as I've privately christened them).

But instead I'm here.

Having all this fun.

'Never go myself,' tall and stocky, City boy Danny (married to Abby, father of Emily) says dismissively. 'Can't be arsed.'

No wonder, I think. His eyes are bloodshot from sleep deprivation and he looks like a zombie. Ever since he arrived, he's been rocking back and forth on his heels in an unsteady fashion, making me suspect that he's either in need of medication, or in possession of an orthopaedic shoe.

'Me neither,' says Willbillphil. 'I prefer pizza.'

I've never met Willbillphil before, but he seems a fairly mellow guy. I didn't catch his name properly and his partner and offspring are also unidentified. For all I know he might not even have any, and simply be an interloper, a hungry, blagging neighbour who just smelt the barbecue and climbed over the fence for some free nosh.

And I don't suppose it really matters if this is true, since the only thing I actually seem to have in common with the other men present is healthy sperm. We're all strangers here. Thank God.

And none stranger than Rory.

'Too many fucking whining kids at markets,' he complains. 'I leave all that to the wife. Especially at the weekend. Quite frankly, I'd much rather stay in bed and have a wank.'

'A wank?' I check, wondering why this man who I hardly know could possibly be telling me this.

'Exactly. Either that or watch some footie on the old Sky Plus,' he reflects. 'Depending on how hungover I am.'

Geoff and Danny nod sympathetically, as if to say, *Yep, we've all been there* . . .

'I see,' I say. And unfortunately I *do* see. In microscopic detail and vainglorious Technicolor. I have an horrendous image of purple-faced Rory the Tory furiously beating his callused meat over . . . over what? A website? Back issues of *Playboy*? Or *Tatler*? Or even his share portfolio, or a signed photo of Mrs Cameron?

'Of course, sometimes,' Rory continues to confide to the group, 'I actually knock one out *while* I'm watching Sky Plus . . .'

'Over the football?' I ask, confused.

Rory screws up his face like he's just been stung on the

nose by a wasp. 'Don't be disgusting. What do you take me for? A dirty gayer?'

A *dirty gayer*? What century does this man think he's in? I find myself too stupefied to reply.

'No, you fucking idiot,' he barks at me. 'I mean I might squirt one out over a film I've recorded. You know, like *Basic Instinct*, where wotshername gets her vag out . . .'

Hmm, I think. *And I'm sure Sharon Stone's sitting at home right this moment bringing herself to a slow and sensual orgasm thinking about . . . you, Rory . . .*

Faith's husband, Craig, snickers like a hyena on laughing gas. He clearly doesn't get out of the house much these days. Which is probably just as well for the rest of the population.

Fortunately, the conversation is prevented from going any further by the arrival of Jan, who squeezes in between Craig and Rory, without so much as a hello, and takes a burger.

She then forces her way back the way she came and stands with her back to us. As her eyes lock on Ben and she begins to hum 'Hickory-Dickory Dock' to herself, I'm looking at her thinking, *You're the reason they invented punk . . .*

That said, compared to Rory and the rest, Jan is a saint, and right now – so long as her continued presence is putting a gag on their previous conversation – she's welcome to stand here for as long as she wants.

When she does make her move a few minutes later – with a rallying cry of, 'Shall we play musical chairs' – I make mine.

I flip the iPod, so that it starts playing 'The End' by The Doors, hoping that a few of these people will get the message, and split.

But then I spot Matt at the kitchen doorway. *At last*, I think, *a human being to talk to . . .*

'Excuse me,' I say, handing the barbecue tongs over to Craig like a poisoned chalice, before extricating myself from the group.

The Godfather

Matt's the godfather. Clearly, I don't mean *the* Godfather, as in Corleone – although Matt is dark-haired and handsome in a vaguely Italian way, and he did once go to Sicily on a two week management course, after he was bumped up to junior partner at the city law firm he works for.

No, Matt's Ben's godfather. Not that we had a christening, and not that I'd ever want Matt to look after Ben if anything happened. On account of the fact that Matt's not a father himself, or in a stable relationship, and his idea of sensible parenting is feeding Ben Skittles behind my back, and interfering with his Action Man toys. (The last time he crashed over, Amy found three stripped-down Marine figurines laid out on the kitchen table indulging in a hardcore gay porn scenario. Or 'Shaving Ryan's Privates', as Matt was later heard to claim.)

Not that Matt's gay. Far from it, in fact. He's just immature. Prone to one drink too many. And a little twisted.

Which are just three of the reasons why he remains my oldest and best friend.

'Who are all these people?' he asks, looking round. 'I don't think I've seen any of them before in my life.'

'Park people,' I inform him.

His brow crinkles in confusion. 'You mean like tramps? You never told me this was a charity event.'

'No, I mean people from the park.'

'Oh, *baby* people.' He notices the gaggle of mums and their children, who have flocked across the savannah of the lawn and are now grazing at the table Amy put the crisps and snacks on. 'Good God,' Matt says, 'it's like watching locusts strip a field of crops. Who's GI Jane?' he then asks.

'Sophie,' I say, gazing admiringly with him at Womb Raider's pert buttocks straining against her combat shorts, as she bends over to pick up her son's Huff Puff Bee.

'So it is possible then,' Matt says.

'What?'

'To still be drop dead gorgeous, even after you've dropped a sprog.'

'Yeah,' I answer, 'of course.'

I say this more defensively than I mean to, momentarily thinking that he's deliberately implying that the rest of the mothers here – *including* Amy – *aren't* gorgeous any more.

But when I look at Matt's face, there's no sign of malice, so either this was a Freudian slip on his behalf, or it's just me inferring a slight where none was intended.

Which means that somewhere in my subconscious *I* must be thinking it too.

I feel guilty about this right away, but not so guilty that I don't find myself now surreptitiously looking from Amy to Womb Raider and back again.

It's impossible, of course, to be objective about the appearance of anyone you love. But still I try.

And, yeah, I can see it, I suppose. Amy has put on a bit of padding. But then again, so have I. And OK, when she smiles, I can see more wrinkles on her face than she once had – but again, the same applies to me. Besides, wrinkles are evidence of a life spent laughing, and there's nothing wrong with that, right?

But do I still think she's gorgeous? As in drop dead gorgeous? If I'd never met Amy and Sophie before . . . if I was seeing them both for the first time right now . . . if I was only interested (like Matt) in sex . . . which one would my inner ape select to further the species with? Would it still be Amy? Would it still be her?

Before an answer springs to mind, my train of thought is derailed by a flurry of motion at the end of the table. Matt and I both watch as Faith's kid barfs up all over her sleeve and down her forearm.

Faith palms the screaming chunder child off on the nearest Coven member, before making a beeline for us.

'Be a love, Jack, and get me some kitchen roll,' she says, sick rolling slowly down her shirt sleeve. 'Hi,' she says,

75

turning to Matt, and reaching out to shake his hand. 'I'm Faith.'

Matt stares in revulsion at the porridgy trail trickling down towards her hand.

'And I'm Chastity,' he says, taking a quick step back.

I duck inside and rush back with a kitchen roll, which Faith snatches from me wordlessly, before hurrying back over to the Coven.

'Since when did that become socially acceptable?' Matt asks me.

'What, not saying thank you?'

'No, acting like being covered with spew is no big deal . . .'

'Oh, I don't know, about the same time it became socially acceptable for people to discuss their kids' shitting habits at the dinner table, I suppose.'

'That happens, too?'

'Oh, yes, Anekin Skywalker,' I smile. 'That and worse. Youngling, a lot to learn, still you have . . .'

Matt takes my hands in his and looks down at them.

'What are you doing?' I ask.

'Just checking you haven't slit your wrists.'

We watch as the Coven rearrange themselves and the children into a circle (or possibly even a pentagram), and 'Ring-a-Ring o' Roses', that old Black Death standard, starts blasting out of the iPod's speakers.

I catch my reflection in the French windows. I look shapeless in faded baggy blue shorts and a white T-shirt with the letters CTU stamped on the front in yellow. I've become nothing but a ghost, it occurs to me, of my former sharp-dressed self.

'Nice shirt,' I tell Matt. He's dressed to impress, as ever, in a new shop-fresh Paul Smith number, and Japanese jeans, which have been razored and prewashed, to save him the trouble of having to wear them in himself.

'I still need to make an effort,' he replies.

I let this dig pass. Matt's always saying how there's an

inverse correlation between the length of the relationship you're in and the effort you make with your appearance. ('It's easy for you married men,' he once told me. 'You can walk round like bin men and still get laid.')

'Talking of effort,' I say. 'Where is she? I thought you were bringing her with you.'

Her. His new girlfriend. It's only casual, he assured me on the phone, but clearly, she's a cracker, or he wouldn't have volunteered to show her off.

'You mean Honey?'

The look of warning he shoots me puts me off asking the obvious, *So is she the sweet and sticky kind? Or just the kind that spreads easily?* It's obviously a joke he's heard before.

'She's still coming, right?' I check.

Matt frowns awkwardly. 'She was. She's just worried about her dress. You know, with all these kids about. It's vintage and she doesn't want it getting trashed. We've got a party to go to later, you see.'

'You mean a real party? A grown-up party. With grown-up food and grown-up music and grown-up talk.'

'Don't be like that,' Matt says, looking around. 'I mean this is fun too.'

I glance across at Jan, who's involved in some quality *traipsing*, even as we speak . . .

'Amy,' she's saying, 'be careful . . . he might . . .'

And I look at Amy, and at Ben who's rolling on the grass, having the time of his life, wearing the Spiderman outfit Jan gave him (a pretty cool present, even I have to admit, especially when you consider the fact that Jan probably doesn't actually know who Spiderman *is*).

And I look at the clear sky and I consider my good health . . .

But in spite of everything I have, I can't help feeling jealous, when I think of Matt being still out there on the Wild Frontiers of the Urban Single.

I suppose it's because it used to be the two of us, with him playing Frank to my Jesse James, and Sundance to my Butch. Whereas my Colt's holstered now, and instead of riding horses, I'm selling their shit, while Matt's still out there robbing banks . . .

'I'm not,' I say. 'It's just . . .'

'Just what?'

'I don't know. It's just that life's pretty fun for you right now, isn't it? Having somewhere else to go to . . . somewhere better . . .'

'I never said that.'

'You never had to.'

'Amy,' Jan shouts. She's got her mitts back on Ben and is holding him up, *turd sniffing* his rear.

Matt digs his wallet out and peels off some notes. 'Here,' he says, pushing them towards me.

I don't accept them. I say, 'What's that?'

'Ben's birthday present.'

'What? You want to give him cash?'

'No, dickhead, I want to give him a toy, but I didn't know what to buy him. I don't know what's cool.'

'So you want me to choose something for him?'

'Exactly. You know, and tell him it's from me.'

I still haven't taken the money.

'Don't look at me like that,' he says, slipping the cash into my pocket. 'It's not like I didn't bother, it's just that . . .' He gazes up at the blue sky, searching for the appropriate words. 'It's just that I don't really know anything about kids. It's a different world. Yours, you know? Not mine.'

5

amy

Dominoes

'No, it's not bloody fine with me!'

Jack's sister Kate turned up late to Ben's barbecue and broke the news that she'd just broken up with Tone, her boyfriend of two years. And Jack has only gone and invited his flipping sister to LIVE with us. *For free.*

'Come on Amy, she's my kid sister,' he says. 'It wouldn't be right to charge her rent.'

Yeah, well, let's see how *right* it feels when she's eating and drinking us out of house and home. I mean, how could he?

But Jack doesn't seem to think it's a problem. He's in the bath with a big blob of bubbles on his head, waiting for me to lift Ben in to him. I'm kneeling on the bathroom mat, removing a disgusting nappy from our son, who's intent on practising beginners' break-dancing, body-popping back-wards away from me leaving a brown smear on the rug.

'What's the big deal, anyway?' Jack asks, as I finish wiping Ben and lift him up. I've got shit up my arms. 'Come to Daddy,' Jack says in a funny voice, taking Ben from me.

'The *big deal*, Jack, is that we live in a flat the size of a *fucking postage stamp*, if you hadn't noticed. Where exactly do you think your sister is going to stay?'

'She can sleep in Ben's room.'

'And have him back in with us?'

'What do you mean, back? He's in with us every night as it

79

is,' Jack says, sitting forward and piling bubbles on to Ben's head. They look scarily alike. 'You've got that mummy of yours right around your little finger, haven't you, Buster?'

I let out a frustrated breath, picking up the stinking nappy and leaning out into the hallway to deposit it in the nappy bin, which emits a throat-grabbingly vile guff.

I'm stung by Jack's insinuation that I'm a pushover mother. How dare he? It's not like *he*'s the one who gets up in the middle of the night to calm Ben down. *He*'s always conveniently fast asleep. With earplugs in.

'So would you rather he antagonises that wanker upstairs?' I snap, staring in the mirror at Jack in the bath, as I scrub my hands and arms in the sink, like a harassed surgeon in *ER*.

But rather than being cowed, Jack glares right back at me.

It looks like we've got our argument dominoes set up. If one of us flips this particular one over, it'll topple into the next and the next and the next. Through a variety of routes, we can make the argument as long as we want, but on the basic route we can get from domino number one (Ben Crying In The Night), through number two (We Need A Bigger Flat) right along to the double six (You Don't Appreciate Me) in a matter of minutes.

We get so little time together these days that even our rows have to be accelerated and conducted in shorthand.

I step away from the temptation to kick it off by reminding myself that this is bath time – i.e official wind down time for Ben. Taking a deep breath, I steer the subject back to my sister-in-law and her imminent arrival. I'm interested in the way in which Jack's offer of free bed and board was made. Could the bottle of vodka Kate brought to the barbecue have had anything to do with it? But Jack's all innocence and brotherly love.

'It's only for a few weeks,' he says. 'Until Kate gets herself sorted out. I thought you liked her anyway.'

'Of course I like her. That's not the point. You should have asked me first, that's all.'

Jack snorts. 'Oh, like *you* asking *me* whether it was OK to invite all of the Coven and your mother over on my weekend? I wasn't aware that I needed to ask your permission for everything. You never ask mine.'

'OK, OK,' I say, annoyed that he's won. I can feel those dominoes really wobbling. If I'm not careful, we'll be back on to bad language and my mother and that argument we started, but never got around to finishing. We both know we can't bring the 'c' word up again in front of Ben.

'Come on,' Jack says, trying to placate me. 'I couldn't say no, could I? Kate is family, and now that Mum's moved to Spain and Dad's in San Francisco, she's the only one of mine we ever really see. Besides, she's out at work all day and she says she'll babysit in the evenings for us as much as we want. You never know, we might finally make it to the cinema.'

The cinema. It's an olive branch, I know. It's as good as being actually asked out on a date. But I can't quite take it. Instead, I walk through to the bedroom, flop out on the blue duvet and lie there listlessly, like a lost ship becalmed on a wide, blue sea.

Just Another Body In My Cave

Men – straight men that is – don't get the whole thing about visitors. I think that's because the comfort of their surroundings never really registers on their radar. When it comes to it, they'd be happy to sleep on a beer-stained sofa in their beer-stained clothes for weeks on end, as long as they have a roof over their head. (And it is from this natural male habitat that most females, in my experience, rescue their eventual mates.)

The problem is, of course, even after you've spent years reprogramming them (to cut, not bite their nails, to actually put those nail clippings in the bin and not leave them on the side of the sink, to leave the toilet seat down, to eat real food from nice crockery, and not packet noodles straight from the pan, to then put that nice crockery in the dishwasher, to put detergent in the dishwasher and to actually turn it on . . .), they could still revert to their natural, slobbish, sloth-like state at the drop of a hat. And they think that this principle applies to everyone else.

Which is why Jack's being so blasé about his sister coming to stay. What's the big deal? It's just a flat, right? Just a cave. So what, he thinks, is one more body into the mix?

To which my answer is: A huge fucking hassle, that's what.

Jack has absolutely no idea what inviting his sister to stay actually entails. He thinks from my point of view it involves a quick vac and, at a push, a squirt of bleach down the loo. As I said, he has no idea.

It's a pride thing, you see. This is *my* cave. *My* life. And I'm not prepared for anyone – especially a relative – to see that the reality of how we live is not quite the same as the paradigm of modern living we attempt to temporarily conjure up whenever people call round.

I'd go to the same trouble for anyone staying in my home, but Kate being female and a relative ups the ante. Along with a general clean, before she arrives, at the bare minimum, I now have to:

Purchase, wash and iron a new duvet cover and pillow cases and towels, and perform a complete overhaul of the bathroom, including mould removal on the grouting and general chucking out of empty product bottles from the cabinet – she'll look, all girls do; at that point hide away bumper-sized sanitary towels, electric breast pump, nipple shields and other items that may terrify an innocent twenty-something; wash, dry and iron sofa covers and rugs (encrusted dried rusk and ancient baby puke not attractive); make space in Ben's wardrobe – this involves finding new homes for the vast array of birthday presents he received, including a mini car from Jack's father sent in a giant air freight box (thanks, we've really got room for that!); and attack the kitchen, clean out fridge, and do a giant shop – I must have a few spare pizzas etc. for emergencies, as I really

82

don't want Kate to find out how many take-aways we consume per week.

'Why don't you relax?' Jack calls from the bathroom, as I get off the bed and noisily root through Ben's drawers for clean pyjamas.

I can tell Jack's trying to make up with me, by reminding me that he's offered to do bath and bedtime tonight.

Ha!

Yes, Jack, why don't I relax?

Because you're a man, and therefore your magnanimous offer to bath our son and put him to bed does not include anything except the actual bathing and cuddling bits. As an offer, it's crap. It's riddled with small print.

Because it's completely futile for me even to attempt to lie down on the bed and read *Heat*, as you would have me do. Because just as I've got comfortable, you'll start shouting questions at me: 'Amy? Can you lift him out of the bath? Amy? Where's his pyjamas? Amy? Where's the nappies? Amy? Where's his bottle?'

Why are men so useless at multi-tasking? It's like asking them to wank and smile at the same time.

I'm muttering all this to myself as I go back to the bathroom. Jack is teaching Ben the ingredients of the Head and Shoulders shampoo bottle.

'Polynaphthalenesulfonate. Methylchloroisothiazolinone. Glycol Distearate,' he says.

'Don't you think it would be better to teach him something simpler?' I ask. 'Animals or something.'

'Jawohl, *mein Führer*!' Jack picks up the plastic bath book and flips through the dripping pages. Then he points to me. 'Who's that?'

'Mummy,' Ben says.

He shows Ben a picture in the bath book. 'And what's that?'

'Moo Cow.'

That's right, Jack says. 'Mummy Moo Cow.'

Ben squeals with laughter. 'Mummy Moo Cow. Mummy Moo Cow.'

'Thanks. Very funny, Jack,' I say, but my husband and son are too busy laughing hysterically to reply.

Airing One's Dirty Laundry

For the first time in my married life, I have a secret. OK, it's only a small one, but the fact is, I haven't told Jack about my appearances on Radio CapitalChat. And now, the longer I don't tell him, the more pleased I am that I haven't.

For as long as I can remember, I've shared every single minute detail of my daily life with Jack, but now that I haven't told him about my regular radio appearances, I'm suddenly aware of how much I don't know about what Jack does when he's out of the flat and what *he* neglects to tell *me*.

I've tried to probe, believe me, but Jack says that by the time he comes home, the last thing he wants to talk about is work. He says it's boring.

But Jack's career is my career by proxy, since it pays my way, so I think it's only fair that I get to hear all the gossipy interesting stuff about the guys he works with. And anyway, what's wrong with being interested? Isn't it my wifely duty to be interested in all things Jack? I thought sharing our intimate moments was all part and parcel of being married.

But not according to my husband. I suppose I have to respect his point of view and not take it as a rejection, but it hurts that he doesn't want to share everything with me like I do with him.

Well now I've got my own back – but it still feels odd that I'm sharing my thoughts with thousands of strangers and not with my husband.

The next morning, I'm on again.

Well, Jessie, I think us girls feel pain just the same as men. The difference is that we're just more grown-up and mature at handling it. I mean, you only have to look at footballers to see what terrible wimps men are.

Men are so dramatic when it comes to pain. When my husband has a headache, it's not a headache, but a migraine. When he stubs his toe, he's fractured a bone. If he gets a cold, it's flu, if he gets a fly in his eye, he's definitely going blind . . .

And they're such hypochondriacs. Jack's got a whole list of on-going ailments that could afflict him at any time: the Dodgy Knee (an old injury that can kick in with devastating consequences and which is responsible on an annual basis for him not being able to enter the London Marathon). Oh, and let's not forget his Weak Achilles Tendon, Clicky Shoulder, Hamster Bladder, Geographic Tongue or, worst of all, The Undiagnosed-but-almost-certainly-Malaria Fever Thing, which curiously always seems to hit the morning after a bender.

But you see, Jessie, I think men have a psychological painometer, that they can turn up and down by will, whereby a bout of knee trouble that renders Jack laid up on the sofa wrapped in wine coolers and unable to so much as lift the TV remote control, could suddenly become slightly less painful were he to be asked down the pub, by his best friend – but on the other hand, it could just as suddenly become rapidly worse and involve indefinite bed rest, should, say, my mother ask us over for lunch.

And as women, we have to be sympathetic. Any wavering from our complete devotion, or the merest hint that we might not be taking them seriously, or suspect them of faking, is met with uncomprehending outrage.

All I can say is that it's just as well men don't give birth. The human race would fizzle out in one generation.

I like being on the radio. In fact, the more I do it, the more I *really* like it. And it wouldn't be a problem, except that I've developed an unhealthy crush on Alex Murray, the producer, even though I've only ever spoken to him on the phone.

It's very unusual for me to fantasise about someone real. Especially someone I've never met.

There are my usual guys, of course who populate my occasional fantasies. There's George, Brad, Damien and oddly, that guy from the ITV news who is weirdly sexy, but they're all safely locked away in my fantasy theme park, where they hang out with their massage oil, and moon-lit hot tubs and private planes, waiting for me to visit (which, to be honest, isn't as often these days as I'd like).

But Alex is different. Alex is from the real world. The world of 'before'. He makes me feel like I could still belong – and, unlike my theme park blokes, he's stimulating a part of me that nobody has got to for a while: my brain.

Maybe it's to do with the fact that, apart from Jack, my day-to-day life is filled almost exclusively with the banal concerns of other women and small children, but talking to Alex gives me a real buzz. I know I shouldn't read too much into it, but Alex makes me laugh and I'm on the ball and witty when I talk to him. I feel stupidly flattered that in the whole of London, I'm the listener he calls.

'It's all very well launching a phone-in station,' Alex explained the last time we chatted, 'but you won't believe the amount of weirdos out there. Producing Jessie's show is a nightmare, but you're a godsend, Amy. It's so great to have found someone I can rely on to give an intelligent, funny response.'

That's me. Intelligent and funny.

And reliable.

His words gave me the confidence I needed.

'Well I'm happy to be on,' I told him. 'In fact, I was thinking, if there's ever an opportunity that comes up for a job at CapitalChat . . . I'm thinking of a career change. I'd love to get into radio.'

Surprisingly, Alex didn't laugh at me. Instead, he told me that he'd bear it in mind, and ever since, I've been secretly excited at the thought of an unexpected job opportunity down the line. I'm determined to keep in Alex's good books.

After the phone-in, I stay on the line to chat to him.

'I know it's a funny question, but do you think I could have Jack's number? Only I know Jessie is looking for a gardener,' he says. 'She's just moved to a big house in Notting Hill and you're in West London, aren't you?'

'Er . . . yeah,' I say.

We *are* in West London, broadly speaking, just not the bit of West London anyone imagines when they think of West London.

'I could fix it up for you. If your fella wants the business . . .'

Wants it? He'd love it. And I'm always on at Jack to start working for himself.

'That would be great, Alex,' I gush.

And it would be. Except that how do I tell Jack that I've got him a job with Jessie Kay without telling him everything I've been saying on the radio? About him. About us. About our dirty laundry? Because there's no chance that Jack would find it funny in the same way that Alex does.

Suddenly, I feel myself flushing with a deep-down guilty feeling.

Blimey. I'd forgotten how complicated having secrets could be.

Easy Like Sunday Morning

It's Sunday morning and I'm in the café in the park with Ed, Sophie's husband. This is a purely accidental meeting, due to the fact that Ripley and Ben spotted each other, and are playing on the wall outside and Ed and I met just now in the queue for coffee. I don't think he can remember my name.

I know for a fact that Sophie would have a fit if she could

see Ripley balancing precariously above a very muddy flowerbed, but Ed hasn't even clocked that his daughter might be in danger of getting dirty, let alone in danger of getting hurt. I notice that she's shrieking and jumping around like a chimpanzee. The tell-tale smudge of chocolate around her mouth and the wrapper in her hand makes me suspect she's high on the most hardcore form of kiddy-crack, aka Milky Way.

'So where's Sophie?' I ask, as I sip my latte and sit down at one of the tables outside.

'Soph? I doubt she'll be up for hours,' Ed says. 'We had a late one last night.'

'Oh?'

'People over. Wrap party,' Ed explains. 'You know, one of those nights that gets a bit out of hand?'

No, I don't, but Ed's obviously very familiar with them.

'I think everyone left at about four or five,' he continues, taking off his sunglasses and rubbing his face. His eyeballs look like eight balls. I think I know what type of 'wrap' party he means now.

Even so, I can't help feeling left out. Jack and I haven't been invited to, or hosted a party – except for Ben – for ages.

Ed yawns flamboyantly, stretching out his arms. His T-shirt rides up and I can see a ruffle of hair coming up from out of his jeans towards his belly button. I quickly look away.

'What did you cook?' I ask, feeling like I should make conversation. I feel so uncool. I sound like my mother, even to myself.

'Nothing. I got caterers in.' He yawns and looks away.

I suddenly see myself from Ed's point of view. To him, I'm clearly one of Sophie's mummy mates in dirty jeans and a shapeless T-shirt, with no make-up on. I doubt it would ever occur to him to think of me in a sexual context, or to secretly fancy me, like I suspect Jack secretly fancies Sophie. The thought of this – that I've warped into someone completely asexual – swamps me with depression.

Ed's clearly not interested in making small talk. He leans back in his seat and, pointing his face towards the sun, shuts his eyes.

This is typical Sunday dad behaviour. I look around the café.

It's anarchy.

There's a couple of four-year-olds upending the sugar tubes into their mouths; a parentless kid is tearing around on a stolen scooter, intent on terrorising the pigeons. A baby howls in the corner, whilst two toddlers smack each other. Their father, oblivious to the scene behind him, is busy checking his pockets for change in order to pay for the mountain of sticky buns he's bought as bribery currency.

Over in the playground, you can see men reading newspapers unaware that their toddlers are hanging upside-down from the death slide like bats.

But the most odious of all the dads now comes braying around the corner. This is Sergeant Major Dad. He's in Sunday civvies: the obligatory chinos, leather boat shoes and pink polo shirt with the collar turned up. He marches towards the café, smoothing his fringe and barking orders at his kids.

'Toby, park the scooter. There, boy, there! Jonquin get the door. And hurry up! Football in fifteen remember. You'll need time to digest, if you're going to have bacon sarnies.'

As Sergeant Major Dad holds the café door open, Running Commentary Woman comes out holding her baby. She is an absolute type. It's like she has an odd form of Tourette's syndrome in which the sufferer feels compelled to run a real-time commentary on everything going on.

'. . . and look we're walking out of the café and we're walking past the tables and look, there's the sun up in the sky. Shall we put your hat on? Yes, let's put your hat on for Mr Sunshine . . .'

She's clearly insane. Somebody put her out of her misery.

I get up quietly. I'm not going to stay next to Ed and

babysit Ripley whilst he has a nap in the sunshine. I go over near the wall to keep an eye on Ben. I tell him that he's got two minutes and then we're leaving.

'Look, Mumma, look,' Ben says, running round to climb up the wall again. He's having a great time.

'Wonderful darling,' I say.

But I don't mean it. He's not supposed to be my responsibility. He's supposed to be Jack's this morning. Tweedle-Dom and Tweedle-Lee are covering the organic market this week. When I heard Jack wasn't working, I was planning on having a morning off and maybe a long uninterrupted bath, or just a relaxing lie-in. Anything that would give me a break from dealing with every whim of my two-year-old, much as I love and adore him.

However, as usual, despite his promises, Jack has failed to get up and now, once again, I'm on the Sunday shift. I know that it's terrible that I'm keeping count, but this is the seventeenth day in a row that I've dealt with Ben in the morning.

But then, Jack works hard to pay for me and Ben, I remind myself, and therefore it's only fair that he gets a lie-in. After all, he's the one bearing the financial pressure of our family. He's the one who has to get up and do a job.

But I still feel resentful. Isn't looking after Ben a job, too? The *Daily Mail* says it is, but no one else seems to think full time childcare and housekeeping really counts.

The only way that Jack could possibly understand how I'm feeling is if he'd got up for seventeen days in a row with a two-year-old and looked after that two-year-old all day. Only then would he ever get close to realising how essential . . . vital . . . some time off is.

But that's never going to happen. Because if I left Jack to look after Ben for seventeen days in a row, on day two *he'd hire a fucking nanny*.

'Come on,' I tell Ben, 'let's go and find Daddy.'

Yes, sod Jack, I think. *We'll go and wake him up anyway.*

'No Daddy,' Ben says. 'Swings.'

90

'No. Come on.'

'Swings,' he repeats.

'No.'

'Why no swings?' He tips his head to the side, his face a picture of disappointment and curiosity. I don't have the heart to explain.

'OK, we'll go to the swings, but just for a bit,' I relent.

'Me. Me. Me,' Ripley says.

'You'll have to ask your daddy,' I tell her.

'I done poo,' she says happily, clutching her bottom.

Great.

I take her over to Ed.

'She needs changing,' I tell him. The air is turning green around us.

He looks at me and it's difficult to tell who's the toddler, Ripley or her father.

'All right,' Ed says, sitting up, but he clearly has no idea what to do. It wouldn't have occurred to him in a million years to bring nappies and nappy wipes with him.

'Well, I'm going to the swings,' I say. 'See you.'

'Amy,' he says, suddenly remembering my name. 'You don't have any of the stuff do you? You know? A spare do-dah. Or a – you know – thingy . . .'

It's like conversing with a foreigner.

I check the bottom of the buggy and hand over a pull-up and wipes.

'So?' Ed asks, 'Where do you do it? I mean, where are the loos?' He looks utterly helpless.

Aha. Not so big and clever now, are you Ed? I think, rather enjoying his discomfort. If only his trendy mates could see him now.

Then I look at Ripley and she looks at me. Can I really leave her in the hands of a man who clearly hasn't had any sleep, or any recent practice at changing a nappy? Let alone a pull-up? Ed wouldn't have the faintest idea that he'd need to take her trousers off and –

91

'Do you want me to change her?' I ask.

For a moment I think Ed might fall on the ground and kiss my feet. 'Would you?' he asks.

'Come on, sweetie,' I tell Ripley, holding out my hand for her.

Afterwards, we go over to the swings and play for a while. I can see Ripley in the sandpit, whilst Ed lies with his feet up on one of the benches, his baseball cap over his face. I feel furious with myself. I should have left him to it.

I'm about to leave when I see Jack coming in through the park gate.

So he read my two-word note, then. It was as perfunctory as I could possibly make it: 'At Park'.

'Hey, Babe,' he says, coming to find me.

'Dadda! Dadda! Dadda!' Ben launches at Jack, as if he's some kind of an amazing superhero. I sit down on one of the toddler play tables and fold my arms, annoyed at the level of adoration Ben reserves for his lazy father.

'What's the matter?' Jack asks me, coming and sitting down next to me.

'Just a bit tired, that's all.'

'Well why don't you go back and have a sleep?'

'Because I'm up and I'm dressed. I'm not sleepy now.'

'I thought you just said you were.'

'There's a difference between being tired and being sleepy.'

Jack looks at me, confused. 'Don't blame me. I thought you were having a lie-in,' he says.

'So did I.'

'Well, why did you get up, then?'

'Er . . . maybe because our son was up.'

'So? Why didn't you just leave him?'

'I couldn't *just leave him*. He'd already been awake for an hour.'

Jack lets out a frustrated breath. 'I can't help it if you're going to be a martyr about this.'

'I'm not being a martyr, Jack. I couldn't leave him on his own to play. He's two. Besides, he'd have made too much noise.'

'Well I'm knackered. I'm sorry I didn't hear him, but you could have woken me up if it was really that important to you. I've had a very busy week at work and –'

'I know. You don't have to tell me.'

We're interrupted by Ben, who comes over with something gooey and disgusting on his hands demanding a nappy wipe. I clean him up.

'So what *do* you want to do?' Jack asks, before yawning.

There's no point in having a go at him. With an enormous effort of will, I force myself to try and sound less hostile.

'Well, I suppose now you're here we might as well all hang out. Have some family time.'

'But family time doesn't kick in until at least eleven thirty,' Jack says.

This is clearly a made-up Jack stat.

'Eleven thirty?' I check. 'Family time doesn't kick in until eleven thirty. How did you work that out?'

'Well look around you. There's only single parents here.'

Yes, I want to say. *The dads. The mums are in bed.*

'There's no point in us both being here. Not this early,' he continues.

'OK. Fine,' I snap, standing up. 'Go back to bed, if that's what you want.'

He grabs my arm and pulls me down next to him on the bench.

It's only when I look at him that I see that he's winding me up, but I'm not in the mood to play along.

'Well? You going?'

Jack puts his arm around me and sniffs. 'Nah. It's not worth it.'

'Why?'

'Because I know you too well,' Jack says in his best Tony

93

Soprano accent. 'Because you'll just bust my balls if I leave you here.'

I bare my teeth at him and make a sudden snapping noise with my teeth. 'Yes, I bloody well will. I won't only bust them, I'll bite them, too.'

'Go on then,' he says, smiling. 'I dare you. I could do with some action.'

Cheeky bugger.

Calamity And Kate

My sister-in-law Kate has been in our flat for a week, before I can stand it no more. I'm not sure what sob story she gave Jack, but she doesn't seem particularly traumatised by the break-down of her relationship with Tone to me. I'm getting the distinct feeling that we've been done over. We're just her sucker relatives, gullible enough to let her stay for free whilst she waits for some big posh flat-share to come off.

Jack won't hear of it, though. He still thinks of her as his kid sister and he likes to act like the big protector, but since she's been living with us, I've discovered that she doesn't need looking after in the slightest. Confident Kate is very much her own modern gal.

Conversely, I can't help feeling that, on her side, her estimation of me has gone down rather than up. Sometimes, I catch her looking at me with a kind of horror. It's clear that I've lost my status as funky fashion industry Amy who married her brother. In her eyes, I have no status at all.

And I think she blames me for Jack ditching his career as an artist. I can't be sure. She hasn't said anything, but there's something about her manner that makes me suspect that there've been family conversations behind my back. I wish she'd just spit the dummy and ask me outright. Because then I'd be able to set her straight.

I suppose I'm being over-analytical, because, if I'm very honest, I'm jealous of her. She reminds me of myself when I was her age, except, annoyingly, she's much cooler. She's got

94

this swanky advertising job in Noho and a wardrobe (Ben's) full of sassy trouser suits and sexy tops to match. As far as I can make out, she's dined out in every single one of London's most exclusive restaurants on expenses and is positively blasé about being invited to join the latest private members clubs.

I find her relentlessly self-absorbed in the way that someone without a partner, kids, or a home to run, can be. She's obsessed with her social life and seems to be surgically attached to her BlackBerry. She's not capable of talking to you without receiving and sending at least three e-mails and texts, most of which are from and to the various men she's 'kind of' seeing.

Call me old fashioned, but 'kind of' seeing someone sounds confusing, but Kate seems to be in no hurry to settle down and find another permanent boyfriend. Instead, she says she's happy being choosy for the time being, hanging out with her gang of trendy mates.

'There's no point in settling down. I've got years and years of fun before I need to do the baby thing,' she told me. 'Ten years, at least.'

It's the trendy mates bit that I'm suspicious of. Kate is still big pals with Sally McCullen, the girl Jack and I nearly fell out over for ever. A girl who's so slaggy, that if she lived in Wales, they'd turf her.

OK, so nearly a decade has passed since Jack's shenanigans with her and now we're happily married with a family, but having one degree of separation away from Man-eater McCullen living with us bothers me – especially since Jack's intent on playing good-time boy with his sister. He's usually snoring on the sofa at eleven p.m., but since Kate's been staying with us, he's pretending that he's the life and soul of the party, cracking open a bottle of whisky for a nightcap whenever she rolls in from whatever trendy gig she's been to.

It's Wednesday morning and Jack is still out for the count after the latest late night session with Kate. I'm about to go to the bathroom and attempt to get dressed, when Kate breezes into the kitchen yawn-talking something about oversleeping and why didn't I wake her.

'Do you want some toast? I've just made some,' I offer.

'No way. Bread is so bloating, and I'm *so* fat,' she says.

What is she talking about? I look at photographs of me in my twenties and remember how much I used to worry about having a flat stomach. Ha! If only I'd known then what I know now: that *that* was as flat as it would ever get, I would have treasured it. I'd have worn bikinis all day. I'd have pierced my belly button and hung sparkling jewels from it.

'You've got a great figure,' I tell her, truthfully. 'Make the most of it.'

'Well I feel fat. Period pain,' she explains, screwing up her face in pretend agony. 'Maybe I should take the day off.'

Period pain? Give me a break. Don't talk to me about hormones or female problems, because, after forty-eight hours of labour, period pain doesn't count. Try a dilated cervix. Or an episiotomy. And *then* you can ask for sympathy.

'I've got some painkillers,' I suggest, helpfully.

She simply can't take the day off work. I'm looking forward to my call from Alex Murray. I'm on Jessie's show this morning talking about people who hoard junk, and since I live with a man who pays for a lock-up because he has so much junk, I think I'm qualified to wax forth about Jack and his inner Del-boy.

'Oh God, no, I've got a lunch,' Kate says, slapping her forehead. 'I'll have to go in. I'd better get a move on.'

I'm about to ask her if she minds me nipping to the bathroom first, but I get distracted by Ben and, when I next look up, Kate's gone and I can hear the bathroom door locking.

The minutes tick by. Then half an hour.

Private bathroom time is a thing of the past for me. I can't so much as pluck an eyebrow these days without Jack or Ben bursting in to ask me a question.

So what the hell is she doing in there?

Please hurry up, I will her. I'm absolutely desperate for a pee. I've been up for two hours already. So it's nearly ten hours since I last relieved myself, and my pelvic floor muscles aren't what they used to be. I'm not sure I can hold it in for much longer.

I put my ear up close to the crack of the bathroom door. I can hear faint tuneless humming. Hasn't Kate got places to go? People to see? I thought she said she needed to get a move on?

Two minutes later and I'm hopping around the flat. There's nothing for it. I creep into Ben's room and ignoring all of Kate's designer clothes, kneel down and rummage under the bed for Ben's new potty, which I'm going to start training him on next month.

I look at the shiny blue plastic. Have I taken leave of my senses? Am I really about to do this? Yes, *fuck it*, I think. I'm too damn desperate.

I squat over the potty. Serenity returns and I close my eyes with sheer bliss. As the old saying goes, there's nothing so overrated as bad sex and nothing so underrated as a good pee.

'Oh my God! Amy? What are you *doing*?'

My eyes snap open. Kate is standing in the doorway, wrapped in my new towel.

'I'm just . . .'

Mortification makes it impossible to continue explaining. I pick up the potty and scuttle past her and bump straight into Jack in the hallway.

The pottyful of my own pee drenches me.

'Blimey!' he says. 'Did the little guy do all that?'

6

Jack

Before The Pastel-Tinted End Credits Roll

I'm in a buoyant mood as I head off to meet Jessie Kay. Today feels like the beginning of something, like I'm rounding a headland, switching tack, like the fickle wind of fortune has finally begun to blow my way.

And it's all thanks to Amy. She's been on my case for months now, to strike out on my lonesome, work-wise, and now she's come up with a chance for me to do exactly that.

Talk about serendipity. Her wanting to call that crappy radio show. Me encouraging her to do it. Me thinking nothing more of it. And then her mentioning the other night that she had called up after all, that they'd liked her enough to ask her to call back whenever she felt like it – you know, with opinions and stuff. So she's been doing just that, ringing them up from time to time to blather on about – what was it she said? – oh yeah, high street fashion and other girlie stuff.

Just what's all this got to do with me? one might ask. Well, the last time Amy rang, the show's producer mentioned that this rich Jessie bird was on the lookout for someone to redesign her garden . . .

Which brings us to here. And now. And . . . *Ta-raaa! Enter stage right, Jack Rossiter, Horticulturist to the Stars . . .*

I should have checked out Jessie Kay's show, I suppose, before coming here to meet her today. In the name of research, not pleasure – obviously, seeing as the show's utter dreck and strictly for chicks.

The trouble is, I'm always at work when the good lady Kay's show is on, and Rupert, my boss, he's got a rule about us not listening to music or shows, even with earphones, while we're meant to be working. 'It looks slack,' he says, and at the prices he charges, I guess he has a point. We should be looking hyper-industrious and professional at all times.

Which is exactly how I intend to look to Jessie Kay today. Hence my clean shaven jaw, combed hair and cut fingernails, and ironed trousers and smart clean shirt.

Hell, I look more like I'm going to meet a date than pitch for business.

But so what? No effort can be deemed too much effort today, because this is my big opportunity – I can sense it – and I mustn't fuck it up.

I mean, what better way can there possibly be for me to start branching out on my own? Come to think of it, Branching Out isn't a bad name for a gardening company, if I actually do go ahead and set up my own legitimate business.

Not that what I'm doing right now is *strictly* legit. I'm currently still working on my boss's time, still getting my ten quid an hour Greensleeves (or Green*slaves*, as I more often think of it) flat rate. I told my boss, Rupert, that I was going to see a prospective client (true). What I didn't tell him was that Jessie is *my* prospective client, not his. Any proceeds deriving from today's meeting are going straight into the bank account of yours truly. And why not? This potential windfall did, after all, come to me via Amy. So why should I share?

From the snazzy address Amy's scribbled down on a scrap of paper for me, I'm expecting Jessie's house to be impressive, and I'm not disappointed.

If Notting Hill really did have a beating heart – as an estate agent I know always likes to claim – then St Thomas's Gardens could be said to be its pacemaker.

I turn into it now – one of those broad, tree-lined streets, full of detached Georgian four-storey mansions.

The houses that I'm passing even have driveways – *driveways!* – which in this overdeveloped, overpriced part of London is like saying they've got *runways*. It's almost as ostentatiously moneyed as having a moat, or a helipad, or a private army.

We're on Porsche, Bentley and Lexus turf here, and most of the models on show are worth more than our flat (a couple of them actually look bigger than the flat as well).

All of which only serves to make me more self-conscious of my own mode of transport. On account of this not being official Greensleeves business, I'm in my own car (aka the Skip, Dadmobile, or General Lee, as in *generally knackered*). It's a fly-abdomen grey, twelve-year-old Citroën estate, which smells like a stale bagel and makes crunching noises whenever you get into it, because of the avalanche of desiccated snacks which Ben has distributed around it over the course of his short life.

There's no CD or MP3 player, but there is a radio which I've got hooked up to an iTrip and iPod. I'm listening to The Go! Team for inspiration.

I check out the mansions on either side as I drive past, searching for Number 5. The view makes me feel like I'm driving through a film set, the kind you always see in British romantic comedies. So much so, in fact, that as I pull up outside the driveway of Number 5, I'm half-expecting to see a suitably bookish Hugh Grant come bumbling, mumbling, muttering and stuttering along the pavement, before bumping into a sophisticated, Chanel-shaded Julia Roberts, who just happens to be an incognito American film star, and who may be outwardly hysterical and histrionic, but inwardly is lonely and just as much in need of affection as everyone else, and who *will* fall in love with wet but wonderful Hugh, but only after they've overcome a number of unlikely comedic misunderstandings (with the aid of several of Hugh's preternaturally wise Oxbridge chums), thus allowing Hugh 'n' Ju to conclude that love not only changes everything, but is also capable of conquering all social, cultural and financial boundaries, a startling insight which occurs to them just in time before the pastel-tinted end credits roll, while a recently-exhumed nostalgic hit by Wet, Wet, Wet starts to play . . .

What I actually witness through the Skip's fingerprint-smeared side window, however, is a thickset, fortysomething man in a dark tailored suit and Aviator shades, marching down the neatly cobbled driveway of Number 5, before slinging a tan Gladstone bag into the boot of a waxed black Porsche.

So far, so James Bond. My Hugh 'n' Ju rom com scenario is clearly a no go. We've stumbled on to staple thriller turf now. Or rather we would have, but for one surreal element.

The man has nothing on his feet. Neither shoes nor socks. Jesus style.

Even weirder, as he slams the Porsche boot shut and opens the driver's door to get in, he seems to be completely oblivious to this fact himself.

Then he hesitates, and his brow furrows as, somewhere in the back of his mind, a red alert bulb begins to flash.

Only then does he stare down.

For a second, my heart goes out to him, as his face crumples and his veneer of manly sophistication dissolves, leaving him looking like a little boy who's about to burst into tears.

Then his fists clench and his expression sets into a mask of belligerent determination. He turns and stares back up the driveway. He takes something from his pocket – a hipflask, it looks like – and takes a swig, then another, then he knocks his head right back. He returns the flask to his pocket and wipes his lips on the back of his hand, before glowering up once more at the house.

No, man, no, I will him. *Don't be a damned fool! Step away from the house. Get into your Porsche. And flee. Flee this accursed place, while your dignity's still intact . . .*

Because it doesn't take Sherlock Holmes to deduce what's going on here. The evidence speaks for itself: a mind sufficiently distracted to allow you to leave the house without footwear; a packed bag; a getaway car at the ready. It all points to the same woeful conclusion.

This man is no spy. This is no thriller. And certainly no rom com, either. No, what we have here is a rom com gone wrong. A non rom com. This is a break-up, a bust-up, the end of the line, and this man is about to commit a howling schoolboy error. He's about to walk back *in. After* he's walked *out.* And as an ex *troubadour d'amour* myself, I know enough to be certain that no good can come of this.

Because it never does.

But the Shoeless Man has other plans. He strides back up the driveway, flings open Number 5's front door, and disappears inside.

Seconds tick past. I wait for him to re-emerge, shame-faced and humiliated, but he doesn't.

The seconds turn to minutes.

I re-check the address Amy gave me, but this is definitely Jessie's house. Which means that, if I *am* right about a bust-up going on in there, then it's almost certainly between Jessie and the Shoeless Man.

I call the contact number for Jessie that Amy gave with the address, but all I get is an automated voicemail. It's two forty-five and I'm already fifteen minutes late for my appointment with Jessie.

I should leave a message and split, but I keep picturing the man's clenched fists, and that angry look on his face, which keeps getting just that little bit more warped, just that little bit more Norman Bates . . .

I vacate the Skip and peer up at the house.

If I were a cop, this is probably the moment I'd call for

back-up. *Hutch: this is Starsky. Call Huggy.* Or *Riggs, this is Murtaugh: I'm sitting on a bomb!*

But I'm not a cop. I'm a gardener, and I somehow think that none of my fellow wage slaves at Greensleeves will be willing to sacrifice the peace and quiet of their own afternoon for the furtherance of some stranger's domestic harmony.

No, this is something I'm going to have to deal with on my own.

Like A TAI-Fighter Caught In A Traction Beam

The front door to Number 5 is still enticingly ajar when I reach it.

I press the burnished brass bell, but it's not working.

What I do hear loud and clear, however, as I step inside the wide black-and-white chequered entrance hall, is shouting. And screeching. And even the occasional agonised bellow, like a cow's giving birth.

I stand here frozen.

The house is so big that, at first, it's difficult to work out where these Dante-esque sounds are coming from.

I also feel disoriented by the switch from bright daylight outside to cool gloom in here, and it reminds me of the time I got lost in the Natural History Museum on a school trip when I was seven and couldn't work out where my history teacher was calling me from.

As my eyes grow accustomed to the light, I see that double doors lead off to the left and right, and that there's a marble staircase straight ahead. A stunning art deco crystal chandelier hangs from the high vaulted ceiling, and the acrid whiff of polish is in the air. It's an old-fashioned-looking place, with plenty of antiques-laden tables and gilded mirrors, but any effect of grandeur is ruined by the chaos of half-unpacked removal boxes scattered across the floor.

And a smashed white wine bottle at the foot of the stairs . . .

There's a pause in the shouting.

'Hello?' I call out, figuring that I should announce my

presence as, technically, I am now trespassing, and if I'm wrong about this being a break-up, and in the unlikely event that the Shoeless Man really is a double-O agent, then he'll be well within his rights to blow me away with his Walther PPK.

The only answer I get is the echo of my own voice.

Then the shouting kicks off again.

As I cross the hallway and the voices get louder, echoing through the air, I hear a 'mouse-cocked mummy's boy', a 'psychotic slut', an 'alcoholic arsewipe', and a 'Botoxed bitch' in rapid succession.

I also realise that these terms of non-endearment are coming from beyond a doorway tucked away to the right of the bottom of the stairs.

My heart skips a beat as I hear something smash and a female shriek.

As I hurry to the open doorway of what turns out to be an enormous atrium, however, I immediately see that I was being presumptuous.

The shriek wasn't issued by a female at all, but a male.

The Shoeless Man from the driveway is now cowering directly ahead of me, behind a rattan sofa, surrounded by shards of broken pottery. He looks like a doomed extra from *Platoon*, who's been pinned down by machine-gun fire.

'Be reasonable,' he shouts.

'*Me*?' comes the response from a woman who's out of my line of sight, around the doorway, somewhere to my right. 'Don't you fucking dare "be reasonable" me, Roland. How fucking *reasonable* were you being when you took your shrivelled septic stump and put it inside that little tart?'

'For God's sake,' Roland starts to protest, 'I already told you –'

I lean forward to peer around the doorframe and get a better look at the woman who's berating Roland, but then I think better of it, as a plant pot hurtles past me at head height, before exploding against the wall behind the rattan sofa and sending another cloudburst of pottery and pulped

104

Aucuba japonica down on the beleaguered Roland's head.

'Right,' he bellows, 'that's a-fucking 'nuff. Just give me the fucking shoes.'

'Come and get them,' the woman snaps.

He twists round, like he's about to toss a grenade over the top of the sofa, then rises up to face his foe like a man.

I have to admit, the timing couldn't be better.

He stands.

She throws.

He ducks.

Too late.

The first shoe (the left, I think) clocks Roland smack on the side of his jaw. The second cracks against his knuckles as he raises his hands to protect his face.

It would be funny if this was an episode of *The Itchy and Scratchy Show*, but Roland is a real person, who's now shrieking out in pain and scrabbling round on the floor, trying to gather up his shoes, like they're as slippery as a brace of fish.

It's even less funny, because no sooner has he pulled his shoes on, than he spots me.

'Who are *you*?' is his first line of enquiry. 'Who the hell is *he*?' is his second, directed to the hidden part of the room, when I fail to reply.

'Who the hell is *who*?' demands the woman who's still out of my sight.

'Er, me,' I say, finally risking stepping out into the open.

It's only now that I get to take in the full magnificence of the room. You could fit a couple of doubledecker buses in here side by side and still have room for a snooker table, but instead it's full of plants, *big* plants. As in *Jurassic Park* big. The kind that look like they might, just might suddenly lean down and bite off your head.

My eyes skip from *Pogonatherum saccharoideum* to *Convolvulus* to *Yucca gloriosa* – before finally settling on her, the woman who's been doing all this shouting.

105

Woof!

She's like a Wonderbra advert sprung to life (a fantasy I have to admit to having indulged in several times before). But this is real. *She* is real. And tall. And dark-haired. And yoga'd up. And in her early forties. And seriously curvy and seriously stacked.

She's also wearing nothing but a white bra and pants.

She picks up a half-smoked cigarette from an ashtray and takes a long, cool drag, before staring past the hanging plant leaves like an Amazonian warrior – at me.

And wow . . . it's quite a stare. I feel like one of the TAI-Fighters in *Star Wars* caught in the Death Star's traction beam. Or a rabbit in the headlights of a speeding car. I know this stare is dangerous, but I just can't seem to move.

It's mesmerising, demanding, irresistible . . .

'How did he fucking get in?' Roland demands, as he hurriedly ties his laces. 'Why has he fucking got keys?'

I'm expecting her to tell him the truth (in suitably fucking vulgar language): that I'm a fucking gardener who's fucking here to fucking talk about her fucking garden, O fucking K?

But she doesn't.

Instead, I notice a vicious twinkle in her eyes as she stubs out her ciggie in a plant pot and snaps, 'It's none of your damned business *who* he is. Who I choose to see hasn't got anything to do with you, Roland. Not any more.'

Whoah, I'm thinking. *Who I choose to see*? This isn't looking good.

I'm no longer a gardener.

I've become a sexual taunt.

I turn to face Roland, who's just emitted the same kind of noise a cobra would if you trod on it barefoot during its siesta.

As he advances towards me, I wish I had my Greensleeves overalls on (and, yes, they do actually have green sleeves). Or that I had some kind of ID I could flash at him, LAPD style.

It's quite all right, sir. There's nothing to worry about. I've not actually been boning the Missus at all. My business here is strictly of a professional nature. I'm a qualified landscape gardener, you see.

But what I actually say is, 'Hey, Dude. You've got it all wrong.'

Roland stares at me like a live bat has just crawled out of my mouth.

'Did you just call me *dude*?' he demands.

I can understand his cynicism and, yes, revulsion, over this term being applied to him. I mean, I can hardly believe I just said it myself. I've never called anyone *dude* before in my life. I don't even know what *dude* means. I must be more freaked out by this situation than I thought.

'I didn't mean to.'

'Well, don't.'

'I won't,' I insist.

But Roland's not listening to me any more. His attention's back on her.

'I knew it.' His face purples in exactly the same way that Ben's does when he's filling his nappy. 'I knew you had someone else as well, you hypocritical fucking bitch.'

Perhaps I should come back later.

I actually mean to say this out loud, but I don't; I actually just think it.

'Don't call her that, you arsehole.'

I actually only mean to think this, but I don't; I actually say it out loud.

The reason I only meant to think it was because, in this context (i.e. a row where this woman's already accused Roland of being an unreasonable, tart-shagging, mouse-cocked mummy's boy), his equally profane language cannot fairly be regarded as an escalation of verbal hostilities.

The reason I actually *did* just call him an 'arsehole' out loud is because the phrase 'hypocritical fucking bitch' was my dad's drunkenly slurred barb of choice in the horrendously unpleasant, downwardly-spiralling, gin-and-tonic fuelled, Punch & Judy period he and my mother went through shortly before he walked out and 'upgraded to a younger bird' (his recent description, not mine).

I never had the guts to stand up to my father then, on account of the fact I was eight, and he was an intimidating, bullying bastard, and even though me and Dad have been civil to each other for most of my adult life, not having it out with him is something I've regretted ever since. So much so, it's now becoming apparent, that my subconscious has decided to go looking for some closure on it.

And Roland is a prime transference target, make no mistake. For starters, he's older than me by at least ten years. He's stockier than me, too, just like my dad. Only where my dad's weight was largely the result of drinking Guinness and guzzling pies, this guy's bulk – I now notice, as he steps up into my face – is of the seriously gym-sculpted variety.

It's too late to back down now.

And besides, how hard can a guy called *Roland* really be?

If he was called Gary, then fine, I'd have cause for concern. Gary's more guttersnipe, more street. Gary might have grown up on an inner city sink estate and know a nasty trick or two. The names Dave or Tel would also set the old danger bells ringing. Hard bastard giveaways, the pair.

But Roland? *Roland*? As in roly-poly-pudding-and-pie. Well, it's not like the annals of history are exactly littered with many Roly the Impalers, or Roland the Destroyers, is it? (In fact, the only Rolands I can even think of are the speccy porker out of *Grange Hill*, circa 1982, and the stroppy one out of *Tears For Fears* – and the only thing remotely frightening about him was his wet gel frizzy mullet.)

'What did you fucking say? *What* did you fucking say?' This Roland really does say this twice, like he might not have been yelling it loud enough at me the first time.

Which he was.

Either that, or he's got a speech impediment of some sort, whereby he's unable to stop repeating himself, in which case we may be here for quite some time.

A fleck of *his* spittle lands on *my* cheek. He's so close to me that I can see his contact lenses (tinted blue, the big faker) and smell his breath (a meaty and foetid tinned lasagne tang, reminiscent of the rancid pigswill Mrs Smith and Mrs Davies, the dinner ladies from Hades, used to serve up at my primary school and laughably refer to as 'lunch').

'You know,' I say, trying to sound simultaneously in control and urbane. 'The fucking bitch thing. It's not nice.'

He looks me dead in the eyes. 'Do you want to know what else isn't nice?'

Well, I've got a whole list, I'm thinking. *There's broccoli, bullies, Advocaat, tripe, Advocaat and tripe combined, divorce, exams, kids' parties, and not forgetting, of course, Roland's pestilential, bottom-popping, bilious Beelzebub breath . . .*

But then I realise that Roland's question is not one in search of an answer. It's the way he says it that's the giveaway. It's rehearsed, like a line he's heard in a movie – and probably a crap movie at that. Probably one starring Chuck Norris, Sylvester Stallone, or Vin Diesel, where Chuck or Sly or Vin distract some credulous, hapless goon with just such a rhetorical quip, a second before they whip back their fist and –

The Florence Nightingale Effect
Splat.

I spin in slow motion, like a ballroom dancer reaching out for his partner's hands, but there's no one here to catch me and I crash ignominiously to the ground.

The room becomes a blur. My head starts buzzing. It feels like it's swollen to ten times its normal size, like a beach ball that someone's just hooked up to a car tyre air pump.

As my vision begins to clear and I lie here flat on my back, I stare up through the assembled atrium foliage at the jigsaw of blue sky far, far above.

I didn't even see the punch coming, I dazedly muse. If indeed it was a punch, I consider, and not an Uzi bullet, or a

109

lead baseball bat wielded by a steroid-abusing gorilla – which is certainly how it feels.

My eyes lock on Roland, who lurches into sight above me now, glaring down.

'Ge–' I say, which is about as much of the phrase, '*Get away from me, you testosterone-tripping, ASBO-warranting, psychotic, sadistic, scumbag from hell*', that my scrambled brain and mouth can string together right now.

Roland's not impressed. He continues to pose in what appears to be a mirror-practised pugilistic stance, with his manicured mitts clenched into fists.

I then watch in shocked amazement, as he gently rocks from one foot to the other, and allows himself a cruel smile of satisfaction. Like he's a pro. Like he's just knocked out the Champ, and we're actually in Vegas, surrounded by the strobing glare of camera flashes, with the referee counting me out. Like all that's left to do now is wait for a bikini-clad glamour model to adorn Roland with his shining federation belt.

Flash git.

'Stay down,' he snarls.

As if I've got a choice. There's a Jacuzzi hissing in my ears, and my legs are cycling feebly, like I'm doing the dying fly.

That's when she grabs him. From behind. Without warning. Like a Ninja. With a pincer grip to the scruff of his neck.

Then she jerks his right arm up behind his back.

It's like watching a naughty school kid being yanked out of a remedial classroom by a no-nonsense PE teacher. Or the moment when the skinny, masked karate guy named Kendo Nagasaki flattens the seemingly unbeatable beardy giant in a wrestling match. Or Uma kicking ass in *Kill Bill*.

It's cool as fuck, in other words.

This woman, she's poetry in motion. And I'm her number one fan.

'You go, girl,' I manage to mumble, feeling every inch the excited teenaged admirer, as I watch in awe as she frog-marches Roland from the room and out of sight.

If I had a flag I'd wave it. Or cheerleader pompoms. I'd wave them too. I'm not proud. I'm a lover not a fighter. Whereas this woman clearly has nerves of steel.

I owe her big time.

And I'm so grateful that he's gone.

I've been hit harder, I suppose – by Sally 'She Who Must Not Be Named' McCullen's ex-boyfriend, Jons, for one – but that was a long time ago, and these days, I'm out of practice. It smarts something rotten.

Two minutes later, and my bra-and-pantied Amazonian saviour is back, helping me to my feet and leading me over to the rattan sofa, where she gently sits me down.

As she pushes her wavy, espresso bean-coloured fringe back from her face, I notice that beneath it her eyes are pretty and blue.

She reminds me of Raquel Welch in *One Million Years B.C.*, and I feel my stomach perform a pancake flip.

As she gazes down at me, her expression fluctuates between pity and anger.

I, meanwhile, try not to stare at her impressive cleavage, which my peripheral vision has already flagged up as being absolutely corking and only inches away.

In an attempt to focus my attention elsewhere, I tentatively touch my mouth and stare at my fingertips. They're red with blood.

'He's split your lip,' she tells me, 'but don't worry. It's not too bad.'

Now that she's no longer hurling abuse, I can hear that this woman's got a nice voice, a posh voice, but one that conveys intelligence too.

'I'll get you some ice. Wait there.'

And just when I was about to run after Roly and teach him a lesson . . .

'One question first,' I say.

'What?'

'You are Jessie, aren't you?'

'Yes.'

'Oh, good. Because I'd hate to be bleeding all over the wrong house.'

She manages a smile.

Less than a minute later and she's back, wrapped – disappointingly – in a fluffy white dressing gown. I feel something cold and hard being pressed up against my lip.

'Whu?' I grunt.

'It's a Magnum ice cream,' she tells me. 'Your face might get a bit sticky, but it will help to keep the swelling down.'

In spite of the ache in my jaw, I nearly snigger at this inadvertent *double entendre*. I take the ice cream from her.

'And there was me thinking that frozen peas were more traditional,' I say.

'I don't eat frozen vegetables,' she tells me. 'They're common.'

She's speaking to the kid here who thought vegetables grew in plastic bags until he left home, but I let it pass.

'I run an organic veg stall in Queen's Park,' I tell her instead. For my boss, I'm about to add, but then I think better of it, and let that slide as well. Because as far as Jessie knows I am my own boss.

'Perfect. Will you be able to give me a delivery here once a week?' she asks.

'Sure,' I say.

'Half fruit, half veg.'

'No problem. No problem at all.'

'You can drop it round when you next come over,' she says.

My heart thuds.

'You mean you want me to work for you?'

'Absolutely. I want you to manage the garden, and all the indoor plants as well.'

'But we haven't even discussed it yet.' What I mean by this, of course, is we haven't discussed the *money* yet.

'We don't need to,' Jessie says.

'We don't?'

'No. Not after the way you tried sticking up for me just now. And I'm happy to pay whatever your going rate is . . .'

There is, of course, no answer to this, and so I keep my trap shut.

But still, I can't help a painful smile.

Because here it is. My first solo gig. Just like that. Branching Out has begun to grow. I can see the business card already.

'Take your shirt off,' Jessie then tells me, starting to unbutton it without waiting for a reply.

'Why?'

'There's blood on it. If I soak it now, it'll come straight out.'

So not only is she a highly paid radio DJ and expert martial artist, but a provider of handy household hints as well. Is there no limit, I wonder, to this woman's skills?

As she continues to strip off my shirt, without even thinking it I find myself breathing in self-consciously and straightening my back. I'm aware that this is inappropriate behaviour, to say the least. I'm meant to be gratefully receiving the caring medicinal attentions of my new employer, not acting like a teenager parading his fledgling torso on a beach for the very first time.

But there's no denying it. There *is* something exposing, something sensual about all of this. As I look down and watch Jessie's fingers working my buttons free, right down to the waist, I can't help thinking that she's clearly experienced at this sort of thing. They move with the speedy efficiency of a crab's claws underwater, as fast as knitting needles – and when I glance up, I notice that she's looking at my face, not her hands. What's she's doing is all in the touch . . .

She only fumbles once, right at the end – and I can't help vainly thinking that this is deliberate – when one of her fingernails (painted vamp red) brushes inadvertently across

113

the smooth patch of skin, just above my hip, the bit that Amy always ends up absentmindedly stroking after sex.

Amy.

The word slams into my conscious like a whip crack. I actually flinch.

'Are you OK?' Jessie asks.

I feign rubbing my jaw. 'Sure,' I say, 'just a twinge.'

Of guilt, I'm thinking. I mean, if Amy was to walk in now, she'd . . .

But *what*, exactly, would Amy do? What, exactly, *could* she do? OK, so admittedly there *is* an incredibly attractive woman who's currently circling round behind me and slipping my shirt off my shoulders. But there's also blood on my lip and blood on my shirt. There's hard evidence, in other words, that everything going on here is strictly above board.

And even if Jessie, with the sunlight filtering down through her hair and on to my face, does look like an angel to me right now, that's probably just a symptom of whatever mild concussion I might have sustained. Or some kind of Florence Nightingale Effect. Which means it's natural for me to think kindly of her. Perfectly natural. And perfectly pure.

Nothing to feel guilty about at all.

Jessie comes back round and stands in front of me, gazing down at my bare chest.

'So do you work out a lot, or is it just the job?' she asks, dabbing at my lip with a tissue, before enfolding it in my hand.

'Er, a bit of both,' I lie.

In truth, the last time I went to the gym, I was wearing Dunlop Green Flash trainers, a John McEnroe tricolour headband, and The Human League were still in the charts.

But judging by Jessie's astonishing physique, she's clearly a fitness fanatic, and even I know that the number one rule of sales is to bond with people, because people like doing business with people like themselves.

'Thanks,' she says, 'for trying to calm Roland down back there.'

'I'd have done the same for anyone,' I say modestly.

'You should call your gardening firm "Sir Gawain",' she tells me.

'As in the Green Knight?' I guess.

'A gardener with a classical education,' she says with a smile. 'I have got lucky, haven't I?'

'More like I just watch too many movies . . .'

I consider telling her the real reason behind my heroic stance was because of my relationship with my dad, not her, but I don't. Why ruin a good thing? What's the point in owning up to the fact that my assumed heroism was nothing more than a spontaneous bubbling up of Freudian rage? Jessie has me down as her knight in shining armour, when I'm more used to being regarded by Amy as a peasant knee-deep in shit. It's an altered image I could grow to like.

'Seriously, though,' she says. 'You were very gallant.' She says this stressing the second syllable, which somehow makes its application to me sound even cooler in my ears. 'Roland's got a black belt in Taikwondo,' she explains.

More like *moron*-do, I think. 'You didn't do so badly yourself,' I say. 'Slinging him out of the house like that. If you ever get bored with the radio, I'm sure you could forge a great second career as a bailiff or bouncer.'

A smile crosses her face, but then it's gone again. 'It was he who got me to take up self-defence,' she says. 'Kind of ironic that I ended up using it on him.'

'Is he always like that?' I ask.

'Like what?'

I wipe at my lip with the tissue. 'Like someone who needs a restraining order put out against them.'

'No, and anyway,' she adds, 'he gets quite enough restraining as it is. That's what we were rowing about in the first place. I found a business card in his pocket. Here.' She picks a small rectangular card off the floor and passes it to me.

There's a picture of a young Oriental woman on it, dressed in a PVC catsuit, with a mortarboard on her head and a cane in her hand. Widow Spankee's Detention Centre For Naughty Boys, reads the legend underneath, next to a mobile phone number.

'I rang the number,' Jessie continues, 'and asked what services they provided. I had to look half of them up on the net, they were so weird . . .'

'And you confronted him with this?'

'Of course. He never was a very good liar, and it all came out. He's been seeing hookers for the whole six months we've been together. The shit.' I notice tears in her eyes. She wipes them angrily away.

'I can come back,' I say.

'No. It's all right. I'm fine. I'll just get dressed and fetch you a T-shirt. Make yourself at home.'

As she hurries away, it's hard to tell whether she's actually crying or not.

36DD

Waste not, want not, I think, unwrapping the Magnum, and taking a bite.

Mmm. It's quite an unusual taste sensation. Blood and chocolate. *Blocolate.* Not as bad a combination as one might suppose. I might even send an e-mail to Ben & Jerry and suggest they add it to their range.

I realise I'm feeling a lot better and risk standing up. Yep, I think, taking a couple of tentative steps forward, I'm definitely on the mend.

Idly, I pace out the room. My kitchen at home, which is by far the biggest room in the flat, is eight paces long. This, I now calculate, is twenty-eight.

This is the kind of house, in other words, I always dreamt of ending up in when I was a kid, but somehow never did. And I can't help myself: I keep seeing glimpses of that other life I might have had.

There's the dinner parties, with Jude, Sienna, Keira and the gang; and the half-finished canvases, scattered across the floor; and the best mate rock star, unconscious in the corner, after a night out on the lash. And, of course, there's my triumphant return from the Turner Prize award ceremony, and being led upstairs by the nanny to see the kids in their Peter Pan style dormitory room, where they've all been lined up to kiss their papa a fond goodnight, before he heads back out to the Ritz . . .

But before I get too depressed by this lost other life, I start picking up the broken plants, and cradling them in my arm like they're babies, carrying them to some empty pots in the corner of the atrium and bedding them in.

'You're obviously a father,' Jessie says, when she returns.

If she was crying when she left, there's certainly no sign of it now. She's dressed like she's off out for dinner, in a strappy black top, long white trousers, and rope-soled mules.

'Yeah,' I say. 'And you? Have you got kids?'

'No, I'm more the career type.'

She throws me a *Close Encounters of the Third Kind* T-shirt and I pull it on. Then she nods towards a cobwebbed glass doorway in the corner of the atrium.

'Let's go outside,' she says.

'Sure,' I say, going over to join her. 'This is a great house, by the way.'

She unlocks the door. 'It was my mum's. She died last month. Which means it's mine now. I don't know anything about plants myself. Roland said I should get rid of them and modernise in here, but Mum grew all of these herself and they remind me of her, which means I want them to stay. Besides, Roland's gone, so who gives a shit what he thought?'

She pushes open the door, so that the sunlight floods in. I follow her through.

It's like the Eden Project outside, or one of the illustrations from that *Country Diary of an Edwardian Lady* book that my sister used to read as a kid. It's the kind of garden that people

117

in the 'burbs and the countryside take for granted, but in this part of the capital might as well be paved with gold.

'So what's the prognosis?' she asks, as we walk around, and I trail my fingers across the plants. 'Is it terminal?'

We stop by a bench next to a potting shed that, like the rest of the garden, has seen better days. Jessie sits down and then blinks, staring up at the evening sun.

'No,' I answer, 'I think it'll pull through.'

Jessie gets up and stretches, and then, kicking off her shoes, does the weirdest thing: a sun salutation, elegant and graceful.

There's something so serene about it, so private, that I end up having to look away. (Although this might also have something to do with her peach-shaped ass, which is upturned less than a foot in front of me.)

'You'll be able to take care of all this for me, then?' she asks, standing with her hands on her hips as she surveys the garden.

'Sure.' I do a quick bit of mental arithmetic, and then promptly double my estimation. 'It'll probably take six hours a week to keep everything in check,' I say.

'That much?' she momentarily queries, before adding, 'Oh, well . . . I suppose it's always good to have a man about the place.' She flicks a glance at me. 'After all, you never know when you might need one.'

I don't know what to say, which she seems to find funny.

'Come on,' she says, 'I'll show you to the door.'

That's what I love about this place, I think, as we meander back through the house. If I said that to her at *my* home, then all I'd have to do was point. Here, it takes us a minute to get there.

'Well,' I say closing the deal as I stand outside, 'I'm looking forward to doing business with you.'

'Me too.'

'I'm a great fan of the show, by the way.'

She looks at me archly. 'More like you're a terrible liar.'

118

I feel myself begin to blush. Talk about rumbled.

'It's all right,' Jessie says. 'My show's not meant for people like you. It's for bored people who are stuck at home.'

I'd take this for false modesty, but she looks like she really means it. I think of Amy and the way her eyes sparkled when she told me how much she enjoyed doing her slots on Jessie's show. I wonder what she'd say if she could hear Jessie now. But she can't. And I won't tell her. Why spoil her fun?

'I want to say sorry again,' Jessie tells me. 'For what happened earlier. Roland's a horribly jealous man, and I think seeing a good looking young man like you calling round . . . well, it just tipped him over the edge.' She flashes me a smile. 'But well done, you, for not letting him scare you off.'

'No problem.'

'It's been lovely meeting you, Jack,' she then says, reaching out to shake my hand with mock formality.

As we shake, I feel something cold in the palm of my hand and, looking down, I see a silver Yale house key.

'It's for the side entrance,' she says. 'The alarm panel's just inside on the right.'

'What's the code?' I ask, both taken aback and gratified by this display of confidence and trust.

'36DD,' she says with a smile. 'Just like me. Feel free to come round whenever you want.'

Smiling, I think quickly. I normally knock off from Green-sleeves at five. 'I'll probably mostly be round early evening,' I say. 'Seeing as it's summer, there'll still be plenty of light, and it's the best time to water the plants.'

'Oh good,' she says. 'That means I'll probably get to see lots of you as well.'

The phone rings inside and she frowns. 'It's probably him,' she says. 'Trying to make up.'

'What will you tell him?' I ask.

'To go fuck himself, because I'm certainly not going to. Not any more.'

119

With that, she's gone, back into the house, swinging the door casually shut behind her, without looking round.

Good looking young man . . .

The words follow me down the driveway like whispered rumours.

I slip the house key into my pocket and walk towards the Skip with my back straight, just like I imagine Sir Gawain might do. I feel good. I feel noble and brave. I feel like I'm on the way up, and I guess I am. After all, I have just started working for myself.

It's only as I'm getting into the Skip that I realise that – even though it was Amy who put both of us in touch – Jessie didn't mention her, not once, not once during the whole time we talked.

Neither did I.

7

amy

Even Educated Fleas Do It

It's eight o'clock in the evening and I'm knackered. Louis and Finny have been here this afternoon playing with Ben and, together, they've comprehensively detonated our flat. They've had all the toys out and the sandpit and topped it all with a food fight. I'm just scooping up the last of the blobs of jelly from the patio, when I realise Jack's home and he's crept up on me.

He enfolds me in a tight hug as I stand up and I turn in his arms and put my head on his chest. It feels lovely and I let out a long sigh. I always forget what an amazing hugger Jack is and how I fit him like a jigsaw piece. Being in his arms always makes me feel like a woman again and not just a robotic dustpan and brush. I listen to the regular, unruffled thump of his heart and, for one second, in my otherwise hectic day, I have a moment of unadulterated peace.

But I can't stop for long. I'm too excited. I'm burning to know whether he got the job doing Jessie's garden.

So I pull back. I'm just about to ask, when I notice his face.

'What happened to your lip?' His lip's thicker at the top. It looks like it's been bleeding too, like he's been punched.

'Oh, that,' he says, touching it. 'Nothing.'

'Nothing? It doesn't look like nothing. What happened?'

Jack wrinkles up his nose. 'You know . . . oldest trick in the gardening manual. I stood on a rake and it whacked me in the face.'

I laugh and stroke his hair. 'Oh, my poor darling. Did it hurt?'

'It took me by surprise, that's all. It was my own stupid fault.'

'You've changed.'

'I have?'

I pull at his T-shirt. It's yellow and it's got *Close Encounters* written on it. 'Where's this from?'

'Oh,' Jack looks down at it for a moment. 'The other one got covered in blood. I had to go and buy a new one.'

'It doesn't look new.'

'Er . . . well . . . um . . . it's not supposed to. It's supposed to look distressed. Retro. It's the fashion.'

'But –'

Jack leans in close. 'Hey, forget about it,' he interrupts, putting his forefinger under my chin and pulling my face up towards his. 'It doesn't matter.'

I always had a bit of a thing for Jack when he used to do his art. I used to find him so sexy when he was all covered in paint, his eyes tired and seductive from concentrating so hard. It was the same when he started working for Greensleeves. I liked him seducing me when he came back from work and was all rugged and dirty, but it's been ages since he last did that. Seeing the question in his eyes takes me by surprise.

He kisses me. His lip tastes tinny and swollen. I pull away.

'Ah . . . ah, you're not going anywhere,' he says, pulling me back.

'Jack –'

'Shhh.' He kisses me again.

'But –'

'Where's Ben?' he asks, softly.

'Asleep.'

'And Kate?'

'Out.'

'Good.'

He kisses me harder. I put my hands on his chest.

'Hang on. Stop-stop-stop-a-minute. Did you get it?'

'What?'

'The job with Jessie, of course?'

'Uh-huh.'

I squeal with delight, and throw my arms around his neck. I'm so chuffed. 'We've got to celebrate!'

'Er . . . excuse me . . . but that's exactly what I *am* doing, Mrs Rossiter,' he says, picking me up and twirling me round. Then he starts kissing me and talking to me at the same time, as he walks me backwards, treading on the back of his boots to take them off and I giggle.

'But . . . but . . . what happened?' I ask between kisses. I need to know more. I need to know all about Jessie. This is too exciting.

'When?'

'At Jessie's place?'

He doesn't answer. Instead, he grabs my bum and pulls me up hard against him. There's no mistaking what's on his mind and in his shorts. He growls and I laugh.

'What's her place like?' I persist.

'OK.' His voice is husky and urgent. He's not taking much notice of what I'm saying.

'Only OK? What about her, did you meet her?'

'Uh-huh.' He pulls at my belt and undoes the buckle.

'And?' I ask, 'What's she like?'

'You know. Nothing special. A bit lumpy. On the turn.'

He kisses me again. 'On the turn' is Jack's expression to describe older women, who, in his opinion, are irredeemably past their best. It's a sexist, ageist, horror of a phrase, but I always find it funny, on account of the fact that he never says it about me.

Jack snakes his hand up my T-shirt and flips my bra strap open. I laugh and let out a yelp, as he manoeuvres me into the sitting room and towards the sofa.

'I shall have you, wife,' he says in a funny posh voice. 'Prepare yourself!'

But I'm not prepared. He can't just bust in on me like this. I've got to pee. I've got to change out of my comfy mummy pants and into something sexier. I need make-up, perfume, mouthwash . . .

Because, unlike Jack's, my libido is still fast asleep. Despite being pleased with his amorous advances and wanting to respond to him, I find it much harder than him to flip into horny mode.

Don't get me wrong, I adore having sex with him, but my sexuality gets constantly battered down by the sheer weight of domestic stuff I do every day. Because, for me, wanting to have sex is totally incompatible with nappy changing and feeding a kid and cooking and shopping and the endless cleaning up I do. It's a whole side of my personality that gets lost and buried whenever Ben's around.

Jack topples me on to the sofa and I yelp again as something digs into my back. Jack looks behind me, and pulls out the Bob the Builder truck from between the sofa cushions and wings it across the room.

'Come here, gorgeous,' he says, in his normal voice now.

I want to feel horny, I do, really. I want this. I want to be the girl Jack thinks of me as, but I can't help it, my mind is still in daytime mode.

So as Jack moves on top of me, all I can think about is whether I've put the dishwasher on, and what we'll have for dinner. I persevere, trying to think sexy thoughts, but I keep coming back to *Prime Suspect* and *Strictly Come Dancing* in my head, and then I'm on to internet shopping. Should I go for that little blouse on the Top Shop site, or would I look ridiculous?

Jack must sense that my head is elsewhere, because after a while he stops. He goes into the kitchen and comes back with a bottle of wine and two glasses.

I pull my knees up under me and smile at him.

'So?' he says and I know immediately that he understands me well enough to sense exactly what's going on in my head. He pops open the wine and pours me a glass.

'I wish you'd tell me more about your day, that's all.'

'What do you want to know?'

'You *know* what I want to know. Everything.'

Actually, what I want to know is whether Jessie mentioned me. Whether Jack knows what I've been saying. Whether she dropped any hints about my rants on her show. If she did, Jack doesn't seem too upset about it.

'I mean, did she talk about the radio show?'

'A bit.' Jack hands me the glass of wine and comes back to sit next to me on the sofa. His hand wanders across my stomach and I instinctively breathe in. Jack leans up and kisses my neck.

'Well? What did she say?'

'I don't want to talk about her. Not now. Later. I'm more interested in what *we* were doing,' he says.

'OK,' I say, kissing his forehead. 'But first . . .' I say, raising my glass. 'To you. For being the most fabulous husband in the world. I'm so proud of you, my Jack.'

We clink glasses and my stomach flips over as his eyes meet mine.

And my libido springs into action.

And I'm all his.

And suddenly, we're lying together naked on the sofa in a sweaty tangle of limbs and it feels great.

'You know, I was thinking . . . why don't we put that DVD on?' Jack whispers.

'The porn one you got off Matt?'

Jack smiles and raises his eyebrows at me. 'Why not?'

'Oh . . . I don't know. I'm not really –'

'Come on. Don't be a prude.'

'I'm not.'

Actually, I'm just really getting into what we're doing. I don't need any distractions.

'Because, believe me, *everyone* watches porn,' he says, moving down between my breasts, kissing the skin across my ribs.

'Do they? Really?' I can't imagine Camilla or Faith watching porn.

'Of course they do.'

'Well, *I* don't know anyone who does.'

'That's because they don't talk about it. Because it's un-PC. No one wants to think that they're doing something dodgy, or supporting something exploitative, but everyone does it all the same.'

'But –'

'Come on, it'll be fun.'

I laugh, as Jack leaps off the sofa and sorts out the DVD. He comes back and sits next to me.

'OK, pick a number, one to six.'

'Five.'

'OK.'

Jack points the remote, presses the scene selection and the film starts. He leans across and kisses me and I kiss him back, but I feel a bit ridiculous, especially when I see what's going on behind Jack's head.

'What's the matter?' Jack asks.

'Nothing.'

'You've gone all tense. What is it?'

'It's just that bloke.'

'Which one?' Jack turns his head to look at the screen.

'The one on the right . . . oh no . . . now he's on the left.'

'Beside the brunette?'

'No, the one with the bunches.'

'What about him?'

'Well it's just it's his . . .'

'His what?'

I bite my lip. 'His, you know . . . willy.'

Jack looks closer at the screen. 'Oh my God! It's huge.'

'No it's not that. It's just . . . well, don't you think it looks a bit like Yul Brynner in a turtle neck?'

Jack bursts out laughing and moves from on top of me, to sit beside me. We watch for a moment and our heads both tip over in unison as we follow the lurching camera angle on screen.

'That can't be very comfortable?' Jack says.

'She doesn't seem to mind.'

'The one with the bunches?'

'No, the one who's just sat on Yul Brynner.'

I pick up my wine and take a sip. 'Do you think they discuss it?' I ask.

'What?'

'What they're going to do. You know, the order they do it in. Like a dance routine.'

'You mean with a choreographer?' He watches the screen for a moment. 'No I reckon it's more improv.'

'What, even the dialogue?' I ask. 'You don't think some-one's scripted it?'

'No, no Rudi,' Jack says, in a ridiculous accent. 'Cut. It is not *lick* pimp. Ve take it from ze top again. Ze line is "Lick my *love* pump." OK?'

'And what about afterwards?' I ask, laughing. 'Do you think they shake hands? And swap business cards. And congratulate each other on a job well done?

'Or even a blow job well done . . .'

We both snigger like school kids.

'Oh well, at least it has a catchy soundtrack,' I say. 'Do you think one could purchase it on Amazon?'

'Now That's What I Call Baltic Porn Classics Four!'

We're having such a laugh, that it's only when I hear a key turning in the front door that I realise that we're both stark bollock naked.

'Hiya?' Kate calls. The front door slams behind her. Jack and I stare at each other, panic struck.

'Fuck! Fuck!' Jack says, catapulting off the sofa and sliding to a stop against the living room door, whilst I scramble into my jeans and shirt.

I throw Jack his shorts and T-shirt and he just gets them on as I dive for the remote control and manage to turn off the TV, a second before Kate enters.

'Why's it all dark in here?' she says, turning on the light switch. Jack appears from behind the door.

'That's funny,' he said. 'I thought the light just blew and now you've made it work.'

He stares at me like a terrified teenager, before scampering into the kitchen.

'Oh. Hi there. Had a good evening?' I ask Kate. My voice sounds weird. I swallow hard, even more freaked out as I notice there's a guy with her. He's balding, but quite good looking and is wearing a scruffy pin-striped suit with a T-shirt and dirty white trainers. I push my hand back through my hair. I must look a right old state.

'This is Simon,' Kate says. 'He dropped me home.'

'Nice to meet you,' I say.

As he reaches out his hand for me to shake, I sur-reptitiously wipe my hand on my T-shirt first. Then he sits down next to Kate on the sofa.

I clear my throat. 'Well . . . um . . . we were just having some wine. I'll go and get some more glasses . . .'

I scoot into the kitchen. Jack's by the sink.

'You offered them a drink?' he hisses in alarm. 'Why did you do that?'

'I didn't know what to do,' I hiss back.

'Do you think she suspected?' Jack asks.

'Yes I do. And that bloke's sitting on my knickers.'

'Make an excuse. I'll see you in the bedroom.'

'No. No. Don't leave me. You've got to go back in there,' I beg him.

'I can't.' He looks down and I follow his gaze to his shorts. I can see his point.

Literally.

But I've committed to entertaining these unwanted guests. I take another bottle of wine and some more glasses into the living room. It hits me that Kate has described my flat as her home, but I don't have time to worry about that now.

'So . . .? Do you work together?' I say, trying to keep my voice calm. My heart is beating fast. Can they tell I'm sweating? I'm very aware of the fact that I'm not wearing a bra and look like I'm going to a peanut smuggling convention.

'Yes, Simon's my boss. He and I worked on the new Adidas campaign,' Kate says. She's obviously showing off to him. 'You know the one I was telling you about?'

I can't think straight. I can't concentrate. I rub my brow. 'Um . . . yes, I think so,' I manage.

'It's airing tonight,' Kate says. 'Hang on. If we turn on, we might be able to catch it and I can show you.'

I watch, in slow motion, as Kate picks up the TV remote and points it at the screen.

She presses the button.

And there we have it.

In Technicolor glory.

Goran and Rudi . . . now joined by another couple of girls with unfeasibly inflated breasts.

In close up.

Along with the sound effects.

We all freeze. Simon, Kate and I stare at the screen.

Then Simon, totally unfazed, puts his hands behind his head, settles back on the sofa, and says, 'I think the technical term for that is tea-bagging.'

Hey, Girlfriend

It's odd listening to Jessie's show, now that Jack's met her. I feel so grateful to her for giving Jack a chance, because since

129

his interview, he seems full of new-found enthusiasm and really serious about Branching Out, his own company.

I know it will mean Jack working longer hours and missing Ben's bed times, but he reckons that if things go right, he'll soon be earning enough to pay for a couple of mornings of childcare. Which means that I can start thinking about what I want to do.

It's so difficult not having someone to discuss it with. I would tell the Vipers that I'm soon going to have a couple of mornings and potentially I could start a new career, but I know what their views on working mothers are: Immoral Whores of Babylon.

Nor can I tell them that I have a secret fantasy about getting into radio, because, even though Alex Murray is 'bearing it in mind', I know how far fetched and star struck it sounds.

But Jack meeting Jessie has given it all a fresh perspective. She sounds so normal. I always imagined her to be a bit of a vamp, but now Jack's described her as lumpy and on the turn it feels different talking to her. I feel sorry for her too. It must be lonely being in her mother's house, with only the plants for company.

Radio CapitalChat
Jessie's Daily Discussion : Are you still close to your girlfriends?
Caller: Amy from West London

I don't know, Jessie. Maybe it's just because I've been married for a while, or because I'm a parent in my thirties, but the intimacy I once had with my girlfriends like some of the other callers this morning, has long gone. But then I no longer need to share every detail of my sex life, or endlessly discuss my problems on a four hourly basis on the phone, and I don't have time for girlie shopping days and lazy weekends away. There's no vacancy for a female keeper of secrets, because I don't have any secrets to keep.

Of course, I'd like to think of myself as someone who could go out every night drinking with the girls if I wanted to, but the reality is

that after a day looking after Ben, most of my evenings involve
flopping on the sofa in front of the TV with my husband.

So I know it's my own fault that I occasionally feel isolated and
like Billy No Mates – but then, doesn't everyone feel like that,
sometimes?

Of course Jack and I do have *friends, don't get me wrong, but we*
mostly socialise with other couples like us. And apart from those
coupley mates, the people I now spend most of my time with –
people like the Vi – . . . people like my other mummy mates – are
convenience friends. We bump along together because we have
proximity and children in common, but none of them are true
friends. If something went seriously wrong in my life – I mean
relationship-wise – I couldn't turn to any of them.

It's just as well that nothing has gone seriously wrong in my life,
because if it did, I'd be stuffed. I'd have no one.

A White Sofa Or A White Knight?

Well, that's not strictly true, I'm thinking later, because I'd
have Helen. She's still technically my best mate. I've had a
date to meet H written in my diary now for two months. It's
the earliest she could manage. We both bemoan the fact we
don't see each other more, especially since we live in the
same city, but our lives don't coincide. Especially not now
she's one of the top directors of the TV company she joined
five years ago.

I'm pleased for her that her career has taken off, even
though I know she finds the responsibility and long hours
hard. She's got an amazing flat over by Borough Market and
a customised convertible Mercedes – the car we both always
wanted – but it makes me sad that we've drifted apart.

H's flat is so spotless, it looks like a hotel. I haven't been
here for over six months, and in that time she's bought new
sofas, rugs and lights and had the painters in. It feels weird
that she made all these decisions without talking to me about
them once.

I generally admire everything, running my hands over the

131

virginal soft furnishings and digging my toes into the thick white carpet. It's the most child-unfriendly place I've ever seen. Has she not been inviting us over because she suspects (correctly) that Ben might trash it?

There are photos of H's life lined up on the mantelpiece in tasteful silver frames. She looks glowing and happy in every one. The biggest one is of me and her laughing on my wedding day. I run my hand over it.

If I were a bloke coming in here, I would never think for a second that H had any need for a boyfriend. But I know different.

H had a doomed relationship with Matt around the time of our wedding. It lasted for about six months, but ended with them hating each other, and she hasn't had a really serious boyfriend since.

'So, how's the love life?' I ask, as she opens a bottle of wine. 'What happened to what's-his-name?'

She pulls a face. 'Utter donkey.'

'Oh no! I thought he was a go-er. What about the other one, Greg?'

'No good. Toff. So the usual . . . you know, Mummy fixation – and he wouldn't stop talking about his boarding school even though he left there twenty years ago. It was blatantly obvious that he'd been buggered in the cricket pavilion, but he was too repressed ever to admit it.'

I have to tread carefully with H. I know she wants what I've got – a husband and a kid and a future together, but the more entrenched she becomes in her single life, the further away it seems. Her life is so ordered and comfortable, that any potential Mr Right has to be amazing for her even to consider giving any of it up. And that's the problem. H is convinced that finding love will involve a sacrifice of some sort, and she's not sure if she's willing to trade in her white sofa for a white knight.

But eventually, over dinner, she relaxes and stops being scary and is back to being my old mate. As the sky turns dark over the London skyline outside, and a bottle of wine sits empty on the counter between us, I feel like I used to, like we're best buddies and I can tell her anything and she'll listen.

'So how's lover boy? Everything peachy perfect as usual? Even after seven years?' she asks me.

What do I tell her? Nobody has asked me how I feel, or asked about the status of my relationship for so long, that I feel vulnerable and exposed. In the safe confines of H's kitchen, I feel like confessing. I feel like telling H that things between Jack and me aren't as peachy perfect as I'd like. That it's hard work. That I don't see him enough, or have sex with him enough, and that now he's working for Jessie Kay, he's got clear ambitions, but I haven't, and it makes me feel jealous and resentful.

But just as I'm about to tell her all this, something stops me. This is just a phase, after all. Jack and I are fine. It feels too sacrilegious to let H into the inner sanctum of my marriage – and besides, I don't really want to inspect in there myself.

So, instead of talking about Jack, I bitch about Kate, which makes me feel a bit better.

'I want something exciting to happen,' I admit. 'I feel a bit run down by my routine.' I lean over and cup her hand. 'What I really need is for you to get married.'

'For me, or the event?'

'The event, of course,' I laugh. 'I'm just bored. I haven't been to a good party and let my hair down for ages. Everyone else seems to have so much more fun than me.'

It's only when I say this that I realise how true it actually is.

'Well, you know as well as I do, that I don't need to be married to be happy, but I kind of hoped that this would be the year . . .' she shrugs her shoulders. 'I don't know. It's so hard finding someone. It was so much simpler when we used to go out clubbing, and then get off with someone and find out whether we liked them afterwards.' She sighs.

'Well, what's stopping you doing that now?'

133

'What, try and go pulling at a nightclub? I can't think of anything worse.'

'Come on, we're not that old,' I say, trying to chivvy her along.

'We're not that young either. Don't you remember watching women our age when we used to go out? They looked ancient. We used to say that they were mutton dressed as lamb and should be dancing around their handbags.'

'What about that site you talked about?'

'What? Give me some cock dot com?' she says.

I know H has paid a fortune for membership of some exclusive dating site. 'Is that what it's called?' I ask, shocked.

'Durr,' she says, pulling a face at me, as she reaches for her laptop and boots it up.

She'll Settle For Ninety Per Cent

I look at the screen and I'm instantly hooked. This internet dating lark is a totally new world for me. How exactly do you sum yourself up and sell yourself as a potential date without sounding arrogant or apologetic, or downright desperate?

I get H to show me the profile she's written of herself. She leans over and reads down it with me.

'Tess and Jodie helped me do it,' she confides, mentioning two of her friends I've heard about, but never met. Or, her 'comfortable-shoe-wearing lady companions' as Jack likes to insinuate.

How comes H has got so many hobbies? I barely have time to paint my toenails, but H holds down an important job and apparently still has time to 'go Salsa dancing' and 'trawl flea markets for vintage film posters'. Not to mention how she 'goes regularly to foreign films', or 'just hangs about daydreaming in the spa'.

Does she mean the spar? I wonder sceptically, because as far as I know, that's the closest she's ever been to a gym.

'But you're not into fine art – or chess – and you're certainly not patient,' I point out, reading on.

'I am.'

'No you're not'

'Yes, I fucking am.'

'And I see you've forgotten to mention that you're a complete control freak,' I add.

'There's nothing wrong with liking order,' she says, shooting me a warning look.

I get to the end of it without commenting that I've known her for all of her adult life and, apart from the odd concert on the hilly bit of Richmond Park, she's never to my knowledge 'climbed mountains' or 'embraced world music', or shown the slightest glimmer of 'a keen interest in wildlife'. Unless you count boy-spotting, that is. But hey, who am I to nit-pick?

'Well, you sound great on screen. I'd shag you,' I conclude.

She flicks me with the tea-towel, but I can tell she's pleased.

'Oh, hang on. There's more!'

I scroll down to the long section detailing H's essential criteria for a possible suitor. It's baffling.

Sensitive and caring, yet manly and independent. Must like the hustle and bustle of city life, but embrace the wide outdoors. Must like staying at home as well as travelling, but also must be the life and soul of any party. Must care about his health, but know how to have a good laugh. Must be passionate about politics and the arts and like arguing in an erudite, yet respectful way. Must remember birthdays and plan amazing surprises. Must love food and wine and appreciate beauty.

And so it goes on.

And on . . .

Real men aren't like that, I think. Try: *Moderately sensitive when reminded, occasionally utter fuckwit. Main hobbies: scratching own balls and celebrating flatulence.*

'You really think you're going to find all this in one man?' I ask.

'I'll settle for ninety per cent of it.'

'*Ninety?*'

135

'OK. Eighty. But he's got to be drop dead gorgeous.'

I whistle. 'We'd better start looking, then.'

The Chocolate Box Effect

After a few more glasses of wine, I really start getting into it. I can see that this could become as addictive as looking through estate agents' websites.

It's like fantasy window shopping. Each new face is a new dream.

'Bloody hell, H, I can't believe the amount of seriously hot totty on here.'

'Yeah, but, come on Amy, don't be naïve. Everyone chooses flattering photos. Most of those blokes don't *actually* look like that in reality. They're all probably older and balder and fatter.'

'But even so . . . why didn't they have this when *I* was single?'

And I mean it. The world has moved on, while I've been standing still.

Suddenly, presented with so much choice, I feel retrospectively miffed because when I was single and I met Jack, he seemed to be my only option. OK, OK, so I fell in love with him, but was that because I was *ready* to fall in love and Jack just happened to be there at the right time?

Then it hits me.

What if I'd fallen in love with someone else? Would I have been as happy? Could I have been *happier*?

If, like H has now, I'd had a wider selection of men to choose from, might I not have chosen someone with whom I could be more compatible? Someone more well travelled and cultured? Someone who could support me and loads of kids? Or someone who wanted to stay at home, while I pursued a fabulous career? Or just someone posh enough to sail me away in his yacht?

Because I tell you, the possibility is all here, right on the screen before me – and momentarily there's part of me that feels like I've settled for a penny chew, when there was a luxury chocolate shop around the corner all the time.

Maybe I'm just a bit drunk. I blink hard, shaken that I've had such a deceitful thought. Jack's not perfect, but he is mine. I'm doing this for H, not for me, I remind myself.

I trawl through the site a bit longer, while she clears up the kitchen.

And then I spot a profile without a picture.

I'm about to skip over it, but instead, find myself reading what Tom has to say about himself. I like the way he's slightly worried that he has to be on this website in the first place, but after several long term relationships, he's found himself single when all his friends are married. The more I read, the more I like him. He's self-deprecating and funny.

'What are you laughing at?' H asks.

'This one. Tom. He's a literary editor,' I say, angling the screen so that she can see it.

'But there's no photo.'

'That's because he says that he doesn't want to be judged on his looks alone.'

'Because he's ugly.'

'Or drop dead gorgeous. Anyway, I agree with him. Love isn't all about the way somebody looks. It's about the way they make you feel. If you ask me, I think you should have done with it and marry this Tom bloke and have his babies.'

H grins at me. 'Mrs Rossiter, I do believe you fancy him yourself.'

'I'm a married woman.'

'But you would, wouldn't you, if you were still single?' she asks, pressing me for a commitment.

'OK. I suppose, hypothetically, if I was in your shoes, yes, I would.'

When The Cat's Away

It's a long way home, especially with a bottle of white wine inside me. I'm exhausted as I open the front door, after one of those soporific late night tube and bus odysseys that make you feel like you're in a gritty art house movie.

As I softly turn the key in the door, I expect to find Jack asleep on the sofa, but there's music, the smell of cigarettes, and the sound of clinking glasses and laughter.

I find Jack in the garden with Kate and three of her friends: Bells and Max and another absurdly thin pretty girl whose name I don't catch, but something poncy and posh, like Persephone or Paris.

'If I'd known you were having a party, I'd have come home sooner,' I say, not meaning it.

My barbed comment is for Jack's benefit. I'm slightly miffed. I haven't been out on my own for months. I was expecting him to take his babysitting duties seriously. I was hoping for a kiss and a hug and for him to ask me how my evening went. I sincerely doubt that he's checked on Ben once.

'We're going out,' Kate announces. 'Pretesh is playing at Urban Wall.'

Like I give a shit. I look through the window at the clock on the kitchen wall. It's one in the morning. 'What? Now?'

'The night is young,' Max says.

'Do you want to come?' Kate asks, but the way her eyes flick towards Jack's makes me suspect it's a loaded question. This has all been rehearsed.

'No. Thanks anyway. I'm knackered. I'm off to bed.'

I'm about to move in and put my hands on Jack's shoulders and claim him back, when Kate says, 'Can Jack come out then? You won't mind if you're asleep.'

'Yeah, he's gotta come, mate,' Max chips in. He's got a stupid haircut and a pierced nose. 'It'll be fly, man.'

I don't want to make a fool of Jack in front of his new 'yoof' mates by reminding him that:

a. He has to get up in the morning for work.

b. He's far too old to go clubbing.

c. It's one a.m and he should have been asleep for at least three hours.

'Jack can do what he likes,' I say to Max. 'I'm not in charge.'

But Jack deliberately takes my comment at face value. He shrugs in a 'What can I do? I've been forced into it?' kind of way.

Kate's phone bleeps. 'That'll be the cab,' she says. 'Oh, it's Sally,' she adds, reading a text. 'Has anyone seen her bag? She thinks she might have left it here.'

Sally?

She better not mean who I think she means. Sally McCullen. That slag who tried to seduce Jack when we first got together?

She was here?

In my home?

The second my back was turned?

Jack catches up with me in the bedroom.

'She was here for five minutes,' he says in a hushed whisper, holding my arm.

But I'm filled with jealous rage. I shake him off. 'Oh, really.'

'Come on, Amy, don't be like this. She came over to see Kate. What was I supposed to do? It's not like I asked her to stay.'

'It never stopped you before.'

'Oh, for fuck's sake,' Jack says, angry now, but still whispering. Ben stirs in his cot. We both stare at him for a moment, but it doesn't look like he's going to wake up. 'Have I ever given you a reason not to trust me completely?'

'Yes,' I remind him. 'Once. With her.'

'But you know I'd never . . . I mean, we're married, aren't we? It's different now.'

'Exactly. Which is why you should understand how I feel about this.'

'Well I don't. I think you're being ridiculous.'

I can hear the others in the corridor.

'Cab's here, Jack. You coming?' Kate calls.

Jack stares at me. I stare back

'Go on, then. Fuck off,' I say. It sounds vicious, even to me.

He holds up his hands. 'You know what? I can't talk to you when you're in this kind of mood,' he says, exonerating himself.

And he turns and walks out.

Bastard.

But He's So Out Of Practice

I lie in bed, fuming. The room is split by a line of moonlight. On the other side of it, I watch Ben's face through the bars of his cot.

I feel like he looks. Like I'm in prison.

I'm full of Why?s

Why is Jack behaving like this?

Why can't he see what a bitch his sister is being?

Why isn't he on my side?

Why does he think it's OK to go clubbing with Sally McCullen?

Why don't I trust him?

There are no answers, and after a while my anger turns to guilt. What if Jack's having some sort of mid-life crisis? Is it because I don't make him happy? Is it because he finds me boring? Is it because we don't have sex enough?

Because maybe we *are* arguing too much. Maybe we *have* got a problem. And if we have, does that mean that Jack might think about having sex with someone else? After all, he's so out of practice with girls, maybe he wouldn't even notice someone like Sally McCullen seducing him.

Until it was too late . . .

Fear creeps over me, like a cold chill.

Images strobe into my mind of Jack in the nightclub. Then it all warps into the porn movie we watched and Jack is with Sally McCullen and some other, fit twenty-something girl with perfectly pert tits and a flat stomach, and I feel sick with jealousy.

I try to remind myself of all Jack's good points, picturing myself and how happy I look in the framed photo in H's flat.

I watch Ben sleeping in his cot and see how much he's the best blend of Jack and me. I look around our bedroom. There's a framed nude of me above our bed that Jack did just after we were married and a teddy bear that he gave me when I first got pregnant. Everywhere I look are reminders of our entwined life. So why isn't he here in bed entwined with me?

It's light by the time Jack rolls in. I hear him lurch into the bedroom and trip over. I freeze and pretend to be asleep.

He comes up the bed from the bottom of the duvet. Even with my head out of the top, I'm engulfed by cigarette and booze and fast food fumes. It makes me want to retch.

His fingers walk up my thigh. I know what that means.

I don't believe it. He expects me to have sex with him. Now?

And despite all my earlier fears, my hackles rise.

He's horny. And he's horny because he's been dancing the night away with sexy, barely clad clubby types who've probably made lewd advances at him all night and made it perfectly clear they'd do it in the toilet. I'm no fool.

How DARE he.

I coil up and roll on to my side away from him.

Jack grunts and sighs heavily. He thuds on to his side of the bed and wrenches the duvet over him, pulling it off me.

I pull it back.

He pulls it back.

I yank it back with as much force as I can muster.

'Stop it,' I hiss.

'So you are awake, then,' he says.

I'm so relieved he's home, but now that he is, my fury has returned. I'm not going to answer him. I'm not going to give him the satisfaction. Besides, I know that ignoring him will get to him more than anything else.

'So, you're not going to talk to me?' he says.

No, I'm fucking-well not. Not until he apologises for being such a thoughtless shit.

'Well just or the record, Amy . . .' he says, leaning over. His breath honks. 'I did try and make it up to you. You're the one that's being childish here. Not me.'

With that, he yanks the duvet completely off me and, holding it in a vice-like grip across his body, promptly passes out.

8

Jack

The Battered Corpse Of Last Night's Contretemps
I'm up near the summit of Primrose Hill. Kites slice across the
sky, and kids yell, snapping frisbees back and forth. There
are so many people lying around on the grass, that I'm
wondering to myself, *Haven't these people got pubs to go to?*

A moped snarls past and a frenetic bass line thumps out of
a nearby SUV. The screeches of caged apes rise up from
London Zoo – and, boy, do I know how they feel.

It's lunch time and I'm lying side-by-side with Amy on a
moth-eaten tartan rug, as incommunicative and stiff as a
couple of recently-embalmed corpses, with Ben curled up
asleep in between us.

I am Jack Rossiter, The Amazing Melting Man. The sun is
beating down and, what with my hangover leaving my brain
feeling like a sponge in the Sahara, I'm so hot I wish I could
take off my skin.

Doghouse, Jack . . .

Jack, doghouse . . .

It's not hard to spot the link.

Which is why I asked Amy to meet me here during my
lunch hour, and then presented her with a surprise picnic
from the posh deli over on Primrose Hill Road, near where
I've been working for Greensleeves on the communal
gardens of a block of swish Regency apartments.

The picnic was meant as an apology, for being such a

143

drunken oaf last night – a self-assessment which I reached at the breakfast table this morning, as a Stolichnaya-induced Russian marching band rattled through their raucous repertoire inside my skull, and Amy glared at me over the Special K box like a Siege of Stalingrad sniper who'd just zoomed in on her latest prey.

I glance warily across at her now, as she flicks an ant off her wrist and shifts position. She settles back with her hands clasped behind her head, and stares up through the leafy branches of an oak tree at the constantly evolving cloud patterns above.

I look up too and search the sky like a soothsayer for omens that might augur well, but as the clouds continue their slow migration across the city from Wembley to Canary Wharf, instead of discerning smiling faces or fluffy bunny rabbits amongst the cumulus, all I can see are jackhammers, warships and guns.

Amy's got mirror shades on, so I can't tell what she's thinking.

Which is just as well, I consider glumly, because what she's probably thinking is, '*Why did I marry such a complete spanner?*'

And, if this is indeed what's on her mind, I have to concede that she has a point. Or rather three points: I *did* get knee-tremblingly drunk; I *did* selfishly sod off out on the tiles and leave her holding the baby; and, yes, she probably *does* deserve much better than me . . .

Not that she's actually said any of this. She doesn't need to, when she knows full well that her silence cuts me deepest of all.

She's hardly uttered a syllable since she arrived half an hour ago. Nor has she touched the food (all of her favourites), which I painstakingly picked out and lovingly arranged on a specially purchased paper plate.

I feel dejected, rejected, deep down black and blue, and I'm beginning to fear that my gesture of reconciliation could well have been doomed from the start.

Then Amy stabs a finger at the sky. 'There,' she says. 'That one over there looks just like a fat milkmaid bending over.'

I can't see Amy's cloudy bucolic figure myself, but I'm sure as hell not about to let the lines of communication be severed once more. 'And that one right behind it looks just like a randy farmer who's about to –'

'Stop it, Jack,' she tells me, twisting round to acknowledge my presence at last. 'Ben's got a filthy enough vocabulary as it is, without you –'

She pushes back her shades and, unexpectedly, grins. It's like watching the sun burst out from behind a cloud and I feel my heart instantly soar.

'I still can't believe he actually said that to Mum,' she says.

She's referring, of course, to the Curious Incident of the C*** in the Daytime on Ben's birthday, the occasion, no less, of our last barney.

It's an unpleasant memory, perhaps, but one that I'm delighted to see is currently being eclipsed by Amy's smile.

A smile which, I'm even more delighted to see, is currently being directed at *me*.

Because this means that Amy *has*, against the odds, decided to forgive me for going out with Kate & Co last night.

It also means, presumably, that Amy's forgiven me for making a mumbling, fumbling pass at her on my return, before promptly passing out . . .

'Do you want to –' I start to say.

But Amy's shades drop back down faster than the visor of a knight who's just been challenged to a joust.

'No, I really *don't* want to talk about it, Jack. Not this time. Not about something so black and white.'

I was actually going to ask her if she wanted to try some taramasalata, but I'm guessing from her tone of voice that perhaps now is not the best time to point out her mistake.

She sighs deeply. 'I'm here, OK? And you asked me here. And bought all this,' she says, gesturing towards the picnic. 'And that's enough,' she adds magnanimously. 'All I want

145

now is for both of us to put what happened last night behind us and move on.'

I don't need telling twice.

'Deal,' I declare.

It feels like someone's just removed a backpack full of lead weights from my shoulders.

It's all I can manage not to grin, but I do resist. The last thing I need is to reignite our row by looking smug.

Bygones appear to be bygones.

And thank God for that.

Amy crawls around Ben, and then sets about rearranging me against the trunk of the tree, plumping me up like an old pillow, before finally leaning back against me, with her face towards the sun.

I link my arms around her waist and smile.

It comes as a great relief, of course, her deciding not to dig up the battered corpse of last night's *contretemps*, since I'm really not sure what, if any, positive purpose would be served by getting into that whole 'Why Jack Shouldn't Go Out Clubbing Without Amy' debate.

For one thing, it would only lead us back to the topic of She Who Must Not Be Named (somewhat pointlessly, as well, seeing as Sally McCullen didn't even put in an appearance at Urban Wall last night).

And for another thing, I don't actually believe there *is* any justification, aside from my extreme inebriation and predilection towards stubbornness, for going out without my wife the way I did.

Not that I'd ever admit this to Amy, of course – on the grounds that I'm a grown-up and should therefore be allowed to go where I want, when I want.

But still, I do already realise that I was wrong.

The 'Why Jack Shouldn't Go Out Clubbing Without Amy' Debate

I mean, sure, I like to get wasted and throw a few shapes on

146

the dance floor every once in a while. What red-blooded male doesn't? But *without* Amy? Just me, bobbing away in a sea of sweaty strangers? Isn't wanting to do that solo rather like just coming out and saying, 'I want to do the dirty with someone who's not my wife'?

Because that *is* the point of nightclubs, isn't it? To screw around. To get laid by a stranger. OK, sure, we pretend it's about other things. *It's about the music. About the exercise. It's about getting drunk and off your head.* But all of these things can be done in isolation, so why not save yourself the cab fare and do them at home? *It's about meeting new people.* Yeah, meeting them and fucking them, more like.

Because with the music turned up that loud, you certainly haven't gone there to discuss philosophy . . .

And if clubs really *are* all about flirtation and sex, then what's the point of someone like me – someone who's *not* looking for any sextra-curricular activity – going there on my own?

It's like reserving a table at a steak house when you're a vegetarian.

Or visiting a car showroom when you don't have a driving licence. You're not planning on going out for a ride. So why *are* you there? Just to look at the gleaming chassis and wonder *what if*?

Because all *that*'s going to do is leave you feeling frustrated and wound up. Like a spring that needs to be sprung.

Which is precisely how I ended up feeling as I stumbled out of Urban Wall last night, in search of some KFC, prior to some TLC back home . . .

As I chowed down on the Colonel's finest wingery at the taxi rank, visions of the fit, available girls I'd seen in the club continued to dance inside my drunken mind.

Fantastical scenarios played out. I felt like I'd travelled back in time, back to my debauched bachelor years, when I'd gone to clubs just like that with only one thing on my mind: to head home with a stranger and put her to bed . . .

147

It was this very mental regression which led me to my ungainly attempt at sex with Amy after I got back to the flat, because, you see, the truth is: it wasn't Amy I wanted to have sex with at all. Not really. It was the girls I'd been dancing with in the club. Those images of them had stuck with me. It was like I'd been remotely fluffed.

Here in the cold light of day, this is not something I'm proud of.

In fact, it makes me feel ashamed.

But it doesn't make it any less true.

It also makes me no better than the city boy braggers I know, like Rory, who spend their evenings in lap dance joints, before going home to their naïve, deceived trophy wives and getting them to finish them off.

Subconscious as it may have been on Amy's behalf, there was justice, then, in her instinctive rejection of me last night.

It was exactly what I deserved.

Although I concede that it's also possible that there may have been some sort of sensory issue involved – on the grounds that I probably stank like a cigarette butt that had been soaked in a vodka still and deep fried in breadcrumbs and oil . . .

Something Like A Phenomenon

But the past, as they say, is the past.

And new days, I think, as I continue to stare up through the branches of the oak tree at the sky above Primrose Hill, are all about turning over new leaves. And the possibility of change. And the possibility – and hope – that even I might one day end up every bit as perfect as I think Amy deserves.

Now, seeing as any further discussion of my nocturnal misadventures has gratefully, wondrously, marvellously, now been deemed strictly taboo, it seems only fair that we talk about Amy's night out instead.

'So how was H?' I venture.

'All of a fluster.'

I dip my head and breathe in the sweet shampoo scent of Amy's hair. 'What about?'

'Boys.'

'Ah . . .'

H's intermittent singleness, much like Matt's, is a constant source of fascination to wedded folk such as Amy and myself. Hearing their trials and tribulations never fails to excite in us a mixture of relief and nostalgia, drawing us in like a couple of ex-combatants pouring over dispatches sent back from the frontline.

'Who's she seeing now?' I ask.

'No one.'

'No one?' Concerning a woman who Matt once described as being 'hungry like the wolf' in the sack, I find this hard to believe.

'Well, no one specific,' Amy says, 'but lots of people . . . potentially . . .'

'How do you mean?'

'She's trying out this new thing. Internet dating.'

'Ah, yes,' I say, 'I haf heard of zis pheeenomenon. I believe eet eeze powered by vot ve call zee electricitee in combination vid ze com-poo-tor.' I drop the cod accent. 'It's hardly new, darling. It's been around for years.'

'Well, it's new to me.'

'You make it sound like you're trying it too,' I tease. 'Don't tell me you're lining up an undercover lover to seduce you on the side?'

'No. I just mean it's dating, Jim,' she says in her best *Star Trek* voice, 'but not as we know it. They do it differently now.'

'I bet they do. In isolation. Hardwired into their laptops. With electrodes up their bums.'

Amy digs me in the ribs. 'Stop being such a Luddite. All I'm saying is they get to know each other virtually first, before they actually meet in the flesh.'

'It still sounds weird to me.'

'Well, it's not. It's a perfectly normal way for people to get together.'

'Yeah, people who like sticking electrodes up their bums.'

Again, the elbow. 'I'm serious. H said it was the way forward.'

'And was her bum vibrating when she said this?'

Amy sighs. 'She's just looking for happiness, Jack, the same as everyone else . . .'

'Yeah, well, she's not going to find it online. It'll be a disaster.'

'Why?'

'Well, for starters, it's like everything online: you don't really know what you're letting yourself in for. Until it's too late. I mean, there's no quality control, is there?'

'Quality control? I'm talking about people here, Jack, not factory parts.'

'Quality control is even more important with people. You've got to be able to differentiate. That's the first thing you learn when you start dating in the real world: to pick the good from the bad . . . the funny from the boring . . .'

'Or in your case, the big tits from the small . . .'

'Maybe. But so what? What's so wrong with the old-fashioned way of doing it, with a bloke walking into a bar and spotting a bird he fancies, and going up to her and seeing if she wants to get it on?'

'Well thank you, Fred Flintstone, for your considered and enlightened opinion. Remind me to catch the first prehistoric bus out of town, the next time I see your Cro-Magnon face coming my way in a bar.'

'It's way too late for that,' I remind her. 'You let me drag you back to my cave a long time ago.'

'I seem to remember it was me who did the dragging . . .'

'Good point, Wilma, but you mark my words, I bet you that all these people H has been chatting up online are real losers . . .'

'Actually, some of them are pretty good looking.'

'How would you know?' There's a telltale pause. 'You mean you've actually looked?' I ask.

'At their photos? Yes. H showed me. She wanted my opinion.'

I laugh. 'You've been choosing boys with her.'

'*For* her. There's a big difference.'

'But you still thought some of them were hot?'

'I suppose, but . . .'

'But?' My heart skips a beat.

'Oh, I don't know. It's just that whole single mentality . . . fancying strangers . . . going out on hot dates . . .'

'Having great sex . . .'

'Sometimes several times a night . . .'

It's my turn to nudge her in the ribs. 'Hey,' I say, 'I was joking . . .'

'And so was I. But, really, all that stuff's so irrelevant to my life now. It's so long ago that I can barely remember it. It might as well have happened to another person, on another planet . . .'

'Yeah.' I sigh. 'I know exactly what you mean.'

'There's no need to sound so wistful about it,' she chides.

'I wasn't.'

'Er, I think sighing does count as wistful, Jack.'

'I sighed?'

'Like the wind.'

'I didn't mean to.'

'It's all right. There's no law against sighing . . . or being wistful, for that matter . . .' There's a pause. Then she takes off her shades and turns round and peers up at me. 'So what *do* you miss about it?' she asks. 'About being single . . .'

I can't tell if she's just being provocative, or mischievous, or what, and then I begin to worry that the 'Why Jack Shouldn't Go Out Clubbing Without Amy' debate might not be nearly as dead as it seems.

'Nothing,' I say. 'Really,' I add. 'I mean it,' I emphasise.

But none of these denials stops Amy from searching the

depths of my eyes like someone staring into a well and making a wish.

Which leaves me with no option, but to take the coward's way out of the spotlight, by quickly turning it back on her.

'Why?' I ask. 'Is there stuff *you* miss?'

'No,' she says straightaway.

This time it's me searching her eyes. She doesn't even blink.

'Well, that's good then,' I conclude.

'Yes,' she says, turning away from me once more, 'it is.'

As we lapse into silence, I gaze down at the top of her head and wonder what she's thinking.

I also wonder why the answer I gave her just now suddenly feels like such a big, fat lie.

The Furry Altar Of Amy Crosbie

Do I miss anything about being single?

When Amy and I got married, I wouldn't even have had to think about this.

Back then, I was a strict adherent to a neat mathematical theory:

$$2 \text{ tits} + 1 \text{ Ass} = 4 \text{ Ever.}$$

It was one of the many things I signed up for on my wedding day. (Not in so many words during my actual church vows, of course, but in theory, at least.)

And it was easy. Monogamy has many advantages. There's the emotional fulfilment, the guaranteed receipt of at least one really good birthday present per year, the thrill of trusting and admiring someone enough to want them to have your kids, the comfort of a warm bed during the winter, and, of course, the clinchers: blowjobs by the dozen; someone who'll kiss you even when you've got flu; and last, but greatest of all, love . . .

But monogamy has its disadvantages too.

The chief one being that you only get to have sex with one woman.

And man is, by nature, as all men know, a fickle creature, a libertine, a pervert, if you will . . .

The urge to propagate as widely as possible is an intrinsic part of our genetic make-up, but it's an urge I've successfully tamed throughout my marriage.

This has been largely down to the facts that I love and respect Amy, but it's also partly a result of my increasing awareness – thanks to a combination of personal observation and my daily perusal of the *Sun* – that shagging around, and adultery in particular, tends to lead to no good.

It comes down to this. Sexual promiscuity is all about the thrill of crossing boundaries – but the problem with boundaries is that the more of them you cross, the more of them you want to cross, just as surely as first base leads inexorably on towards fourth . . .

If you're unfaithful once, chances are, you'll do it again. If you try a threesome, you'll want an orgy. Then, the next thing you know, you're down in a dungeon club, watching your wife peeing on a dwarf, while a tax accountant from Hull called Clive, in a black leather gimp suit, slowly drips candle wax on to your balls . . .

Or so I've read.

Playing around, in other words, can seriously damage both your marriage and your health.

Which is why Fidelity's a road block halfway down Temptation Alley that this particular married man has never broken through.

I prize what I already have too much to risk tearing it apart. I still fancy Amy and, emotionally, nobody comes close. There's no one I'd rather talk to than her, and no one I'd rather confide in (apart from over these current doubts, obviously). She's the only one I love, and the only one I ever will love. She's therefore the only person I'm ever going to have sex with. Full stop.

Where my cock was previously an intrepid explorer, an adventurer, a kind of phallic Phineas Fogg, or Phalius Fogg, seemingly destined to travel the world in eighty lays . . . it has become a monk, devoted to one furry altar and one furry altar alone . . .

The Furry Altar of Amy Crosbie.

In spite of this seemingly irrevocable spiritual conversion, however, my worry now is that Phalius never really went away at all. Instead he's simply been biding his time, lurking beneath the monk's austere habit . . .

And now he's started itching to get out.

It's because of this itch, this Seven Year Itch, that when Amy asked me if there was anything I missed about being single, I was unable to tell her the truth.

Because the truth is this:

What I currently miss most about being single is . . . all the other women I could be having sex with . . .

This is clearly not a good answer, either to say or to think.

It's the kind of answer that might even merit a slap.

But there's no denying it, because the evidence is here. First, in my mistaking the babysitter for Amy . . . then, in my eyeing up of the girl in The Greyhound . . . next came that charge of eroticism that leapt up inside me like an electric eel as Jessie stripped off my shirt . . . and last night, the Urban Wall girls and all those *what if*s that started running through my mind . . .

Now I don't for a second believe that The Seven Year Itch is in any way a real phenomenon – or think that the current length of my marriage is anything but coincidentally linked to my recent wandering eye – but an itch of some sort is undoubtedly upon me.

And I should therefore be wary.

Because what an itch wants most of all is to be scratched.

And that's the one thing I mustn't do.

I must be on my guard. I must wait for this itch to pass. And, in the meantime, I must be careful to see my cock for what it is: a beast which wants to sew its seed on foreign fields, a beast which will betray me if it can.

154

Or, to put it more eloquently:

> *The Fifth Column*
> *between my legs,*
> *the mauve toad*
> *with hairy eggs,*
> *garlic sausage*
> *with an appetite,*
> *my magic wand*
> *of dynamite*

Which is part of a poem that Matt once e-mailed me, by a prize-winning poet called Duncan Forbes, who clearly knows a thing or two about the trials of manhood.

Strictly On A Professional Basis

It's Sunday night and Amy and I are lying on our bed, drinking hot chocolate out of the *Desperate Housewives* mugs I gave her for Christmas. Our old Toshiba laptop is booting up on the bedside table and we've got an Amazon.com DVD at the ready to put in.

We're in here because Kate and some new chap are in the sitting room, alternating between channel hopping and sticking their tongues down each other's throats. ('Like a couple of ENT surgeons performing simultaneous biopsies,' as Amy succinctly put it.)

It comes to something, I suppose, that Amy and I have been driven into using our bedroom as our main living space, in addition to sharing it with Ben, who's currently softly snoring in his cot at the foot of the bed.

In fact, I think I had more personal space when I was a child myself.

In spite of our cramped conditions, Amy and I are at least both in reasonable moods. We're getting on, and being polite to each other, albeit in a fake kind of way, like a couple in a 1950s public information film. I haven't made the error of going out with Kate & Co again, and we haven't fought since our chat up on Primrose Hill. In theory, then, things are getting better between us, not worse.

Even so, there's still a level of tension between us that's never been here before. It's like we both know that all we've done is wallpaper over the cracks in our relationship, without actually filling them in.

Which makes me feel like I'm on probation, like any second now, it could all kick off again.

'What time do you think you'll get home tomorrow?' Amy whispers, not wanting to wake Ben. She rolls back the duvet and slips underneath. 'Only if you're going to be late,' she warns me, 'then I'll probably take Ben over to Sophie's for tea.'

'The usual,' I whisper back. 'Five.' But then it hits me. 'Oh, no. Seven. I've got a couple of hours of work to do at Jessie's.'

'Oh. I didn't think you were seeing her till Wednesday . . .'

'I'm not. Just her garden. She gave me a key,' I explain.

'You're quite the honoured employee.'

There's no suspicion in Amy's voice when she says this, and why should there be? I've been careful to keep my relationship with Jessie strictly on a professional basis. Not that Jessie's actually been at the house on the two occasions I've been back, but my good intentions are there, all the same.

It's all part of the new leaf I've turned over.

It's all part of my determination to ignore The Itch.

Nevertheless, I do now find myself shifting uncomfortably as I sprawl here, with Jessie suddenly a subject up for debate.

Because I've not exactly been honest with Amy about her.

For starters, I lied about how I got the cut on my lip, the one that I actually sustained during my ruck with Roland in the atrium – or 'The Rumble in the Jungle', as I now can't help thinking about it.

I lied to Amy about the T-shirt Jessie lent me, too.

But at least these lies were selfless, insofar as they were for *us*.

Because if I had told Amy the truth about the fight, she'd only have worried about me, and tried to get me to stop working there, and that's something I can't afford to do. Or she'd have quit her spots on Jessie's show, and that would be crazy, especially as Amy thinks they might possibly lead to something more regular, maybe even something that pays . . .

No, I don't regret those white lies one bit. The lie that's bothering me is this:

I lied to Amy about Jessie's appearance. I made out she was a moose.

And I did it instinctively, without thinking.

Why would my subconscious make me do that?

There's only one possible answer. I did it to hide the truth from Amy: that I don't actually think that Jessie's a moose at all.

I did it to hide the truth from Amy: that I actually think that Jessie's a babe.

No sooner have I thought this, than – flash! – in the blink of an eye, I find myself picturing Jessie – and it's not the kind of picture you'd find in a Sunday newspaper supplement. It's more like one you might find in a magazine hidden under a teenage boy's bed. With the pages stuck together.

But a blink is only a second. Then she's gone again.

I'm glad, because when I open my eyes, Amy fills them once more. My Amy, right here, right now, not in any private fantasy space, but one hundred per cent real . . .

I quickly hug her.

'What's that for?' she asks.

I run my hand through her hair. 'Just because.'

She settles back against the pillows. 'Do you think Jessie'll recommend you to anyone? I bet she's got loads of rich mates with whopping gardens.'

'Anything's possible, I suppose,' I say, putting in the DVD and hitting Play.

She doesn't answer and I stare across at our two dressing gowns, which are lying in a heap by the door, with their arms intertwined. They're ancient thefts, stolen from our honeymoon suite in Bangkok. They used to be fluffy and pristine white, but now they're threadbare and stained. This sight depresses me more than it should.

I get in under the duvet and we lean back and press our heads up close together, so that we can each use an earpiece of the single pair of earphones that are plugged into the computer.

I switch out the bedside light.

The film's called *Contact* and stars Jodie Foster. It's about a scientist sending electronic signals out into space, hoping to make contact with someone else from another lonely planet.

An hour and a half later, I'm watching the end credits roll with tears in my eyes, while Amy's beside me, fast asleep and softly snoring.

Like A Bull In A Field At The Side Of The Motorway

'Have you got time for one more?' Jessie asks.

She's crouched like a tigress in the open doorway of her kitchen fridge, with two bottles of Asahi in her hands, and she's dressed in what she informed me (after I casually remarked on how well it suited her) was a Diane von Fürstenberg dress, D&G sunglasses and a vintage Hermès headscarf from Relic.

'I'd better not,' I say, nodding at the two empty bottles already on the table. 'It'll put me over the limit.'

This is a good answer, an answer I can be proud of, particularly in the light of the blue images of Jessie that have been popping up unsummoned into my mind these last few days.

This is exactly the kind of answer a man resisting The Itch should, in fact, give.

'But I thought you said you were meeting your friend in the Portobello Gold?' Jessie says.

'I did.'

'Well, that's only a five minute walk. So why not leave

your car out in the driveway and collect it in the morning?' She smiles at me slyly. 'Go on, it'll give my nosy neighbours something to gossip about.'

Without waiting for a reply, Jessie stands and closes the fridge door behind her with a practised swing of her hips. Instead of being annoyed at her, for subverting my attempt to leave, I find myself smiling instead, thinking how girlish she suddenly looks.

'What?' she asks, catching me staring. She does the hip swing thing again, to check the fridge is properly closed. 'Oh, that?' She blushes slightly. 'I know, it's a childhood habit I should grow out of, but that's one of the problems about moving back here into Mum and Dad's house. It's such a time trap that it makes me feel like I'm a teenager all over again.' She smiles across at me. 'And makes me want to act like one too.'

She expertly pops both beer bottle tops on a magnetic opener on the fridge door, then grins.

I smile back. She looks good and she knows it. In the same way I used to know it when I was single, and the same way Amy did when I met her. Not that Amy doesn't look good now. Of course she does. It's just a different kind of good, that's all. It's more a comfy kind of good, instead of the look-at-how-cool-I-am good, that Jessie's working right now.

Weird, now I come to think of it, that in spite of Jessie being older than Amy, she somehow strikes me as seeming much younger as well. Her remarkably wrinkle-free brow has something to do with it, but it's also because she laughs more than Amy, and she stresses less. She's fun to be around.

'Cheers,' she says, perching on the edge of the old teak inlay table I'm sitting at, and pushing a bottle of beer into my hand.

Today is Thursday and it's a week now since I picnicked with Amy up on Primrose Hill. This is my fifth visit to Jessie's house, but only the second time we've met.

She was already here when I arrived this afternoon,

sunning herself on a deckchair in the garden. It's now seven and we've been sitting in the kitchen for the last quarter of an hour, ever since the sky clouded over and I finished my work. The radio's on (noticeably it's *not* Radio CapitalChat, but instead its altogether raunchier rival Emotion FM).

I follow Jessie's gaze as she looks around the kitchen. It's a large L-shaped room, leading out into the garden in one direction and off towards the drawing room and atrium in the other. It's not hard to see what Jessie means about it being a time trap.

The units are clean, but dated, with 1980s farmhouse-style wooden doors. There's a black Aga in one corner and not a single piece of stainless steel in sight. Even the calendar on the wall above the wilting aspidistra in the corner is three years out of date and flipped over to December, like someone just stopped caring about the passing of time.

Jessie notices me staring. 'Dad died before Mum. She slowly shut down after that. They were really in love. Right to the end.'

'They're lucky.'

Jessie looks horrified. 'To be dead?'

'No . . .' I start to protest, but then I realise that she's teasing me. 'I mean they're lucky to have been in love for so long.'

'I thought that was the whole point about marriage,' she says.

'It is.'

'Is that how it is for you?'

The directness of this question throws me for a second.

'You mean with Amy?'

She nods. 'Unless you've got more than one wife . . .'

'Er, no. Yeah. Things between us are great.'

'So where is she now?'

'You mean right now?'

Again, that nod.

'I don't know.' I check the time on my phone. 'At home. Probably bathing Ben.'

160

'Your son . . .'

'Well, I don't mean the lodger,' I joke. 'She really enjoys doing her spots on your show, by the way,' I quickly add. Since this is the first time either of us has even mentioned Amy, I figure that the least I can do is give her a plug.

'Yeah, my producer likes to get normal people on from time to time. He thinks it keeps it real.'

Normal people? Is that how Jessie sees Amy? As somehow less than her? Is that how she sees me? Is that why she's talking to me now, because she's keeping it real, because she's got me down as a piece of rough, on account of the fact that there's dirt under my fingernails?

Then she diffuses my suspicions by saying, 'And I think he's right. It's good to have someone with a bit of life experience on. There are already far too many media luvvies like me hogging the airwaves.'

'If you say so.'

'Were you there with Amy?' she then asks. 'When she gave birth?'

'Yeah. Why do you ask?'

'She was talking about it the other day . . . on the show . . .'

This comes as news to me. Quite how childbirth could have featured into Amy's high street fashion slot is beyond me. She must have been talking about maternity clothes, I suppose . . .

'What was it like?' Jessie asks. 'I mean, from your point of view.'

Vietnam, I'm thinking. The November Revolution. Waterloo. 'Amazing,' I say out loud.

She stares at me over the top of her beer. 'And what about after you got home? How were things then?'

'You ask a lot of questions.'

'I'm a journalist. It's my job. Anyway, I'm interested. I've always wondered how people cope with a sudden shift in lifestyle like that. I've always wondered what it would be like . . .'

161

'Well,' I say, taking a moment to think about it. Then, perhaps emboldened by the beer, or perhaps because her in-your-face attitude is becoming contagious, I decide not to give her the PC version, but to tell her the truth instead. 'OK,' I say, 'well, you've heard of alien abduction, right?'

'Yes, but I don't believe in it.'

'Well, you should.'

She laughs.

'I'm serious,' I say, 'because it's for real. It happens to thousands of pregnant women every day. They go into those hospital maternity wards perfectly sane, only to come out, well, temporarily *changed*, altered, not quite themselves . . .'

'That would certainly explain why one of the foremost experts on motherhood was called Dr Spock,' Jessie suggests.

I smile, taking another swig of my beer. 'Exactly, and after Amy got home from the hospital, that's how it was . . . like I was observing *Amy Through the Looking Glass*, or *The Twilight Amy*, like she'd become somehow separate from me, alien, and totally wrapped up in her own new world.'

'It sounds horrible.'

'No, it was just weird. Just different.'

I know I should be feeling guilty about telling Jessie all this, because it's personal to Amy and me. but I don't. Now that I've started, I can't seem to stop.

'Was she on meds?' Jessie asks.

'No, but she acted like it. For weeks. She just kept staring at Ben, and right through me.'

'Surely that's only natural. After a trauma like that.'

'Yeah, well trauma's the right word, but people don't use it. People think you're callous if you use it. Miracle. That's what people like to hear. The miracle of birth. But trauma's what it is, all right. For men and for women. I swear, I've seen horror films with less blood in them.'

'Wow . . . maybe we should get you on our show, too . . .'

'No, because I don't want Amy ever to know . . .'

'What, about how you felt?'

162

'Yeah. I never told her any of that. I mean, how could I?'

'When she was the one who'd gone through all that pain . . .'

'Exactly. I mean, I was fully aware what my role was meant to be in all of this. I was meant to be interested, sympathetic and supportive, and I *was*. And I *am*. And I *do* respect Amy for carrying Ben and giving birth. Just like I *am* grateful to her for quitting her job to look after Ben, so that I didn't have to quit mine. Just as I also recognise that childcare is hard work in itself . . .'

'You sound like quite the model husband,' Jessie says.

I laugh. 'Plus if I *had* accused her of being a hormonal nightmare after the birth . . .'

'She'd never have spoken to you again . . .'

'Exactly.'

'So what you're saying is . . . you're not as close as you were . . .'

'No.' I frown. 'No, I'm not saying that at all.'

She holds up her hand. 'Sorry . . . old DJ habit . . . putting my words in other people's mouths.'

I feel a jolt of panic. 'But still, that's what it sounded like to you?'

She nods. 'A little.'

A silence settles between us.

'I think I've probably said enough,' I then say.

'It's OK. We're only talking. And people don't talk enough. About personal stuff. Don't you think?'

'I suppose . . .'

'It's the same for me.'

I smile awkwardly. 'Oh, come on, you're on the radio all the time. Talking personal's what you do for a living.'

'I don't mean on air. That's all fake. I mean intimately. One on one. Like this.'

Again, the silence drops.

'How about you?' I then ask, figuring I've said more than enough. 'Have you ever considered having kids?'

'I'm too selfish. I like having fun too much.'

'But you said before that you've always wondered . . .'

'You've got a good memory.' She runs her forefinger pensively round the rim of her bottle, and then continues, 'But I suppose, yes, it is always out there. As a possibility. Not that I think you have to have kids. Not that I think you're incomplete in some way without them.'

'Or maybe you just haven't found the right man yet.'

'Or maybe I'm just having too much fun looking . . .'

'Maybe . . .'

'How about you, Jack?' She peers into my face. 'Are you still looking?'

'I'm married.'

'That's not what I'm asking.'

Her words – and the look that accompanies them – leave me feeling stumped. I stare down at the ground and tap my toe in time with the tune that's playing on the radio, unable to look Jessie in the eye.

The thing about it is, I'm no longer used to being regarded sexually in this way – if that is indeed what's going on here. I'm more used to being disregarded by women, in fact, and have been ever since I became a dad.

Women have a sixth sense for it: *dadness*. It's almost like they can smell the baby on you. To them, you're like an old bull in a field at the side of the motorway, harmlessly chewing the cud, watching the world race by, nothing like the wild buffalo stock from which you came.

You've got a ring on your finger, but you might as well have one through your snout. You're domesticated, desexualised. You're no longer seen as predatory, to the extent that women discuss stuff in front of you that they'd never dare to discuss in front of a single man, for fear of becoming desexualised themselves.

I remember how I once had the misfortune of sitting in between two mothers on a pigeon-crap-stained bench beside the kids' sandpit in Queen's Park, as they openly

164

discussed the symptoms of a particularly virulent vaginal yeast infection that one of them was suffering from – like I wasn't there . . .

As I look up now, I notice that Jessie's very much staring right at me, still waiting for a reply.

I open my mouth, uncertain just what it is that she wants to hear, or just what it is that I'm going to say.

Then my phone rings and I quickly take it out and answer it.

It's Matt: 'I don't care what you're doing,' he says. 'Wrap it up and get your arse down here. You're late.'

I shrug apologetically at Jessie, as I tell Matt, 'I'll be there in five.'

'It looks like we'll have to pick up this conversation another time,' Jessie says as I slip my phone into my pocket and reach for my jacket. 'Which is a shame,' she adds, 'because it was just getting interesting . . .'

I pull my jacket on. 'Right . . .'

She raises her bottle to her lips. 'I'll look forward to next time,' she says. 'Cheers.'

A Right Old Casanova

We're at our usual corner table in the Portobello Gold and Matt's holding forth about why he's taking everything with Honey one step at a time (or one lovin' spoonful at a time, at least . . .).

'I tried that whole "Find The One" thing with H and it didn't work,' he's telling me. 'I wanted to fall in love, but I just fell apart. I learnt my lesson. You can't plan to fall in love with someone, and it's the same with fidelity. You can't plan to be faithful to someone. You just have to find yourself suddenly doing it. That's how you'll know you're with the right person. Like you and Amy.' Matt laughs. 'I mean, who'd have thought you'd ever settle down with one girl? But you did. It just happened. It just came right at you, when you weren't looking, right?'

165

There's a pause.

'Right?' Matt checks.

'Oh, yeah, sure. I mean, of course.'

He looks at me curiously. 'You've still got your work head on. You need to relax.' He taps my glass with his. 'See that one off and I'll get you another.'

As I watch Matt walk away with our empty pint glasses and merge into the crowd at the bar, my mind returns to Jessie.

Did she make a move on me? There in the kitchen, just before Matt rang. *Did* I read those signals right? Because I didn't exactly hang around long enough to clarify her intentions. And I'm out of practice. It's like trying to remember my French irregular verbs. I think I'm right, but I might be wrong.

Which is why I don't need to mention this to Amy, I decide. Because there might not be anything *to* mention. And even if there is, I passed and I walked away. I walked out of Jessie's life and back into my own.

In other words, whatever this is, or isn't, whatever either *is* or *is not* going on, I'm handling it just fine. Right?

Right.

And the only reason I'm getting stressed about it at all is because I'm tired. Matt's right. What I need is to have a few beers and relax.

In an effort to distract myself, I pick up Matt's phone, remembering that he mentioned he had a picture of Honey as his screensaver, but even in this simple matter, I now see that he's been a typical lawyer, mincing his words.

There's actually only part of Honey on display. Or two parts of her, at least. Instead of the photograph of Honey's face that I'm expecting, or maybe a nice shot of her smiling at Matt over a candlelit dinner, what I actually get are boobs.

Honey's boobs.

At least, I'm assuming they're hers, because the jpeg is a close-up, and I can't see her face.

166

The breasts, as a result, seem strangely nonsexual and disembodied, reminding me of those cheesy old postcards outside the tourist shops in Piccadilly Circus, the ones of women's tits painted to look like cartoon characters, or puppies, or pigs . . .

I've always wondered how the models concerned, potentially grandmothers in their seventies by now, feel about these artistic curios.

'Oh, yes, that was a giggle. I was going out with a biker called Dave at the time, who used a tin of boot polish to make my tits look like Pepe Le Peu . . .'

Similarly, I can't help wondering how Honey feels about Matt carrying this shot of her round on his phone to show to his friends.

'Pervert,' I tell him, as he returns with our pints.

He snatches the phone from me. 'Don't blame me,' he protests. 'She's the one who took the picture – *and* told me to have it as my screensaver. She sends them to me. Snaps of herself. At work. In meetings. It turns her on. It's just some-thing she does. Still,' he reflects, staring admiringly down at the phone, 'you can't beat a nice pair of twentysomething norks, eh?'

Apart from a great pair of fortysomething norks, my subconscious automatically pipes up, once again tossing up an image of Jessie the first time I saw her, trussed up in a Wonderbra, with a burning ciggie in her hand . . .

I shake my head to dispel the image and take a deep swig of my beer.

'Who are *they*?' I then ask, nodding towards two very attractive girls, a blonde and a brunette, who've just walked into the pub, and who are now waving as they walk towards us.

'Oh, didn't I tell you?' Matt says, standing up, and loosening his tie. 'I asked Honey to pop along if she wasn't busy, and it looks like she's brought a friend.'

I don't bother telling Matt that, no, he didn't tell me this, or reminding him that the whole idea (his idea) behind this evening was for a quiet boys' night out.

'Honey, meet Jack,' Matt says proudly, kissing the blonde on the lips, before turning her round to face me. 'Honey works in art,' he explains.

And is clearly something of a work of art herself.

'Nice to meet you,' I say, keeping my eyes fixed on hers, unwaveringly, refusing to let my stare drop even a milli-metre, on account of a problem I've got.

The problem is the jpeg of Honey on the phone, and the fact that my brain keeps playing this trick on me, substituting the photo for Honey's actual ample glittery-T-shirt-covered chest.

'This is my mate, Carmen,' Honey says, introducing the brunette, who shoots me a wide, bright smile. 'You'll have to watch this one, Car,' Honey giggles. 'Matt told me that back in the days before he got hitched, he used to be a right old Casanova . . .'

Back in the days . . .

What next, I wonder? Is she going to 'Hey, Daddio' me, or start referring to me as 'old-timer'?

I don't know what stories Matt's been telling her, but it seems to have completely slipped her notice that he and I are the same age.

'Married, eh?' Carmen says, looking down at my ring finger to check. 'That's a shame, eh?'

A shame . . .

I can't help feeling a tiny thrill of gratitude and pride at this compliment.

The old bull in the field seems to have some juice in him yet.

In fact, I feel more like the wise old bull in the old joke, the one who's standing at the top of a hill alongside an impetuous young bull, with both of them staring down at a field of cows.

'I'm going to run down there and fuck one of them,' says the young bull.

To which the old bull answers, 'I'm going to walk down there and fuck them all.'

Not that I'm planning on fucking anyone, of course, but still, it's nice to know that perhaps I still could . . .

On the back of my ego boost, I ask the girls what they want to drink. I notice there's a spring in my step when I walk up to the bar, like I'm suddenly several years younger.

As I wait to get served, my phone rings: it's Amy. It's so noisy in here that I don't bother answering – or that's the excuse I make to myself anyway. The truth is, I don't really *want* to answer. I'm happy and relaxed and I don't want anything spoiling my good mood. What's the harm in that? It's only for a couple of drinks. So I switch the phone off and glance back at Matt and the others instead.

Regarded sexually twice in one day . . . I don't know quite what to make of it. Is my lucky star in the ascendancy? Or is this just a quirk of circumstances? Do I just look good in these jeans? Has my hair accidentally reached some optimum pulling length and style? Is my whole being suddenly *in*?

Or more likely – it then hits me with a worrying thud – and worse, much, much worse, have I become like Jodie Foster in that film I watched the other night? Have I started sending out signals myself? Have I started wanting, and watching for, replies?

9

amy

Beware The Chicken Fricassee

I'm watching re-runs of *Will and Grace* on the TV, as the clock on the video ticks over to 1.38 a.m. I get up and start pacing the living room rug. Then I sit down again. This is ridiculous. I should just chill out, I tell myself. Jack's been out late loads of times before. Getting uptight isn't going to make him come home any sooner.

I pick up my empty glass and go to put it in the sink. The flat seems oddly quiet and I look around the kitchen and think how pokey it is. A feeling of hopeless depression washes over me.

Things haven't been back to normal between Jack and I since our lunch on Primrose Hill and we haven't had sex since Kate and Simon walked in on us. In fact, now that I think about it, we haven't really been getting on since Ben's barbecue.

I don't know what's gone wrong, but we're always snappy and quick to find fault with each other, and lately I've found myself childishly sticking out my tongue at Jack behind his back, silently furious at some thoughtless oversight he's made.

Of course it doesn't help that we're accidentally living with possibly the most thick-skinned selfish female on the planet, but despite all the hints I've dropped, Jack still refuses to ask his sister to move out.

But tonight we were supposed to be alone. Just us. Kate's gone away on a work jolly for a few days and Ben's asleep, put to bed early under protest, so that I could get ready.

Because tonight was the night that all the rows and recriminations were due to stop and the romance that's been missing for the last few weeks would be rekindled. Because Jack and I both agreed that we needed quality time together.

So I've really pulled out all the stops.

And it's all been for nothing. The chicken fricassee I made sits untouched in the pan on the hob, the vegetables chopped and raw on the board. On the table, the candles are unlit, the ironed napkins still folded, and the remaining two of our best wedding crystal wine glasses, empty.

It's dark outside. I can see my reflection in the glass of the kitchen doors. My hair is dishevelled where it's fallen out of its clips. I'm wearing a low-cut top and the necklace Jack gave me, but instead of looking sexy and alluring like I did seven hours ago, when I was expecting Jack to come home, I look crumpled and tired. I've had too many vodka and tonic top-ups and I feel drunk and unsteady. All I want to do is go to bed and fall into a deep black sleep, but I'm too wound up.

I check my mobile phone again, but there are no new messages. Jack sent a text earlier to say that he was going to Jessie's, but he'd forgotten he'd promised Matt that he'd meet up with him for a drink afterwards. When I called him back, he didn't pick up. Then, at ten o'clock, he sent another text to say that he was staying later with Matt and he wouldn't be home for dinner, after all – and that I shouldn't wait up.

I'm so busy imagining all the places he might be, and working out my eloquent speech about how unfair it is that he gets to have all the fun, that I nearly jump out of my skin when he creeps into the kitchen and throws his keys on the side.

'Oh, so you're finally home,' I say, flicking on the lamp next to me. He freezes like a burglar who's just been caught.

'Jesus! I thought you were in bed.'

'Well, I'm not Jesus, and I'm not in bed.'

'It's really late.'

I can tell that he's drunk. His eyes look bloodshot and, even though I'm slightly squiffy too, there's no way I'm going to let him off the hook. I can feel myself rapidly sobering up, like a tape on fast rewind.

'I'm well aware that it's *really late*, Jack.'

'Sorry, babe. I didn't realise. My phone ran out of juice.'

Like he's going to get away with that! 'Oh, really?'

Finally, Jack cottons on that I'm not in a great mood.

'What's the matter?' he asks.

'Oh . . . nothing in particular. Only that I spent all day preparing a special meal for you, because you said you'd be home, and because we'd agreed that we'd have a nice evening in together. Quality time. "To reconnect" I think was what you said. "On our own." '

He looks at the kitchen table all laid up, and the penny drops. 'Oh. You should have said.'

'It was a surprise.'

'Well, I kind of double booked. We can have the meal tomorrow night,' he says, coming forward and trying to reach out to me, but I shrug away from him and fold my arms, leaning back against the unit.

'Look, I couldn't do anything about it, I promised Matt, and I hardly ever see him, and Honey said –'

'You went out with Matt *and* Honey? You didn't mention that *she* was there.'

'Didn't I?'

'No you didn't.'

I can feel the hairs standing up on the back of my neck. Personally, I have no desire to meet this Honey person, not after she refused to come to Ben's birthday party on the grounds that her dress might get ruined. Uh! Excuse me, but *how* much of a princess? But the thought of Jack and Matt and Honey, bantering away all night in the pub, fills me with indignation. It used to be Matt, Jack and *me*.

'So what's she like?' I ask, drumming my fingers on my arm.

'The usual. Blonde . . . big tits.'

'Really? How interesting of her.'

'She's got a filthy sense of humour, too,' Jack laughs, and he looks like he's about to share something Honey said, but when he sees my thunderous expression, he obviously thinks better of it and the smile fades from his face.

'Well, we'll have to invite her over to dinner,' I say acidly. 'That's if she can stand coming here in her designer clothes.' *And if her tits will fit through the door.*

'She's not like that, really. She's very down to earth. Her and Carmen –'

'Carmen? Who's Carmen?'

'Honey's best friend.'

'A girl?'

'Yes.'

Oh, this is just getting better and better.

'I see. So how come you didn't mention her either?' I say.

'I didn't?'

'No. You didn't.'

Jack goes over to the sink. He takes a glass from the cupboard and fills it from the filter jug. Even from behind, I can tell he's hiding something. His jacket seems to be radiating guilt.

'Oh, yeah. Well, Carmen turned up with Honey, and she was hungry, which is why we went to the restaurant.'

I glance across at my pan of lovingly prepared chicken fricassee.

'Oh? You went to a restaurant?'

'Yes.'

I'm pursing my lips so hard, I can feel them hurting. I can't believe he went out to eat. I can't believe I actually made him his favourite pudding (crème brulée) and burnt my finger blow-torching the top. When all the time he was at a restaurant. Now I wish I'd blow-torched *him.*

173

'Which restaurant?'

'Oh. That place. You know. Park Lane. That . . . um . . . that posh one.'

He can't possible mean what I think he means.

'You mean Nobu?'

'Yeah. That's it. Carmen works there. She managed to wangle us a table. Cool, huh?'

I put my thumb and forefinger on my temple. I can feel my heart thumping in my chest.

'So, let me get this straight. You went to Nobu. You went to Nobu – one of the most exclusive London restaurants there is. Without me.'

Jack turns round to face me. He swallows a gulp of water and puts the glass down.

'It's not what you think. It's all alright, you see. Matt paid.'

'I don't care who fucking *paid*. What I care about is that *you* went to Nobu *without me* and *with* some fucking girl called Carmen.'

'You're making it sound like it was a date.'

'Well, wasn't it? Because that's what it sounds like to me. A double date. Matt and Honey. Jack and Carmen. How very fucking cosy.'

'It was an accident. It just turned out that way –'

'What was it, Jack? Four spoons. One pudding.'

'A pudding? Are you kidding? After the chef's tasting menu. Christ no. None of us even had room for a wafer-thin mint.'

'Don't you fucking dare make a joke of it.'

'Oh, come on? Nobu? Would you have said no?'

'Yes!' I shout it at him.

'Amy. Be reasonable. Please. Come on. It wasn't my fault –'

'No. You be reasonable. Last week it was clubbing all night with Sally McCullen –'

'She wasn't there. I swear it –'

'And now you're out dining in the restaurant that *I've* always wanted to go to, the restaurant *you* said *you'd* take me

174

to, with some girl who sounds like she works in a lap-dancing club.'

'So you're pissed off about the restaurant? Is that it? You'd have been OK if we'd eaten in the pub?'

'No, you moron.' I'm shouting louder now and tears are coming. I will them away. I hate getting emotional when I'm trying to get my point across, but I can't help it.

Jack looks at me, totally exasperated. I can see that he has no idea why I'm upset.

'I'm sorry. Is that what you want me to say?'

'No. I want you to mean it, not just to say it.'

'I don't see why you're shouting at me. I've done nothing wrong. It's not a sin to eat.'

I stare at him, and for a second he seems like an absolute stranger. Doesn't he care at all? Does he really take me so much for granted, that he can't see how I feel?

I can't bear to look at him any longer. I turn and put my hands on the side of the unit. I can feel anger boiling in my chest.

'Fine. Do what you want then,' I say.

'What's that supposed to mean?'

'Well, it's very obvious that you don't want to spend any of your free time with me.'

'Why would I, when all you give me is grief?' He mumbles it, but I hear it as clearly as if he'd shouted it in my ear.

How DARE he!

Something inside me snaps.

I pick up the pan of chicken fricassee, spin round, and hurl it as hard as I can on the floor. The pan clatters spectacularly and chicken splatters everywhere.

Jack stares at me, astonished.

Ben starts crying in the bedroom. I shove past Jack and open our bedroom door. I pick Ben up and cradle his head. I'm shaking.

'What did you do that for?' Jack asks, standing in the doorway.

'Kate's not going to be back tonight,' I tell him, hardly managing to control my voice. My face is wet with tears. 'You can sleep in Ben's room.'

'What?'

'You heard me.'

'You're throwing me out of the bedroom?'

'Since you seem to have lost all respect for me, I don't see why I should share a bed with you. So, yes!'

Take Your Positions, Please

The next morning, I wake up with a hangover, still in my clothes. When I look in the mirror, there are tramlines of mascara down my cheeks like Marilyn Manson. I think of H and what she would say if she could see me. She'd no doubt recite our favourite JR quote from *Dallas*: '*Sue Ellen, you're a tramp, a drunk, and an unfit mother, and that's what my daddy said before he died.*'

I get up and go into the bathroom before Ben wakes up, so that I don't scare him with my appearance. He stirs in his cot as I quietly open the door.

In the hallway, I freeze, listening for any signs of Jack. I creep along the carpet to Ben's room, where Kate has been sleeping. The door is ajar and I peer through the crack by the hinges. The bed is untouched.

I go through to the lounge and stop in the doorway. The cushions of the sofa have been pulled off, revealing a patina of raisins, miniature cars, loose change and one of my missing earrings on the sofa shell. The sofa cover and all the cushions are heaped up on the floor, like a collapsed kids' den, but Jack's no longer in his nest.

It's the indent of his head on a cushion that makes tears spring to my eyes. It's not that I'm sorry for over-reacting and throwing him out of the bedroom. Or that, for the first time in our marriage, we've broken one of our sacred rules and gone to sleep on a row. It's just that the dent signifies the absence of Jack, and I know what that means.

176

It means that he's taken his position.

And when I go into the kitchen and see the chicken fricassee congealed on the floor, I know exactly which position that is: far far away in the Land of the Unjustly Treated. He's an illegal immigrant there, let's not forget, but he's there all the same.

As the day progresses and I don't hear from him, I feel worse and worse. I have such a battle going on in my head that I can barely function. I dither in the supermarket aisles, I burn Ben's lunch and, to top it off, I dye the white washing grey. All before midday.

And all along I know that Jack's at work and actively not thinking about me. How can he just switch off? Doesn't he care that we've reached such a low point? We've never had such a sustained period of arguing before.

Eventually, when Ben's having a nap, I relent and call Jack to see if he's ready to say sorry.

'Oh,' he says, when I tell him it's me. His voice is cold and unfriendly.

I take a deep breath.

'Look. Can we just sort this out?' I ask. 'Can we talk later? I really think we should.'

'Well that depends, Amy,' he says.

'On what?'

'On whether you're going to be able to behave rationally. I mean, how can I be sure that you're going to be civil and not turn into a psycho and start smashing the place up?'

'I –'

'Because, I tell you, how you behaved last night was totally out of order.'

How I behaved, indeed. I wouldn't have thrown the bloody chicken fricassee if it wasn't for him, but Jack seems to have forgotten all about the fact that he was the one in the wrong.

I wish I'd never called him.

There's a long silence on the phone. My eyes well with tears.

177

'I'll see you later, then,' I say.

'Maybe you will, maybe you won't.'

Mystery Woman

At lunch time, I walk up to Gracelands. It's Ben's favourite café and, as it's a Friday, there's bound to be a friendly face. Being out of the flat calms me and puts things a bit more in perspective, but as I walk up the pavement, I still feel bleak. It's a hot, sunny day, but inside I feel cold. An arctic freeze has settled over my relationship and it's altered everything.

Most of all, I hate the way that Jack has twisted things round, that it's all come down to the frickin' chicken fricassee.

Was it really so much of an over-reaction on my part? My head says, yes, that probably it was, but my heart doesn't. My heart is still wounded by the fact Jack thinks that all I give him is grief. And if that's really what he thinks, then throwing him out of the bedroom just made it ten times worse. The more I think about it, the more tied up I get. The way Jack sees it, I'm completely in the wrong. But I'm not. I know I'm not.

The café is all high ceilings, brickwork walls, wooden floorboards and rustic tables. Behind the counter is a huge array of salads and delicious looking moussakas and lasagnes, but because of my hangover, I can't face anything.

Camilla and Faith are on the far table. They wave and I go and join them. Despite their warm welcome, however, I feel like I'm gate-crashing their lunch. There's something conspiratorial about them, as if they've stopped talking because I'm there. Ben shoots off to find Amalie and Tyler in the play area in the corner.

'It's nice to see you up here. We weren't expecting you,' Camilla says, smiling brightly as the waitress deposits two plates on the table in front of her and Faith. I order a strong coffee. It's all I can handle.

Camilla doesn't look at me, but my gossip radar is up. She's got something to say. About me.

178

'What?' I ask, as our eyes finally connect.

She glances at Faith, before asking, 'So are you meeting Jack for lunch, then?'

'Jack? I wasn't planning to. Why?'

'Oh. Because we just saw him. Just a minute ago,' Camilla says.

My heart leaps. Is Jack here? Has he come to find me?

'Where?' I ask.

'He was in a car.'

'A car?'

'An amazing car, actually,' Faith chips in, nodding at Camilla. I notice mischief sparkling in her eyes. 'A Lexus convertible. Customised. Brand new.'

I don't know anyone with a Lexus convertible.

'We couldn't believe it when we saw them zooming past. They looked like they were having a right old laugh,' Camilla says.

They?

'She must have a *fortune* to be able to afford one of those,' Camilla adds.

She?

I can feel a blush rise in my cheeks.

'Oh yes, I've just remembered, Jack's with one of his clients today,' I bluff.

Faith looks at me. Then she looks at Camilla. 'They were probably going to the garden centre, then?'

'I guess,' I say, but the truth is I don't know where Jack was going, much less who he was going with . . .

Accidental Skin Contact

Elvis's 'Suspicious Minds' is playing loudly, as I sit and wait for H. It's a Thursday night in Soho and the pub is nearly full.

How bloody apt. Jack and I can't go on with suspicious minds, either. I'm not sure how we've managed to come to this stalemate. We're having to be civil to one another because of Ben, but all affection has been turned off like a tap.

179

I'm not getting so much as a drip of kindness or remorse out of him.

We're sleeping in the same bed, because Kate is back from her work trip, but Jack won't even look at me, let alone touch me. Also despite it being furnace-like in our flat, for the first time in our whole life together, he's taken to wearing his old pyjamas to make it clear that accidental skin contact is strictly forbidden.

Even so, I've hardly seen him all week. He's been out of the flat, claiming that he's working long hours. I only know what he's doing because he tells Ben when he'll be home.

The more he ignores me and is mean to me, the more indignant I feel. He should apologise. And explain himself. Who exactly is this beautiful client of his? If indeed it is a Greensleeves client. Or is it someone Jessie recommended to him? One of her rich friends?

And why is he driving around in the sunshine in her convertible all the time, when I'm feeling *this* bad?

I would ask him outright about the mystery woman, but since communication between us is at an all time low, I've hardly had the opportunity.

Never, ever have we sustained an argument this long and not made up – and the worrying thing is that now it's technically stopped being an argument. It's warped into something else. It's more like an on-going form of torture.

Maybe this is how marriages go wrong. I can really see how it happens now. You have an argument. You don't sort it out, but life keeps on happening. After a while, you lose your moment to recap and find the path together out of misunderstanding and misery. You find that you can't access the emotions you felt so strongly when the argument started, because they've distilled down, evaporated into a drop of poison and, like sulphuric acid, it hisses and burns a little hole in everything that's good and true.

Which is why I need H. I need to hear it from her that I'm right not to back down – that my strategy of holding the line until Jack cracks will work – but I also need to discuss how long this might take, because at this rate, there's every chance I'll crack first. And if I can't get Jack to apologise, then I need to work out a surrender plan that will minimise my losses and won't set any precedents.

More importantly, I just need to be out of the flat. Kate's there tonight and I can't bring myself to discuss my problems with Jack with her, even though I know she's itching to. She keeps looking at me with hangdog sympathetic eyes, that make me want to punch her. It infuriates me that she thinks of herself as an expert on relationships when she's only just broken up with someone herself.

So I agreed to meet H after work. It was perfect timing, she assured me. She wanted me to act as chaperone for the date she's fixed up with 'No-photo' Tom off the website. The idea is for us to meet before the date begins, so we can have a proper chat and then, as soon as he turns up, I leave. That is, unless he turns out, as H suspects he might, to be minging, at which point we have a pact to both run away.

So, all well and good in theory, except that now I'm here in the pub and H has failed to show up. I've been sitting here like a lemon on my own for half an hour. I've read the *Metro* twice and now, as I drain my drink, I know for sure that my window of opportunity to discuss my problems with H has closed.

Why is H doing this to me in my hour of need? I need to talk it all through. I need to tell her about the mystery woman Jack was seen with in the Lexus convertible. Who was she? What does it all mean? Should I be worried? How do I get the image of Jack laughing with a beautiful woman – who I've now built up in my imagination to look like a cross between Grace Kelly and Jackie O – out of my head?

I look around the pub. There are gangs of after-work drinkers and I'm reminded of the nights I used to go out with the girls from Friers. How we used to promise each other that we were just staying for the one, but would end up crawling

181

from bar to bar. Sometimes Jack would join us and we'd go somewhere cheap to eat. Those were the nights when I was full of beans at seven in the evening and not on my knees with exhaustion. Nights that were no pressure, because there wasn't a babysitter at home. Nights where I'd throw on something skimpy and fun that I'd bought in my lunch break and stay out dancing until two.

Suddenly, all those spontaneous good times seem like aeons ago.

Everywhere I look, people seem to be having fun. Everyone has someone to talk to, and they're all laughing. There's a hen party at the table next to mine and they sing along to Elvis, waving their feather boas in time.

They're all older than me and have dressed up the hen in a fairy outfit. She's got flabby arms and an old tattoo and keeps phwaaah-ing like a pantomime dame. Various phallic objects litter the space between their empty snake-bite pint glasses. They look like the kind of hardened women that don't give a damn about what anyone else thinks of them. From what I've gathered from their conversation so far, they all smoke, they all watch *Coronation Street* and *EastEnders* with a devotion that's almost religious, and they're off to bingo later. But I admire them in a way. They seem to have being happy sussed. You wouldn't find any of them tying themselves up in knots like I am.

They all laugh uproariously as the song finishes.

'Waiting for your hubby?' one of them says. She's the nearest to me and has a light blue feather boa and lips that are lined in a dark maroon liner with metallic pink filling. Her cheeks are flushed. She must have noticed me staring at them all.

'No, my best friend,' I say, embarrassed.

'Girlie chat is it?'

'Something like that.'

I can't explain. I can't stay and talk to a bunch of strangers. I grab my bag, ready to go.

Drop Dead Bloody Gorgeous

But just as I'm about to stand up, I notice a man at the bar on his own. He seems to be surveying the room, searching for someone and, when his eyes meet mine, he comes over to my table.

'Hey,' he says. He smiles. His teeth are perfect. His green eyes twinkle with question marks. 'Are you Helen?'

My throat goes tight and my palms start sweating.

Oh my God. It's him! It's Tom. H's internet date.

Well, so much for H's no photo theory. My instinct was right all along. *He's absolutely drop dead bloody gorgeous.* He's tall with shaggy dark lustrous hair and he's tanned. He's wearing a short-sleeved linen shirt with nice shades tucked in his top pocket. There's a kind of magnetism to him, which renders me incapable of speaking.

'Um, well . . . I'm, er . . .'

'Mind if I sit down?' he says, pointing to a stool opposite mine.

I'm blushing. I know I am. I can't help it.

'Are you . . . ?' I say.

'Tom,' he says. 'Tom Parry. My friends call me Tommo.'

He smiles again and holds out his hand to shake mine. His grip is firm and warm. His Irish accent speaks of heather strewn mountains and lazy lock-ins in country pubs.

'I'm not H . . . Helen. I'm not the right person,' I blurt. 'I mean, I sort of am. I'm her friend. I was supposed to be meeting her earlier, and then I was going after you arrived, but she's not here and . . .'

'Oh,' Tom says, looking a little put out.

'I'm Amy,' I say.

'Well, Amy,' he says, smiling again. 'I'm delighted to meet you. Do you fancy staying for another one, whilst we wait for H to get here?' He nods at my empty gin and tonic.

This is all wrong. I should say no and make an excuse – but H will probably turn up any minute, and Tom is so relaxed. He's behaving as if this is all totally normal.

'Come on. Say yes. Don't leave me.' His eyes flick towards the hen party who are ogling him unashamedly. I think he's sussed that if he stays on his own, they'll eat him for breakfast.

'OK,' I say, sitting down. 'Just one, then. Thanks.'

He goes to the bar with my glass.

'You don't waste much time, do you?' blue boa lady says, laughing with the others.

'God, this is embarrassing,' I say, covering my face.

'Phwoar, got yourself a looker there, love, eh?' the hen says. 'If you don't want him, I'll have him.'

'And I'll have him twice!' one of her friends screeches. They all crack up laughing.

I look at Tom at the bar. As if sensing me, he turns and smiles.

My stomach flips over.

Where is H? It should be *her* getting the smiles from the bar. I've met the guy for twenty seconds, but he's fantastic. Perfect for her. Tom's a ninety per center.

At least.

I check my mobile. There's a voicemail. Shit. How didn't I hear my phone? I dial to get the message. It's H.

'Babe, sorry, sorry, sorry, sorry, can't make it. I'm completely stuck at this meeting. Can we meet up another time? Sorry. I know you're going to kill me. Anyway, you're not picking up, so I imagine you're on your way home. If not and if you do bump into that Tom guy, tell him I'm sorry. I'll e-mail him later and re-arrange.'

'I can't believe it. She's not coming,' I tell Tom as he comes back to the table with my drink. 'H. Helen, I mean. She says she's really sorry, but she's got held up at work . . .'

'You're kidding? Just my bloody luck,' he says. 'You see, this is my first time. I've never done this internet dating thing before . . .'

'Me neither,' I say, before realising my blunder. 'Not that I'm —'

'It's not a great start to be stood up, is it?' Tom says, but he's smiling.

I notice the hen party nudging each other and looking at me and Tom. The blue boa lady gives me a meaningful look.

'Evening ladies,' Tom says, raising his pint to the hen party. They collapse into flattered giggles.

'Cheers,' he says to me, leaning forward. Now that he's up close, I notice how nice he smells – kind of musky, but clean. Not like Jack, who doesn't smell of anything any more, not to me, on account of the fact we both use the same deodorant and Ben's shampoo and bubble bath. But Tom . . . he smells different. Other. New. And – I can't deny it – sexy as hell.

'So . . . she's not very reliable, this mate of yours, is she? Sounds like she's let us both down.'

I feel I should stick up for H. 'She's great, honestly, you'd really like her.'

'I'm sure.'

And H would like him. He's good looking enough to model, but rough enough to satisfy her rugged outdoors-man fantasy.

'She's just got this important TV job and she's the boss,' I insist.

'Oh.' He doesn't sound very impressed. 'What about you, then? What do you do? Are you in TV, too?' He says 'TV' as if he thinks it's a ridiculous job.

'I used to work in fashion, but I've got a little boy now, so I'm just a mum . . .'

'Congratulations,' he says. His eyes twinkle at me as he sips his pint. 'Lucky fella. Your husband, I mean.'

I take a sip of my drink.

'So you're a literary editor, right?' I ask.

Tom raises his eyebrows. 'Oh? So you read my profile, too?'

'Yes, I kind of helped H choose.'

As soon as I say it, I realise how bad it sounds. Like *I'm* the one who chose him. I hold my breath. I feel totally rumbled.

185

There's a beat.

'So . . . I bet it's hard work, parenting full time?' he says, letting my comment pass. When I glance up at him, his eyes are dancing with smiles. George Clooney eat your heart out.

'Yes, but it's not like it's real work, is it?'

'Hey, don't do yourself down,' he says, suddenly serious. 'In my opinion it's the most important job in the world, and the least appreciated. People don't realise the sacrifice it involves. My mum brought us all up herself and I couldn't have more respect for her.'

And that's it. Maybe it's just that my stalemate with Jack has starved me of conversation for a week and that I'm desperate to talk to someone . . . anyone. Or maybe it's more that Tom is so easy to talk to. Suddenly, we're chatting as if we've known each other for years. We seem to cut straight to the chase. All the nervous preambling small talk simply vanishes. Instead, we dive headfirst into meaty, interesting topics.

Before long I've learnt all sorts of fascinating things about him: that his soul home is the west coast of Ireland, that his last girlfriend was a musician who went to America to record an album and promptly ran off with her producer, that his grandfather owned a printing press and that's how his passion for books came about.

Then we talk about how he loves challenges, and how he helped organise a rally last year and took part in a vintage Bentley and drove all the way through Europe. His life seems dynamic and interesting and filled with quirky adventures.

'So what do you do to let off steam?' he asks me.

I laugh. 'You know, these days, not much. Apart from phoning up radio stations for kicks.'

'Really? Which one?'

'You won't have heard of it.'

'Try me.'

'It's . . . it's just quite a new one. Radio CapitalChat.'

'No way!' he says, putting his pint down on the table. 'I love CapitalChat. I have it on all the time.'

'Really? My husband, Jack, thinks that the only people who listen to it are bored housewives and nutters. I'm delighted that you've disproved his theory.'

And I am.

'Who do you phone up then?' Tom asks.

'Jessie Kay's show. I like her.'

'Me too. I love all her Conundrums and My Rant stuff. Hang on,' Tom says, pointing at me. His face lights up with a question. 'You're not . . . you're not Amy from West London?'

I cover my cheeks and nod as a net of butterflies is released in my stomach.

'You're kidding, right?' he says.

'I don't believe this,' I say. 'You've heard me?'

'Heard you? I think you're fabulous! I always listen to that show, just to see if you might come on. That thing you said about blokes hoarding junk . . . about the inner Del-boy? I was quoting you all day.'

'You were?'

'Of course I was. It was hilarious – and so true.'

I am stupidly, shamelessly, breathtakingly flattered.

All of a sudden, for the first time in ages, I feel like I have an identity. That I really *am* Amy from West London. A person with opinions and things to say that people want to listen to.

Soon it gets too loud in the pub to continue our conversation. When Tom suggests we leave, I get up to go with him, but I get to the door and Tom's not behind me. I look back and he's at the bar talking to the barman. I see him showing Tom a bottle of champagne and Tom nodding, before handing over two twenty pound notes. The barman takes the champagne to the hen party.

'Why did you do that?' I ask, as he joins me on the pavement. 'That was so sweet.'

'Sometimes, you have to restore people's faith in mankind.'

It's worked. My faith is restored, let alone the hens'.

'So, what are we doing now?' he asks, rubbing his hands together. Standing next to him, I realise how tall he is. He towers above me and I notice for the first time how fit he looks. I can see the muscles on his arms.

I know I should go home. Every brain cell I have is screaming at me to end this thing right now. It feels too good to be anything other than utterly sinful.

'I've got to go . . .' I mumble, half-heartedly.

'Come on. You don't mind keeping me company, do you? To be stood up once is bad enough, twice is looking careless – and anyway, I can't believe my luck that I've met Amy from West London.'

'Stop it –'

'Look, I booked a restaurant up the road, just in case, you know, and now I'm starving. I hate dining on my own. What do you say?' His accent is irresistible.

'I . . .'

'Come on. What harm can it do?'

'But I hardly know you.'

'So?'

'So,' I point out. 'I don't usually do that kind of thing.'

'What? Eat?'

I laugh, embarrassed.

'It's OK. I generally behave quite well in restaurants. You can trust me.'

I think about Jack going to Nobu with Matt, Honey and Carmen. He didn't think it was a problem, did he? 'It's not a sin to eat.' That's what he said. And why the hell *shouldn't* I have some fun?

My First Internet Date

It turns out that the restaurant Tom has booked is in a private members' club in a ramshackle town house in Dean Street. It's one of those places that you'd never guess was there unless you were 'in the know'. There's a discreet panel on the door and I feel a thrill of excitement as we're buzzed in.

We're shown up some rickety dark wooden stairs to a beautiful dining room. It's all crisp white table-cloths, candles and pretty chandeliers. I haven't been somewhere this tasteful for years.

'They know me here,' Tom says, as we're shown to the best table in the corner. The waitress visibly swoons at him.

'How are you, Anna?' he asks.

She smiles. 'Fine thanks, Tommo.'

'Is the English asparagus risotto on tonight?'

She nods.

'Then my lovely companion here must try it,' Tom insists and Anna looks me up and down with an expression of curious admiration.

I feel myself standing taller. I like being described as Tom's lovely companion. I like his calm confidence and the way he makes everything seem exclusive and exciting.

'So tell me about Jack,' he says, when we're settled at our table and he's ordered an expensive bottle of white wine. 'He must be a hell of a guy.'

I shake my head. Sitting in this restaurant with Tom, I feel like I'm on a date, and I can't quite handle it.

Tom must sense my confusion. 'You don't want to talk about him?'

'No. Yes. I –'

'It's OK.'

'Is it?'

Tom gives me a reassuring look. 'You can tell me anything. I mean, we'll probably never meet again, so what have you got to lose? And anyway, I'm a good listener.'

He is. I don't feel self-conscious at all, but even so, I don't tell him about my on-going row with Jack and the incident with the chicken fricassee. Instead, I tell him that Jack *is* a great guy, but he's a great guy who works most of the time, and I find myself admitting that I'm lonely and that I find parenting hard, and that Jack and I have got so used to each other and so domesticated that we hardly

189

ever find time to remember why what we have is so special.

In other words, I tell him *way* too much.

'Oh God, I'm making out that we're not happy,' I say. 'I am. I mean we have our rows, but we are happy, I think.'

'Well at least it doesn't interfere with your internet dating.'

I look up and see that he's teasing me.

'This must look really bad to you, Tom.'

He shrugs. 'No. It's just fate.'

'Fate?'

'Is it really so bad to step outside your life once in a while and do something way out of the ordinary? Just to let your hair down and live a little?'

'You don't think I should feel guilty about this?'

'No. Not at all.'

Maybe Tom's right and this *is* all fate. Maybe he's been sent to me. Maybe I've bumped into this perfect stranger to help me think things through.

'It's not all so bad,' Tom says. 'To be honest, I'm envious of you. I'd love to have kids. I'd hang out with them all the time. I've got loads of nieces and nephews and I'm always up in the mornings with them, building camps and taking them for adventures.'

The way he talks about it makes parenting sound fantastic. Exciting. Like I once imagined it would be.

'But I think the trick is to have loads of kids,' Tom says, after describing what seems like a perfect idyll in his family's farm in Galway. 'A big gang.'

'I'd love to have more,' I confess.

Tom leans across towards to me. His smile is charm itself. 'And you should. People as pretty as you should breed as much as possible.'

The Cinderella Moment

It's nearly twelve by the time we leave Tom's club. We've been talking all evening like long lost friends and I've only

190

just realised the time. We've discussed everything from politics to art, and books of course. I've given Tom my e-mail address, for him to send me some recommendations. I feel stimulated and wide awake, like my brain has suddenly remembered what it's there for – to soak up all this cultural knowledge and wisdom.

'I'm going on the Bakerloo line,' I tell him, as I shrug into my jacket on the pavement. I've drunk too much and I'm worried that I'm going to miss the last tube.

'I'm going on down to Charing Cross to catch the train. You could walk with me and catch the tube there?'

The night air is balmy, red buses and black cabs idle in the distance on Charing Cross Road and we're standing in a pool of lamplight. Suddenly, I've decided that if I miss the tube, I'll get the night bus. Our eyes connect for too long.

'OK,' I say, but my heart is pounding. Why don't I just go home?

We head towards Trafalgar Square. We walk side by side down the steps in front of the National Gallery and on between the fountains. There's a full moon and the face of Big Ben shines below it in the distance. The clock is striking midnight, echoing towards us. There's something magical about it. Something that reminds me of Peter Pan.

'What are you thinking?' Tom asks. It's only then that I notice him staring at my face.

'That it's so easy to fall out of love with London, or anywhere for that matter, when you only pound the streets of one square of the *A–Z*. You forget that there is all this other stuff that makes you feel so alive. Tonight has made me remember what I love so much about living here.'

'And what's that?'

'That it's full of possibilities.'

I can't hold his gaze. I can't tell what he's thinking. Did that sound provocative to him? Did my comment about possibilities sound like I meant me and him?

Is there a me and him?

'What about you? What do you love about the city?' I ask, desperate to keep the conversation going, or steer it somewhere else, I no longer know which.

'Ah, well, everyone thinks the countryside is inspirational, but I'd say the city's the place for dreams,' Tom says.

'I guess.'

'So what are your dreams?' he asks.

'I don't know. I don't think I have any, not any more.'

'You never run out of dreams, surely?'

'I always dreamed of getting married and having kids.'

'What about other stuff? What do you want for yourself?'

'Just to keep it all afloat. To try and be happy.'

'OK, but say that was a given, then what would you really want?' he asks.

To be with Jack. That's the answer my heart gives. In a flash. Then I remember everything that's happened. How far removed my fantasy for us is from how we actually live.

And the fact that we're not even talking to each other.

So I tell Tom that I'd like to do something interesting with my life, before it passes me by. That I'd love to get involved in the whole world of radio, except that I have no idea how to do it. I tell him that I feel stupid for even thinking I could get a job, with no experience – but rather than agreeing with me, like Jack would, Tom seems to think I should go for it.

'If you had your own show, I'd listen every day,' he says.

My own show, indeed. Even the thought seems crazy. Crazy, but wonderful, too.

'So you *do* have dreams, after all,' he says, smiling at me. 'You see, I knew you did.'

'I've never really discussed it. I've been too embarrassed . . .'

'You shouldn't be. Why shouldn't you do it? Why shouldn't it be you who gets a lucky break?'

'Because I'm not a very lucky person.'

'You're not?'

'Well . . . I haven't won the lottery yet.'

Somehow, my words sound hollow. Being with Tom has made me feel very lucky indeed, like I've been blessed in some way.

It's been so long since I've had this kind of conversation, contemplated the bigger picture of life and put everything into perspective. It's been a while, too, since I've met anyone who lives life like Tom does. Who reaches for the stars and gets there.

'I wish I could be like you,' I blurt out. 'You know, doing what you really want to be doing and travelling and . . . I don't know, you just seem to have it all sussed.'

'I don't know whether that's true. I haven't got it all sussed, but I suppose I do believe that you owe it to yourself to make your life amazing.'

We have reached Charing Cross and stand outside by the entrance to the tube. It crosses my mind that this is the exact central point of London. That when you see London 65 on the side of the motorway, it means sixty-five miles to here. I get the impression I'm right at the centre of the universe.

People rush all around us, but Tom and I stand quite still. I feel strangely emotional. I don't want to say goodbye. I don't want this bubble to burst.

'I had a good time, tonight,' I tell him.

'Me too. It was a blast.'

'Well . . . bye then, Tom,' I say, but my heart is hammering. As I look at him and his eyes meet mine, I feel incredibly, intensely alive.

'Thanks for dinner.'

He nods. 'You'll be OK getting home?'

'I'll be fine.'

But I don't move. My feet won't move.

'I'll tell H you're a great catch,' I say, but my voice sounds funny.

Neither of us move.

We stay staring at one another.

And there's no point in denying it any more. The thing I've

been trying to ignore all night is suddenly glaringly obvious and right in my face.

I fancy the pants off him.

Plain and simple.

My body is aching with desire.

And he must feel it too, because I seem to be watching myself in close-up as the space between our faces closes.

Then his lips are on mine, and I feel like there's a tornado in my head.

We stay still, our lips pressed together in the softest kiss, and I feel as if my feet have left the pavement and I'm floating. Then his arms fold around me and I'm surrounded by him. His smell, his body. I'm blown away by his difference. Like the feeling of stepping out of a plane when you land somewhere hot and exotic in the middle of winter.

Then his tongue presses into my mouth.

And the tornado blows the top of my head off. I remember everything.

Jack.

Me.

Ben.

I stumble backwards, away from Tom.

'Sorry,' he says, holding up his hands. 'I didn't mean . . .'

I'm so flustered, I'm trembling all over.

'It's OK, I understand,' he says.

But how can he possibly understand? That I've totally taken leave of my senses. That this shouldn't be . . . *can't* be happening.

'I'm . . . I just . . . haven't felt this kind of connection before, that's all,' he says.

Neither have I, not since I first kissed Jack, but I can't tell Tom that. I can't speak.

'I didn't mean to . . .' he repeats.

I put my fingers to my lips and shake my head. A small whimper escapes. I feel like there's a spotlight shining down on me.

Then he steps towards me and holds the top of my arms.

'The thing is, I don't think you realise how amazing you are, Amy. How beautiful . . .'

'Tom. Please. Don't.'

I look at him now, and as his eyes connect with mine, I want to cry, because he seems confused too. As if something bigger than us both has overtaken us.

And then he says, 'Listen, I know this is crazy, Amy . . . but . . . can I see you again?'

10

Jack

Up On The Roof

I'm sweating like a racehorse in the winner's enclosure, after carrying ten sacks of potting compost up ten flights of stairs. Without pausing for breath, I drain an iced bottle of Evian. Then, slowly, I exhale.

From where I'm standing, I can see the Houses of Parliament and the top of the Millennium Wheel. I'm on the newly teak-decked rooftop of an eight-storey Covent Garden office building, and the sun's beating down on my bare back. Distant aircraft cross the clear sky like ice skate blades on a frozen pond. The steady hum of traffic rises up from the street below, mixed with the occasional shout and beeping of horns. Traces of the nearby fast food joints reach me on the warm breeze: pizza, garlic bread, burgers and fries . . .

Yet where I am, it feels more like an oasis than the centre of a city of ten million souls.

The rooftop's perimeter is lined with a lush variety of tall and hardy standards, like bay, bamboo, chusan palm, euonymus and hibiscus, all of them in terracotta troughs and pots. In the middle is a beach shack constructed from corrugated iron and driftwood, which is fitted with a bespoke, curved wooden bar that's shaped like a surfboard.

Behind the bar are two glass-fronted drinks fridges and a row of optics, which make me want to pull on some surf

196

shorts, kick back with a cocktail, and laze the rest of the day away.

In other words, it's extremely funky and enticing up here. But then I would say that, seeing as I designed the layout myself.

This building's owned by an ad agency called Pep Talk, a slick, hipster operation, headed by an extremely short and chubby Hawaiian named James Peters, who went to boarding school with my boss Rupert.

James, or 'Slim Jim', as he perversely likes to be called, wanted a little slice of his homeland here in London to use for corporate entertainment, and that's exactly what I've given him. He came up to see the finished article ten minutes ago, and gave it, and me, a rapturous reception.

Which means Rupert should be indebted to me too. Which is no bad thing, what with my annual review coming up next week. Who knows? I might even get a bonus – and with that bonus, I might even pay for some business cards of my own and lease myself a van . . .

I feel proud as I look around, but not as elated as I expected. I think it's because there's no one here to share the moment. Or no one important. Meaning Amy. Because normally, on something this big, she'd be the first person I'd want to show it off to. I'd want her opinion and I'd want her to think it was cool. Because that would make me feel cool too.

Dom and Lee – both of them South Africans in their early twenties, with sandy shoulder-length hair – are leaning over the rooftop railing, smoking roll-ups and watching the girls go by below.

'Hey, Boss,' Dom calls out to me, 'come and check out this chick. She's got a cleavage you could chuck a Coke can down, without it touching the sides . . .'

Hmm. A mammary recycling unit. An original and intriguing concept, to be sure, and yet, somehow, I can't quite see Westminster City Council incorporating it as an integral part of their refuse disposal scheme.

'And she's got an arse like a ripe peach,' adds Pete, another of my Greensleeves colleagues.

Normally, I'd be right there alongside them, merrily leering away. It's pathetic, I know, but every man has an inner wolf-whistling builder that needs letting off the leash from time to time.

But not today.

Today, sex is the last thing on my mind. In fact, the way I currently feel, you could stick me in Hugh Heffner's Playboy Mansion with a bunch of nymphomaniac Bunnies telling me how my every horny wish is their desire, and what I'd actually ask them to do is put their crotchless panties and peephole bras back on, and leave me alone with a nice hot cup of cocoa and an *Inspector Morse* DVD.

To feel desire for someone else, I think, first you need to feel desired yourself.

And after last night, I feel about as attractive as a pair of skid-marked Y-Fronts.

Last night, Amy went out to see H. It was only meant to be for a quick drink, but she didn't get back until gone midnight. During her absence, she didn't call me once. Then when she did finally come home . . . nada. Not a *Hello*, or an *Are you still awake?* Nothing at all.

She didn't even undress in front of me. Like a shy room-mate on a school trip, she retreated into the bathroom fully clothed. I listened to the shower running for what seemed like an age. When she came back, she was wrapped in a dressing gown, which she kept on as she lay down on top of the duvet, right at the edge of the mattress, as far away from me as she could.

How long can a row go on?

That's what I want to know.

Because this one's gone far, and wide, and deep.

I used to think of my relationship with Amy as a beautiful mountain that we were climbing together, but now I find myself sliding back down its sharpened scree alone, with my fingertips raw and bloody from where I've been trying and failing to hold on . . .

I've been waiting for Amy to reach out to help me back up. But she hasn't.

And I don't know if I can climb back up to the summit alone. Particularly, as I'm not sure that Amy even wants me there beside her any more.

If she doesn't want me there beside her, then I don't know if I want her.

If it was just sex and physical affection she was withholding, if she was just punishing me in some crazy Victorian style, like when she told me to sleep in the spare room the other night, then I could handle it.

If we were fighting, I could handle that too. If she was calling me every name under the sun, I could soak that up like a sponge.

Even if she was sulking, I could weather it. Because at least then I'd know that I could tease her out of it. Or that at some point, she'd crack.

But we're not fighting. Or sulking. We're just . . . *co-existing*. Like mushrooms in a darkened room. Or goldfish in a bowl.

That's what I can't handle: her indifference.

The way she looks at me like she no longer cares – like she'd rather be somewhere else instead.

It pisses me off. It makes me want to ignore her too. So that's what I've been doing. And why shouldn't I? *She*'s the one in the wrong. *She*'s the one who flew the chicken across the kitchen. It's *she* who won't back down.

So the attitude I've been sending back at her is this:

Well, hello, Immovable Object, I'm the Unstoppable Force . . .

Which is why it comes as a surprise when my phone buzzes, and I see that it's Amy's name that's flashing on the screen. It's the first time she's called me at work in days.

I say, 'Hi.'

She says, 'I need to see you. There's something I need to talk to you about.'

Not, *Why don't we meet for lunch?* or, *Do you fancy hooking up for a quick coffee?* Nothing so casual. She emphasises the word *need*. Twice. As in, *This is necessary. It's something we have to do. Whether I want to or not.*

No sooner have these words left her mouth than the hairs on the back of my neck – the primeval warning mechanism put there by nature to alert me to the approach of famished sabre toothed tigers, rabid mammoths, falling trees, and other mortal perils – stiffen like a porcupine's spines.

My heart thuds. 'Are you all right?'

'Yes.'

But I can hear the tension in her voice. Then Ben starts to cry in the background. 'Is something wrong with Ben?' I demand.

'No. I just need to speak to you. Face to face.'

Face to face?

My heart begins to race.

First *There's something I need to talk to you about . . .* and now: *Face to face . . .* Even in isolation these phrases would be unnerving. But paired up like this? Well, it's like putting Smith and Wesson together. Or Kung and Fu. Or Celine and Dion.

They're downright unpleasant and threatening, in other words, and I don't like them one bit.

You don't reach my age without having mastered a few basic survival skills, and recognising the inherent danger posed by these two phrases is about as basic a rule as 'Don't eat the yellow snow' is to an Eskimo.

Amy might as well be sitting here in front of me, with a John Malkovich unhinged smile, loading bullets with my name on them into a gun.

Because the plain fact is that *There's something I need to talk to you about* and *Face to face* are invariably followed by a *because*. And that *because* is rarely a nice *because*. It's hardly ever a *'Because I wanted to tell you how much I love you'*, or *'Because I've bought you a cuddly-wuddly kitten as a present'*.

200

It's more usually a nasty kind of *because*, like: *Because Jane Sanders told me you fingered her on the school trip to St Fagan's Folk Museum last week, you lying, cheating bastard."*(Clare Fleming, my then girlfriend of two weeks, to me in June 1987, a second before she tipped a blue raspberry Slush Puppie over my head, and told me that I used more hair mousse than a girl.)

Or:

Because I don't want to go out with you any more, because I want to go out with Brian Wilkinson instead, because his nob's the size of a Swiss roll, his balls are as big as haggises, and his dad's just bought him a brand new Renault 5. And because Clare Fleming's right: you do use more hair mousse than a girl. (Jane Sanders, my then girlfriend of six days, to me in July 1987, a second before she got into Brian 'Whopper' Wilkinson's factory fresh Renault 5 and he wheelspun her out of my life.)

'Can you meet me or not?' Amy asks.

Wearily – because that's exactly what this row's doing to me, draining me of energy, like a vampire draining me of blood – I check the sky for forks of lightning, sudden eclipses of the sun, and swarms of bats. My ears strain for the sound of melodramatic piano chords, blasting out *Duh! Duh! Duh! Duurrghs!*

But none of these traditional portents of imminent doom are present, and so, reluctantly, I agree.

After all, this could be the breakthrough I've been waiting for. She could be about to admit that she's wrong.

Pummelled By A Succession Of Body Blows

A sense of apprehension balloons inside me as I approach St James's Park. Rather than an ordinary civilian strolling to meet his family in one of London's prettier Royal Parks, I feel more like a lone gunslinger advancing nervously down the dusty deserted main street of a lawless Wild West frontier town. From which direction will the first shot ring out? Will I survive till sundown, or end up in a shallow grave?

201

As I cross the wide expanse of the tree-lined Mall, I glance over at the ugly hulk of Buckingham Palace. I bet Princes William and Harry don't get snagged up in webs of female trickery like this. They probably outsource their emotional entanglements to a butler or faithful family retainer instead:

'Chop chop, Jeeves. Find out what the wilful wench wants – and if she persists in buggering one about, then lock her up in the Tower for a decade or two, until she sees the error of her ways. Oh, yes. And in the meantime, Jeeves, prithee fetch me a bevy of buxom peasant girls and my jewel-encrusted fornicating sheath. For I do believe I have the right royal horn.'

In the eighteenth century, St James's Park was a notorious spot for gentlemen to go a-whoring, but these days it's dedicated to far more civilised pursuits.

I walk past a bony bunch of pensioners practising t'ai chi, and a fat guy wheezing on the ground doing press-ups, being chivvied along by a personal trainer who looks like she's just stepped out of a salon. In the distance, there's a woman lying on the grass in a pink bikini, like a Barbie doll left behind after a children's picnic.

As I get nearer to the café where Amy and I have arranged to meet, I scan the well-heeled mothers out parading their posh kids in their posh prams, until I locate The Blue Gingham Buggy from Hell, which sticks out like a Sinclair C5 in a Grand Prix starting line up.

Amy's standing in the shade of a giant sycamore tree. She's wearing a long white skirt and a black vest top, with her hair tied up. I smile, as I watch Ben stumbling ineffectively after a squirrel, like a drunk chasing a ten pound note that's been snatched by the wind.

I wave at Amy, but she doesn't seem to notice me. Or if she does, she chooses not to wave back.

If I were a weatherman and Amy was a weather front, my forecast would be: frosty to begin with, with a high possibility of gale force winds and electrical storms to follow . . .

In other words, I'm prepared for the very worst.

202

I'm fully expecting, for example, to be confronted with what I've privately come to think of as Amy's 'Munch Face', on account of the fact that it bears a striking similarity to the renowned Norwegian artist's most famous painting, 'The Scream'.

Amy's version is a microsecond-long look of horror and revulsion that I've noticed greeting me several times in the last few days, before her face has had the chance to revert to its more customary mask of general indifference.

But what I actually get as she sees me now is something far more ambivalent. It's less Edvard Munch, and more Leonardo da Vinci. Much more 'Mona Lisa', than 'The Scream'.

Hope bursts inside me. Could that really be the trace of a smile playing at the corners of Amy's mouth? Are we really about to dump all our discontent behind us and move on?

And then, suddenly, Amy *does* smile, and it's not a shy smile either. It's the kind of smile a donkey would be proud of.

Or, more kindly, one that might feature in a TV toothpaste advertisement for whiter, brighter, healthier teeth.

I should smile back, of course. And I do try. But I can't.

My problem is that, as with the smiles in the TV ads, I can't help thinking that there's something fake about Amy's. It's all teeth, you see. Not eyes. The eyes have an altogether darker look to them – one that, if I didn't know Amy better, I might almost mistake for fear . . .

They're certainly not the eyes of someone who's about to apologise, or back down in any way.

'My Daddy, my Daddy, my Daddy!'

Ben charges at me like a pigmy rhino, and it's such a treat, seeing him at this time of day, that, for a moment, I forget all about Amy as I sweep him up into the air.

'Hello, my Ben,' I laugh, as he stretches out his arms and legs like a freefalling skydiver.

'I flying, Daddy! Look, Mummy! Looka me fly!'

'Daddy's going to be flying soon, as well,' Amy says.

'What's that meant to mean?' I ask defensively, because it sounds like a threat.

'I'll tell you in a minute.'

'Tell me now.'

'No. I think you should sit down first.'

Those hairs on the back of my neck prickle again, springing to attention like a football crowd that's just witnessed a shot on goal.

Which is hardly surprising, considering that *I think you should sit down first* is an even more ominous phrase than *There's something I need to talk to you about* and *Face to face*. In fact, you'd have a tough job finding a more ominous phrase in the whole English language (barring *Today is a good day to die* and *Hey you, boy, my redneck buddy, Bubba, here thinks you look mighty puhrty in them thar jeans* – neither of which, thankfully, you encounter every day).

In fact, the only reason someone ever asks you to sit down before they break news to you is because they think that the news might make you faint.

I lower Ben to the ground and hold his tiny hand in mine as I follow Amy to a nearby cast iron bench and sit beside her.

She hands Ben a box of Sunmaid raisins and then turns to me and says, 'I've got some exciting news.'

The smile is back, I note, and, if anything, it's grown in intensity. There's a maniacal edge to it now, like Jack Nicholson's in *The Shining*, when he broke down the bathroom door with an axe.

I suddenly feel like I've just swallowed a rock.

'You're not pregnant, are you?' I ask.

And I really think I will faint if she answers, *Yes*. Because – and I hate myself for thinking it – her being knocked up really is the worst thing that could happen right now. We're skint and we're not getting on. And our flat's not big enough, and a baby won't solve a thing, and –

I'm just about to blurt all of this out, and more, when Amy laughs.

And the second she does, I do too, because it's only then that it strikes me how ridiculous my question actually is. Because not only is Amy on the pill, but our sex life is now such that, if it were being monitored on a cardiogram, with its increasingly sporadic peaks, any watching consultant would predict that it was only a matter of time before a complete flatline occurred.

'No,' she confirms.

'Then what?'

'I've won a competition.'

'A what?'

'A competition. For a shopping trip to New York.'

My face screws up in a frown. 'You're joking.'

'I'm not.'

'My God.'

'I know.'

'But how?'

'On the back of chocolate wrapper.'

I feel like a boxer being pummelled by a succession of body blows. 'But I didn't think anyone actually ever won those things.'

'Well, they do, and I have, and so have you.'

'What do you mean?'

'It's a trip for two.'

'But you said it was a shopping trip . . .'

That toothpaste ad smile shines out once more. 'Men *can* shop, Jack. I mean, I know *you* don't, but you could learn.'

This is all coming at me too quickly. I stutter, confused. 'But don't you want to . . . I don't know . . . take someone else?'

'Like who?'

'Like H.'

'No, I want to take you.' Suddenly, the smile vanishes. 'Why?' she asks. 'Don't you want to come?'

I realise, I should, of course, be jumping up and down with excitement, or even whooping for joy, like Charlie Bucket after he won his golden ticket to visit Willy Wonka's Chocolate Factory.

After all, a gargantuan piece of luck like this doesn't come along every day.

And, of course, I do feel a buzz, as Amy's news slowly begins to sink in, but I can't, I *won't*, quite allow myself to go whoopee.

In fact, it's sitting about as well with me as a bloody rump steak in a vegan's gut, because forget where Amy and I might be going, thanks to this competition. What about where we are right now? We're in Desolation Drive, Miseryville, that's where. In a condemned property, with the bulldozers revving up outside . . .

So, instead of shouting, 'Of course!' and bursting into a spontaneous rendition of 'Congratulations', whilst simultaneously waltzing Amy across the freshly mown lawns of St James's Park, what I say instead is:

'But –'

And that one word, interrupted as it duly and inevitably is, is enough to resurrect Amy's 'Munch Face', just for a second, making me think that it never actually went away at all.

'What do you mean, *but*?' she demands. 'There are no buts.'

'But what about Ben?'

'I've already sorted it. Mum says she'll look after him.'

The words *fait* and *accompli* spring to mind. As do the words *How come Amy told her mother before me? Is it because she thinks my opinion counts for shit?*

'For three days?' I check.

'Yes.'

I don't even bother getting into the risks inherent in leaving 'The Precious' with Jan for that long. (Although, automatically, I'm thinking that *Manchurian Candidate* levels of brainwashing, affection manipulation and loyalty reprogramming are highly likely to occur.)

I'm too busy thinking of how being away from Ben for that long will affect us.

'But won't you miss him?' I ask. I know I will. The longest I've ever spent away from him is a night, when I went on Ug's stag do to Swansea. And even then, when I woke up at seven in the morning and stared in dismay at the unfamiliar Artexed ceiling of the pub dormitory we were staying in, I found myself pining for my son like a dog that had just given up its pups.

'Oh, come on, Jack. It's a holiday. A *free* holiday.' I watch as the excitement fades from her face. 'Or maybe it's not the holiday that's bothering you,' she suggests, 'or spending three days away from Ben. Maybe it's just that you don't want to spend three days with me.'

'I never said that.'

'No, but you're not denying it, either.'

Before I get the chance to right myself over this Freudian slip that Amy's spotted, Ben asks, 'Wha-be you going, Daddy?'

'Daddy's not going anywhere.'

'I can't believe you're just going to turn this amazing opportunity down,' Amy snaps. 'That you want us to stay here and stew in the flat, and watch fucking TV with your sister, when we could be in New York instead.'

I wait for the shock waves of this mini-explosion to subside.

'Actually,' I then say, keeping my voice calculatedly calm. 'I was telling Ben I wasn't going anywhere *at this exact minute*. Because I'm guessing, on account of the fact that he's too young to have any concept of time, or international travel, that that's what he was asking me. But thanks a bunch,' I conclude, 'for letting me know how you feel about our life in London all the same.'

She stares at the ground. 'I'm sorry,' she then says.

She looks like she's going to cry, and suddenly I feel all churned up as well.

'I'm sorry too,' I admit.

'For what?'

'For not getting more excited about this . . . It's just . . .'

'Just what?'

'I don't want us to go there and find that things are exactly the same as here . . .'

'You mean between us?'

'Exactly.' I feel sick, sick at saying this, sick that we've reached a point where I feel I *have* to say it.

'And how *are* things between us?'

'I don't know.' It's my turn to stare at the ground. 'Flat.'

'Flat?'

'That's one way of putting it,' I say. And a nicer way than *crap*, which is how I actually feel.

'So we'll make them not flat,' she says.

She sounds – and looks, I now see, as I glance across at her – like she really means it.

My heart skips a beat. 'You think we can?' I ask, because I've got my doubts. Love's not like a Sodastream. You can't just switch the fizz on and off at will.

'We can try,' Amy says. 'We can make an effort. And I will.'

'Then so will I.'

Part of me thinks it's ridiculous, this verbal brokering of peace between us, this edging towards an agreement. It's so formal and so far removed from the way we used to be. Our relationship was once self-governing, and not something that had to be monitored and adjusted and planned. Whereas now a part of me is almost tempted to shake her hand.

I make myself smile instead. And Amy smiles back. And this time it doesn't look like a toothpaste ad at all. It looks genuine. And lovely. And real.

'OK, then,' I say, 'so let's do it. Let's go to New York.'

'Do you mean it?'

'Yeah. Let's go there and have fun. I'll even let you teach me how to shop. Come on,' I say, taking her hand and pulling her up. 'Let's go for some food and talk dates.'

We get a table outside the café and buy some sandwiches and drinks. Ben feeds crisps to the squirrels.

And, finally, we start to work things out.

'I'd better get going,' she says half an hour later.

The agency organising the New York trip have given Amy a choice of dates. We're taking the first one available, as that's the one that suits her mum for babysitting. It's next weekend.

I settle Ben in his buggy. He's half-asleep, weary from the heat and all the running around he's been doing.

I ask Amy, 'How are you getting back home?'

'Tube.'

'I'll walk you there.'

'OK.'

We set off up the path, away from the café, and back towards the Mall.

'So how have the internet dates been going?' I ask.

Amy half-trips over a stone. She stops. 'What?'

'The internet dates . . .'

She freezes and stares at me like I've just told her there's a spider in her hair.

'You know,' I remind her, 'all those guys H had lined up. Don't tell me she didn't fill you in on what's been happening with them.'

'Oh, yeah.' She nods her head, understanding at last. 'Yeah, she did.'

We start to walk again. 'And?'

'It's like I said: it might as well be another planet.'

'So where did you and she end up last night?'

'Oh, a restaurant.'

'Which one?'

'Zuma.'

'Oh, yeah, Matt was on about that the other day. How was it?'

'Fine.'

'Just fine? What did you eat?'

'A Pad Thai thingy . . .'

'But I thought it was Japanese?'

'It is but –'

209

I laugh. 'So what are they doing serving Thai food?'

She turns on me. 'What is this?' she snaps. 'Twenty fucking questions?'

The sudden aggression hits me like a gunshot. I stop dead in my tracks. I can't look at her for a moment. On the back of getting along with her just now, I feel more hurt than I otherwise would. It's like the moment I drop my guard, smack, in comes the killer punch. Anger surges through me. I fight the desire to flare up right back at her. I count to five. I will it all away.

And I'm right to wait.

'I didn't mean to,' she says, briefly pressing her hand on mine. 'I'm just tired, OK?'

'It's all right.' I carry on pushing the pram. I don't look at her, in case I don't like what I see. In case I see that nothing's really changed at all. 'Let's just forget it. We're both making an effort, remember?'

'OK.'

As we reach the Mall, I turn left, towards Trafalgar Square.

'Where are you going?' Amy asks.

'Charing Cross station.'

'I was going to go up to Piccadilly.'

'Charing Cross is closer and it's on my way back to work.'

In spite of the common sense underlying my suggestion, an awkward silence reasserts itself between us, as once more she falls into step beside me. We walk beneath Admiralty Arch and cross the road on to Trafalgar Square.

It's only then that I glance at her. She's gazing at the ground, like a prisoner on the march. I feel my heart sink.

I hope she is just tired.

I hope we both really are going to make an effort to get through this.

I hope.

'I love it here,' I hazard, as we walk past Nelson's column. 'Shall we get an ice cream and just chill out for five minutes?'

She doesn't break her stride. 'No.'

Not even a thank you.

We cross the road and walk up the Strand to Charing Cross station.

And that's when I notice it again, the thing I've dreaded the most: the disinterest. I briefly kiss her lips as we come to say goodbye, and I see it's returned to her eyes like a veil.

She's looking through me, not at me, again.

I watch her walk with Ben into the station, and I wait for her to wave, or blow me a kiss, like she always used to. But she does neither. She doesn't look back. She disappears into the crowd.

And what I'm left with is a feeling of great fragility. A feeling that, any second now, Amy and I might once again snap.

The Beginning Of The End

Amy's out and Kate's still at work, and I'm back at the flat with Ben, and loving every second of it.

I've converted the kitchen into a giant den, by draping blankets and bed sheets over the kitchen table and chairs. Ben's scrabbling around beneath the table, while I'm pretending to be a monster, stomping up and down outside, listening to him squeal with fear and delight.

His favourite album, *No!*, by They Might Be Giants, is cranked up on the sound system, and there's melted chocolate ice cream all over the worktop, from where we made Häagen-Dazs milkshakes earlier on, to go with the biscuits and crisps he had for tea.

Amy told me to give Ben some of the vegetable casserole that's in the fridge before five thirty, but Ben said he 'hungry now' at five and that he 'no like gevetchtable carole' and that he 'want eat crips instead'. So I caved in. Which was just as well, because judging by how quickly he wolfed down all the chipsticks and Jammy Dodgers I gave him, the poor mite must have been half-starving.

And it looks like there's no damage done, either, because

211

now, at just gone six, he's certainly full of energy. And wide awake. Whereas, normally, when I get back from work, more often than not he's half-asleep.

If you ask me, there's too much fuss made about kids' sugar intake. I mean, their baby teeth fall out anyway, right? So who cares if they've got a bit of plaque on them when they do?

Still, I don't suppose I'd better let on to Amy what I've been up to. Parenting is, after all, meant to be her area of expertise – and, despite our uneasy truce in St James's Park, things still aren't exactly great between us. The last thing I want to do right now is rock the boat.

'Home alone by any chance?'

I jump like I'm being stalked by a monster myself, and Ben screams even louder under the table, thinking it's all part of the game.

Kate's standing in the kitchen doorway, taking off her white suit jacket.

I survey the carnage around me and smile. 'Now whatever makes you say that?' I ask.

She rolls her eyes and walks over to the sink and fills the kettle.

'Good day at work?' I ask.

'So so.'

Ben braves peeping through a gap in the sheets, and clocks that it's Kate, not a flesh-eating monster, that's joined us.

'Kay-kate!' he yelps, scrabbling out and running over to give her a hug.

'Hey, gorgeous,' she says, kissing him on the top of the head.

'Tweenies?' Ben then asks, looking over at me and nodding managerially, before ramming another Jammy Dodger into his mouth.

'Of course,' I say. 'Why not?'

'Do you want tea?' Kate asks.

'Please.'

I go and put *Spirited Away* on for Ben in the living room. And when I come back, Kate's folded up the blankets and sheets and stacked them on one of the chairs.

'Where's Amy?' she asks.

'Out. Shopping. You know, for our trip to New York.'

Kate hands me a cup of tea and we both sit down at the table. 'Oh, yeah. Only two days to go. You must be really excited.'

'Delirious.' The level of involuntary sarcasm in my voice leaves me appalled. 'I didn't mean it to sound like –'

'Like you don't want to go?' Kate says.

'Yeah. Because I do.'

Kate looks at me the way only a sibling who's grown up trading bullshits with you over the past three decades can: like she doesn't believe a word.

She's not wrong. Because I *am* a little wary about the trip, and still feeling a little kidnapped. It's all happened in such a rush, and so far it's not brought us any closer than we were before. Nothing has been mended. The fizz Amy promised never arrived. I feel as flat as a bottle of milk, and more deflated than elated at the prospect of spending three days with Amy, *mano a mano*.

Kate blows on her tea and peers at me over the top of her mug. 'Am I right in guessing that things aren't so good between you two at the moment?'

Of course, I want to contradict her, and tell her to back off and butt out. I want to laugh in her face and tell her she's way off mark. And I wish that I could.

Instead I say, 'It's that obvious, is it?'

She nods sadly. 'Like a turd in a cake shop.'

Her lack of hesitation knocks me. I thought I'd done a fairly good job of masking all my worries and doubts from her, but maybe I'm not the one who's been giving the game away, I then think, as a fresh fear creeps across my skin.

'Did Amy say something to you?' I ask.

'No. It's just . . . you know how you have a mental picture

213

of somebody? Like Dad? I always picture him with a pint in his hand. Or Mum. I always think of her crying when Dad left . . .'

'Yeah . . .'

'Well, the picture I've always had of you and Amy was of the two of you laughing. You know, side by side. With your arms round each other . . .'

I sigh. That's always been the picture I've had too.

'But now I hardly even see you in the same room,' Kate continues. She reaches across the table and takes my hand. 'I want you to be honest,' she says. 'Is it me? Being here. You know, in your space . . . Because if it is, I can move out right away . . . into a hotel . . . The last thing I want is to make matters worse . . .'

It's an offer worth considering, I know, but there's a desperation in her eyes when she says it, and there's no way I'm going to accept. Besides, she told us last night that she's got a room lined up at a mate's place in two weeks' time. It would just be mean to kick her out now.

'No,' I tell her. 'It's nothing to do with you.' Or if it was to begin with, I think, then it's not any more. 'It's me,' I admit. 'Amy just seems to get pissed off at everything I do. If I go out, she gets angry, but if I stay in, she goes out herself.'

'She still hasn't forgiven you for going to Nobu with Matt then?' says Kate.

'No.'

'Have you tried saying sorry?'

I shrug. 'Sorry is my middle name.'

'I mean a proper sorry. Not just a pragmatic one to try and end an argument.'

'There's a difference?'

'There is if you're a woman. We can tell if you mean it, or not.'

'I'll bear that in mind,' I say, 'but really, this isn't about sorry. It's gone way beyond that.' I rub at my eyes, suddenly

214

feeling very tired. 'We're just not making each other very happy at the moment.'

'So tell her about it. Tell her how you feel.'

'Thanks for the tip, Billy Joel.'

'I mean it.'

'I know, and I've tried. I told her that I didn't think things were good between us, when she told me about the New York trip. She said she'd try to make things better. That we both should.'

'Well, that sounds pretty positive.'

'That's what I thought at the time, but ever since . . . whenever I do talk to her, it's like . . .' I struggle to find the words. 'It's like talking to a telephone operator. You ask a question and you get some information back, but there's no emotion in the exchange . . . That's how we are at the moment. Our conversations are perfunctory. We talk about putting the bins out, or what's on the TV, or how Ben needs a new pair of shoes, but on anything emotional, it's like she's totally distracted. Honestly, Kate, we might as well be work colleagues – and work colleagues who don't even like each other very much at that.' I shake my head sadly. 'I don't want our marriage to turn into a business arrangement.'

'No. Of course not. It's got to be about you two loving each other, and loving Ben.'

I look at my sister, my little sister, and I see that she looks worried as hell.

I tell her, 'That's how I always thought it would be. Me and Amy against the world. I never thought we'd win – you know, because you can't, because the world grinds everyone down in the end, everyone gets old or sick, everybody dies – but I did hope we'd give it a damn good run for its money. Not just quit.'

'And that's how you feel? Like you've both given up?'

'I don't know. You know how it is. You spend your life discussing how things are going to be next year. And the year after. And what will happen when you get that new job. And

215

what kind of house you'll move into, and all the cool places you'll go to on holiday . . .'

'Yes, but surely that's half the fun.'

'Well, that's just it. Amy and I don't discuss that kind of thing any more. We've stopped making plans. It's like instead of looking forward, we're standing still. Or looking back. And I don't know which is worse.' I chew down on my lip. 'I just know that it's making us both miserable.'

'But every relationship goes through its ups and downs,' Kate points out.

'I'm not talking about ups and downs. I'm talking about downs and downs. I mean, sure, we've had rough patches before. Like after Ben was born. But not like this. I hate it. I hate what's going on between us. I hate her shutting me out. But what I hate about it most is that it's like yawning. It's contagious. It makes me want to do it to her too.'

That's how it feels, I realise. Like we're in love and in hate at the very same time.

'That's how it was with me and Tone towards the end,' Kate says. 'Before he told me to pack my bags and go.'

I grimace. 'Oh, cheer me up, why don't you?'

Kate clamps her hand over her mouth, then says, 'Oh God. That sounded awful. I'm not saying that's how it's going to be between you and Amy,' she hurriedly adds. 'You two are totally different. You've been together for ever.'

People used to say that to me about Zoe Thompson, I suddenly think, simultaneously realising that I haven't really thought about Zoe for years. Not since we broke up in 1995, after going out with each other for two years.

But the reason I am thinking about her now makes perfect sense. It's because Zoe and I stopped talking towards the end, just like me and Amy have now.

My stomach lurches.

Is that what this is? The beginning of the end? Have Amy and I already started acting out our relationship, instead of inhabiting it for real?

'I bet it'll all blow over,' Kate says. 'You probably just need a change of scene.'

'Well, New York here we come,' I say, trying to sound positive. 'Make or break.'

'Just look on it as a fresh start,' Kate says encouragingly. 'Draw a line under all the bollocks that's going on now.' She comes round the table and stands behind me, squeezing my shoulders. 'You will get through this, big bro. I know you will.' She hugs me and I lean back into her.

'I know,' I sigh. 'I'm just letting off steam. You're right: New York's the place to move things on.'

She hugs me again, harder this time. I look up into her eyes. She suddenly seems so grown up, and I suddenly feel so young.

'Never feel like you're on your own,' she tells me, 'because you're not. You've always got me.'

But the way she says it, the way she hugs me so hard when she does, I know that she thinks my fears are real fears, and that what I dread might be happening to Amy and me actually *is*.

11

amy

Age-Defying Hands

Radio CapitalChat
Jessie's Daily Discussion: What would you say is the most
important thing in a relationship?
Caller: Amy from West London

As always, it's been very interesting talking to you Amy. So,
to recap for the listeners, you're saying that honesty is the
most important thing in a relationship.
Yes. Whatever the problem, or issue, honesty is always the best
policy.
And you're totally honest with Jack? Always?
Of course.
And Jack's honest with you?
Yes . . .
You don't think he might have told you a few white lies along
the way?
Well . . . maybe . . . but I trust him.
And he trusts you, I'm sure. Maybe we're getting somewhere
here. I don't want to put words in your mouth, Amy, but
maybe you're saying trust *is what's more important. More*
important than honesty, perhaps? What the eye doesn't see,
the heart doesn't grieve over and all that . . . But I want to hear
some more of your thoughts, listeners. After this ad break . . .

'That was great,' Alex says to me, when I stay on the line after I've been on air.

But I feel soiled. Phoney. For the first time, I've called in just to get on the radio and not because I believed in what I was saying. Because all that – everything I've just said on air – is a lie.

'Jessie's giving me the thumbs up from the studio,' Alex continues. 'Honestly, you should see her. I think she even has her hands done.'

'Her hands? What do you mean?'

'You know. Botox. Or plastic surgery. Those hands of hers are so bloody perfect they don't seem real. We're all sure of it. She's definitely had work . . .'

Botox? Plastic Surgery? Jessie? That certainly doesn't fit with my image of a lady 'on the turn' living a spinster's life in her mother's old house. And why would she have work done on her hands and not the rest of her? It doesn't make any sense, but I'm not given a chance to enquire further, before he says, 'So you're off to New York? How exciting. I wish we could come with you and do an OB.'

'OB?'

'Outside broadcast.'

'I can't imagine Jack would like that,' I tell him. I'm not even sure that Jack really wants to go. And to be honest, I'm not sure I do either. It's like everyone else is excited apart from me. The Vipers went nuts when I told them about the trip yesterday. Camilla went into overdrive about discount designer stores and Faith, who apparently worked there for a few years before she got married (which was total news to me), started listing off tips. Now, today Alex too is telling me how lucky I am. But I feel doomed.

'Well, whatever,' he continues. 'You're going to love it. All that shopping. And it's all included in the prize?'

'Flights, hotel and a thousand dollars spending money,' I say, but my enthusiasm sounds false.

'Lucky lucky you. I could spend that in a second in New

219

York. Oops, gotta go. Jessie's cracking the whip again. That's her problem, Amy. She thinks she's God! Speak to you soon, darling. Tatty bye.'

When he puts down the phone, I ring straight back and speak to the CapitalChat receptionist.

Suddenly, I want a photo of Jessie Kay.

Telling It Like It Is

It's six o'clock in the evening as I come out of the tube at Green Park. The workers are spilling on to the pavements and I'm just another body in the crowd on Piccadilly, yet I feel as conspicuous as if I had a neon arrow above my head pointing down at me.

I walk around the corner to the cobbled streets of Shepherd Market. My head is telling me that I shouldn't take one step further, but something that I don't understand, and certainly can't fight, compels me to walk on. I've made the decision to do this in person and that's the right thing to do. The decent thing to do. Isn't it? I'm the one who thinks that honesty is the best policy. I said so on the radio, after all.

I spot him straightaway, as I approach The Grapes, the pub where we've agreed to meet. He's wearing cream linen trousers and a loose cream linen shirt, and he's sitting at one of the tables outside, reading a book. He's surrounded by men in grey suits standing up, drinking beers. In the late afternoon sun, Tom Parry looks almost saintly.

For a moment, I'm tempted to turn and flee, but, as if sensing me, he looks up and waves. Like a fish on a hook, he reels me towards him.

'Amy from West London,' he says, standing up and smiling. 'You came.'

He doesn't touch me, but I feel his body, as if it's radiating out towards me. I bite my bottom lip and look down at my feet, holding my handbag against my knees. I'm wearing my new red wedges especially. Can he tell how much effort I've made with my appearance?

220

I think of all the lies I told Jack so easily in order to get here. The fictitious theatre trip with Ali – the spare ticket becoming free at the last minute. It was as if everything just fell into place, so that I could be standing here, right now.

'I'll get you a drink,' Tom says, smiling at me and holding up his hands, like I'm some kind of flighty creature. 'Don't go away. OK?'

I nod. I can't look at him. I can't look at his lips. They'll be forever locked in that midnight moment and the kiss that I can't forget. Just the thought of it turns my insides to jelly.

It occurs to me that Tom and I share history that no one else knows about, and that we're making more history at this very moment. Despite all my resolve, it feels wonderfully, decadently selfish, because since I met Tom, for the first time in over seven years, I feel like I'm living *my* life. Mine. As if I've connected to a part of myself I'd forgotten about, the bit that isn't a wife, or a mother, or a daughter, or friend. The bit that's just me.

Then I remember why I'm here.

I'm here to tell him how it really is.

I sit down at the end of the bench and stare at the table, listening to the group of men in suits behind me.

'That place? The art gallery. You know it used to be a brothel,' one of them says.

'How things have changed.'

'Not really, there's still loads of hookers around here.'

'Shhh.'

There's a small silence, and I notice them looking at me. Oh my God! Do they think I'm a hooker? I hope not, but, I have to admit, there's some part of me that feels like one. I look down at my red skirt. Maybe I should have worn my black one instead.

Tom comes back outside, carrying my drink. He smiles, and there it is again . . . that feeling of lightness.

'What are you reading?' I ask, nodding to the book on the table.

'I've just finished it. It's by an author I'm meeting tomorrow,' he says.

'Is it any good?'

'It's brilliant. Why don't you take it? I'd be interested to hear your take on it.'

He pushes the book towards me and I reach out for it. As I do, his finger brushes over mine. I feel it like an electric shock and I move my hand away quickly.

What am I thinking? I feel sick with nerves.

'Amy?' Tom says, searching out my eyes.

I shake my head and look down again, forcing myself to remember the speech I've rehearsed. 'You know I told you I wasn't lucky and I never won anything?'

He nods.

'Well, I was wrong. I just won a trip to New York for two.'

'Wow! Are you going to take me?' he says. His eyes dance with smiles. 'I love New York. It's one of my favourite places. I could show you round.'

'No, no,' I stutter, thrown by the casualness with which he's made this suggestion. 'No, it's this weekend, and I'm going with Jack. We're going together.'

I'd planned out what I was going to say next, but sitting opposite Tom, I feel tongue-tied. I feel like I should apologise.

I swallow hard. 'So what I came to tell you is –'

'Amy?'

I look at him now. His gaze is so intense that I can't look away.

'Please don't say any more. It's enough that you're here.'

He smiles and it's a beautiful smile – and all at once, I realise what a stupid, silly cow I'm being. How, once again, my ego is getting the better of me: because to know that someone as attractive as Tom finds *me* attractive is possibly the most seductive boost my ego has ever had – and, like a junkie, it's crying out for more, more, more.

I sigh, still looking at him, giving in.

'Oh God,' I say, smiling despite myself. 'Look Tom,

whatever this is, it's ridiculous. We've only met once and –'

'Sometimes it only takes once: to realise that you really like somebody. It has for me. Somebody told me that when you know, you know. I never believed them until now.'

'You can't, I mean –'

'Just listen to what I've got to say,' he says, reaching across the table and holding his hand over mine. It feels warm and strong.

'But Tom, I –'

'You see, I haven't been able to stop thinking about you. Not for a moment since we met.'

I can tell how much he means it. I shake my head, flustered and confused. My eyes fill with tears.

'You don't understand,' I say.

'What don't I understand?'

'I'm married. To Jack. Don't you know what that means?'

'Yes, but I don't think you're in love with Jack. Maybe once, but not any more. Things change, Amy. It's no one's fault, but people grow up and they want different things. You let me kiss you, Amy. You let me kiss you, because you wanted me to.'

I shake my head again. Just hearing him say the word 'kiss' makes it even more vivid than ever.

'Please, Tom, don't say all this.'

He nods. 'OK, I'm sorry.'

I pull my hand from under his. 'It's just . . . I'm not sure why I came. I shouldn't have.' I take a deep breath. 'But I wanted to tell you to your face. We can't meet again. We can't have any kind of future. That's why I'm here.'

There, it's out. I've said it. I've told him how it really is. I've done what I came here to do. I've told him this has to end.

But Tom smiles. He doesn't seem to have heard me.

'I'm not going to pressure you, much as I want to, much as I want to take you back home and make love to you right now. As much as we *both* want to. Because, you do, don't you, Amy? Haven't you been thinking about us too?'

223

I feel a deep blush rising up through me. I feel sick with fright. I stand up. I'm shaking. I think of the underwear I'm wearing. *The sexy, new, matching silk underwear that I'm wearing.* Of course, I kidded myself when I put it on that good underwear would make me feel better, but maybe Tom knows me better than I know myself. Once again, I feel stunned by his ability to cut to the chase – to speak the truth.

'I'm going,' I tell him.

Tom stands up too. He puts his hand on my arms and looks down at me. 'I don't mean to scare you, but I understand if I have. Amy, this is big for me, too, you know.'

I pull away from him. 'Goodbye,' I say. 'This is goodbye.'

He blocks my path.

'Think it over whilst you're in New York,' he says, softly. 'Promise me. Just promise me that before you go.'

A Dose Of Tough Love

I'm in the underground car park of H's office building, having convened an emergency meeting. I have her undivided attention from London Bridge to Islington, where she's chucking me out before going on to a friend's dinner party.

She points her keys at her car and it bleeps unlocked. It echoes around the concrete walls and pillars. I jump and make a yelping sound. My nerves are all shot.

She pulls down her sunglasses and gives me a stern look over the top.

'Get in,' she says. Clearly, the scant details I've given her so far about why I need to see her haven't been met with as much sympathy as I'd hoped.

I sit in the low bucket seat, feeling claustrophobic. I put my hands between my knees.

'I'm afraid the hood's broken,' H says, turning the ignition. The chunky charm bracelet she's wearing jangles as she steers the wheel. 'Damn thing. It's being repaired next week.'

I feel like a churning mass of emotions as we drive up to street level and H pulls confidently into the traffic.

'OK. I want it all,' she says. 'From the top. Every detail.'

So I take a deep breath and I tell her everything. I tell her about my argument with Jack and then I tell her how amazing meeting Tom was. I tell her about the dinner, about how I really opened up to him, about how he filled me with confidence. I tell her every detail of our conversations and our romantic moonlit walk. I splurge until there's only one thing left to say.

As we stop at the traffic lights by the roundabout on London Bridge, I tell her about the kiss.

'You kissed him!' she says. She's staring at me, aghast.

I cover my face and nod.

'Fucking hell, Amy.'

'I know, I know. Oh H, I'm so confused. I feel sick with guilt. I've never even *thought* about being unfaithful, until Tom. If Jack ever –'

'Jack? It's not about Jack,' she says, throwing me off track. 'How about the fact you stole my internet date?'

'I didn't steal him, H.'

'You did. You went on *my* date.'

'Only because you didn't turn up.'

'Pardon me for having a job.'

The lights turn to green and she wheel spins away.

'I don't believe you did that.' She snorts at me, outraged. The river stretches away in both directions. I can see the blue paint of Tower Bridge sparkling in the last of the evening sun. 'But I suppose you were always going to steal him,' she continues, nodding her head with righteous indignation.

'What? Don't be ridiculous. I –'

'You were. You fancied him when you read about him on the site. Don't deny it.'

'Oh fuck off!' I say. She's being ridiculous.

'No, you fuck off.'

We might as well be having a cat fight on Jerry Springer. Thank God she's driving.

'Just you remember,' she stabs her finger at me. '*I* paid for

225

the subscription to that website, not you It's not fair. Tom was my only lead.'

She makes it sound as if she's a detective on a case, not a girl looking for a potential boyfriend.

'Calm down, OK? I'm sorry. If I could take it all back, I would.'

'Well you can't. And anyway I don't want him back. Not now. I might be desperate, but I don't need your sloppy seconds, thank you very much.'

I look at her. Is she completely mad? How did she get to be this self-absorbed? I'm tempted to get out of the car, but I'm in too deep and I've told her too much. She might be a mad, jealous, twisted old cow, but she's all I've got.

'Look, you've got to help me out. I'm so confused.'

'Poor you.'

'H! Please. Just listen. There's more.'

So I tell her about the trip to New York and how bad things are between me and Jack. And I tell her about the meeting I just had with Tom in Shepherd Market. How I meant to break it all off with him, but how it all got out of hand, and that now, rather than having finished it, he's hanging on for me.

'What did you expect? You're giving him all the wrong signals,' she says, rolling her eyes at me. 'You actually *turned up* looking like that,' she nods at my outfit and I feel every inch the hussy in my Wonderbra, 'to tell him you never want to see him again. Er . . . hello? What's the guy supposed to think?'

'I know, but –'

'If you want to fuck up your marriage with *my* internet date, so be it – but don't expect any sympathy from me,' she says.

'H!'

'Well, what do you want me to say? At least you've *got* two men to be torn between.'

'Look, I'm sorry. I didn't intend any of this to happen.'

'So, do you want him, or don't you? Make your bloody mind up.'

'I thought I had – but there's something about Tom . . . I don't know, H. Maybe he's right. Maybe I did want him to kiss me. Right from the first moment we met. And when he said he hadn't been able to stop thinking of me . . . well I've been like that too, about him. I feel, I don't know . . . connected to him.'

'Connected? My fat arse. It's just someone giving you attention for the first time in ages. Someone who wants to get into your knickers.'

Man, she's brutal. I wish I'd never told her. I wish I'd never said anything.

'Get real, Amy. Do you think you'll still feel this "connected" to him when you tell Jack about him. Or when he meets your mother? Or for that matter, your son? I mean, what are you proposing? That you run away to some rural backwater in Ireland with him? Aren't you forgetting that you already have a life?'

'It's not like that, it's . . .' But all of a sudden, I don't know what it *is* like. Apart from a huge bloody mess.

She glances over at me. 'OK, answer me these questions. Honestly. Did he, or did he not mention sex?'

'He called it making love –'

'Euch! Pass me a barf bag. OK, question two: is he, or is he not, used to getting his own way?'

'Well he's a successful businessman, if that's what you mean, so, yeah, I suppose –'

'And did he, or did he not tell you that he likes a challenge?'

'Well . . .'

'And do you, or do you not think it is out of order for him to prey upon women who are clearly already married? Especially one with a very young child?'

'He didn't mean to. It was just fate.'

'Fate? Do you think he hasn't used that line before? I mean, come on, that's about as corny as "to be stood up once is bad enough, but twice is looking careless". He did say that, didn't he? That *is* a direct quote?'

I squirm, blushing. I wish now that I hadn't been so accurate in my retelling of events.

'Look, Amy, what we have here, is a man approaching forty, who is still single and clearly terrified of any sort of long term commitment, demonstrated by the fact that he makes a bee-line for totally unsuitable women.'

'But,' I say, 'but he knew about you off the website. What are you saying? That you're totally unsuitable, too?'

'Apparently, yes,' H grunts, 'but this isn't about me any more, Man Thief. This is about you.'

I put my head in my hands. I don't think he's like she's describing him. I don't. But something niggles me. What if H *is* right? What if Tom's been feeding me a line, right from the start?

'Sorry to piss on your bonfire,' H continues, clearly enjoying being in her stride, 'but he sounds to me like your typical bastard – and before Jack, you were a renowned bastard magnet. Even Jack was a bastard when you met him. Excuse me, but have you forgotten *Nathan*?'

I shudder at the memory of how I got suckered in by Nathan. How he was good-looking, charming and a complete shit with it. How he kept me dangling, never committing himself, always unreliable, always unfaithful.

And H is right, he wasn't the first. I'm shocked that she remembers my past. It shocks me too that she sees me in the context of my relationships, of which Jack is part, and now Tom is the latest. It's been so long since I've considered myself in that way. I thought my relationship history had stopped the moment I did, at the altar.

'But Tom didn't seem like that at all,' I insist. 'He seemed lovely. *Really* lovely.'

'Which is a bastard speciality, of course.' H looks pleased with herself, as if she's just solved some sort of puzzle.

I'm still not buying it.

'So you don't think he meant anything he said?'

'I think he's using sophisticated tactics to get you into bed, because currently, he can't quite have you. So what he'd like more than anything is for you to crack. For you to sleep with him. Then he's got himself lined up with a nice married fuck buddy, who won't intrude on his social life, or move in with him, or anything else apart from shag him on the side.'

'That wasn't how he was. The way he was saying it, he wasn't talking about a tawdry affair. He was telling me to make a decision between him and Jack. And besides, this isn't about Tom,' I say, steering the conversation away from the impossibility of such a choice. 'It's about me. It's about the fact I wanted him as well.'

'You can't help your hormones, honey, but you can resist them. I'm not denying that sex with a tall dark handsome Irishman might be knee-tremblingly fantastic, but do you really think he's going to stick around and take on all your baggage, once he's had his wicked way with you?'

She looks at me and I fall silent. As we head up towards Farringdon, I can feel my head trying to argue back – to come up with a scenario in which Tom is a hero, but the brief intense passion I've been feeling is suddenly ungraspable, like a fading vapour trail.

'So what do I do, then?'

'You've already crossed a line with him,' she says in a warning tone. 'You told me once that there's a very big gulf between *not* kissing someone and kissing them; and a very *small* step from kissing them to sleeping with them.'

'Did I?'

'Yes you did. So you need to think carefully about where all this is going. All this talk of emotions is just that . . . talk. It hasn't actually gone anywhere yet. You've still got time to jam on the brakes.'

She's right, of course. Having sex with Tom would be like

exploding a nuclear bomb in my life. I can't imagine the fall-out.

And, to be very honest, I can't imagine the sex either. I mean, do I actually *want* to have sex with him? Sitting here, I'm not actually sure that I do. I just want to be swept up in him, and romanced by him, and that's not the same thing.

It's been so long since I've had sex with a stranger. Would it really be fantastic? It could equally be embarrassing, or clumsy or just plain awful. What if I just blindly followed on down this path and let fate decide and the sex was rubbish? Then what?

Or what if the sex turned out to be great, but he didn't? What if he turned out to be another Nathan in disguise? After all, what do I really know about him?

More importantly than *all* of this, there is the ultimate, six million dollar question: what would having sex with Tom mean for me and Jack?

And there it is. The answer. Looming large.

Like a sky-scraper.

Like the Hollywood sign, all lit up.

The D word.

All of a sudden, I feel like I'm going to throw up.

'Oh God, H,' I say, groaning. 'What have I done?'

'Well, I guess it's not surprising he slipped in under your radar. You're out of the loop,' she says, 'and it *is* a jungle out here.'

I feel like I've been on drugs and I've come crashing back to reality. I open my eyes and look at the traffic and the buses and the adverts. Everything seems very real and harsh and out of my control.

'But it was all so . . . I don't know . . . like a fairy tale. Romantic, you know?'

'Romantic shmantic,' H says. 'Hasn't it occurred to you that it's very easy to be romantic when there's no reality involved? It's a fantasy, Amy.'

230

My heart aches and I'm welling up. 'I know, but I really wanted it. *Needed* it.'

'Everyone needs romance, and everyone likes the feeling of giving in to temptation. That's why chocolate sales are so high.'

How can she be so clinical? So . . . practical?

'But how come *I* was so tempted when Jack –'

'Jack's not tempted?' she interrupts, looking at me. 'How do *you* know?'

I'm silent. I feel I don't know anything about Jack any more. About us.

H's phone goes off and she answers it. The conversation blares on speakerphone in the car, but I'm not listening. Instead, I think about Jack in that convertible Lexus. With that woman. Is there something going on with him as well? Isn't it possible that he could equally have become embroiled in a situation with someone else, like I have with Tom?

The thought of it, just the possibility of it, makes me breathless with fear. But no. Jack wouldn't. He couldn't.

Could he . . . ?

I look out at the darkening sky and the buildings we're passing by. All these people, all living their lives. Are theirs as complicated as mine? Why is this happening to me. To us?

H finishes her call and pats me on the knee.

'Come on, buck up,' she says. 'It's not the end of the world.'

Isn't it?

'Just do yourself a favour,' she continues.

'What's that?'

'Don't see Tom again.'

'I won't.'

'And for fuck's sake, promise me that you never, *ever* tell Jack. What's done is done. You can't take that kiss back, but you *can* pretend it never happened. And don't feel all guilty and emotional about this, or start banging on about honesty. For once in your life, Amy, just do the pragmatic thing.'

I pull my hair back from my face. 'I promise.'

231

'And it's a promise you better not break, because I'm telling you, you'll ruin everything if you tell Jack. You'll totally fuck up your marriage forever. Men don't forgive that type of thing. They're territorial. Like dogs. You tell Jack about Tom and it'll turn into the biggest pissing contest you could ever imagine. So you're just going to have to take this on the chin and chalk it up to experience. Think of it as a blip.'

'A blip?'

'Well, maybe just more of a warning that you need to start looking closer to home for your answers. You and Jack are great together.'

'Are we?'

'Yes you are. *Were.* Now get your shit together, girlfriend,' she warns me, 'and bring that magic back.'

We've reached Islington and she pulls to a stop by Angel tube station. She leans over and gives me a hug.

'Thanks for the talking to, and the lift,' I say.

'All part of the friendly service.'

'I mean it. Thanks,' I feel a huge wave of emotion. I guess it's relief. 'I think you might have just saved my life.'

'That will teach you to steal other people's dates. Now, go home, make up with Jack and have a great time in New York.'

12

Jack

In Love With A Brazilian

I knock on the door to Jessie Kay's study and she answers, 'Yes!'

The second I enter, I smell it: *eau d'Amsterdam*, Portobello Road *parfum*, skunk, dope, grass, call it what you will.

Jessie's sitting at an antique writing bureau. She's on the phone and frantically waves at me to come in, then stabs her finger towards a brown leather armchair next to the double bay window which overlooks the garden. She's wearing Gucci shades and a pearly translucent shirt, the top two buttons of which, I note, are unbuttoned, revealing a black coral necklace beneath.

The smart clothes make me think of Amy, who's in the West End today. She's seeing a show with Ali, then going shopping for some new tops and a bit of costume jewellery. Though quite why she's going shopping now, when we're about to head off to New York, I don't know. Women. There are some things about them I'll never understand.

I take a seat and gaze out at the trees, making a mental note to cut back the Virginia creeper, as it's started encroaching on the window and blocking out the light.

In spite of the gloominess, the room has a pleasant, relaxing feel to it. Granted, this probably has something to do with the bonfire reek of dope smoke, but it's also down to the old world atmosphere of the place. As with the kitchen, it's clear that Jessie hasn't yet had a chance to redecorate in here.

There are a couple of oil paintings of ships in storms on the walls, both derivative of William McTaggart, who I like, and both badly in need of a clean. The bookshelves are strictly PG (pre-Google), crammed with various encyclopaedias, dictionaries, atlases and other reference books, along with at least a dozen old bound volumes of *Punch*.

A wooden Bang & Olufsen stereo in the corner is playing Simon and Garfunkel's 'America', and I listen to that, instead of earwigging on Jessie's conversation, which is work-based anyway, something to do with advertising revenues for her show.

I do, however, hear her call whoever it is she's talking to a 'chickenshit' and 'dinosaur', before she finally terminates the call by slamming the receiver down.

'My fucking producer, Alex,' she complains. 'Honestly, he's driving me insane.'

I stand up, as she walks over towards me.

'How are you, darling?' she asks, kissing me on both cheeks. 'Sorry I didn't come out to say hello before, only I've been stuck in here all afternoon, dealing with bloody idiots.' She beams at me. 'But enough about me. How are you?' She nods towards the window. 'I was watching you working out there. It's looking great.'

'Thanks.' As I follow her stare, I notice a marijuana plant on the windowsill, about a foot high. Glancing across, I see that Jessie notices me noticing it too. 'I see you've been doing a bit of gardening yourself,' I say.

'Oh, that. It's Roland's. *Was* Roland's. I don't even know how to harvest it.' She nods towards a small bag on the desk. It's transparent and through it I can see a pack of red Rizlas and a bunch of green. 'That's his as well,' she explains. 'I found it in the bedside table drawer. It seemed a shame to let it go to waste . . .'

As if to prove it, she then collects a half-smoked spliff from an ashtray on the writing desk, and sparks it up. She blows smoke in my direction and smiles slowly, like a cat. She offers me the spliff.

'Want some?' she asks.

'Not if it's got tobacco in it.' I quit smoking when Amy got pregnant and vowed I'd never touch a cigarette again.

'It's OK,' says Jessie. 'It's pure.'

Warily, I accept. I say warily, because I've got no head for hash these days, on account of the fact that I don't smoke enough. Judging from how badly this joint's been rolled, Jessie's clearly no big smoker either. Plus, she doesn't seem remotely wasted, which means it's probably not that strong. So I think what the hell, and take a couple of hits, before handing it back.

'Thanks.'

As she smiles at me again, I notice that she seems shorter than usual. Looking down, I see she's barefoot, clearly going the whole hippy mile. She's wearing a short plum-coloured skirt that shows off her well-toned calves, and there's a silver bangle round her ankle. She looks knockout, in fact. The biz.

She returns the lighter and joint to the ashtray, which I now see is resting on the piece of A4 paper which I covered with a rough pencil sketch for Jessie of an arbour. I reckon it would look gorgeous at the end of her garden, between the oak and the copper beech.

'Have you had a chance to look at that yet?' I ask.

'What? Oh, yes.'

'And?'

'I adore it,' she says, pulling the sketch out from under the ashtray, like a magician whipping off a tablecloth. She holds it up before her and cocks her head to one side, appraisingly. 'You're very good at drawing, you know,' she then says.

'Thanks.' I feel myself start to zone out a little, as the dope kicks in.

'Were you trained?'

'Housetrained, certainly,' I joke. 'I haven't peed on a carpet for years.'

She raises her shades and rolls her eyes at me. 'No, I mean did you train professionally as an artist?'

She sits in the armchair and I lean against the desk, and I fill her in on my background, about how I used to work in a gallery, about the paintings I sold, and how it all then fell apart.

'So you see, there was no money it,' I conclude. 'Or not for me, anyway. I guess I wasn't good enough.' I'm feeling pleasantly high now, and can't be bothered to make excuses for myself.

Jessie can. 'Just because you didn't make a living out of it doesn't mean you weren't any good, Jack. There are plenty of famous artists . . . like Modigliani and Toulouse-Lautrec . . . who never made a bean while they were alive.'

'Yes, but they both committed suicide,' I point out, 'after becoming impoverished, depressed and chronically addicted to absinthe. And,' I continue, 'as appealing a prospect as that is, I guess that, when push came to shove, I decided to follow a more conventional path instead. Besides, I had a wife, and a child on the way. I made the only choice I could.'

She wags a finger at me. 'Ah, but all choices can be unmade, Jack. *All* of them,' she repeats, in such a way that I'm left wondering if we're even talking about painting at all.

I stare out of the window, and wonder what time it is, and contemplate the fact that I really should think about getting home soon. Then I picture Amy in our tiny kitchen, fixing Ben's tea, and I wonder what kind of mood she'll be in. I imagine the wan greeting I'll receive, and suddenly staying right here strikes me as so much more pleasant an option. I reach for the joint and relight it.

'You don't mind, do you?' I ask.

I take a long, deep drag and watch Jessie as she walks across the room and stops in front of a large oval wooden mirror. She removes her sunglasses, pushes her hair back, and her reflection flashes me a smile.

'I've never had a portrait done,' she says.

'No?'

She stares at herself. 'Do you think I'd make a good study?'

'Sure.'

'Why?'

'Well . . .' I half-laugh, embarrassed at being put on the spot like this. 'I don't know . . . because you've got an interesting face . . .'

'Interesting?'

'Er, yeah . . . you know . . . an expressive face.'

'Do you mean you find me attractive?'

I laugh. 'Well, yeah, sure . . . or rather, yes, you are . . .'

She turns round to face me. 'Would you paint me?'

'No. No, I couldn't.'

'Why not?'

I wouldn't normally say anything, but my tongue feels loosened by the dope, so I tell her the story of Sally 'She Who Must Not Be Named' McCullen. Sally was the last woman whose portrait I painted. This was back when I first started seeing Amy. When Amy discovered that Sally was actually modelling for me in the nude, she freaked. But not half as much as she did when I admitted that Sally had set upon me orally during my sleep – an indiscretion which, to this day, I swear occurred accidentally and through no fault of my own.

After Jessie's finished laughing, her eyes quickly narrow, and she says, 'So you haven't always been such a good boy then.'

Such a good boy as *what*? I'm tempted to ask, but I don't. For fear of where the conversation might lead. I'm in danger enough already, because, as I watch Jessie look me coolly up and down, once more I feel The Itch, and Phalius twitches inside my britches, awake.

'It's time I headed home,' I say, pushing myself off the desk and standing unsteadily before her, feeling suddenly quite high.

She ignores me. 'Well, if you won't paint me,' she says, 'maybe you could give me some advice.'

'Sure.'

'It's upstairs.'

'What is?'

'The thing I need advising on . . .'

She opens the door and beckons me towards her with her forefinger.

'Come on,' she tells me. 'Don't be shy . . .'

'I really do need to –'

But she's already gone.

I follow her out into the chequered entrance hall.

'Can you leave your shoes downstairs?' she calls back down the marble staircase. 'The carpet fitters came yesterday.'

I'm actually wearing flip-flops, but do as she says, leaving them in the hallway, before joining her. I've got every intention of making my excuses again, but I never get the chance, because as soon as I reach her, she sets off again, and I find myself giving chase.

It stinks of paint upstairs and there are dust sheets on the floor of two of the bedrooms we pass. We head up another flight of stairs, taking a right at the top, and continue down a long white corridor overlooking the garden which, if anything, appears even more magnificent from up here.

'This was my bedroom when I was a kid,' Jessie explains, as we reach a steep wooden staircase and continue our ascent. 'I've been camping up here while the decorators have been fixing up the main bedrooms downstairs.'

A few steps from the top, Jessie stops without warning, and I walk straight into her. She pushes her bum back against me, so that I'm forced to step down.

'Oops,' she laughs, before hurrying on.

What have you got yourself into now? You should have left, I tell myself. *You should never have agreed to come up.*

I rack my brain for excuses, for a reason to turn right round, but I'm having trouble concentrating. The dope's left me feeling unfocused, and Jessie's short-skirted rear is now level with my eyes. It's shaped exactly like a peach.

The door at the top of the stairs is plastered with Garbage Pail Kids stickers and a sign that reads 'Keep Out! This Means You!'

'Ta-da!' Jessie says, flinging it open and disappearing inside.

I follow her into what still looks exactly like a teenager's bedroom. There are *Smash Hits* posters of 1980s pop stars on the wall: Kajagoogoo, Duran Duran, The Belle Stars, and the like.

Jessie walks up to a photo of Simon le Bon and kisses him on the lips.

'Bloody hilarious, isn't it?' she says. 'It's like I told you last time you were here: this whole house is like a time trap – and this room in particular. For me, it's like turning back the years . . .'

I nod, looking around. There are clothes scattered across the stained cream carpet: a pair of inside-out jeans, a crumpled white dress and a black pair of knickers. An open copy of *Vogue* lies amongst the scrunched up sheets on the folded out sofabed. On a school desk in the corner of the room rests an Amstrad computer, covered with cobwebs.

Jessie opens the door just past the desk and steps out on to the wide, railed balcony beyond. I join her and look out across the rooftops of West London, towards the setting sun.

'It's beautiful,' I say.

'That's what I need your advice for. I want to start doing my yoga up here, but I'm going to need some plant cover, because I prefer to do it without any clothes on.'

I list off some plants that will do the trick. They're pretty much the same ones I used for Slim Jim's Covent Garden rooftop, hardy and densely foliaged, but Jessie doesn't seem to be paying much attention. Soon we go back inside.

'That's quite a gallery,' I say, staring at the walls, which are covered with photos. There must be hundreds of them pinned there.

She plucks off a framed photo, and hands it to me. It's a black-and-white wedding shot. 'My parents,' she says.

'Your mother's very beautiful.'

'Do you really think so?'

'Yes.'

'Everyone's always told me that I look exactly like her.'

I can't help smiling, embarrassed by the way she's twisted my words round into a compliment for herself.

'Nice outfit,' I tease, noticing a photo of Jessie in her early twenties in a black and red jacket with sharp pointed shoulders. She's wearing fishnet tights and red velvet boots, and her figure hasn't changed a bit. 'You look like an extra out of *Thriller*,' I say.

She blushes. 'Batwings were very fashionable back then, I'll have you know.'

'And who's that?' I ask, nodding at a handsome looking guy standing next to her in another photo, where she looks younger still, maybe eighteen, tops.

'Duncan Musgrove.'

'Old boyfriend?'

'My *first* boyfriend. Or my first *real* boyfriend, anyway,' she confides. 'I lost my virginity to him.'

'Oh.'

'In here.'

'Ah.'

She sits on the edge of the sofabed. 'On this very mattress.'

'Ah-ha.'

'Right in front of that mirror on the wall,' she adds, glancing at her reflection.

'Is that a fact?'

She winks at me. 'Well, surely you didn't think you were the first boy I've smuggled up here, did you?'

I should, of course, be shocked by Jessie's frankness, and tell her that I really don't think such revelations concerning her sexual history are appropriate in the context of our employer/employee relationship. And then I should, of course, leave.

240

I do neither. Because being here feels . . . I don't know . . . right . . . and mellow . . . and easy . . . and cool . . . I feel like something of a teenager myself. Everything seems so fresh.

I walk over to the mirror and stare at my own reflection. It might be an effect of the spliff, but the Jack I see staring back at me seems suddenly altered, and, without wanting to come over all Alain de Botton, it makes me wonder: have I changed? *Do* we change? Us? As people? As we get older, do we alter and grow and sometimes grow apart? And if I really have changed, then isn't it likely that Amy has too? But what if we haven't changed in tandem? What if we've gone in opposite directions? What if we no longer belong together at all?

Because that's how it feels . . . like Amy's a million miles away . . .

'Duncan was older than me,' Jessie continues. 'Have you ever been with someone older than yourself, Jack? Because you should. It's educational. It's something you should try at least once.'

I don't reply. I turn round and stare at the photos again.

'Don't tell me you're embarrassed.'

'No.'

'Do you want to know what was really weird about Duncan?'

'What?'

'His willy was shaped exactly like a toadstool. I mean *exactly*. Right down to the pointy round end.'

She starts to giggle, and so do I. Contagiously. This dope's obviously stronger than I initially thought, because, without warning, we both collapse on to the sofabed, with uncontrollable tears of laughter running down our cheeks.

The next thing I know, we're swapping secrets like a couple of Cold War double agents. I tell her about losing my virginity to Mary Rayner and lasting less than twenty thrusts. She confesses to having secretly slept with her best friend's boyfriend when she was seventeen, and then with the same woman's husband last year.

241

And on, and on, it goes.

Until we've got very little left to tell.

But even then, after our sexual Glasnost is over, the conversation keeps flowing, unstoppable now, like the river when it hits Niagara Falls. It's like we're a couple of sci-fi characters, who've just gone through some kind of Accelerated Friendship Vortex. Things between us will never be the same again.

Of course, it's partly the drugs, but it's something else as well.

I never get this kind of fresh intimacy with Amy any more. This feels all new, like popping a spoon through the foil on a coffee jar, whereas, with me and Amy, it's so much more familiar than that, more like scraping the last of the Marmite out of the jar.

Amy and I know too much about each other. There's nothing left to discover. Whereas this reminds me of dating. I feel young – and horny as hell.

Inappropriate phrases start to queue up in my mind (like flashers, queuing up to jump out of a bush): *For an older bird, you've got cracking knockers; Are they real?; Can I feel?; With muscle toning like that, I bet you're dynamite in the sack.*

I don't say any of them, of course, but I want to. I want to very much.

Then Jessie goes for a pee and, in her absence, the effect of the spliff seems to drop off, like my ears have popped on a plane coming into land, and whatever spell it is I've been momentarily under breaks.

I stand and stare at myself in the mirror again. How long will it be before I start looking old, even to myself? Because it *will* happen. Early middle-age will lead to late middle-age, And onwards and down, until one day I'll look in a mirror and I'll be grey, or bald. My skin will look like creased up baking paper, and my balls will be hanging round my thighs like a pair of Argentinian rancheros' bolas, while my cock will look like a half-smoked, stubbed-out Cuban cigar.

It should depress me, this thought, but what it actually does is fill me with fire. Because I'm still young. I've still got what it takes. I've still got it in me. Which means I should be fucking at every opportunity I get. While I still can. These days are precious. I shouldn't be letting them go to waste. I don't want to be sitting there in some rest home, looking back on my life with regret. I want to be sitting there smiling, knowing that I had just as good a time as I could.

And I do feel good, here in Jessie's room, acting the way I am. I can't help grinning at my reflection. I'm flirting. I'm flirting and it feels great. It's like exercising an old muscle: the more I work it, the easier it becomes. I feel like I've just graduated from Charm School, like I've got this woman wrapped round my little finger.

Then the smile falls from my face and I slump back on to the sofabed, because I also know that being here isn't right. In fact, it's plain wrong. I'm no longer a free sexual agent. I'm Jack Rossiter. Married to Amy. Father of Ben.

I've got to get the fuck out of here, before I do something I regret.

I sit up on the edge of the bed. I move to stand.

Only then I freeze.

Because Jessie's back.

She's standing in the doorway with her hands on her hips, and I'm so shocked by the sight, that all thoughts of escape, and everything else for that matter, fly from my mind. Until all that remains are two numbers – and two letters.

36DD.

A mystery, it seems, has been solved. Ever since Jessie first told me that the code for her burglar alarm was the same as her bra size, I've wondered whether she was joking, or whether it really was true.

I need wonder no more.

I can see for myself.

And – *Hey, Breast-o!* – what I can see is this: Jessie, naked as the day she was born, foxy, and fanciable, and gorgeous as can be.

If certain parts of her are too perfectly rounded to possibly be true, so what? If her plastic surgeon was here, I'd have no option other than to congratulate him on an awesome piece of work.

And I'm not the only one who's impressed. Phalius has just fallen in love with a Brazilian.

Suffice it to say, my Itch is on fire.

'What are you doing?' I say.

'What does it look like?'

I hold my hands up as she walks towards me. 'No.'

'Don't be silly. You know you want to.'

'I don't,' I say. Which is a lie, because I do. It's just that I *can't*.

She stops right in front of me and leans forward, her hands snaking down her bare thighs.

'I don't believe you,' she whispers. 'Not after everything you just told me . . .'

'But that's all in the past. I've changed.'

'No one ever leaves their past fully behind, Jack,' she tells me, kneeling down, 'and especially not someone like you, someone who used to be such a naughty boy . . .'

She pushes me back on the sofabed and reaches out for my belt.

'It's all right,' she says with a wink. 'I promise I won't bite.'

If there's one thing I know for certain right now, it's that this sentence could only be less convincing if it were being spoken by a lion.

13

amy

The Erotic Bath Bomb

'I feel like we're in a movie,' Jack says, as the yellow cab pulls to a stop outside the hotel on Thompson Street.

'Here we go,' I say. 'The Big Apple.'

I slide up the black seat and swivel out of the cab's door and on to the sidewalk. I look up at the façade of the hotel stretching towards the starry sky and all my tiredness and anxiety vanishes.

'Good evening folks and welcome to New York. I'm Stephan and I can organise your luggage for you. Just one moment, please.'

Jack and I stare at the absurdly handsome porter, who has just addressed us. He's wearing an earpiece and a black designer suit.

'OK,' I mumble. 'Thanks.'

'You're welcome, Ma'am.' He flashes me a bright smile.

Inside, the concierge is waiting for us like we're long lost friends. She's over six foot and has the most piercing green eyes and flawless skin I've ever seen. She walks regally in front of us, and I watch Jack's eyes widen as he tries to take in the impossible length of her legs.

The hotel lobby upstairs is gob-smackingly cool. There's funky music playing and everything is uber-chic and large – even the flower arrangements are made of whole branches of cherry blossom trees. As we wait by the desk, I notice a group of trendy models lolling over the designer sofas, slurping iced lattes through straws, at the end of a photo shoot. Jack squeezes my hand, clearly as amazed and excited as I am.

In no time at all, we're shown to the top of the hotel in the sleek black lift and then into our suite. Jack tips Stephan, who has brought up our luggage, and manages to keep a straight face, until Stephan leaves, closing the door gently behind him. The second it shuts, we both look at each other, then squeal like little kids.

'Bloody hell!' Jack exclaims.

The suite we're in is bigger than our entire flat. Jack kicks off his boots and we both leap up and down on the bed. I've never seen one this size before. We lie down side by side and practise rolling together on it, before dissolving into giggles.

It's the closest I've felt to him for so long, and we stare at each other, suddenly embarrassed by the intimacy. For a second, I think we're going to lose it again and retreat into the separate shells we've been living in for weeks.

But then Jack smiles.

And I smile back.

And I know that this *is* going to work, that we're both really going to give this a go. Everything is going to turn out right.

Jack kisses me and grins. 'Let's party,' he says.

He hops off the bed and flings open the mini bar. It's fully stacked, and in a moment he's popped a mini bottle of Laurent Perrier. Meanwhile, I check out the drawers and cupboards.

'Oh my God! Look at this stuff.' There are goodies of all descriptions. I unscrew the jar of aromatherapy massage oil and offer it to Jack. 'Smell that.'

'Look at this,' Jack says, undoing a plastic bag with his teeth. 'Wey-hey! It's a shag bag! I mean it,' he laughs, 'it's actually got it written on the side.' He pours out condoms, and a small packet labelled clitoral stimulant gel, a scented candle, an erotic bath bomb and a specially compiled chill-out CD on to the bed. 'This is awesome.'

I undo the erotic bath bomb and take a sniff. 'Let's give it a whirl,' I tell him. 'Honey, I think we've just got time for a freshen-up before our complimentary cocktail in the private members' rooftop bar,' I remind him in my best New York accent, as I guzzle champagne and unwrap one of the Hershey's Kisses from the packet Jack opens.

I feel euphoric. Dizzy with excitement. I haven't felt like this since . . . well, not since our wedding night.

I take the bath bomb into the bathroom.

'Wow! Check it out in here!' I call.

There's a walk-in shower with jets at all angles and a seat, plus a giant Jacuzzi bath with room for about ten. There are twin basins and a pile of blindingly white towels and two of the fluffiest dressing gowns hanging from pegs set in the chic brown-black tiles. There's not a plastic duck in sight, or a tub of chewed foam letters half filled with old bath water, or leaking bottles of kids' shampoo, or any wind-up plastic submarines and boats.

In other words: It's Heaven.

It takes me a full minute to work out how to put the water on in the bath, but once it's on, I go to the mirrors by the basins. They are lit with film-star bulbs. There's a pot full of complimentary Mac make-up, so I open the eyebrow pencil and start experimenting.

Jack appears at the door. He's holding a piece of paper in his hand.

'What's that?' I ask.

'The price list.' His face is grim.

My hand freezes as my eyes meet his in the mirror.

'So far, we've been in the hotel for seven and a half minutes and we're . . . two hundred and eighty-five dollars down.'

'Shit.'

I follow him back through to the bedroom and watch from behind as he picks up his glass and downs the champagne. I don't know what he's thinking, but I suspect that this could

247

be the start of a row. I know how suspicious Jack has been all along about our 'free' trip, and I've been the one saying it's going to be fine.

I can't bear it if we're going to fight again. Since I got back from my chat with H, I've been making a super-human effort. Every time we've even veered towards tension, I've done a U-turn.

I didn't complain when he took ages to leave the flat and we were late getting to my mother's. I didn't rise when he accused me of forgetting his iPod, or fight back when he told me off when I got the directions wrong to the airport carpark. I even beat down my feelings when he told me to stop talking about Ben on the plane.

So now, if that's our moment of fun over and he starts making a fuss, I'm all out of energy. I can't keep treading on eggshells.

But Jack turns and hands me my glass.

'Oh well, we might as well enjoy it,' he says. 'I guess we can take the chocolate home for Ben.'

I take the glass, weak with relief.

'Oh Jack, do you think he'll be OK?' I ask.

Time is doing funny things, now we're the other side of the world from Ben. Being with him in my mother's kitchen earlier today feels like it happened a month ago.

'No, of course I don't,' he teases.

'Don't. I'm finding this really hard.' And I am. I feel the pull to my child like a physical ache. 'I've never left him for this long before.'

'I wish you'd chill out. Your mother's going to spoil him rotten and undo every bit of our good work. He'll have her eating out of his hand by now.'

'Do you think?'

I picture Ben, sobbing like his heart was breaking, his fists clinging to clumps of my hair, as he screamed at me not to leave him.

'Come on,' Jack says, smiling. 'We're here to have fun,

remember? It's a Friday night in New York. Let's forget the bath and hit the rooftop bar. What do you say?'

Back On My Comfortable Reef

I wake up and the sun is streaming in through the bedroom window. Jack is sitting on the windowsill and the sound of New York waking up billows in with the net curtain.

I feel my heart flip over. For the first time, for as long as I can remember, Jack is doing something amazing. He's sketching. He's totally absorbed and he doesn't notice that I've woken up.

I watch the way the sunlight falls on his face.

My Jack.

I smile, images of last night coming back to me. How we strolled hand in hand through the streets of SoHo, diving into a steak house with red-and-white chequered tablecloths and ordering the most massive meal we've ever had. Then walking more and finding a bar where we drank tequila and played pool and met some guys who took us to a jazz club, where we danced until we fell over with exhaustion just as it was getting light.

We had more fun in one night than we've had in five years.

I feel winded – breathless – when I think of the mistake I might have made with Tom. Now it's all over, I feel like a fish who just poked its head above the confines of the nice, comfortable reef and nearly got eaten by a shark.

What was I thinking?

Lying here, it seems utterly absurd, unfathomable, but I'm not going to dwell on it. I'm not going to even let it into my head. That's all in the past. H was right. It was just a blip. A warning. This is a new dawn of my relationship with Jack.

I yawn and stretch, luxuriating in lying like a starfish under the Indian cotton sheet. 'What time is it?' I ask.

Jack turns and smiles at me. 'Early, but it doesn't matter. Isn't it great?'

He comes and lies down next to me on the bed. He holds

my hand and we listen to the sounds of distant traffic and beeping cabs and voices drifting up from the sidewalk.

'It's so weird,' he says. 'So urban, but so peaceful at the same time.'

'I love it,' I say. 'It's the first time I've woken up and not had Ben jump on my head for as long as I can remember. And I don't have to empty the dishwasher. Or make cereal. Or clear up. Or find shoes . . .'

I roll over and make gleeful noises into my pillow, kicking my feet.

Jack laughs and strokes my back. 'Poor Amy,' he says. 'It's sometimes a bit of a mindless slog for you, isn't it?'

I turn and look at him. It's the first time Jack has said anything that remotely acknowledges my day-to-day life. I didn't even realise he'd noticed.

'I know I've been rubbish,' he says. 'When we get home, I promise I'll get up more, and take care of him more. You know, being away from him, I miss the little guy.'

I reach up and kiss him. I feel strangely moved. 'Do you?'

'Yes, it's weird without him. Nice, but weird.'

'Shall we call?'

We dial up my mother's house and I hold the phone, our heads pressed together, as my mother puts Ben on at the other end. His voice sounds babyish and confused.

'Are you being a good boy?' I ask him.

'No,' he replies, and Jack laughs.

My mother shoos me off the phone with hardly any information about how Ben is coping without me. 'It's an International Call,' she reminds me. She's shouting and enunciating, even though the line is perfectly clear.

I put the phone down.

'You see,' Jack said. 'I told you he'd be fine.'

But I press my lips together.

'What's the matter?' he asks, smoothing my hair behind my ear.

'Nothing,' I say, laughing and flapping my hand over my

mouth, as tears start rolling down my face. 'I'm fine.'

Jack hugs me. 'It's OK. It's OK to miss him . . . but you know – I've got an excellent way of taking your mind of it . . .'

After an hour of fabulous, sensuous, satisfying, uninterrupted *morning* sex, a full half an hour on my own in the bathroom, listening to music and putting on make-up, and having left the hotel in less than a minute, on account of the fact that I didn't have to pack nappies, juice and select a particular toy truck, I feel marvellously refreshed as we hit the streets.

I've turned down the corner of nearly every page of the *Time Out* guide Faith gave me just before we left. I'm amazed by how well she knows this place. I can't imagine Faith living here, let alone clubbing and drinking in all the places she's recommended, but I guess I must have underestimated her. If I'd had a funky previous jet-set life, I'd have made sure Camilla and the rest of the Vipers heard all about it, but Faith has kept schtum. I had no idea she once held down an international job. Maybe she's not so thick after all.

I've made a long list of things we want to do: Bloomingdales, Saks, the Mac Shop, Kheils, Donna Karan . . . the list is endless. However, Jack's not getting into my shopaholic vibe. He wants to do the Frick Collection, the Guggenheim and the Flat Iron Building. We're never going to do it all.

We wander out of the hotel on to the sunny sidewalk, awestruck. I've planned a route around all the shops I want to visit, but Jack's hungry, so we breakfast on bagels and smoothies as we walk along and, almost immediately, we get lost.

For once, it doesn't matter. Being in New York makes me feel injected with coolness. I'm wearing my favourite halterneck sundress and my new shades, which look like they're designer, but were actually a tenner in Tesco's. Jack's wearing three-quarter length trousers and flip-flops and his funky baseball cap, which we picked up in a store last night.

I so rarely walk anywhere with Jack in the daytime on my

own that, as I catch sight of us in the reflection of a shop window, strolling hand in hand, I'm surprised at how well we match.

Every time we walk around a corner, there's a new sight and more things going on. I feel effervescent with the sheer spontaneity of it all. I love the yellow cabs and the old buildings with their zigzagging cast iron fire escapes and the unfamiliar font of the street signs. I love the crowds of people – the dazzling array of clothes and the flamboyant mix of races and accents.

On Spring Street, there are stalls everywhere on the wide sidewalk and Jack buys me a spotty silk headband which matches my dress. We both stop and look at the street art for sale. I fancy an impressionist painting of the skyline, done in thick oils, but Jack turns his nose up.

'I could do that,' he says, dragging me away.

I'm delighted to hear it, because he's right. He could.

He's outraged by the street hawkers' prices. 'Remember that ghastly "Study in Yellow" I did for Dad's office? Even that was better than any of these.'

'Ten times better. At least,' I tell him. 'I wish you hadn't given up. I know why you did, but I miss you being an artist.'

'Hey! Maybe we could move here,' he says, smiling at me. 'Think about it. We could have a little SoHo loft and live the bohemian lifestyle.'

I laugh, sucking on my smoothie straw.

'I could flog big canvases to the tourists and you could make fabulous clothes and sell them to these posh boutiques. Oh, and maybe we could both keep Branching Out going, and charge a fortune for planting up people's window boxes.'

'It sounds great – but darling, haven't we missed the boat a bit? I mean, how would we get Ben into a school and what about lifting the buggy up all those stairs?'

Jack looks crestfallen. 'Yeah, I suppose you're right,' he says. 'I guess we're too old.'

'But never say never,' I tell him. 'Why the hell shouldn't we do something mad and live somewhere different? I don't want to live in our flat in Kensal Rise forever, do you?'

Jack looks at me. 'You'd really move? Leave all your mates?'

'What, the Vipers? They're not mates, Jack.'

'But you seem . . . I don't know, so entrenched.'

'Well, I'm not. Not for a second. Why do you think I do the lottery all the time? Because if I won, I'd get us out of there in a flash.'

'You would?'

'Of course I would. I always dreamed that we'd have loads of adventures together. I always thought we'd be the type of people who would live an exciting life. That it would be like . . . like *this* all the time,' I say, gesturing around us.

'And it's not?' he asks.

'Don't say it like that.' I can tell I've offended him.

'Well, that's what you're implying, surely? I do my best, you know.'

I sigh. I don't want to argue with him. I take his hand. 'I'm not criticising you, Jack. All I'm saying is that we owe it to ourselves to make our lives amazing. Don't you think?'

Jack gives me a funny look. 'Where did you get that from?'

'What?'

'That. You don't usually say that kind of thing.'

I can't speak. I feel queasy with guilt, as if by accidentally quoting Tom, I've brought him here with me. My secret suddenly feels as tangible as if it was Tom standing next to me, holding my hand, and not Jack.

Shocked, I lift up Jack's hand and look at my fingers wrapped around his. My wedding ring glints in the sun.

'Forget it,' I tell him. 'Look there's a sign for Grand Central Station. Let's check it out.'

Tourists

Even before we've reached the station, Jack's on a roll, naming all the films he's seen the grand hall featured in, but

when we get inside, the only bit I recognise is from the kids'
cartoon, *Madagascar*.

Jack makes me stand by the staircase so that we can take a
photo for Ben. Then he comes in closer and tells me to sit on
the steps. He takes a close up of me, but as usual, he takes
ages about it.

'Amy, don't do that, OK?' he says, looking at the screen on
the back of the camera.

'What?'

'Pull your photo face.'

'I've got a photo face?'

'Yes,' Jack says, 'and it really annoys me. Every time I take
a picture of you, you do this staged smile.'

'I do?'

'Yes, you do. Now look normal.'

I try to look neutral, but I can't help feeling the moment is
ruined. I don't feel like smiling now anyway. People walk
past me, down the steps, and I feel crowded in and annoyed.

'There,' says Jack, looking at the image of me on the digital
camera. 'Got you.'

'Let me see,' I say, reaching out. He shows it to me.

'That's horrible!' I protest. 'I look awful.' And I do. Like a
cardboard cut-out, with no emotion on my face.

'No, you don't.'

'Delete it,' I insist, but Jack snatches the camera away from
me.

'You worry too much about the way you look,' he says.

'I don't.'

'Yes, you do. You're so hard on yourself. You're always
starting these unrealistic diets and complaining all the time
about your flabby tummy and your wrinkles. I mean,
where's the magic for me?'

I fold my arms. I feel like he's telling me off.

Jack unfolds my arms. 'Don't get defensive. I'm just being
honest.'

'But you're having a go at me.'

254

Jack sighs. 'OK. Then tell me what annoys *you* about *me*. That's fair.'

'No.'

'Why? There must be things that I do that wind you up?' He sits down next to me. He puts out his hands. 'I'm serious. Let's hear it.'

'I wouldn't know where to start.'

Jack laughs nervously. 'OK. Well, we've got all day. We're in as good a place as any. Shoot.'

I look at him, and then I look down into the vast, cavernous space and the thousands of strangers with places to go, and up to the stars painted on the ceiling. And he's right. We're in a great place to do this. The petty things that annoy me at home seem insignificant in a space this size.

'OK, and this is in no particular order. First off, you always expect me to find things for you. *That* annoys me,' I tell him.

'But you're better at finding things. You're one of life's great finders. And besides, you've always moved the things I'm trying to find –'

'Jack. You're not supposed to get defensive. I'm just telling you.'

'OK,' he relents.

'And you never tell me what's going on at work.'

'Mmm-hmm?'

'Camilla said she saw you driving around with some woman in a sports car,' I say, without thinking.

All this time I've wanted to ask him and now I've brought it up as if it's the most normal thing in the world. It feels like such a relief. 'And I didn't know who it was,' I continue. 'I mean, I presume it was one of your clients, but you didn't tell me, and that hurts because I end up assuming the worst . . .'

Jack looks at me blankly, like I just asked him to tell me pi to the fiftieth decimal place. 'I have no idea what you're talking about.'

'Camilla swore it was you. In a Lexus convertible, apparently.'

'Well, Camilla should keep her silly posh nose out of other people's business, and I shall tell her as much, the next time I see her. That interfering cow.'

I'm surprised at the vitriol with which he says it.

'Please don't. Forget it. She just made a mistake.'

'Yeah, one which left you "assuming the worst". And what worst is that, Amy? That I'm having an affair?'

I can feel my heart hammering, because I *did* think that. Or at least I suspected him of something – I'm not sure what. Now that he's so adamant about his innocence, I feel even more guilty for doubting him, and when I look at him again, all I can think is that he's the strong one and I'm pathetic in contrast. I remember H's warning and vow to myself that Jack must never, ever know about Tom.

'No, Jack, no. I'd never think that, because I know you never would.'

The blood fades a little from his face.

'Well, OK, then,' he says. He forces a smile. 'So I'll try and be more communicative – but you know, sometimes it's the way you ask . . .'

'What do you mean?'

'Sometimes when I'm tired, you ask me loads of questions. You make it like an interrogation.'

I take this in. He's right. I do badger him.

This feels liberating. It feels like we're really communicating for the first time in ages – and now I know that all that stuff I thought in London about Jack and the woman in the car was rubbish, I feel more determined to put all that behind us.

As we sit on the stairs, we cover all sorts of topics, from the fact I'm too obsessed with ironing, to the fact he gives Ben too many treats.

Then we discuss our car arguments and the fact that he always shouts at me for directions and then ignores what I tell him to do. We agree that when we can afford it, we'll get an in-car navigation system.

'Let's go and eat oysters and drink champagne to celebrate,' Jack says eventually.

'Celebrate what?'

'The fact I annoy you that much and you're still with me.'

We both stare at each other for a second. Then laugh. Then he kisses me.

King Kong

After that, everything is perfect, and the kisses and laughter keep on coming. Somehow we slip into an easy togetherness which reminds me of how we were when we first got together. We have a long lazy lunch and then brave Macy's, until I can tell that Jack is bored. So we hail a cab and explore the Meat Packing District, stopping for a few pints in The Spotted Pig.

Time drifts by in a haze. In the evening, we shower together in the hotel, and talk about the first shower we had together in a B&B in Brighton and how we flooded the place. Reminiscing about our early days makes us both laugh and, in a buoyant mood, we head out to a comedy show. Later on, we have a midnight feast, like little kids – sitting cross-legged on the bed and sharing peanut butter sandwiches and pretzels. It feels like I'm on the best adventure of my life.

The next morning, we brunch in Greenwich Village. We scoff pancakes and maple syrup, sausages and bacon, and talk to the all-American waitress, who plies us with black coffee. When she mentions that she has a little boy, it occurs to me that I haven't even thought about Ben all morning, and whilst I feel a moment of total guilt, at the same time I feel as if some part of myself has been restored and redefined.

After brunch, Jack wins the flip of a dime and decides on the Empire State Building as our next stop.

'But what about Bloomingdales?' I ask.

'We've got to do the Empire State,' he says. 'It would be a sin not to.'

I'm too happy to argue.

Inside, there's a huge snaking queue and we both fall silent, people-watching. I can't help feeling that none of these people can possibly feel as content as I do.

Last night, on our stroll from the comedy club, Jack suggested that we list things we like about each other – the stuff that makes us happy. At first, it was embarrassing and awkward, and it felt too much like therapy, but by the end I felt wonderful. It was such an obvious thing to do and, as I contemplate all the people around us, it occurs to me that I might never have told Jack that he makes the best chilli in the world, or that it makes my heart melt when he sings to Ben in the night, or that I love the doodles he does when he's on the phone.

In return, Jack told me that he loves listening to me and Ben playing, and that his favourite smell is me after a bath and that he always kisses me on my eyelids if he leaves for work before I'm awake.

They're only little things, but telling them to each other has made me feel like there's still so much to know about him, and it makes me feel like he still notices me.

I squeeze Jack's hand and sigh to myself. Being together like this is sheer bliss.

And then, in the Empire State lift, I see him.

For a second, I really think it's him and my stomach feels like it's plummeted all one hundred and two floors down the lift shaft, but when the man turns round, it's not Tom. Just someone who looks like him. And there it is again, the feeling that Tom's just under the surface, lurking in the shadows.

I want him gone. I want him out of my head.

I didn't kiss him, I reason with myself, trying to dispel my panic. I sort of did, but I stopped. I didn't go all the way. I didn't really snog him. I have nothing to feel guilty about.

Go away, I tell Tom, mentally. Stop bugging me. *Fuck off.*

We head out on to the viewing platform. Jack stands behind me to protect me from the crowd and we stare down at Manhattan. It's awesome.

'It's funny to be here. I always imagined it to be a bit like in *King Kong*,' he says.

'I hope you're not going to lift me up to the very top,' I tell him, 'and beat your chest.'

He smiles and then is silent. 'Why not? It's a great place for a love scene, don't you think? It's so epic.'

'Even with all the crowds?'

'The crowds don't matter,' He puts his arms around me and nuzzles into my neck.

I cross my arms over his in front of me and we stare in silence for ages at the view.

So, here we are. On our own, with no place to be, other than on top of the world. I'm so aware that this should be an amazing experience – a top five moment for the memory banks.

The problem is that suddenly I don't feel on top of the world. Instead I've hit rock bottom. I thought I'd be able to dismiss the whole thing with Tom, 'chalk it up to experience', as H said I could. I really hoped that I'd be able to make myself forget, and I've been trying . . . *really* trying. But I've failed.

Because now I've remembered and rekindled all the good things about my marriage, I feel racked with horror and guilt, and standing here with Jack, my heart beats faster, because, no matter how much I try and tell myself otherwise, retrospectively my liaison with Tom feels so much more than a tiny, fleeting infidelity. It feels a betrayal. Not just of Jack, but of me. Of us. Of everything that we are.

'I love you, Amy,' Jack whispers, squeezing me tighter. 'I really, really love you.'

I close my eyes.

I can't speak.

Milords And Milady's

It's late by the time we've finished at the Empire State Building and we head to the Guggenheim, but neither of us can face the queue, so we end up strolling through Central Park.

It's odd being in a park without a buggy. We walk for ages, stopping to listen to some jazz buskers and to watch the roller disco. Eventually, we find a spot by the lake and, in the late afternoon sun, I lie with my head on Jack's lap, looking up at the sky. I feel tiredness pinching my eyes.

I gently run my hand over Jack's.

'Tell me one of your happiest memories?' I say.

'Why?'

'I don't know. I just wondered what they are, that's all.'

'When Ben first said "Dadda". That was a biggie for me. And . . . I don't know . . . I'm pretty happy right now.'

'Do you remember that first holiday we had in Greece?' I ask him. I haven't been planning on asking him at all, it's just popped out of my mouth.

Immediately I know I'm on dodgy ground. It's rather a taboo subject with us, since the holiday ended so badly, after Jack crashed our moped and confessed to spending the night with Sally McCullen. I'm not sure why I've brought it up.

'Of course I do.'

'I remember looking at the sky on that beach and feeling this happy,' I tell him, trying to make light of it, as if it's now OK to talk about it. But I'm not quite sure that it *is* OK.

Jack reaches inside the top of my dress. 'I remember that beach,' he whispers.

I giggle. 'Jack, stop it! Somebody will see.'

'Come on,' he says. 'Let's go back to the hotel.'

But by the time we get back to the hotel, I feel hungover and woozy. The jet lag has really kicked in.

I run a bath with the erotic bath bomb and try to get all sexy with Jack, but we end up having a perfunctory, familiar shag, and I can't say that it's satisfying for either of us.

Afterwards, we both fall into a fitful sleep. I have a headache when we wake and I'm shattered still, but I force myself to get up.

260

'Come on,' I tell Jack. 'Let's get going. Why don't we try that restaurant you chose in the guidebook? Balthazar, isn't it? That French brasserie?'

Despite my best efforts to chivvy things along, Jack seems to have slumped into one of his brooding moods. We go to the restaurant, but somehow we don't gel and Jack spends most of his time talking to the waiter about English bands, whilst I drink most of the wine.

Afterwards, we stroll back to the hotel and stop in a bar called Milady's for a nightcap. Jack orders a Dark and Stormy – very appropriate, given his mood.

I'm not even sure how the row starts. Maybe it's because we're both dog tired and a bit drunk, but I don't stop myself from complaining that he spent more time talking to the waiter than to me, even though I know that it'll annoy him.

'Well, if you took an interest in popular culture,' he says, 'then perhaps you'd have been able to join in.'

How dare he be so pompous? I read *Grazia*, every week. I know more about popular culture than he does. Would he be able to name all the winners of *Big Brother*? No, I don't think so. So he can spare me the lecture.

'All I'm saying, is that I didn't come all this way to spend the evening talking to someone we're never going to see again.'

'Why not? Why are you so judgemental? You're saying he can't have decent opinions because he's a waiter?'

'No, of course I'm not saying that.'

'Maybe you think the same about gardeners . . .'

'No, Jack, no.'

'At least he has a job.'

I can feel my hackles rising. It was a jibe at me, and we both know it.

'He was just after extra tips.'

'So what? I don't mind tipping someone who interests me, who takes an interest in what I'm interested in.'

'And I don't interest you. Is that what you're saying?'

I've raised my voice, and there's a palpable lull in the murmur of voices around us. My cheeks begin to burn.

Jack sighs. Then he rubs his face.

'Enough,' he says. His voice sounds loaded with weariness.

I'm silent. We look at one another.

'All we ever do is row,' he states, 'and I've had enough of it. We said we'd try to make things better, but they're not better. They're worse.'

I wish he'd take it back. I feel like he's broken something. Some sort of pact.

'How can you say that? Things *are* better. They've been great. We've had so much fun today and yesterday.'

'So how come we're rowing now?'

I'm stumped, because he's right. We are, and it was so easy. Too easy.

'And anyway,' he goes on, 'I'm not talking about today and yesterday, or being here in New York. Anyone can have fun on holiday. I'm talking about our real life, not a fantasy life won from the back of a packet. I mean next week, next month, in ten years' time.'

He pauses. I can't look at him. Then he sighs heavily.

'Things have got to change, Amy.'

The way he says it scares me. I look up at him. 'How?'

I'm frightened of where he's taking this. If only we could have had this conversation two weeks ago, a month ago. Not now.

Looking at Jack, I feel stalled. How can we start talking about how to improve our relationship, when Jack doesn't even *realise* the state of it? When he doesn't know what's been happening. When he doesn't know – and can *never* know – about Tom?

'I want to get back to us. The old us, that used to hang out all the time like we have been here in New York. The old us that used to love spending time together, and having fun. The old us that used to always tell the truth.'

262

He glares into my eyes. 'I mean, are you really honest with me about what goes on in your head. What you really think about?'

'What?' I ask. My heart is going crazy. I can't breathe. Is it really that obvious? Has he sussed about Tom? Has he suspected all along?

'Because I'm not honest with you,' he continues.

'You're not?' I ask, confused.

'No.' His voice cracks.

'What is it?' I ask.

'Well . . . there's something you should know . . . about Jessie and me.'

14

Jack

There's Something You Should Know . . . About Jessie And Me

The moment this self-betraying serpent of a sentence slithers past my lips, I know there'll be no turning back. I feel breathless and light-headed, as if I'm being strangled by my own words. Then like a soldier stopping for a pee in the heat of battle, I instantly find myself oscillating wildly between dread and relief.

My relief springs from the fact that I've begun my confession. Which means I'll soon have exorcised this horrible guilty secret that's been festering inside me all weekend.

I've chosen to seek salvation by putting the integrity of my relationship above all else. I'm holding it before me, like a torch to light my way. I'm going to do what I know Amy would do in my place: I'm going to tell the truth.

Then my fear kicks in. What if I'm wrong? What if Amy's wrong? What if the truth isn't a great healer, as she's always claimed? What if it's an executioner instead? What if my confession, rather than proving to be a revitalising tonic that resurrects our relationship from its current bi-polar state – whereby we veer between happiness and hatred at the drop of a pin – instead proves to be an horrendous act of self-destruction, akin to ramming a hand grenade into my own mouth and pulling the pin?

Amy stares at me. Behind her, pool balls clack across the table.

I wish I still smoked. Now would be the perfect time to nip out and buy a pack of Marlboro . . . and never come back . . .

All of a sudden, I feel incredibly weak.

'You and *Jessie*?' Amy says.

'Yeah.'

'Jessie Kay?' she checks.

I nod, as my throat dries out, like I've just swallowed a handful of dust.

'Oh, Jack,' she groans, instinctively grabbing my hand. 'She hasn't fired you, has she?'

Amy's groan is one of sympathy, not anger. She's groaning for me, not for herself – not because I might have forfeited her fledgling radio career, but because I might have lost my one and only client and source of recommendations.

She's groaning, because she thinks that Branching Out has just been felled.

This is an example of Amy's generosity of spirit that, quite frankly, I could do without right now. Why can't she be bitchy instead? Or damning? Or have spinach in her teeth? Or a big zit on the end of her nose? Why does she have to be so caring? And look so beautiful? Why does my heart choose this exact moment to start aching with love?

'I didn't get fired.'

'Then what is it?'

My voice thickens, as misery swamps me. I look into her eyes and tell her, 'I'm so sorry . . .'

Amy and I are both old enough to know that any story that starts with a sorry is almost certain to end in tears.

Unsurprisingly, then, her voice is loaded with suspicion, as she demands, 'What have you got to be sorry about?'

One of the pool players behind her glances up from his sniper's position over his cue. His gold front tooth glistens in the gloom. I feel my chest tighten, like I've been bound with barbed wire. Sweat breaks out across my brow.

'I never meant for it to happen,' I say. 'Between Jessie and me.' My voice doesn't sound like my own. It sounds like a child's.

Amy's face locks into a frown. The sparkle dies in her eyes, like a pissed-on fire.

'What do you mean, *Between Jessie and me?*' she asks.

'I promise you. None of it was planned. You've got to believe me, Amy. Please . . .'

She snatches her hand from mine. 'What do you fucking mean?'

She spits the words at me like curare darts and, for a second, I think she's going to take a swing at me, Rocky-Balboa-style.

A barman pops up out of nowhere and glares at me suspiciously. 'Are you OK?' he asks Amy.

Which comes across as a bit like the captain of the *Titanic* saying, 'Did anyone else feel a bump?'

Amy tells him, 'Yes,' and, as she watches him walk away, her whole face seems to sag.

'But I don't understand . . .' She says it like she's talking in her sleep. 'I never even thought . . . no, not for a second . . .' She peers at me in confusion, like I'm a stranger who's just sat down. 'You told me she was lumpy . . . on the turn . . .'

'I lied.'

'What have you done?'

My chest heaves at the sound of pain in her voice. I can't bear to look at her any more. I wish I could dash outside, and come back as someone else, someone better. I wish I could duck into a phone booth, and turn into SuperJack, and then fly so fast around the world that I was able to reverse its spin and turn back time.

I wish I could undo the things I've done.

'Tell me, Jack,' she demands. '*Everything.*' Again I hear that panic in her voice. 'Tell me,' she says, 'right bloody now.'

So I do.

Because this conversation was my idea. Because our

relationship's been so messed up recently, and entangled and confused, that I know that keeping on telling lies is only going to make it worse.

Because I've got no choice.

Because, like the bra of a Page Three model at a photo shoot, this is something I've just got to get off my chest.

Confessions: No. 5. Attic Attack

'No one ever leaves their past fully behind, Jack,' she told me, kneeling down, 'and especially not someone like you, someone who used to be such a naughty boy . . .'

She pushed me back on the sofabed and reached out for my belt.

'It's all right,' she said with a wink. 'I promise I won't bite.'

If there was one thing I knew for certain right then, it was that this sentence could only have been less convincing if it had been spoken by a lion.

Jessie wasn't just planning on biting me.

She was going to eat me alive.

I stared down at her pampered skin, toned muscles, coiffed hair, manicured nails, trimmed pubes, perfectly rounded, surgically sculpted breasts, and watched as her lewd and lascivious tongue flickered lightly across her bow-shaped lips.

Her fingers began to unbuckle my belt, displaying the same astonishing dexterity as when she'd taken off my blood-stained shirt the first time we'd met.

I felt Phalius twitching like a ferret in a sack, straining against my jeans, like he wanted to rip them in two.

Any second now, and the sexual Rubicon would be crossed. There'd be no turning back. My seminal legionaries were ready for battle, and it was only a matter of time before they'd be flowing in triumph through the Gates of Rome.

Jessie popped the top button of my jeans.

I heard myself groan.

I'd thought about this, about *her*. I'd pictured this moment in my mind a dozen times, and now here it was – my fantasy fuck – only seconds away from becoming real. And I wanted it. I wanted *her*. I wanted to do it right now.

My Seven Year Itch was screaming like a mosquito bite to be scratched.

What kind of a man could possibly resist?

My next decision took only an instant to make, but I immediately knew that it would affect me for the rest of my life.

'Don't,' I told her, grabbing her wrist.

She looked up at me, startled. 'What?' she asked, but then she smiled mischievously. 'Oh, I see . . . so you want to whip it out yourself, eh?' She sat back, grinning expectantly, watching my crotch. 'Go on, then, big boy. Let's see what kind of weapon it is you're packing down there . . .'

'You don't get it,' I told her, shuffling quickly sideways. 'I don't want to whip it out at all.'

I'd love to be able to claim that the reason for my unexpected reticence was because I'd suddenly remembered where my true loyalties lay. Say, because I'd been stung by a mental image of Ben waiting for me at home. Or because my wedding ring had unexpectedly flashed in the evening sun. Or any other such honourable and noble qualm.

But I can't.

Similarly I wish I could say that my guilty conscience had stepped in at the last moment and tripped my erotic fuse, thereby cutting off the supply of hormones and endorphins to my loins, and sending Phalius scuttling back into the darkness from whence he'd come.

But that's not true either.

I *did* still want to have sex with Jessie. Not only did I want to jump her bones, but I wanted to tickle her tonsils too. And twiddle with her bits. And brush up on my Brazilian linguistic skills. Not to mention have her up against the mirror. And draped across the desk. As well as out on the balcony, cheekily from behind.

No, the reason for my sudden reticence was neither a surfeit of scruples, nor a lack of desire.

It was the dope.

It was the fact that I was fuddled. And muddled. And horrified at the thought of making any decision, let alone an emotional one, or one that required a rational weighing up of pros and cons, or a choice between right and wrong.

What happened was this: I panicked. I fell back on the one thing I had left: my instinct. And my instinct told me to keep my todger in my pants, and get the heck out of Dodge.

Which would have been fine, except that Jessie's agenda was radically different to mine.

'Where do you think you're going?' she demanded.

'Away.'

'Away where?'

'Anywhere. Home. I'm sorry. It's not your fault.'

I'd have apologised a thousand times, if that was what it took to get me out of there. All of a sudden, I felt like I was trapped in a bad dream. *Let me out, let me out!* a voice inside me screamed.

But the further I shuffled sideways along the sofabed, the further Jessie shuffled sideways as well across the floor. Until we were eyeballing each other above my unbuckled belt, like two crabs locked in a stand off over a piece of meat.

'It's too late for second thoughts now, Jack,' she warned me.

'Look. I've said I'm sorry, and I should have said something before, but I've really got to go.'

'Before when?' Jessie asked, half-smiling now. 'Before I walked in here naked?'

I looked to the ceiling, suddenly wishing she was dressed. 'Yes.'

'Or do you mean before you lay down here on the bed with me and told me all about your sex life?'

I looked to the door. 'That too.'

'Or what about before you decided to get stoned with me downstairs and started flirting with me?'

I looked to the window. 'Yes, before that as well.'

'So you do admit you *were* flirting with me?'

I looked to the floor. 'Yes, but –'

'Good, because I'd hate to have somehow misunderstood what you meant when you told me that you thought I was attractive. Or to have misread your intentions when you pressed yourself up against me on the way up the stairs . . .'

I finally looked back at her. 'Now hang on a minute. You were the one who –'

'But most of all, Jack,' she cut in, 'I'd really hate to have misinterpreted the significance of that swelling in your jeans just now, when I was trying to unbutton your flies . . .'

Her eyes glinted, like someone who knew she'd just won an argument. Like someone who knew she was about to get her way.

But she was wrong. Because this wasn't about debating prowess. Or logic of any kind. This was still about what my instinct was telling me. And my instinct was still telling me to run.

I tried to stand up. She pushed me back down.

'You're not going anywhere,' she said. 'We're going to finish what we've started, and you're going to thank me for it too, because I know it's what you really want . . .'

Even though I wasn't moving, my heart had started pounding like I was running for a bus.

Then I did move. And fast.

I rolled back across the sofabed and bolted for the door.

'Come back!' Jessie yelled.

No way, José. I was running for my life.

I stumbled through the doorway and half-fell, half-sprinted down the first flight of stairs. As I landed in a heap at the bottom, I yelped out in pain, and clutched at my right ankle, which I'd twisted on the way down.

Jessie appeared at the top of the stairs, like a villain in a slasher movie. She glared down at me as I squirmed.

'Look at you. You're pathetic. And you call yourself a man?'

With all the swagger of a gladiator closing in on a wounded opponent to deliver the *coup de grâce*, she strode down the stairs. A flash memory hit me of the ease with she'd dealt with Roland. This woman was a Taikwondo queen. She could probably snap me in two.

'How dare you not want to screw me!' She planted her hands on her hips.

'You got me stoned,' I groaned, as I tentatively tried putting my weight on my right foot, and winced. 'It's not my fault, and I've already apologised. What more do you want?'

But she wasn't listening. 'And don't you dare tell me that you'd rather be with your stupid frump of a wife, with her stupid frumpy, suburban life . . .' Jessie glowered at me with all the arrogance and contempt of a catwalk model. 'Because I won't believe a word . . .'

The one advantage of the pain in my ankle was that my head had suddenly cleared.

Which in turn had led to the realisation that Jessie was behaving in a not dissimilar fashion to Glemn Close in *Fatal Attraction*.

She was also dissing my wife.

'Don't talk about Amy like that.'

'Fuck Amy,' she snapped, 'and fuck you. And you know what?' she sneered. 'She's welcome to you. Because looking at you now, I've no idea what I saw in you to begin with. You're not even that good looking! *And* your hairline's receding. *And* you've got BO.'

Anger raced through me, flushing out whatever remaining intentions I'd had of extricating myself from this situation with politeness, dignity and calm. So she wanted to make this personal? Well, fine. Two could play that game. Taikwondo, or no Taikwondo, I was going to say my piece.

'Oh, yeah?' I snapped back, struggling to my feet, before firing back the most sophisticated insult my mind could conjure up at such short notice. 'Well, your minge looks like a burnt fishfinger.'

Her face turned puce. *Oh yeah, baby,* I thought to myself. *Welcome to my world . . . Now you see what happens when you tangle with the Jack-meister . . .*

She pointed down the corridor and bellowed, 'Get out of my fucking house!'

'Oh, I'm gone,' I answered, hobbling away as fast as I could. 'And you're right,' I yelled back. 'I do think your show's shit.'

She caught up with me at the bottom of the next flight.

'You've got bad breath and teeth like Austin Powers',' she hissed.

I spun round to face her. 'Yeah, well you should fire your plastic surgeon, because your tits don't match.'

'You're a fucking liar.'

'No, I'm fucking not. Look for yourself. The left one's bigger than the right, *and* you can see the scars.'

This was complete crap, of course, but boy, did it hit the mark. Old Boss-eyed Boobs let out a bestial scream.

'Wanker,' she shouted after me, as I hurried to the top of the marble staircase.

'Cow.'

She ran after me, then stopped.

'You're fucking fired,' she said.

'No, I'm fucking not, because I fucking quit.'

As we glared at each other, panting, it occurred to me that, not since Aaron Wilson had bitten the head off my Darth Vader figurine in the playground in 1979 and told me that my shoes smelt of wee, had I engaged in such a vitriolic slanging match.

But there was something else about this situation that was appallingly familiar too, and what Jessie said next revealed exactly what it was.

'Mouse-cocked mummy's boy,' she spat at me, as her eyes narrowed to slits.

So here it was, the exact same phrase she'd used to describe Roland on that fatal day when first we met.

A phrase designed to emasculate. A phrase designed to bring a man to his knees.

That's when it hit me with absolute clarity. This wasn't about me. This was about her. If it wasn't me standing here, it would be someone else. This was Jessie's *modus operandi*. This is what she did.

Jessie Kay was a Manipulator of Men.

She was a puppeteer and I was just her latest toy.

Now, because I'd refused to do exactly what she wanted, she was throwing me out of her cot.

All of which meant that Roland was no longer my sworn mortal enemy, but my Brother-in-Arms.

I quickly considered redeploying some of the abusive phrases he'd tossed her way ('psychotic slut', for example, struck me as a particularly apt initial volley).

Then I clamped my mouth shut.

What did any of this actually matter? I *wasn't* Roland. I was Jack Rossiter. Jessie wasn't my girlfriend. She was my boss. And even though I'd come close – damned close – I hadn't actually done anything with her. Which meant I didn't have to deal with her now, or put up with any more of her shit.

There was nothing, in other words, to stop me from turning my back on her and limping away.

So that's exactly what I did.

I kept my mouth shut and closed my ears to the machine-gun rattle of insults that chased me across the hallway and out of the front door and down the drive.

I kept walking, and I didn't stop until I reached the Skip, which was parked on the other side of the street.

It was only then that I froze in my tracks, and my brow furrowed, as somewhere in the back of my mind, a red alert bulb began to flash.

I stared down. And that's when I saw it: I had nothing on my feet. Neither shoes nor socks. Jesus style.

I'd left my flip-flops in the house.

I had become the Shoeless Man.

I stared back up the driveway at the front door of Jessie's house, which even from here, I could see was still ajar.

I took a step towards it.

Then stopped.

I'd been about to make the same howling schoolboy error as Roland. I'd been about to walk back *in*. *After* I'd walked *out*.

And if there were two things my short-lived relationship with Jessie Kay had taught me, they were these:

There are some things in life that aren't worth going back for.

There are some things in life that are worth leaving behind for good.

As I drove away, I remembered once more what my estate agent friend had always liked to claim: that if Notting Hill really did have a beating heart, then St Thomas's Gardens could be said to be its pacemaker.

Well, during my time here, I now realised, I'd been nothing but a clot.

It Ended With A Kiss

I stare desperately at Amy across the table in Milady's.

My heart's pounding with adrenaline. My chest feels tight, like I'm gasping for air. All this nastiness I've told Amy . . . all this nastiness I'm trying to leave behind . . . it makes me feel like I'm trying to out-swim a shark, and Amy's my only hope. If she doesn't reach out for me now, if she doesn't forgive me, then that's it; I'm fucked; my life's not worth a damn.

'You mean you didn't actually do anything?' she says.

She's staring at me with tears shining in her eyes.

I knock back my glass of Dark and Stormy.

'That's not the point. I wanted to, and I nearly did. And I promised you once that I never would. Never again. Not after Sally McCullen. Don't you get it? I thought I had Phalius under control, but I was wrong. And –'

'Who the hell is Phalius?' she interrupts.

274

I screw up my face, a little drunk, a lot confused, astounded that I've really just said that name out loud. 'Nobody.'

'Who?'

'It doesn't matter.'

But from the expression on Amy's face, it's clear that it does.

'My cock,' I admit.

'Your cock.'

'Yes.'

'Your cock has a name?'

'No. I mean, not specifically, but yes, I suppose . . .'

Amy stares at me in astonishment. 'After seven years of marriage, you tell me this? Who do you think you are, Jack? D H Fucking Lawrence?'

D H *Fucking* Lawrence? I'm guessing that she's not referring to a porn star, but to the famous novelist and poet who wrote *Lady Chatterley's Lover*, where the two main characters used to refer to their genitals by nicknames.

'No, of course not,' I say.

'But you really do call your cock Phalius?'

'Not actually call, no. Not out loud. That would be ridiculous. Not to mention schizophrenic. But, yes. That is how I sometimes think of him.'

'*Him?*'

'Well he's hardly a her . . .'

She growls. 'Whatever. Look, I don't want to talk about Penius –'

'Phalius.'

'Can you please just shut up about him – *it* – for one minute?'

'Of course.'

'And think about the facts. Which are that you got yourself into a bad situation with Jessie – but probably only because you were stoned – and you still managed to get yourself back out. You still acted on instinct. You still came back to me.'

She's looking at me with the same mixture of deter-mination, anxiety and distress you might encounter on the face of a veterinary student shoving their hand up a cow's arse for the very first time.

I stare back at her, dumbfounded. Why is she being this nice to me? If it was the other way round, I'd go spare . . .

'You mean you're all right about this? You mean you don't mind?'

'Well, I'm not exactly delirious about you hanging around in strange women's bedrooms, no, but there's nothing to forgive. You taught yourself a lesson, Jack, and everyone messes up from time to time. Everyone.'

Everyone except you, I think

I don't deserve her. I really don't.

I feel my heart leap and I grab her hands.

'God, I love you,' I tell her.

Exhilaration and relief run through me hand in hand, like lovers through a field of summer clover. I feel like I'm sitting here naked. I've said it. It's out. I've got nothing left to hide. Amy *was* right, I realise, as I stare gratefully into her eyes. Just like Amy's *always* right. The truth *does* heal. It *does* make things better, not tear them apart.

I swallow hard, tears in my eyes. Now that I've got her back, I don't want to risk losing her again.

'I don't *ever* want to come that close again,' I tell her, 'to messing things up between us. That's why things have got to change. We've got to start taking more care of each other. No matter what happens. No matter what it takes. We've got to make our lives great again. And I swear to you now, if I'm ever tempted to do something stupid again, then I'll tell you straightaway.' I squeeze her hands in mine. 'I want to be a good husband, Amy, and a good father. I don't want to end up like my dad. I don't want Ben to end up hating me. I want to spend the rest of my life with you. I want to make you happy and give you everything you deserve.'

I'm saying all this to make her feel good, but she actually starts to cry.

Panic leaps inside me. 'What is it?' She won't look at me. 'You said you were OK . . . You said you –'

'I –' She tries to speak, but she's too choked up to get the words out.

'I'm sorry,' I tell her. I hate myself for having hurt her like this. 'I'm so sorry. Please, Amy, please don't cry . . .'

She buries her head in her hands and starts to shake.

'I love you, Amy. I love you and everything's going to be all right. I swear it to you. I swear that I'll –'

'Stop it,' she tells me, looking up. Her eyes are blood-shot and raw 'You don't understand. It's not you who's messed things up. It's me.' She blinks heavily and a tear runs down her cheek. 'Can't you see that, Jack? It's *me*.' She looks like she's about to be sick. 'I'm the one who's ruined it all.'

I feel like all the air's being sucked out of the room.

'What are you talking about?' I ask.

What she says, she says quickly. Her words topple over each other, like pennies falling off the shelf in an arcade machine. There's something about an internet date. A guy called Tom who works in publishing. Trafalgar Square at night. A kiss. And then another day. Another meeting. Where she tried to break it off with him. But didn't.

I feel like I'm suffocating.

Promises and assurances wash over me. Bullshit that I don't want to hear.

Amy did what I never did.

She kissed someone else.

I don't care about the rest.

When I stand up, I stumble and sway, like a man on the deck of a sinking ship.

As I look down at her and she continues to speak and continues to cry, I hear nothing, and I feel nothing.

I don't even know who she is.

I turn my back on her.

I walk towards the door.

I don't bother looking round to see if she's following, because I don't want to look at her at all.

Turn Around

I break into a run, the second I'm outside.

I sprint past packed cafés and bars. There's music all around. People are laughing and drinking at tables on the sidewalk. Basketball players rush up and down a floodlit court. Cars hiss by. Sound systems blare. I pound the sidewalk until my lungs feel like they're going to burst.

I slump in the doorway of a diner. Then I see the light of a cab and I stick out my hand.

As soon as it pulls over, I climb in.

'Where d'ya wanna go?' the Mexican driver asks.

All I get is a slice of his face in the rear-view mirror, like he's staring at me through a letterbox.

'I don't know,' I say. 'Just drive.'

'What?' he wisecracks. 'Like in the movies?'

'Yeah. Like that.'

He shrugs. 'Sure, man. Whatever you say.'

He flicks on the meter and we pull out into the traffic. I curl up in my seat.

I feel dazed, like I've been hit repeatedly over the head with a sledgehammer.

I can't believe what she's done. I try running it through my head, but it makes no sense.

How can this have happened? How can she have pulled the wool over my eyes like this? All this time, I thought *I* was the threat to our family, when all along it was her.

I think about Ben.

I think about Amy.

I think about me.

But I can't think about us together. Not any more.

I gaze through my half-reflection in the cab window, at the

278

neon lights of the New York stores. At the strangers all around. At the strangeness of it all.

As we enter Times Square, I think about John Voigt in *Midnight Cowboy*, and how it was for him when he first hit town. That's what I'm like now. Only a lot less gay, clearly, and without a stetson on my head. But just like him, I'm lost in a place that I don't understand. Just like him, I'm lost.

The cab passes a subway station, and I remember the customer satisfaction questionnaire I filled out on the train journey to Heathrow Airport on the way out here.

At the beginning, where they ask you to tick the demographic box, I'd noticed that I'd moved up an age bracket, from 25–34, to 35-50.

Well, maybe that's what this is: the end of the last stage of my life, and the beginning of the next.

I wipe the sweat from my brow on the back of my hand, and I notice my wedding ring. In the gloom of the cab, it looks like a groove that's been cut into my flesh, right down to the bone.

I feel so sick, it's all I can do not to spew.

I can't get away from the facts, and the facts are black-and-white. She's wrong and I'm right. We've got nothing left to say to each other.

We've got nothing left.

For a married man, with very little money to his name, no luggage, and a free flight ticket home back at the hotel he's meant to be staying at with his wife, I then do a very strange thing.

But for me, after what's happened, it's the only thing I can do.

I check my jacket pocket to see that both my wallet and my passport are there, And then I say to the driver, 'Can you please turn around?'

'You wanna go back to SoHo?' he asks.

'No,' I tell him. 'Take me to the airport. Take me to JFK. As fast as you can.'

279

Because that's where I'm going: home.

Or to London, anyway.

Because I don't even know what the word home means any more.

15

amy

The Everest Of Moral High Ground . . .

It's Tuesday and I'm in my mother's kitchen and I'm high with exhaustion. I'm actually not sure how I've managed to get myself here, but if nothing else, the last twenty-four hours have proved that I'm more resilient than I thought.

I've come straight here from the airport, by train and cab. I haven't slept – except fitfully on the plane – since Jack left me in Milady's on Sunday night. That seems like it happened in a different universe.

At first, when Jack stormed out, I thought that he'd gone on a New York drinking bender. So I went back to the hotel room to wait for him. I sat on the bed, watching the door, paralysed. *He may hate me for what I've done*, I told myself, *but he can't hate me forever. Can he?*

By the next morning, when Jack hadn't shown up, my fear about our relationship had warped into something else entirely. By lunch time, I'd convinced myself that Jack had been mugged and didn't have any way of getting back to the hotel. By mid-afternoon, he'd been brutally murdered in the Bronx. Which is when I got the hotel staff involved, and they in turn called the NYPD.

It was only when I was about to cancel my flight on Monday night, and Officer Delancy was about to file a missing persons report, that Matt called, and I discovered that Jack was already back in the UK and wasn't dead at all.

Which is when I got angry.

It hadn't even occurred to me that Jack would ever do that. That he would be so *stupid* and *selfish* to do that.

That he would send me to hell and back.

Putting aside my obvious embarrassment, about having to explain the situation to the exhausted hotel staff and apologise for wasting NYPD time, I'm still incensed that Jack didn't give me the chance to explain myself. After I'd been so understanding about Jessie, the least he could have done was hear me out.

I may have been stupid – delusional even – in the whole affair with Tom, but Jack leaving me in New York, is worse. Much, much worse.

How dare he walk out on me?

How dare he ruin our trip like that?

I must be the only person in the world who could win a trip to the shopping Mecca of America and fail to buy anything. I even came home with *change*.

So I'm staggered that Jack has claimed the moral high ground – and we're talking The Everest of moral high ground – when he's got no right to have even made it to base camp.

And to add insult to injury, my longed-for reunion with Ben just now was also a total disaster.

'Wabby Daddy gone?' he asked me, by way of hello.

I tried to gather him up into my arms, but he punched me.

'I want my Dadda!'

'Daddy's not here, darling,' I said, catching his wrist, before he hit me again. 'Haven't you got a kiss for Mummy?'

'No.'

I stayed crouched on the floor, my arms outstretched towards him, as he stomped away from me into the garden.

Then I burst into tears.

Mum immediately went into action mode. Which is why I'm now sitting at her kitchen table, with a cup of tea and a box of Kleenex in front of me on the floral plastic tablecloth.

'He'll come round,' she says, setting the teapot down. 'He's probably just trying to punish you for leaving him for so long. You're lucky he didn't bite you. Some children do that to their parents, you know. When they've been left.'

Honestly, can she make me feel any worse? I detect a slight note of satisfaction that Ben has rejected me.

'Anyway, I should imagine you're exhausted. Now that you're here, why don't you have a sleep, darling?' she says. 'I can make up your old bed and –'

'No, Mum. Thanks anyway, but I really have to get home.'

I watch Ben in her back garden on the new slide she's bought for him, next to the huge sandpit. He's clearly been having the time of his life. He obviously hasn't missed me at all.

Am I really that dispensable?

Apparently I am. The men in my life seem to think so. They're deserting me in droves.

'Just give him a few days,' Mum says. 'By the end of the week he'll have forgiven you.'

'What?' I ask, homing back in on her. 'Don't worry, Mum. I'm not really upset about Ben. It's just . . . nothing. It's been a fraught few days, that's all.'

'Did you have a wonderful time?'

'Yes and no.'

There's a pause. I take a sip of my tea. I don't want to tell her. I'm determined not to involve her. I've already lied once and told her Jack isn't here because he had to go straight back to work, but I can feel my resolve crumbling. The need for someone to be on my side, to feel sorry for *me*, feels overwhelming.

'So . . . do you want to tell me what happened?' she asks, gently.

I blow my nose. Exhaustion has left me weak and defenceless against my mother's probing stare. 'Jack and I had a silly row in New York, that's all. And Jack . . . he left and came home . . .' I describe my day from hell yesterday.

She puts her hand to her mouth. 'He did that? Jack

283

really did that? Of all the mean, cowardly, ungentlemanly things –'

'Mum, please . . .'

'But . . . but . . . but . . . *anything* could have happened to you. Doesn't he *care*?'

'It's OK. I'm a grown-up. I was fine,' I lie.

My mother's reaction has made Jack's behaviour seem much worse. Even more indefensible. Even less forgivable.

But I still feel I should back-track. Somehow, by grassing him up, I've crossed a boundary, taken myself out of the Jack and Amy team and realigned myself with my mother, and I'm too long in the tooth for that. Added to which, I've clearly trashed Jack's fragile relationship with his mother-in-law. She'll never forgive him for this. I can see it in her face.

'I don't want you to worry, Mum. It's nothing. Jack just wants . . . he just needed some time on his own.'

But the truth is that I don't know what Jack wants or needs. Certainly not any contact with me or his son. Apparently, he's decamped to Matt's house and, according to Matt, has thrown his mobile phone away. Jack has been back in England for twenty-four hours and hasn't bothered to come to pick up Ben.

'It's another woman, isn't it?' Mum says.

'Mum! It's not like that –'

'Because your father was the same. He had the roving eye. I know what it's like . . .'

'Jack's not –'

'But to *leave* you! I mean, what's he playing at? You're the *mother of his child.*'

She puts her hand on her chest and looks poignantly out at Ben. I roll my eyes. This is what years of watching day-time soaps does for you.

'It wasn't Jack, it was me,' I say, which stops her in her tracks. 'I told him about something that had happened between me and another man and he . . . well, he didn't react too well.'

284

Mum looks me over, trying to take in what I've just said. I can't hold her gaze. She leans across and puts her hand over mine.

'Has he been hitting you?'

'What?'

'Jack. You can tell me if he was. Domestic violence is very common you know, darling. You wouldn't be the first woman to find comfort in the arms of another man. Angela Dixon down the road . . . her daughter –'

I rub my face and sigh. 'Mum, please, you're just making this worse. It's nothing like that.'

She takes a sip of tea and looks at me. I hadn't realised how old she looks these days. Will *I* look like her soon? Are those crow's feet going to come home to roost on my face any day now? Is my brow going to become creased from a permanent distrust of the opposite sex? Is that where I'm heading?

'You and this other man . . . has it been going on for long?' Mum asks me, in the pinched, pretending-not-to-care way she does. I remember her asking me whether I'd been having sex for long with my first boyfriend, at this very table. Experience has taught me, it's best not to answer.

'No. Look. It was nothing. I shouldn't have said anything. Please don't worry about us. Jack and I have just had a tough few months that's all, and –'

'I'm not surprised it's tough. Living in that grotty flat. In London. It would be so much better if you lived nearer me. You could have a proper house then. Ben has positively thrived in all this fresh air, with a big garden –'

'I've told you before, we can't afford to move –'

'But if you lived near me, you could get a part time job, and I could look after Ben.'

She's obviously got it all figured out. I can't believe I'm in the middle of the biggest relationship crisis of my life and, somehow, it's all about *her*.

'I couldn't get the type of job I wanted around here,' I say, dismissing her scary suggestion. 'Look, it's no problem,

Mum. I like looking after Ben. I thought it was what *you* wanted me to do?'

'I do, but I hate to see you scrimping and saving. If that husband of yours got a proper job, instead of mucking about doing all that gardening for next to nothing . . .'

'It's not mucking about, and it's not for next to nothing,' I say, feeling my hackles rise. I thought she was pleased that Jack was working for Greensleeves. 'Jack gave up his dream of being an artist so that he could support me and Ben. You can't ask for more of a sacrifice than that.' I stand up. 'And I'd appreciate it if you didn't use this opportunity to start picking apart our marriage, because, for your information, Mother, it's a very good one.'

'Not from where I'm sitting, it's not. You might not want to hear it, Amy, but it takes two to tango. You might have made a few mistakes, but why? That's what you've got to ask. Because that so-called brilliant husband of yours wasn't paying enough attention, that's why.'

'Can you just stop making assumptions?'

'And as for him taking parenting seriously? Well!'

There's no stopping her. She's on a roll.

'Will you shut up! Jack's an excellent father. Ben worships him,' I shout at her.

'So where is he? Where is he when it counts?'

My chin wobbles and tears fall down my face. It's checkmate. I hate her.

Facing The Enemy

My mother has clearly not followed any of my instructions whilst I was away. Ben's routine is out of the window, and he's fast asleep by the time we get to the flat, even though it's nearly tea time.

Jack must be back, I tell myself, in spite of the fact that I've already called the home phone five times and only got his voice on the answer machine.

I will him to be there. I will him to have come to his senses

286

and left Matt's house. I open the door, struggling with my bag and Ben, who is like a deadweight on my shoulder. I haven't carried this much for years and my muscles scream with agony.

Hearing the thump of the front door behind me brings my familiar world back in a sudden rush, washing away New York, breaking the whole experience from me like a piece of driftwood.

'Jack?' I call out. 'Jack?'

I'm exhausted. I'm on my knees.

I need him.

He must have calmed down by now. He must have realised how bad I'm feeling. He must be desperate to see Ben, if nothing else.

I strain my ears, desperate for him to call out my name, for the hysteria of New York, the misunderstandings, to be washed away too, for sanity and normality to be returned.

The flat is empty.

I put Ben in his cot in our room. I watch him stir, but he doesn't wake up. I lean down over him and stroke his face. I'm glad he's home. I'm glad he's back with me, where he belongs.

I look around our bedroom. At first it all seems normal, and then I notice that the alarm clock from Jack's side of the bed has gone, along with my favourite framed picture of Ben. I open the wardrobe and gasp. Jack's taken most of his clothes. The only thing that remains is the suit that he got married in.

I grab the arm of it and hold it to my face.

And I swallow. My throat feels scratchy and dry.

This is real, then. I haven't returned to normality, at all. Jack has gone.

Frantically, I search the rest of the flat. There's no note, no communication at all. There's a message on the answer machine from Kate, telling me that she's away, but has heard what's happened and will be home tomorrow to chat. Like I need her advice.

287

I leaf through the pile of mail on the hall table, and in amongst all the pizza flyers, I spot an envelope addressed to me.

I rip it open.

Inside is a signed photo.

The photo I requested from Radio CapitalChat.

Of Jessie Kay.

I stand and stare at her for ages, feeling sick. She's smiling, her sultry eyes transmitting a knowing intelligence. She has perfect make-up, perfect teeth, glossy hair and a neckline that plunges to a perfect cleavage. So much for being 'lumpy and on the turn'. She's undeniably gorgeous. The kind of woman men of all ages drool over.

I look up and see my own reflection in the mirror on the wall. By contrast, I look creased and washed out. I've got blobs of make-up wedged in the corners of my bloodshot eyes, which are lined with deep gothic shadows. My hair is greasy and pulled back from my face and I've got a smear of ketchup down my white T-shirt. When I breath in, I realise that the nasty smell in the flat is *me*.

Is half Jack's upset to do with regret? Is he pissed off that he didn't do anything with her? That he had the opportunity to fuck the living daylights out of a woman like Jessie and he didn't do it? And now he feels a fool and wishes he had, because he knows that while he wasn't kissing her, I was kissing someone else.

Maybe that's why he's not here. Maybe he's intent on revenge. Maybe he's gone on the rampage, to find someone to be unfaithful with, like his lying, cheating wife.

Maybe he's even gone back to Jessie. Maybe he's there right now.

I'm too miserable to eat anything and nothing in the fridge appeals. I open a bottle of wine and pour myself a large glass.

I sit at the kitchen table, feeling totally at a loss. Without Jack here, it doesn't feel like a home. It feels like a cramped little cage.

I sigh and put my head on the table.

This is intolerable.

I get up and retrieve the picture of Jessie Kay. Then I take one of Ben's felt-tip pens and draw a moustache on her face. Then I rip it into tiny pieces and throw it in the bin.

I'm not sure why I hate her so much. I'm not sure which is worse: that she tried to seduce Jack, or that she failed. Because the fact she failed, when Tom didn't, means that Jack is stronger than I am – and that's something I can't live with, because he'll never let me forget it.

I boot up my laptop and get on line. Just as I suspect, there's an e-mail in my in-box from Tom.

Amy from West London – are you back? Did you have a chance to think? I'd love to see you again . . .

A wave of revulsion and annoyance sweeps over me. He's like an over-enthusiastic puppy. And H is right. He hardly knows me. How dare he think that I'll just give in to him. If it wasn't for Tom, I wouldn't be in this mess.

There is nothing to think about, I type back. *I'm sorry if I confused you and gave you the wrong signals, but I am not the girl for you.*

I stare at my message. Then delete the word 'girl' and replace it with 'woman'. And then, to make sure I don't leave any room for manoeuvre, I add: *Don't ever contact me again.*

I press Send, and then I delete his details from my mail list. Just like that, he vanishes back to cyber-space.

Action Stations

A few hours later, H is pacing in my kitchen. I've poured my heart out to her and told her everything that's happened.

'Didn't I warn you?' she says, clearly exasperated.

'I didn't think he'd go off the deep end, like that. I thought . . .'

I fizzle out. What *did* I think? Or didn't I think at all? At the time, I certainly didn't think about the *consequences* of spilling the beans. All I wanted to do was the actual spilling. I felt so dreadful after Jack's confession, I just couldn't help myself. But it seems that H was right. All I've succeeded in doing is making a giant sloppy mess.

'You stupid, stupid idiot, Amy.'

She sighs and shakes her head, then she looks at me and her features soften into sympathy as yet more tears start leaking out of my eyes.

'You've got to help me get him back, H. He won't listen to me, but he might listen to you.'

'Where is he?

'He's moved back in with Matt. He must know I'm home, though. He knew the times of my flight. I thought if we went round there . . .'

I look at her, expecting her to refuse. I know how she feels about seeing Matt. After their tempestuous relationship ended, they've done nothing but bitch each other off. But to my surprise, she nods.

'Let's go.'

She's amazing. Cometh the hour, cometh the woman. I feel stronger with her by my side.

Swallowing my pride, I ring up Camilla and ask to borrow Yitka. Camilla makes it perfectly clear that this is a huge favour I'm asking, and I don't have any choice but to suck up to her. Ten minutes later, Yitka turns up to look after Ben, and I leave with H.

It's odd being back in a car outside the converted pub where Matt lives. I feel like we're teenagers and we're out stalking a boyfriend.

'You ready?' H asks.

I nod and get out of the car.

But despite knocking on the door, Matt's not home, and if Jack's in there, he's not answering.

'What do we do now?' I ask.

'I'll call Matt,' H says. I'm surprised she still has his number on her phone.

I can see the lights on inside. 'Jack,' I call. 'Jack, it's me.

Open up. I've got to talk to you.' I kneel down and look through the letterbox.

'I know he's in there. I just know it,' I tell H.

'Matt will be here soon,' she says. She's spoken to him. 'Then we can get this thing over and done with.'

I sit on the doorstep with H, looking out at the traffic. It always used to be so quiet here, but since this area's become more and more gentrified, it's busier than ever.

'Do you ever think about Matt?'

'Sometimes.'

'Any regrets?'

'No we both tried, but the timing was all wrong. I wanted things to go to the next stage and he wanted to go back down the pub.'

'Are you nervous about seeing him?'

'No. Only annoyed that I'm not wearing a big fuck off engagement ring to shove down his throat.'

Right then Matt pulls up in his BMW, and when I glance at H, rather than looking like she would carry out such a threat, she looks like a breathless schoolgirl. We both stand up.

Matt's as flash as ever, in a trendy Paul Smith suit, with sunglasses on his head. He smiles, as he jogs towards us.

'Wow, H. You're looking . . . great.' He stops and stares at her. She stares right back.

'Thanks.'

'Good. Good,' Matt says, obviously at a loss. He's usually so full of sarcasm and banter. They still haven't broken eye contact with each other.

'Hi,' I say.

Matt looks at me, as if he's only just clocked me. 'Er . . . yes . . . Jack. I hope you've come to take him home. I don't want him.'

We're still standing on the doorstep.

'Come in,' Matt says, unlocking the door.

I haven't been to Matt's place for ages. He's redecorated, and I miss the old shabby décor, but still the smell of the place

– the onslaught of memories of when I first got together with Jack – hits me like a slap.

I watch Matt disappear upstairs and H and I stand in the living room. The bar's still there and the dartboard.

I wonder if she's having a similar attack of nostalgia. She runs her hand along the back of the tatty old leather sofa and doesn't speak.

Matt comes back down a moment later. He flexes his fingers together. 'He won't come out of his room,' he says.

'Oh, for God's sake!' H says. 'Tell him to grow up. Make him come out.'

'I can't. He's not answering and the door's locked.'

'What the hell's he doing in there?' H asks.

'The usual. I expect. Listening to shit music. Drinking my booze. Playing guitar badly and becoming a borderline depressive. He's been like that since he got back. In other words, he's reverted to type. He's doing exactly what he used to do in the old days, whenever he broke up with someone . . .'

I see H glare and him and flick her eyes towards me.

'Oops,' Matt says. 'I meant to say whenever he *rowed* with someone.'

'Let me speak to him,' I say.

Matt moves to come with me.

'Alone.'

'Sure. Of course, of course. Go right ahead.'

I walk down the corridor to Jack's old room and knock.

'Jack? Jack? It's me.'

Nothing.

I put my ear to the door. I can hear the radio playing inside. I picture him sitting on his old bed, listening to me. Just feet away.

'I know you can hear me, and I just want you to listen.'

I rest my forehead on the closed door. This is so hard.

'I want you to come home, Jack. I'm asking you to. For me and for Ben. For us all . . .'

Nothing.

292

I sigh.

'Listen, I know you're upset and angry, but the thing is . . . that whole thing with that other guy? With Tom. I wish you had have let me explain. I wish you hadn't left me in New York, because you don't need to feel as angry as you are. I know I made a mistake. I knew that almost right away. I never intended it to happen, I swear it.'

It's odd having this conversation with Jack, knowing he's listening. I feel oddly encouraged, that I'm able to get my argument out, without him interrupting me for once.

'Maybe it did happen because we'd been growing so far apart, but I know that I never want that to happen ever again, that I will do everything in my power to make sure we get back on track.'

I can feel tears welling up. I just want him to open the door.

'We've both done stupid things, Jack,' I feel my throat tighten, 'and I understand why. I know that you're angry and hurt . . .'

I wipe tears away from my eyes.

'But those days in New York – before we fought – they were some of the best times of my life, and they made me remember how good we are together. How right.'

'Amy?'

My heart leaps at the sound of my name.

Then I realise it's coming from behind me, and not in front. It's Matt whispering. He's at the end of the corridor. I wave my hand at him, to tell him to go away. How can he be so insensitive? I press my head back against the door, willing it to open.

'You're the person I want to grow old with, Jack –'

'Amy?'

I flap my hand more vigorously at Matt. Can't he see I'm in the middle of the most important conversation of my life?

'All I want you to do,' I say, sniffing, 'is to open this door and we can start our future together. Jack, please. You remember? The future we always –'

'Amy?'

'Go away,' I hiss to Matt, before realising that he's right next to me.

'But he's not there,' Matt whispers, then clears his throat, and says in a normal voice, 'I mean, Jack's not there.'

'Not there?' I look at the door. The door I've just poured my heart out to. 'Well, where is he?'

'Dartmoor.'

'Where?'

'Dartmoor.'

'But what's he doing there?'

'Fishing.'

'Fishing?'

'And camping. He left a note,' Matt says, holding out a piece of paper towards me. 'I've just found it. He says he needs time to think. And he really has gone. I've checked. He's taken his tent and his rod.'

'I didn't even know he had a tent.'

'Oh yeah, one of the many things he's left cluttering up my house since he moved out. He was a great one for the boy scout thing, before he met you. He and I used to go camping at least once a year together. He loved it, said it always helped him think. I guess that's why he's gone. Because he's got a lot of thinking to do . . .'

I fight back tears and nod. Matt gives me a hug.

'Hey, don't worry. He might think he's the big outdoors type, but Jack doesn't really like his own company very much. He'll only last a couple of days, tops – and besides,' he adds, with a knowing smile, 'the weather forecast is shit.'

The Waiting Game

The next day, Ben is full of energy, but I can barely function. Despite my mother's prediction that it would take until the end of the week for my son to forgive me, he's full of affection and cuddles. Somehow, it only makes me miss Jack more.

294

I can't believe he's gone to Dartmoor. By himself. I imagine him sitting at the river's edge with his fishing rod, lonely and cold in the rain, thinking only that his wife has betrayed him, that the bond of trust we had is severed forever.

Then I go to Sainsbury's and Ben kicks off. As I battle with my thrashing, spitting son, who refuses to sit in the trolley at the check-out, I picture Jack sitting at the river's edge in the sunshine and, mentally, this time I push him in.

How dare he leave me like this!

I didn't do *anything* that justifies this level of punishment. He's being way out of line. This meting out of dispro-portionate revenge is, after all, how wars start. I mean, where is he planning on taking this? Are we going to end up swinging from a chandelier, like in *The War Of The Roses*, not content until we've killed each other?

The cashier is running the black cherry yoghurts I've chosen for Jack, through the scanner, and I stop her and tell her I don't want them. She scowls at me, but I don't care. Jack can buy his own fucking black cherry yoghurts.

Kate is in when I get home. She plays with Ben, while I put away the shopping. Then I put on a Teletubbies DVD and follow Kate into Ben's bedroom. She's in the middle of packing her bags.

'Where are you going?' I ask.

'I've decided it's better for you guys if I'm not here,' she says. 'I'm staying with Simon and then I'm moving next week. I don't want to get in the way.'

'Get in the way of what? There's only me and Ben here.'

'No, honestly, I think I should go. You need your personal space.'

A week ago, I would have found this magnanimous statement irritating in its sheer irony, but not now.

I never thought I'd think it, but with Jack not here, I rather wish Kate would stay, so that I don't have to spend another night on my own.

There's an awkward pause.

'Ben will miss you. He's enjoyed having you around. You're so good with him.'

'It's easy when it's someone else's kid.'

'Yes, well, for what it's worth, I think you'll make a great mum, one day.'

Kate laughs and then looks at me as if I'm crazy. 'Not me. I'm never going to have kids,' she says, shaking her head. 'Come to think of it, I don't know any of my friends who want one.'

'What . . . never?'

She shrugs.

'But don't you realise that having a child means experiencing the most powerful form of love there is?'

'So, if you feel like that, why do you moan about how hard it is all the time?'

Kate's comment hits me like a lorry-sized home truth that's just reversed into the flat.

'Do I?'

She nods.

Oh God. Maybe she's right. Maybe I am a big moaner. And it's not just Ben I've bellyached about, but Jack, too. On the radio. To thousands of listeners.

Did Jessie Kay home in on him because she thought I didn't love him? Did she feel sorry for him, when she heard what an ungrateful wife I was? I mean, all that stuff about him being a hypochondriac . . . and worse . . .

If Kate could get the impression that I don't love being Ben's mother, when nothing could be further from the truth, couldn't Jessie Kay have got the impression that I don't love being Jack's wife?

'You know,' Kate says, 'you and Jack . . . I really hope it works out for you both.'

'How can it, when he won't talk to me?'

'You'll just have to find a way to make him listen. He's a stubborn bastard, Amy. He always was. None of us can believe you have the patience to put up with him. But if he won't listen to you, or see you, then you're going to have to find another way.'

Then it occurs to me . . . . I *do* have another way.

I pick up the phone and call Matt. I've got a radio frequency for him to write down. To give Jack when he gets back. In time for my next slot on Jessie's show.

I'm Not Afraid To Speak My Mind

Radio CapitalChat
Jessie's Daily Discussion: What's the point of being married?
Caller: Amy from West London.

I think there's every point in being married. Because you don't really realise what it means, until you have a family. And until you're challenged. And people . . . people like you, Jessie Kay, should respect people who are married more, because sometimes it's difficult to tell how much two married people mean to each other. Because it's just not done to shout about how much you love your husband. I mean, people wear T-shirts saying I Love New York, or I Love Chocolate, but they never wear one saying, I Love My Husband. And us married lot – we don't snog in public any more. And people think we're boring and stuck in our ways. And yes, sometimes we are guilty of getting boring, of not taking care of our relationship, of forgetting to do something exciting once in a while. **Er . . . hang on a minute. Is this Amy? Amy from West London?** *And I may sound emotional, but I know that after seven years, my greatest achievement, by far, is my relationship with my husband.* **Well, Amy, I'm afraid this is a radio show, and we're debating the relevance of the institution of marriage in today's society. Not focusing on individual marital spats. I'm sorry, but this is not the place to sort out your personal problems –** *Isn't it, Jessie? Well, I'm sorry, but didn't you make it personal when you tried to sleep with my husband?*

Ooooo-kaaay. Thank you for your call. And next up . . . let's move on to some music –

Because you did try and seduce Jack, didn't you Jessie? In your house? Didn't you strip off naked and shove your big, false tits in my husband's face?

Alex? GET HER OFF MY SHOW –

But you know what? He wouldn't do it with you, Jessie, would he? Because he's got something that you'll never have: integrity. And Jack, if you're listening, you will never realise how much I respect you for that, and I want you to know that I'm sorry. Truly, deeply, terribly sorry for letting you down. For letting us down. I would give anything to take what I did back.

Alex. DID YOU HEAR WHAT I SAID?

But you've got to know that I've never, ever stopped loving you, Jack. Not for one second. In the whole time we've been together.

I'm sorry listeners, but my producer seems to be fast asleep. Amy get off the line. Now.

Oh, don't get your G-string in a twist. I'm going. I've said all I want to say. Apart from one other thing. Jessie Kay . . . Go fuck yourself!

I put the phone down and I'm shaking.

Almost immediately, the phone rings again. My heart leaps. It's Jack, I know it is.

'Hello?'

'Wow! Amy, that was incredible. I've been waiting for someone to sock it to the old bitch for ages. The entire production team is whooping here.'

'Alex?'

'She's going mental,' he laughs, 'absolutely mental.'

'I'm sorry, Alex. That was totally out of order. Are you going to get into trouble –'

'Of course I am – I was the one who was meant to pull the plug – but Jessie Kay deserves everything coming to her. She's been treating me like shit for years.'

'I'm still sorry.'

'Look I've got to go, but one more thing . . .'

'What?'

'Is it OK if I give you a call sometime in the next week? I haven't got time to talk now, but I'm moving to another radio station, a new one a friend of mine is setting up, and I think I might be able to use someone like you. You know, as part of the team. I haven't forgotten you mentioned getting into radio, and I need someone honest, who can suss out the bullshitters and who isn't afraid to speak her mind.'

'Are you serious?'

'I'm not promising anything right now . . . and there are some people I'll need to speak to first, but yeah, I really hope we can work something out. So . . . can I call you?'

'Yes. Definitely. And Alex, thank you. For everything.'

'You're welcome. And Amy. I want to hear all about Jack. My boyfriend Linus can't wait to find out what happens next.'

I put down the phone and stare at it, stunned.

You've Got To Have Faith

But nothing does happen next.

I pace around the flat. Every time a car goes past, I jump. I stare at the phone and check it for messages all morning, but in the end I can stand it no more.

I'm still shaking as I take Ben to the park. We head for the sandpit and he jumps out of his buggy and leaps in with all the other kids. It's crammed today. Fortunately, at least Ben seems totally unaware of my marital crisis.

I look around me and feel completely isolated. There are no men here, as usual, only women, and suddenly I'm terrified.

Is that it? Is Jack really not going to forgive me?

I can't believe that the unimaginable has happened.

I'm standing somewhere so familiar, and yet I feel like an alien. Everything has changed. I've just crash-landed into my future, and it's not how I expected it to be at all. It's barren and lonely and never-ending.

Then, just when I think I can't feel any worse, I see Faith and she waves.

Of all the people in the world, why did I have to bump into Faith today?

'Hi, Amy,' she says, as I slump on to the bench next to her. 'You look dreadful.'

'Thanks.'

'How was New York?'

'Don't ask.'

'What's the matter?'

'You really want to know?' *Oh Faith*, I think, *you're just going to love this, and you're going to rub my nose in it forever more . . .*

'Well, you know what?' I say, 'You're here and I need a friend. So you'll just have to do.'

'I don't understand?'

I take a deep, shuddering breath. 'Well, Faith, I think my husband's just left me.'

She stares at me, open mouthed.

There's a long pause.

And out of nowhere, wet, soggy, blubbering, uncontrolled sobbing overtakes me. Faith puts her hand on my arm. Then she hugs me.

'I'm sorry,' I tell her, eventually, blowing my nose and wiping away my tears. 'I've made a right bloody pig's ear of everything. I'm sorry to break down on you, like this –'

Faith smiles at me, then she positively grins.

'Oh Amy, thank fuck.'

'What?'

This is not the reaction I'm expecting.

'Don't you see?' she says, holding my wrist.

'No?'

'You have emotions after all. Thank the Lord. You're normal. You're not one of them.'

'Who?'

'That stupid group of bitches.'

'You mean the Vipers?'

'Is that what you call them? Very appropriate. Man, they make me feel so inadequate.'

'Me too,' I admit.

'Well I thought you were one of them. The most stupid cow of the lot, actually,' she says, but her eyes are kind.

'Me?'

'I thought you were perfect and nothing ever went wrong and you coped with everything all the time.'

I wipe my eyes and smile. 'Er . . . no.'

'You know, I've tried so hard to do this Mum thing. I thought it would be easy, but it's so difficult being so . . . so inane.'

I smile at her through my tears. 'Don't do yourself down, Faith. You're pretty good at being inane.'

She laughs.

'I just wish we could all be honest, like we're being now,' she says, 'because you know what? If it's any consolation, my life's not so great either.'

'Isn't it? You always seem to be in control to me.'

'That's all bollocks. I'm not in control at all. Far from it. And sometimes I get really low. Sometimes I really can't cope with doing all the childcare. I really can't cope with the person I've become.'

I can't quite take it in. Glancing at her now, I see she looks different. Like an ally, rather than an enemy.

'Really? You feel like that too?'

She nods.

I blow my nose, suddenly feeling much stronger.

'So what happened with Jack?' Faith asks, gently. 'You don't have to tell me, but . . . it might help.'

So I tell her all about Tom and Jack and what I said to Jessie Kay this morning on the radio, and she listens carefully and then tells me I've done the right thing.

The relief of telling Faith makes me feel more solid. I want to hug her for being such a good friend.

'Wow,' I say, after my confession. 'Well, if nothing else, I guess I'm glad you know now that I'm not like Camilla.'

'Half the time, I want to kill that stupid cow,' Faith says. 'The way she stirs everything up. The way she keeps us all in a group. It's not right. Why should having babies at the same time mean that we should have anything else in common?'

And we pick apart everything we hate about the Vipers. And it cheers me up no end.

'You know, Faith, I've just been wondering,' I say. 'Is there any way we could share some childcare? Because I'm hoping to go back to work.'

'Great idea,' she says. 'I was thinking of doing the same thing. I think work will keep me sane. Looking after Amalie full time is sending me over the edge.'

For the first time in days, as we discuss how we might make it work, I feel almost normal.

Then I see him.

He's walking into the playground and I watch him in slow motion as he comes in through the gate, and I'm on my feet and running.

And Ben spots him too.

And we both race towards him.

Jack scoops Ben up and kisses him. Then he puts Ben down.

Ben goes running back to Faith, who gives me a none-too-subtle thumbs up, before steering him over towards the slide.

I look into Jack's eyes and everything around us feels like it's fading away. The other people, the sound of children screaming and laughing and crying – everything – until it's just Jack and me. Face to face.

My man . . .

I think . . .

Because I can't tell if he really has come back to me. If that's really what this is. All I know is that I feel like there's a chink in the clouds and the sun is starting to poke through.

'I heard what you said to Jessie Kay,' he says.

302

'You listened? I wasn't sure if you would.'

'Matt didn't give me the choice. He locked me in my old room and told me to switch the radio on and why. He told me that if I didn't, he was going to leave me there to rot.'

'Are you serious?'

'Yes, and I believed him. You know how stubborn he can be.' Jack catches something in my expression and blushes. 'Almost as stubborn as me . . .'

I don't know what to say next. I said it all on Jessie Kay's show, and Jack's already heard all that. I just know what I want to hear. I want to hear that I'm forgiven. That I forgive him too. That this is over. That we can start again. Together.

'Did Matt tell you where I went?' he asks.

'To Dartmoor. Fishing. How was it?'

'Shit. All of it. The weather. The fishing. The campsite. All of it.'

'I'm sorry.'

'It was shit because you weren't there,' he says, his eyes on mine, 'and Ben wasn't there. Just me. Stuck with all these stupid words and arguments spinning around my head. And you know what?'

'What?'

'After a while, I realised that none of it mattered, because no matter what words I tried to use to tell myself that what I'd done was right, I still felt wrong.'

'You did?'

'Because all I cared about, all I wanted to do, was to come back to you, and to be with you and Ben and never leave again.' He sighs heavily, like he's suddenly out of breath. 'Only after ditching you in New York like that, I didn't know if you'd want me back . . .'

'Oh Jack.'

'And all I want to know is whether you do really feel like you said on the radio?'

'Oh Jack. Yes, yes,' I say, throwing my arms around his neck. My face is wet with tears.

He wraps me in his arms and lifts me off my feet, and then he smiles down at me. 'In that case . . . watch this for snogging in public.'

And what follows is the most gorgeous, sensuous kiss of my life. Indecent and majestic and wonderful, and it last for ages. Long enough so that, one by one, I hear all the women by the sandpit start clapping, and by the time we've finished, I look round and Faith is on her feet and applauding too.

'Come on,' Jack says, pulling away and grinning at me. His eyes are shining and his cheeks are pink. 'I think it's time we went home.'

And Now For The Pastel Tinted End Credits

'You call this fun?' I shout at Jack.

'It's going to be fun, believe me,' he shouts back.

'You don't look like you're having fun.'

'I am. This is my fun face.'

'It doesn't look like it. It looks like your "I'm about to puke" face.'

'OK, so it's a little bit scary. But it's symbolic, what we're about to do. That's the point. We said we'd do more exciting things, and you can't call this dull.'

I feel a tap on my shoulder. 'You ready, guys?'

Jack takes hold of my hand.

I look out of the airplane door. The land below is far, far away. I think of Ben down there, with H and Matt in the airfield base, where Jack and I did our training.

'I love you,' I tell Jack, kissing him and smiling. Our goggles clink with each other.

'I love you, too, Mrs Rossiter.'

'OK, after three.'

'There's one more thing,' I tell him, as we shuffle to the edge of the open hatch. 'Something I've got to tell you.'

'What?'

'I'm late.'

'What do you mean late?'

'You know, late late. I didn't want to mention it before, but I think I might be –'

But suddenly we're holding hands and freefalling, watching each other fly. Together. Into the great unknown.